THE GHOST AND THE GREYHOUND

BRYAN SNYDER

Lost Souls Publishing, Ltd.

Paperback: ISBN 978-1-7348970-2-9

Ebook: ISBN 978-1-7348970-3-6

Cover art by Carey Blindenhofer

Lost Souls Publishing, Ltd.

www.summerdaysaga.com

CONTENTS

AUTHOR'S NOTE

The story you are about to read is not an easy tale. It touches upon trauma and the difficulty of moving beyond grief into a place of acceptance. Other themes are explored within, including matters of diversity and how humans respond to the possibility of a pandemic. In the course of editing the final draft of this book, the human world was struck by the very real virus COVID-19, which put several elements of the plot in a very different context. The similarities to current struggles were unintentional, but it goes to show how fiction and reality can overlap and inform each other in the most unexpected of ways.

The greyhound came crashing out of the forest as he always did, sending sticks and pinecones flying as he raced to return to his owner. He skidded to a halt, shook his muzzle and stared up at the boy with an unusual intensity.

Piers ignored the look. "Nixon! I'm gonna stop letting you off your leash if you're going to disappear like that. We need to go home."

He tried to scratch the coffee-colored markings on the dog's forehead, but Nixon shrugged the hand away, then licked it a few times.

"*Ugh.*" Piers wiped his fingers on his jacket. "C'mon, Nix. My mom's going to be stressed out." If his mother wasn't already having one of her bad days, a little anxiety might push her over the edge.

Piers hadn't meant to stay in Nicol's Park for so long or to let Nixon run free, but his dog's whimpering had worn him down. As it usually did. He pulled the leash from his pocket and reached for Nixon's collar. The greyhound dodged his fingers, then leapt away when he tried a second time.

"Hey! No games... I'm serious, Nixon!"

But the slender dog wagged his tongue at him and bounced in a circle, staying just out of reach. Piers lunged once more with the leash and missed. That set Nixon off again. He ran in a wider arc, tearing up the freshly-mown grass and flinging dirt behind him as he gained momentum. Then the greyhound shot back into the forest, a blur of white and brown fur that soon disappeared among the trees.

"Nixon!"

Piers ran forward but hesitated on the edge of the city parklands. He'd been warned to stay away from the woods after the second body had been discovered. It wasn't safe.

He blew out a long breath and glanced behind him to reassure himself. There were enough joggers, picnickers and frisbee players manning the pathways and pavilions that a short trip into the state forest seemed to pose little danger. Even if the forest *did* extend for thousands of acres.

Piers threw on his backpack and dove ahead.

His running speed was no match for that of his unfaithful companion, and his feet hit the ground far less gracefully. Still, he managed not to trip over roots or slip on fallen beech leaves as he plunged deeper into the woods. Gradually, the well-worn pathways became more obscure and littered with fallen branches, forcing him to jump and dodge the accumulated obstacles. *This was a dumb idea,* Piers thought. *I need a slower pet. Like a turtle.*

He dropped to a walking pace, wiped the sweat from his forehead and then almost called out for Nixon again before deciding it might attract the wrong attention. Instead, he listened. Although faint, he could still hear an occasional referee's whistle trilling sharply in the soccer fields. This far from the city park, the sounds of civilization were almost as soft as the wind that murmured through the branches overhead. His ears picked out the chittering of chipmunks and the punctuated chirps of an irritated sparrow. No dogs, though... no crunching of leaves beneath canine feet. Only his own footsteps, and–

A branch cracked, not far away. Piers spun around and raced uphill toward the noise. Ahead came a second snapping sound, louder than the first. He crested the rise, then skidded down a steeper slope into a wide gully. As he was shaking debris out of his sneakers, a muffled grunt pulled his attention up the ravine.

Oh no. Eighth-graders.

Three large boys were stationed around a crude fortress of logs and sticks they'd built beneath an overhang where the slate bedrock protruded from the side of the gully. The largest wore a grimy trenchcoat and was busy weaving dead branches into the walls of the enclosure. A second, skinnier kid appeared to be carving letters into a log above the entrance with a pocketknife. The third teenager sat, legs dangling, on the shelf of rock above the others, distracted from his management duties by a text on his cellphone. Piers held his breath and turned downhill. Maybe he could sneak away before his presence was noticed...

"Whatdaya know? A surprise visit by the one and only Piers D-d-d-davies!"

Too late. Piers blew out a breath and turned back slowly. The blond boy atop the fortress had brushed aside his bangs, revealing a wide grin and a predatory stare. *Brock Townshend.*

The stocky eighth-grader in the trenchcoat glanced at Piers with less interest. "Hey, kid," he muttered, then snapped a branch in half and shoved the pieces into a gap between the logs.

"Oh! H-h-h-h-hi," Piers stammered, his voice failing. *As it always did.* He took a few tentative steps forward. "I'm l-looking f-f-f-for..."

Brock picked up two sticks and began striking the rock underneath him. He found a rhythm and began scatting, "P-p-p-p-p-p-p-Piers! D-d-d-d-d-d-d-Davies!"

Blood crept into Piers' face as the shame of the schoolyard came rushing back. Although the boys were two grades ahead of him, they had somehow found the time to make his first year of middle school a living hell.

Brock ended his performance with a flourish of strikes, then set down his sticks. "So, Davies... whatcha think of Dwarviss' new high-rise here? Penthouse suite's mine, I'm afraid. I wanted to give it to you, but Dwarviss said no retards allowed."

"I did not," the large boy protested. "Give the kid a break. Looks like he's had a hard d-d-day."

Brock sniggered. Dwarviss immediately looked a little sheepish. He flicked away a few leaves that had lodged themselves in his thicket of curly hair and mumbled, "Sorry."

Piers tried again. "I'm l-l-l-looking for Nixon."

Dwarviss called out, "Anyone seen the dog?" But Brock had returned his attention to his cellphone. Ripal, the scrawniest member of the gang, continued to notch letters above the entryway.

"I wouldn't be out here alone," Dwarviss told him. "They keep finding dead animals. And you heard about the new body, right?"

Piers shook his head.

Dwarviss snorted. "Really? Well, they found a dead body at the edge of the park. And I'm not talking about the homeless guy they found dead last week. This college kid—"

Without setting down his knife, Ripal corrected, "High school senior."

"Okay, this high school senior had no wounds, no nothing. They're thinking heart attack."

"Or the ghost girl!" teased Brock from his perch.

A single "G—" escaped Piers' lips before he stopped himself. Despite his curiosity, he didn't want to get his tongue tied up with difficult consonants.

Brock climbed to his feet and placed a hand to his ear. "I'm sorry, D-Davies... Can you be a little clearer with your q-questions?"

Dwarviss decided to show some pity. "People have been seeing a ghost here in the woods," he confided. "A little girl or something."

"Who scares her victims to *death*," Brock whispered, opening his eyes freakishly wide.

"Apparently," said Dwarviss.

Brock resumed his usual tone of fake sincerity. "Hope your dog doesn't scare easily."

Piers took a slow step backward. "I have to g-g–" He swallowed and tried again. "I have to leave, look for N-Nixon."

"Hold on, Davies," said Brock. He stepped from the rock overhang onto the hillside and slid down the carpet of leaves to the base of the fortress. "You haven't thanked us yet for this valuable information."

"I–"

The eighth-grader selected a fresh stick from the ground and moved closer. "Say, 'Thanks, Brock.'"

Piers looked down at his feet. "Th-th-th-thanks, Br-Brock."

His tormentor wasn't done. "Say, 'You're the greatest.'"

"Y-y-you're the g-g-g-g-g –"

"C'mon, D-Davies! You gotta practice, or you'll never get any better!"

"G-g-g-g–" Piers' vocal cords felt tight as a clenched fist.

Dwarviss dusted off his trenchcoat and stepped over. "Let's keep working, Brock."

Brock was too absorbed to quit now. "Come on! You've almost got it!" He started whipping Piers on the back with his stick as if he were trying to knock the words out of him.

"G-g-g-g-great–" Tears of frustration spilled onto his cheeks.

"Spit it out, Piers!"

"G-g-g-g–"

Dwarviss tried again. "Brock..."

The blond teenager abruptly stopped. "Bah," he said. "Guess I'm not cut out to be a special ed teacher." He tossed his stick away and walked back to the fort. "Back to work, Dwarviss!" he called over his shoulder, kicking a support beam. "I don't think our fortress is "code compliant" yet."

Piers turned and ran.

He didn't stop until he reached a glade where the trees gave way to a patchwork of grasses, moss and bare bedrock. Piers sunk to the ground and wiped his eyes. Moisture from the damp moss slowly seeped into his clothing, but he didn't care. He felt angry, and angry at himself for being so angry. All summer he had managed to avoid those bullies or kids like them. Of course, he'd had to quit the soccer program to do so. And the drama program. And swim team. But he'd felt guilty for taking the time away from his mom, anyway, and she never objected. Unfortunately, having done all that, now Nicol's Park felt unsafe, too.

A slight disturbance caused Piers to whip his head around. At first, he thought he might have heard something, but it had been less of a noise than a sensation of being *watched*. Not the eighth-graders. Something more subtle. And yet the surrounding forest looked empty.

Piers got up and ran from the glade. By the time he stopped, he had completely lost his bearings. He leaned against a tree and forced himself to slow his breathing so he could listen for sounds from the park. But all seemed quiet. No horns, whistles or screams of hyperactive children cut through the whispers of the forest.

There. He heard a commotion in the distance, growing steadily closer. It sounded like a herd of wild buffalo, and he imagined that a multitude of beasts would come crashing across the landscape at any moment. Piers let out his breath when he finally recognized what was coming. *Nixon.*

The long-limbed creature tore through the forest like a crazed comet, closing the distance between them in seconds before skidding to a complete stop. He sat in front of his owner, panting and gazing up at him with an unidentifiable expression.

Piers sighed. "Nixon. I'm tired of this stupid forest. I need to go home."

Nixon suddenly leapt up like an excited puppy, mouth open wide. With an explosion of leaves and twigs, he took off running once more, looping around Piers in tighter and tighter circles. Strange noises seemed to be emanating from the dog that Piers had never heard before.

"Nixon, would you get ahold of yourself?"

The greyhound finally rushed up to him and bounced up and down with unbridled joy.

"I *knew* the boy could talk!" Nixon shouted. "I *knew* it! I *knew* it!"

2

Piers stood there, stunned. "Are you...? Are you...?"

But Nixon sprinted off into the trees again, unable to restrain himself. Piers called after him, "Nixon, come back here!"

The greyhound's trajectory curved back around, and Piers swore he could hear him saying, "I *knew* the boy could talk! I am a smart dog, and I *know* these things!"

"What?" Piers shouted after the relentless canine.

Nixon paused in front of him, and Piers took the opportunity to grab the dog's pointed face and pull it close to his own. "Nixon, are you seriously talking right now?"

"Nixon?" the animal said. "You mean *me?*"

When the dog spoke, Piers felt like he was hearing and seeing two different things at once. He could hear Nixon making whuffs and barking noises, but at the same time, his brain registered the sounds as human speech and convinced him that he was seeing the dog's lips curl to form English syllables. "Yes, you!"

The greyhound looked slightly befuddled. "I thought *you* were Nixon."

"What?" Piers blurted.

"You keep making this sound – 'Nixon'. I thought it was *your* name."

Piers scratched his scalp. "No, my name is Piers. *Your* name is Nixon."

"Nixon?" The dog cocked his head.

"Nixon."

"Nixon?"

"Yes." Piers let out a long breath.

Nixon sat back on his haunches. "*My* name is Longpaw Leafcrasher."

A shrill voice cut through the forest. "More like *Long-butt Butt-crasher!*"

Piers whirled around. "Who's there?" He looked past a crouching squirrel, searching for someone hiding behind a tree trunk or concealed in the branches.

The squirrel stood on her hindquarters and waved at him. "Hey! Down here, monkey boy!"

Piers stepped over to have a look at the rodent. Brownish-gray fur cloaked the diminutive figure, and a pair of beady eyes stared boldly up into his own.

"You're a... squirrel?" Piers mumbled.

The creature shook her head in disgust. "Oh, *there's* a real insight. I'm *soooo* glad you brought us out here to meet this genius, *Nixon.*"

Piers took another step closer. "I've just never–"

"Hey!" The squirrel jumped back and dashed up a maple sapling. "Back off, human!" she hollered from a low branch. "You try to run me over and I will gnaw your head off and use it as an acorn dispenser."

The boy stopped. "Who said anything about running you over?"

"I will rip out this tree and smash you so hard even the moles won't know where to look for you."

Piers ran a hand through his hair. "Okay, I'm really not–"

"Leafcrasher!" The squirrel tapped a foot against the spindly branch. "Why in oak's name would you try to recruit one of these murderous idiots to save the—"

The greyhound cut her off. "Scarlet, he's *my* human. I get to ask him!"

The tiny figure threw up her hands in disgust – a gesture Piers wasn't sure had really happened, as his eyes simultaneously observed her twitching in place like a normal squirrel would do. His mind was playing tricks on him, translating slight physical cues into the body language of a human.

"Piers." The greyhound pulled the boy's attention back to earth. "I have something to ask you."

"Yes, Nixon?"

"It is very important, Piers. I am an important dog, a *good* dog, and this is very important."

Piers took a deep breath. "I'm listening."

The hound cocked his head and said, "Why do you call me Nixon, Piers? You say it, and in my mind, I can see myself, and I can kind of see a human with a long nose sneaking out of a big, white house."

"Ummmm..." Piers thought quickly. "In human language, it means, "strong leader"."

"Oh." Nixon jumped up. "Oh! Then that is my name, because I am strong, and I am a leader because I lead my human to many places!"

"*And* you led a gullible squirrel clear to the other side of the forest to hear a moss-headed, babbling human. Congratulations, *Nixon.*" The squirrel scurried up to a higher branch and looked down her furry nose at them.

Piers got down on his knees in front of the greyhound.

"Nixon. What is going on? Why can I understand what you're saying?"

A wind stirred the trees overhead and a few rogue leaves tumbled down.

The dog spoke, "Piers, I am going to tell you a very important thing. I need you to lift up your ears and listen carefully."

"My ears don't do that, but okay."

"Are you listening?"

"Yes!" said Piers. "I'm listening!"

Nixon leaned in close. "We are talking to you because... we need you to help us save the world."

3

"Wait, what?" Piers wrinkled his brow. "I'm supposed to help you save the world? How do I do that?"

"Badly. Stupidly. Ineffectually," the squirrel offered.

Nixon lowered his eyes. "Maybe Emlee should explain. I am a really smart dog, but I might mess it up." The dog walked a short ways away, then looked back. Piers stood up and reluctantly followed.

"Nixon, we need to go home. My mom's going to be really worried."

The squirrel hopped down the tree and planted herself behind Piers. "Keep walking, Hairless. And don't even *think* about running me over."

Piers turned to stare at her. "I *can't* run you over. I don't have a car. I don't even drive!"

The animal pointed two fingers toward her narrowed eyes then turned them outward towards Piers – the classic *I'm watching you* gesture. Piers sighed and followed after his dog.

After catching up to Nixon, he asked in a low voice, "So, what's up with the squirrel? Is that... Emily?"

"*Emlee*," the greyhound corrected. "No. That is Scarlet."

"*No*, the name is *Scarlettail Thistleclaw*."

Piers turned to see the squirrel keeping pace behind them. "But your tail is gray. Like the rest of you, pretty much."

"It's scarlet!" Her fur bristled. "Do all humans have weak eyes like you?"

Piers kept walking. "Looks gray to me."

"*Scarlet!* It's just... we're in the shade, that's all."

Piers leaned down toward Nixon and whispered, "It's gray, right?"

The dog continued forward. "I do not know, Piers. I am not really into colors."

Colorblind. Right. Piers returned to the subject. "I thought you always chased squirrels, Nix. Why are you hanging out with this one?"

"We have a truce." Nixon stopped and sniffed the air a few times. "We are here. I have used my nose, and I have brought us back here."

Nixon looked upward. Piers glanced around but saw nothing. "Uh. Are we supposed to meet someone?"

The dog kept staring in the same direction. "This is Emlee."

Piers followed Nixon's gaze again, and his eyes began to perceive a misty, translucent shape floating in mid-air about five feet in front of him. It became slightly more substantial until he could finally focus on the outline and identify what it was. *The Ghost Girl.*

"Yaaaa!" Piers bolted behind the nearest tree, startling Scarlet, who scurried up an adjacent cottonwood. It was *her*... the one Brock had warned him about. Piers clutched his chest, wondering if his heart was going to burst. He forced his breathing to slow down and carefully peeked around the tree trunk.

The ghost's colorless form hovered above the greyhound. She appeared to be conversing with the dog, and her long hair and the hem of her dress billowed outward as they spoke, as if stirred by

BRYAN SNYDER

an invisible wind. Then without warning, the specter turned and looked in his direction.

Piers jerked his head back. *I should run,* he thought. After a few seconds, he risked another look. The apparition had closed half the distance between them, wordlessly advancing with unblinking eyes. Piers ducked behind the tree again. The next time he dared to check, the ethereal figure was gone.

He eased back against the base of the tree, allowing himself to rest for a moment. Then he noticed Scarlet on the ground beside him, and he sprung upright before his brain could recognize who it was. A curse nearly escaped his lips, but he regained his composure and mimed for the squirrel to stay quiet. Scarlet gave him a hard look, then slowly pointed a finger upward. Piers craned his neck. Directly above where he was crouching, the ghost's head protruded through the trunk of the tree. She was staring straight at him.

"Hello," the ghost said.

"Yaaaa!" Piers fell to the ground, flipped over, jumped back up and then promptly fell backward again. The girl floated over and paused. Her face, instead of being filled with malice, held an expression of genuine curiosity.

"I'm terribly sorry to have startled you. Are you able to understand me? Am I talking too loud?" She leaned closer and whispered, "How about this? This is my first time talking to an Unborn. I'm very honored and terribly excited. Please say something."

"I d-d-d-d—" Piers could not get the words out.

The apparition pressed her hands together. "Oh, my. That's very interesting, but I'm not sure I understand." She turned to Nixon, who had joined them. "Is this one damaged?"

Scarlet hopped onto Piers' chest and looked down at him. "That's probably an understatement."

Piers brushed the squirrel aside so he could see the ghost again. The girl looked roughly the same age as him, with mono-

14

chromatic skin and clothes that glowed with a faint bluish light. Her hair and the hem of her antique dress drifted slowly around her frame as if she were suspended in liquid.

"Y-y-y-you're the Ghost Girl!" he sputtered.

"A ghost?" The girl looked puzzled and backed away. "You mean you think I'm... dead?"

Nixon spoke up. "Piers, this is Emlee."

"She's just a floaty version of a human," said Scarlet, "and not nearly as ugly."

Piers sat up. "You're the ghost Brock s-said was in the woods. The one that's been killing people."

"Oh, dear, no," the pale girl said. "But that's what we needed to talk to you about." She glanced at Nixon worriedly. "Are you sure he can help?"

"Oh, yes!" said the greyhound. "Piers can do simple tasks like feeding and scratching and opening doors. He should be able to let us in."

Piers stood up and brushed off his shorts. He wished he had the slightest clue what was going on. "Nixon, where did you find a ghost?"

Emlee frowned. "There's that word again. I'm not sure I like it."

"You mean *Nixon?* That's his name."

"No. *Ghost.*"

"You're a ghost!" Piers argued. "I can see right through you!"

She circled slowly, studying him. "You seem to know my kind. Have you met other ghosts?"

"I've seen plenty in movies."

"There's another fascinating human word – *movies*. That's when you take humans and put them inside flat cages for display.... Do you steal my people for your movies too?"

"No!" he protested. "They're just made-up stories. Not real people... or real ghosts."

Emlee glided closer. "Hmmm... Let me try to explain." Her

voice had an airy, singsong quality as if she were narrating a children's book. "I am one of the Awakened, to put it formally. Just as you are of the Unborn."

"The Unborn?"

"Yes. When an Unborn's body is ready, they crumble. And then sometimes, someone like me is born."

"When someone like me dies."

"Yes," she responded.

"And they become a ghost?"

"If you'd like to call it that. Usually, they don't become one of the Awakened, but yes. I guess if you're lucky, *you* might someday."

"Lucky?"

Scarlet jumped onto Nixon's back and said, "Look, if we want to stop all this death from happening, we need to speed things up a little."

"Quite right," Emlee said. She floated upward and began to drift away. "It should be easier to explain once we're there."

Piers remained in place. "I'm sorry.... did the squirrel just say, *death?*"

Emlee looked back. "Do the Unborn usually talk in questions? It must be extraordinarily hard to communicate. You'll have to teach me how that works someday."

The ghost girl glided ahead. Piers trailed after her, with Nixon at his side and Scarlet scampering close behind.

"Nixon, what's going on?" the boy whispered. "Where are we going?"

The dog thought for a second. "It's sort of a... dark place."

Piers called out to the misty apparition. "Emlee... where are you taking us?"

The girl floated down to earth, tucked both sets of fingers through a point in mid-air and pulled them outward as if she were stretching a rubber band. In the space between her hands, one foot above the ground, a dusky circle appeared through which

Piers could glimpse the forest beyond. It seemed identical to their present location but dimmer, as if a shadow had passed over that part of the woods.

Emlee looked back at them and smiled.

"We're going to *my* world."

❦ 4 ❦

Emlee's translucent form slipped through the circle. Once she was on the other side, Piers could only see her body within the perimeter of the portal, as if she had indeed entered some other dimension. The ghost continued to hold the edges of the circle to keep it from closing.

Nixon nudged him with his nose. Reluctantly, Piers got on his knees and crawled through. He expected his skin to tingle or something, but the only odd sensation occurred when his shoulder brushed Emlee's arm and passed through without resistance. He climbed to his feet and shivered involuntarily, rubbing his shoulder as he examined his surroundings.

The forest of oak and maple surrounding them looked identical but darker, as if a cloud had passed in front of the sun. "This is... this is the same place, the same forest, right?" Piers asked. "I feel like I'm wearing sunglasses."

He watched Nixon jump through the invisible opening, and the dog seemed unaffected by his passage. After Scarlet followed, the ghost girl released the portal, which contracted back to half its original size.

Emlee rose into the air. Her pale figure glowed more brightly in the dimmer light. "As far as I can tell, this *is* the same place as your human world, except that here, the humans – the Unborn – never talk. Not in ways we can understand, at least."

"And there are more ghosts here?"

"There are more people like me, yes."

Piers gathered some sticks and arranged them into a triangle beneath the collapsed portal. The brighter scene on the other side was barely noticeable, and he did not want to find himself stranded here. *Wherever here was.* "So are we going to meet these friends of yours?"

"We are." Emlee's face grew serious. "But we have to be careful. There's a new... *ghost* in the forest. One that should not be here."

Emlee drifted off through the trees. Nixon immediately followed, but Piers took the opportunity to pull out his cellphone and check the screen. *Oh, good. It still works.* He shuffled after the others while texting his mom a short, apologetic message. She probably wouldn't see it, but he didn't want her to hesitate to call if she needed him.

Nixon noticed that the boy was lagging and circled back. He pulled up alongside the human. "Since you are smart now, I wanted to ask you something. Why do humans have such boring toys?"

"Toys?" Piers looked up from his phone. "You mean this thing?"

Scarlet caught up with them. "It's just a pet, dummy. All humans have to take care of one. You see it all the time."

Piers turned the device so they could see the screen. "This is just my phone. It lets me communicate with my mom."

The greyhound gave him a funny look. "Is that a human joke? Do you pretend the toy is your mom?"

"No." Piers hopped over a fallen tree and pushed through a patch of dense brush. Wherever Emlee was leading them, she wasn't choosing the easiest path for human feet.

Nixon had less difficulty with the terrain and trotted ahead. "Sometimes I pretend that sticks are squirrels. That way I can practice chewing their outsides off so they become dead squirrels."

"Gross."

The dog glanced back at him. "But that is how I protect you from squirrels. If one killed you, I'd be sad."

"A squirrel isn't going to kill me," Piers argued.

A shrill voice piped up from behind. "Don't be so sure about that, human."

The forest opened up again, and Piers went back to texting. "Anyway, I'm just telling my mom that I'll be late getting home. I don't want her to worry about me."

Nixon circled back once more. "Did you know I am a really good barker? That is how I communicate." He gave a loud bark, which Piers' brain interpreted as the words, "Like this!"

The boy finished his text and hit SEND. "I guess this is like barking... it lets me communicate really far... all the way to my house, where my mom can hear me through her phone."

They reached a well-worn trail, and while Piers looked around and tried to get his bearings, Emlee swooped back to scold the greyhound.

"Leafcrasher!" she whispered. "That's not safe when we don't know where he is."

Nixon's ears and tail drooped. He looked up at Piers. "Emlee says I have to be a careful barker, or we'll be dead."

"Wait, what?" Piers sputtered.

Just then, two joggers came running down the path toward them. Piers stepped out of the way, but Emlee didn't seem to notice or care as the joggers ran straight through her wispy form without breaking stride. They disappeared around a corner, and Emlee simply resumed her travels through the trees.

Piers ran to catch up. "They didn't see you!"

Emlee turned to face him. "Those were just some Unborn.

They don't notice any—" She put her hand to her mouth and widened her eyes. "Oh, I see! This must be strange to you. It's very strange to me, too. I have so many questions! But we'd better keep going."

The ghost moved on. Piers followed once again, the greyhound at his side.

"Nixon, how did *you* start talking? Is it something that the ghost girl did?"

The dog cocked his head slightly. "Well... I was kind of chasing squirrels, and it really was not my fault, because I am a good chaser, but I got my head stuck in one of those holes. Then Emlee found me."

Piers pointed to the creature hopping behind them. "Was that the squirrel you chased?"

"The squirrel that outsmarted him, yes," Scarlet boasted, "and the *first* being to discover this world of floating, talking humans!"

"I found it first!" Nixon gave Piers an aggrieved look. "Squirrels do not count."

Emlee paused in her flight to survey the local trees, and Nixon took the opportunity to sit and give himself a good scratching. Apart from it being a little rockier, Piers didn't see any difference to this part of the forest. The trees along the border of Nicol's Park had been logged several times, and none of the second-growth oaks and maples around them matched the giants that supposedly grew deeper in the woods.

Before Piers could ask Emlee what she was searching for, Nixon commented, "This is a strange place. The animals do not talk."

"Yep," Scarlet added. "They're as dumb as humans here. The regular kind. Watch this!" She shouted up to another squirrel in a nearby oak, "Hey, sapsucker! I just stole all your nuts and shoved them up the nose of this talking human. What do you think about that?"

The squirrel chittered and moved to a higher branch.

"See?" said Scarlet.

"Spooky," said Nixon.

"Emlee," said a third, unfamiliar voice, "what in the world is going on?"

Piers jumped. Scarlet bolted up the tree, triggering a frenzy of titters from the other squirrel. Behind them stood the ghost of a young man in a long jacket and scarf, his translucent form composed of the same spectral blue substance as the ghost girl. Nixon growled, but Emlee wore a big smile as she floated over to join them.

"Vinst! I was looking for you," said Emlee.

The man crossed his arms and eyed Piers and the animals suspiciously through a mop of hair. Unlike Emlee, he appeared to stand rather than float, although his feet didn't quite make contact with the ground. "Why are these animals talking? And the Unborn?"

"It's a really amazing and very long story," Emlee said. "They're going to help. Piers, this is Vinst. He's one of the seven in my Circle."

"I d-d–" Piers paused to get his tongue under control. His stutter always became worse when he felt self-conscious. "I don't know what that m-means, but... *hi.*" He extended an open hand, but the ghost ignored the gesture.

"What happened to it?" asked the specter. "Is it Born or Unborn?"

Emlee floated between them. "Vinst, this one might be able to learn how the Obsessed escaped his Circle. The dog says Piers can get into the North Tower."

Nixon looked up at Piers. "She means the house with the old humans."

"The nursing home, where my mom works?" Piers looked from the dog to Emlee and back again. "Is that why I'm here?"

Emlee's attention remained fixed on the other ghost, and Piers had to suppress his irritation. "Where have you been, Vinst?" she asked. "I haven't seen you in days."

"Hiding." The ghost's frown deepened, and he floated around the group with his arms clasped behind him. His feet never moved, so he looked like he was standing on a circular conveyor belt. "Aredo told me that Rima was eaten by the thing. And I fear Aredo might be gone now, too."

Now that Piers had a better look at the apparition's clothing and hairstyle, he thought Vinst could have been plucked from a college campus in the 1960s. The ends of the young man's scarf drifted about his head, defying gravity much like Emlee's hair.

The new ghost stopped in front of his counterpart. "Emlee, he's close. And he's been growing."

"Show us," she responded. "Piers needs to see."

Vinst glanced at the others. "Come with me, then." He drifted away through the darkened forest, and the group moved to follow him.

Piers caught up to the ghost girl and whispered, "Emily?"

"It's Emlee."

"Sorry. Emlee." Piers had a thousand questions, but he decided to start with this one. "What's an Obsessed?"

The girl considered for a moment before answering. "Well... when one of us – *ghosts*, as you say – gets too focused on a particular human or group of humans, we call them Obsessed. They may try to interfere with a human or a human's environment."

"They haunt people."

"Yes, you could say that."

Vinst suddenly shushed them. He gestured for the group to duck behind some foliage. Piers crouched next to Emlee and peered through the branches, trying to see whatever had alarmed their new companion.

"In this case," Emlee continued, "the Obsessed seems to want to *kill* humans."

A shadow emerged from the woods.

The thing that strode into their vision was a giant – at least twice the size of a human – and it flickered with the same dull, ethereal blue light as the other ghosts. As it floated across the forest floor, its legs slowly lifted and came down in vague imitation of a living person's movements. Its skin rippled disturbingly as if it were made of jelly, not flesh.

"Don't move," whispered Vinst. "He kills my kind, too."

"And animals," said Nixon.

"And smart animals," added Scarlet, "like squirrels."

Although the monstrous ghost wore some kind of work uniform, there was nothing civilized in the bulging, ravenous eyes that searched the forest. Piers did not want to be seen by this creature.

"He's growing," Vinst said.

He. Piers acknowledged that it *was* a man, or at least it used to be. As the boy watched, the towering figure raised his head and fixed his gaze on a crow perched in an oak tree. Wordlessly, the ghost approached the animal, stretched out his arm, and his fingers flattened and elongated to encircle the unwitting bird.

"No!" Emlee gasped.

"Can't it see him?" asked Piers.

Emlee shook her head sorrowfully. "The crow... it's not in our world. Not in *my* world."

The bird continued to preen its feathers even as the giant closed his transparent fist around it. There was a quick contraction of fingers. The crow let out a muted squawk, and a ripple shot through the ghost's arm and reverberated across the rest of his body. The feathered creature fell lifeless to the ground.

"Terrible," said Emlee, shaking her head.

Nixon let out an angry "whuff". Piers grabbed his snout, but it was too late. The giant's head swiveled in their direction.

Everyone crouched as low behind the foliage as they could. Piers let go of the greyhound and flashed him an angry look.

Nixon wrinkled his nose. "Smells bad. Like dead things."

After a tense moment, the aberration turned and slid back into the trees. The others waited for a minute, then carefully followed.

Piers felt on edge. Something intangible had changed about the forest, or maybe the shift from daylight to perpetual twilight was finally getting to him. He knew one thing for certain: true danger walked in these woods.

Before he could gather his courage and ask about the thing they'd seen, Vinst held up a hand, and the group halted. The outline of Vinst's body had become tattered and windblown. The ghost's scarf fluttered sideways as if being stirred by a light breeze, though to Piers, the air felt completely still.

"This is the edge of my Circle," Vinst said.

"You can't go past here?" asked Piers.

"No." The apparition stared ahead. "But I know where the Ender is going. The North Tower."

"The *Ender?*" Piers repeated. But he was ignored again.

Emlee floated over to Vinst and clasped hands with him. She seemed unaffected by whatever winds were buffeting her friend. "We'll see you soon. Don't be such a good hider."

Piers wasn't sad to leave the other specter behind. Something about his stuffiness irked him. They continued without Vinst and soon came to a chainlink fence at the edge of the forest rimmed with barbed wire. Beyond the barrier, they saw the strange, gargantuan ghost drifting across a mowed clearing toward a white, fortress-like brick structure. *Aspen Home.* Where Piers' mom worked.

Emlee hovered in front of the fence but did not pass through. "We are close to where my own Circle ends. I should not go further."

"So that's why you need me," Piers said. "To go into the nursing home and..." He had a sudden burst of panic, thinking his mom might be in the building at that moment. He clutched at the chain links but then relaxed as he remembered it was her day off.

The ghost girl moved in close to Piers. "Leafcrasher tells me you have access to the Tower."

"On days my mom is working. Not today. Is she in danger from that thing?"

"I don't know, Piers. Have the Unborn been dying in there?"

His mom *had* mentioned something about the residents expiring at a faster rate lately. A virus, they suspected. "Yes. But just the old ones."

"Idiot," said Scarlet.

Piers looked down at the squirrel and scowled. "Excuse me?"

"Oh, not *you,*" Scarlet clarified. She pointed beyond the fence. "I'm talking about the *other* idiot."

Piers turned toward the nursing home and saw the tail-end of Nixon. The dog was heading straight for the spectral giant.

"Nixon!" Piers shouted, raising his voice as loud as he dared, but the greyhound was too far to hear. He looked at the barbed wire atop the fence, then whirled back to the ghost girl. "Emlee, you have to stop him!"

Her eyes widened. "I... I can't go there!"

Piers frantically gestured toward the fields. "He'll be spotted! Go!"

Looking flustered, Emlee passed through the chain links and headed after the greyhound. Piers was about to attempt the barbed wire when he spotted a tree a short distance away that had fallen on the fence – not hard enough to crush it, but enough to cause the lower edge to bow inward. Nixon must have slipped through there, he realized. Piers ran to the breach, grabbed the links at the base and lifted them so he could crawl underneath.

Once through, he jumped to his feet and saw that Emlee had only managed to move twenty feet from the fence. Her hair and outline were being battered by winds far stronger than what Vinst had experienced, and she stared back at Piers, looking sad and helpless. He sprinted past her across the open grass until he had almost caught up to the greyhound. "Nixon!" he hissed. The sleek animal stopped and turned toward him, just as the Ender slowly did the same. Piers leapt onto the canine, grabbed him by the shoulders and pulled him to the ground.

Nixon let out a yelp as Piers buried his snout in the grass. The boy sprawled as flat as possible, hoping the undulating contours of the field would be enough to hide them.

"Stay down!" he ordered. "He'll see us."

"I am staying down, Piers," Nixon said, eyes wide. "We are staying down now."

The grass tickled Piers' nose. He ignored it, though he wished the blades were taller and could conceal them better. He couldn't see ahead from where he lay, but looking backward, it seemed that Emlee had wisely dropped out of sight. After a minute, he dared to raise his body and gaze across the meadow. The Ender had his back to them once more.

They both got up quickly. Piers held onto Nixon's collar and didn't let go until they'd returned to the fenceline. "What were you thinking?" Piers scolded as he pushed Nixon underneath the gap where the tree had fallen.

"I am sorry, Piers. I thought we were going to the Tower."

From the other side of the fence, they watched Emlee rise from the earth where Piers had seen her last. Strange winds whipped her long hair and dress about, though they did not stir the grasses beneath her. As she flew toward them, the turbulence subsided. She passed through the chain links and blurted, "I couldn't go any further! I tried to tell you."

"It's okay. I don't think–" Piers paused when he suddenly noticed the Ender was gone. The ghost must have sped up and reached his destination. "I don't think he saw us."

Emlee glanced back at the white turrets and windows of Aspen Home. It really did look like a medieval fortress from this angle. "He keeps returning there. It must be his Center, where he was Awakened... that is to say, born as a person like me."

Piers plopped to the ground. "Okay, Emlee..." he started, before taking a deep breath. Nothing about today fit into his conception of how the world worked, and his brain felt like it was on the verge of shutting down. "So you need me to see what the ghost is doing?"

"And report back," said Scarlet from atop the fence, "so we know how to kill it."

Emlee nodded. "Myself and those in my Circle... we're at a loss. We need some clue about how he became so powerful and escaped his own Circle."

Piers mulled it over. It sounded like less of a time commitment than what Nixon had requested. *Something about saving the world, wasn't it?* He responded slowly. "I guess I can look. I haven't gone there in a while. But I can't until tomorrow."

The ghost girl swirled once around the human, then settled in front of him, smiling brightly. "Thank you, Piers!"

He stood up and looked at the others. "I should go home now. Nixon and me. I have to let my mom know I'm okay."

"Mom. Mom." Emlee's brow furrowed as she tried out the

word. "An interesting attachment. Yes, of course! I'll find a hole for you."

The ghost darted back into the forest. Piers caught up and tried to keep pace with her. "So," he began, "have you been haunting humans for a while?"

"No, I only recently discovered the holes to your world, and theirs." She indicated the dog and squirrel. "I tried to stay out of sight so I could listen to the humans talk. They tended to run away if I didn't." Emlee tapped her finger against her lip. "Actually, Leafcrasher showed me the holes first."

Scarlet jumped onto Nixon's back, bristling.

"Hey, I went through to Ghost Land before *he* did! Scarlet, Discoverer of Worlds!"

Nixon looked up at Piers. "I chased her into here. Where Emlee lives. I am a good chaser."

The squirrel climbed onto Nixon's head. "*I* was exploring. *You* got your stupid muzzle stuck in the hole, and she had to pull you out!"

Piers decided to change the subject. "How many holes are there?"

"Honestly, I don't know," said Emlee. "But they started to appear about the same time as the Ender first came to the forest."

"And they all go here, to the ghost world?"

"I think so."

"We haven't explored them all," Scarlet said. A shrewd expression slowly crept onto her pointed face. "Come to think of it... you should pay *our* world a visit."

Piers hesitated. "I-I-I really need to check on my mom."

"Maybe another time, Scarlet," said Emlee.

The squirrel hopped down to Nixon's back. "But I need to... see my mom, too! That's right, she'll be worried sick. Just a quick hello, introduce the human to a few friends, and then we're off."

Before Piers could react, Scarlet launched herself at his leg. She latched on, then scurried up to his shoulder.

"Ow!" he yelped. "Claws! Watch the claws!"

Scarlet stood and murmured into his ear. "Think about it... a whole world of talking animals. It'll blow your simple little human mind."

Piers glared at her. "Don't *ever* do that again."

"So... *yes?*"

Piers knew he should go straight home, but...

He sighed. "A quick trip."

"Spec-tac-u-lar!" Scarlet jumped back onto Nixon's back and muttered to the dog, "You think he'd be honored."

The squirrel then hopped to the ground, and Piers and the others followed her downhill to a more rugged patch of forest. She searched among the mossy rocks, muttering about "it" being around somewhere until Emlee descended and grabbed something undetectable to the eye a few inches above the ground. The ghost widened the space between her hands, and Scarlet jumped between them.

To Piers, the small animal looked different when she landed on the other side of the portal. It was as if Scarlet had lost the subtle signs of higher intelligence, moving and behaving just like any other backyard squirrel. She scurried up to the base of a nearby tree and scratched at an exposed root. Seconds later, another squirrel popped its head out of a hole high above her where a dead branch had fallen away from the trunk. They chittered back and forth, and Piers had no idea what was going on.

Emlee pulled his attention away. "It really is amazing to meet you, Piers. I have so many questions." Her translucent form bobbed restlessly, like a jellyfish in the ocean. "I'm glad Leafcrasher knew you, and of your abilities."

"Abilities?"

"To go into the North Tower! Since it's inside your Circle, we have a chance to learn where the Ender came from. I always suspected human Circles were much bigger than ours."

Piers took out his cellphone and turned the camera on. "I don't think we *have* a Circle."

"Really?" The girl looked stunned. "But you have a Center, right? Always in some human-crafted building. And you have resting periods, like other animals."

Piers pointed the camera sensor at the ghost, but her image failed to appear on the screen. He lowered the device. "Emlee, you really don't remember being human?"

Before the girl could answer, Scarlet hopped back through the portal and announced, "Okay, we're ready!"

Piers raised his phone again to record video of the squirrel. "Scarlet, who's *'we'*?"

"Uh... my mom and stuff," she mumbled.

Emlee began to float down to the portal, but Scarlet moved to block her way. "Maybe you should stay here, your ghostliness, and guard the hole. Remember how you scared everyone off the last time?"

The girl looked disappointed. "I'll stay."

"That's the spirit!" Scarlet looked over to Piers. "Ready?"

Without waiting for an answer, the squirrel hopped over to the portal, stood on her back legs and held the upper edge in her claws. Her beady, black eyes twinkled mischievously.

"Welcome to *my* world, human," said Scarlet.

❦ 6 ❧

Scarlet jumped through the hole, then turned and chittered back at Piers. The boy crouched down and felt for the opening with his fingers. Somehow, it eluded his grasp, and Emlee had to float over and take hold of the portal for him. Piers reached for it again, but his hands still passed through whatever she was holding.

"I can't touch it!" he complained.

"I don't think you can feel the outside edge," Emlee said calmly. "Put your hand here, along the inside."

Piers moved his fingers to where Emlee was pointing and found the inner edges of a small circle. It felt bitterly cold to the touch, like metal in winter, and the resistance increased the further he stretched it. Awkwardly, he slipped through the portal and held it open so that Nixon could follow.

Once the three of them were through, Piers stood and rubbed his hands together. The forest had changed again. Compared to the twilight atmosphere of the ghost world, the woods here appeared well-lit, although the quality of light had a rusty brownish cast. Scarlet's tail looked a little redder, but then again, so did everything else. The place also felt busier, like he was back in Nicol's Park, catching fragments of distant conversations. Emlee was gone from view, but a second squirrel hopped over to join them.

"Everyone's ready," the newcomer said, "though they're a little skeptical."

"Not for long," boasted Scarlet. "Fleastriker, this is my human, Piers. Piers, this is my cousin Fleastriker."

Piers waved. Scarlet looked mildly annoyed at him.

"Say something, human," she prodded.

"N-nice to meet you?"

Fleastriker's eyes went wide. He fell over, did a quick roll and popped back up again. "Wow! I think we should have doubled the admittance fee."

"Admittance fee?" Piers blurted.

Scarlet scampered behind Piers and pushed at his shoes. "Let's go! Move your big feet."

Piers walked forward. Nixon whuffed in annoyance and followed. They soon came to a big boulder, and Scarlet instructed Piers to wait behind it. She then turned to Fleastriker, gave him a rough push and said, "Do the introduction!"

The other squirrel hopped around the boulder, and Piers heard him attempting to make an announcement. "Attention, one and all! Sit down, Grunter! You too, Gravelfoot! This is a day that will change your lives *forever*. I now introduce the three-time nut hoarding champion, Dominator of Dogkind..."

Nixon gave a loud snort.

"Discoverer of... of Something. And... uh, I forgot the other stuff."

Scarlet spat. "Fah. Human, bend down for a second."

Puzzled, Piers knelt.

Fleastriker continued, "The, uh... the one and only Scarlettail Thistleclaw!"

Scarlet jumped onto Piers' head, then up to the boulder. She scurried to the top and stood tall.

"Yes, friends! Thank you, thank you. In this — I swear if you don't shut your mouth, Cloudcutter, you'll be scavenger-hunting for your own teeth! *Ahem.* In this dark hour, I have done what no other creature has dared to do. I have made contact with both humans and otherworldly forces, and tomorrow, we will begin our quest to seek out and destroy the Ender!"

Piers heard what sounded like several animals stomping the ground in approval. One heckler shouted, "You couldn't destroy a one-legged centipede!"

"I'll destroy your *face* in a minute, Toadbiter! Anyway, now is the moment you've been waiting for..."

"And paid for!" said another critic.

"Prepare to have your mind shattered into a thousand pieces as I present..." Scarlet paused again. "What are you... *Oh, great.* He's right behind me, isn't he?"

Scarlet turned and saw that Piers had peeked around the side of the boulder. The entire congregation of mice, squirrels, deer, rabbits, raccoons, skunks and a large bear were all staring at him. She crossed her arms and glared at the human. "Sheesh. You really know how to blow a dramatic entrance, huh?"

Piers waved weakly to the crowd. "Hi."

A rabbit stood up on its hind legs, then promptly fainted and fell over. The other rabbits looked at the first rabbit, then fainted themselves, in unison.

"*Ta da,*" said Scarlet underwhelmingly. "Well, human... why don't you come out so they can get a good look at you."

Piers walked around to the front of the boulder. He noticed a small pile of roots and nuts arranged between him and the audience. "Scarlet, I *thought* we were just going to visit your mother."

The squirrel shuffled her feet atop her rocky perch. "She.... couldn't make it." Scarlet turned her attention back to the crowd. "All right, who wants to ask the first question?"

A raccoon raised his hand. "Ooooo, me! How did—"

"Donation first!" Scarlet demanded.

As the rabbits regained consciousness and righted themselves, the raccoon produced a hazelnut and placed it on the pile. "How did you learn to talk?" he asked.

"I don't know," said Piers. "Sesame Street?"

A rumble of confusion arose from the assembled animals. "Doesn't matter if the answer makes sense or not," declared Scarlet. "Next question!"

A skunk meekly added another nut to the mound of offerings. "Is it true you keep Domestics in your den until they're big enough for you to eat them?"

"You mean *pets?*" the boy asked. "No, we don't eat our pets... at least not the indoor ones." He glanced back at the emcee again. "Scarlet, did you put me in some kind of Talking Human Show?"

The squirrel wouldn't look him in the eye. "I don't like to explain my process. Next question!"

A junco flitted down and deposited a sprig of berries onto the pile. Before the bird could pose a question, Scarlet barked, "Hey Nightpouncer, quit lurking back there! Pay up or get out!" A fox stepped out from behind a tree, sniffed with feigned indifference and padded away.

The little bird fluttered to the ground in front of Piers. "Is it really the humans who are responsible for the deaths in the forest?" she asked.

"What deaths?"

"Healthy birds that are found dead with no scratches, no wounds," the junco explained. "Other creatures, too."

"No, it's a ghost," he explained.

The bird cocked its head. "You mean a... dead human?"

Scarlet cut the boy off. "Don't answer that." She threw the junco a stern look. "That's two questions! Next!"

Nixon trotted up to Piers' side just as a trio of squirrels began fighting over who would interrogate the human next. A rabbit appeared to pass out from the excitement for a second time.

"Something smells wrong," said Nixon.

Piers nodded. "This whole thing is wrong. I need to get back home."

One squirrel chased the others away, and another rabbit tipped over. The victorious squirrel came back and asked, "How do you make granola bars, and do you have any with you?"

Piers turned to Scarlet, still perched atop her boulder. "Scarlet, we need to go."

"Sure, just ten more questions, then we'll wrap it up."

The greyhound sniffed the air and repeated slowly, *"Something... smells... wrong."*

"Now, Scarlet," said Piers.

"Okay, *five* more questions!"

A deer in the audience suddenly collapsed. Everyone went silent. One of the raccoons crept over to look at the prone creature.

Nixon looked up at Piers.

"He's here."

7

Animals bolted in all directions. Scarlet leapt down to the food pile and began shoving nuts into her mouth as fast as possible. Piers grabbed her with both hands and ran.

"Jufft one mmmre!" she protested, cheeks bulging.

With Nixon at his heels, Piers raced back to the portal site and dropped the squirrel. "Where is it?" the boy shouted.

Scarlet sniffed around the rocks for a moment, located a spot in midair and hopped through. She then bounded away without looking back. Piers grabbed for the hole, but his fingers felt nothing.

"Scarlet," he roared, "get back here!"

The squirrel ignored his calls. Desperately, Piers clawed at the air until his fingers finally caught the inner edge of the portal. He held the perimeter with two hands and stretched it wide.

"Nixon, go!"

The greyhound bolted through. Piers suddenly began to feel the air compress around him. He threw his upper body into the hole, but as he was wiggling his torso through, he sensed an invisible force clutch at one of his legs. The pull felt soft, like a river current, but nearly strong enough to drag him back. Piers kicked and struggled, finally flopping down onto the shadowed surface of Emlee's world. Something still had hold of his leg. Heart racing, Piers flipped over and saw... *the Ender.*

The spectral giant towered overhead, and as the ghost leaned forward, his eyeballs bulged further from their sockets. His chin and jowls sagged as if made of dough, and when he opened his mouth, his lower jaw stretched horrifically wide.

"MORE," the monstrosity intoned, with a voice that gurgled up from cavernous depths. Still clutching the boy's calf, he extended another rubbery hand, reaching down toward Piers' chest. Piers recoiled and dug his fingers into the earth, trying to gain enough purchase to yank his leg away. He could not free himself... and he was going to die.

A brown and white creature streaked out of nowhere, unleashing a deafening bark as it leapt onto the Ender. *Nixon.* Piers was ecstatic. Unfortunately, the greyhound passed through the transparent flesh without resistance and landed awkwardly on the other side, tumbling into a heap.

Emlee rushed to Piers' side, eyes frantic. "I'm sorry! I didn't see him coming!" Piers threw up his arm to grab Emlee's hand, but there was nothing solid to hold onto.

The Ender, distracted briefly by the smaller ghost, fixed his horrific gaze upon Piers once more. His massive hand reached out and touched the boy's chest.

"Get him off me!" Piers cried.

The giant reared back, and his eyes locked onto Piers with newfound intensity.

"HUMAN.... YOU... LIVE!"

Piers realized for a split second that his leg was free, but the ghost's arm lashed down and hit him like a sandbag, pinning his lower half to the ground. The other hand extended toward his chest again, becoming more substantial the closer it came to his heart.

Suddenly, with a high-pitched scream of fury, Scarlet leapt

from the trees onto the Ender's grasping hand. Her body quickly sunk into the hand like it was a cushion, but she whirled about, scratching and biting the oversized fingers. Gradually, the appendage became more and more transparent, causing the squirrel to sink deeper until she fell through to the ground.

Nixon dashed up to the arm holding Pier's legs and bit into it repeatedly. The dog's jaws penetrated further and further into the limb until it also became completely insubstantial, allowing Piers to yank his legs free. He scrambled to his feet and ran from the Ender as fast as he could. The others followed close behind.

Nixon took the lead, propelling his streamlined body across the slopes in the general direction of what Piers hoped was Nicol's Park. When Scarlet's speed began to falter, Piers scooped her up and placed her on his shoulder. He tried to keep pace with the greyhound on the uneven terrain, shooting backward glances as much as he dared without tripping over downed logs and branches. Emlee soared effortlessly through the canopy above, unhindered by leaves and twigs. Her long, phosphorescent hair streamed behind her.

They reached a ravine, and Piers plunged down it, not recognizing where he was until he found his path blocked by a trio of humans. *The eighth-graders?* He skidded to a stop, while Scarlet hastily abandoned her perch and scampered out of sight. Nixon pulled up next to Piers in the shadow of the bullies' makeshift fortress, panting heavily.

The tallest of the three humans stepped forward, his face blank of expression. Piers thought it odd that he could not read any of their faces, nor could he focus clearly on their features. He assumed the tall one to be Brock – a guess that felt confirmed when the bully reached out and shoved him backward. The whole action seemed strangely impersonal.

Brock opened his mouth. "Fsoijoij sfoiaepwdv afsdgyuadg adsvc adsfii afored ad!" The noises made absolutely no sense.

Piers tried to communicate, though his tongue seemed to fail him again. "B-b-brock, you h-h-have to get out of h-here."

"Isfd aefs afssdiojds!"

Emlee floated down and whispered, "He can't understand you. You're not in his world."

Piers glanced anxiously behind him, and his breath caught in his throat. The Ender stood at the lip of the ravine, gazing downward, his distorted features warping into a sadistic grin. Slowly, the ghost leaned forward, his fluidic mass oozing into his face and shoulders until he resembled a cresting tidal wave. One rubbery leg lifted up, and then the entire mass dropped into the ravine and came surging toward them.

Piers felt another push against his chest, and he whipped his head around. The other two humans, who must have been Ripal and Dwarviss, stepped closer. Piers waved frantically to get everyone's attention and pointed back at the monster. "Look at him! If you stay here, you're going to die!"

The teenagers continued to stare at Piers, even as the Ender came rushing toward them like a raging mudslide. In desperation, Piers shoved Brock in the chest. He found himself instantly knocked to the ground. Nixon bared his teeth and growled, while Emlee rushed to Piers' side.

"You can't save them. We have to go!"

The larger human rumbled, "Osdfio weaedfs wei afsdgads agd," and Brock snarled, "Csbafwe!" back. Piers couldn't understand anything that the eighth-graders were doing, only that they weren't leaving, and the Ender was almost upon them.

Piers rolled to his feet, dashed to the fortress beneath the rock overhang, and ripped loose a log holding a support beam. The fort collapsed. He bolted down the ravine before the teenagers had a chance to grab him.

Piers wasn't sure why he had done what he did, but he had no time to think about it; the cries from the bullies pursued him through the trees, getting closer and closer until the trio was right on his heels. One almost seized the back his shirt, but Nixon dashed between them, throwing his pursuer off and giving Piers a few extra seconds of distance. *If he could just make it to the park...*

Piers nearly ran through the ribbon of yellow police tape before he realized it was there. He skidded to a halt. Before him lay the remains of a homeless encampment. Tattered tarps hung between trees, while blankets lay strewn across the ground amid trash and discarded belongings. He had just half a second to wonder why the camp was enclosed with police tape before he was tackled to the ground.

Someone was punching him. Piers threw up his arms to block the blows. In the midst of the attack, his brain dimly registered shouting noises – incomprehensible but growing nearer. His assailant stood up and stepped back, and Piers dared to open his eyes.

Two police officers, both male, were advancing quickly onto the scene. Dwarviss and Ripal turned and fled, while Brock, his attacker, was cornered against the police tape perimeter.

Emlee drifted down to Piers's side. "Are you all right?"

Piers put a hand to his face and sat up. "Yeah." His lower lip felt tender and was probably bleeding.

Nixon came up and licked his hand. "Next time you should try to bite him," the greyhound said.

"Sure, Nixon."

The policemen approached and confronted Brock, though Piers had no idea what anyone was saying. Emlee whispered to him, "If you're quick, there's a portal to the human world inside the yellow ribbon."

Piers raised himself to a crouch. "Show me where."

Emlee flew past the police tape into the homeless camp and hovered over a bundle of blankets. Piers gave one more look at the officers, then ducked under the yellow ribbon. He raced over to where Emlee held the invisible portal, replaced her hands with his own and stretched the opening wide. "Nix, are you coming?"

BRYAN SNYDER

The dog dashed into the perimeter and squirmed through the hole. Piers looked around for Scarlet but saw no sign of the squirrel. Brock, however, was shouting and pointing at him, and the officers turned in Piers' direction. Soon, the policemen were shouting as well, advancing toward the boy, and Brock used the distraction as an opportunity to run away.

Piers scrambled through the portal, and the gibberish spouted by the officers instantly resolved into English.

"Isf aawe agsddo lk-immediately! Walt, we need to grab this kid," said one man.

"Watch the dog," directed the other.

The hole collapsed to a smaller size as soon as Piers let go. He sprang to his feet, but the second policeman seized his arm before he could escape.

"I'm s-s-s-s-sorry," Piers stammered. "We c-c-c-can't stay here."

The officer was unmoved. "*You* can't stay here. You're in an active crime scene."

The uniformed duo marched Piers outside the perimeter. Nixon kept his distance, and Emlee was nowhere to be seen.

One officer – Piers thought he had heard the name *Walt* – kept hold of his arm, while his bearded partner stopped Piers and looked him in the eyes.

"Why didn't you come out when we told you?"

Piers swallowed. "Th-th-th-this is where the h-h-h-h–"

"The homeless man, yes," said the one holding him. "And it's still under investigation, which means you broke the law going in there."

"We're going to have to take him in," said the other.

"I c-c-c-c-c–"

The officer with the beard bent down. "Easy, kid. We'll call your parents once we're back at the station. You got a leash for your dog?"

Piers realized he couldn't remember where the leash ended up.

He froze, not knowing what to do or say. He had failed his mom. He had failed everyone. The words wouldn't come out, and in his frustration, they began to push out tears.

The policeman looked visibly uncomfortable. He awkwardly patted Piers on the shoulder and said, "It's okay. Forget the leash."

Walt asked, "Want me to stay here?"

"We have to go together," said the other man. "Rules. And the dog might be an issue. I think I have rope back at the car." He stood straight again and gave Piers one last clap on the shoulder. "All right, let's talk as we walk, kid."

Piers tried to protest as he was led away from the encampment. They had only walked a short distance when the bearded officer suddenly stopped and clutched at his chest. He grunted with obvious pain.

"You all right, Steve?" asked Walt.

"I think..." The officer took a few quick breaths. "My chest..."

"You having a heart attack?" Walt let go of Piers' arm. "Hold up a minute. Let me call—"

Steve took a few steps forward. "Wait. It feels better if I keep moving." He walked in a small circle. "There. Must be nothing." The officer paused again in front of Piers and tried breathing deeply while he stretched his arms. Then he let out another cry of pain and bent over.

Walt put a hand on his partner. "Steve, this is serious!"

The ailing officer took a few more steps and seemed to breathe easier. "Okay, call," said Steve.

Piers and Nixon slipped away in the confusion. No one shouted for them to come back, and Piers wouldn't have turned around if they had.

$\maltese$ 8 $\maltese$

P iers stopped in front of his back door, brushed the bits of leaves and dirt off his clothes as best he could, then slipped inside with Nixon. He closed the door behind them, and the click of the latch bolt sliding into place never sounded so good.

Classical music permeated the house, and Piers breathed a sigh of relief. Music meant his mom was having one of her better days.

He walked through the kitchen into the living room and saw his mother lying on the couch. Long brown hair covered half her face, and the one exposed eye stared upward, unfocused. Maybe she wasn't having such a good day after all.

Nixon padded over and sniffed the woman's feet. Piers went to the cabinet across the room and turned down the radio. "Hi, Mom," he said.

His mother didn't move. "Hi, Piers."

"Park was good. Sorry I'm late. Did you get my text?"

She paused as if she were remembering where she was. "No. It was jumbled up."

"Oh," said Piers. "Weird. Well, I'll get back to working on the garage, like I said."

He turned the music back up and left the room. In his gut, he felt the familiar pang of guilt at having pulled his mother out of whatever memories she'd taken comfort in.

Nixon followed him to the garage. "Piers, was I supposed to say, "Hi, mom," too?"

The boy picked up a broom. "No. I don't think it's a good idea to talk to her." He began sweeping the concrete floor. "Probably ever."

Chores would take a while. There would probably be dinner in a few hours. Or he'd make something simple for them to eat. In the meantime, he had a lot to think about. And a few things he'd rather not think about at all.

He coughed at the dust billowing up, but he didn't put down the broom, and he didn't open the garage door.

Later that night, Piers was haunted by dreams. Students were vanishing in his school, one by one, and nobody but him could see the grey shadow roiling and seething at the far end of the hallway. Whenever he tried to warn someone, the words stuck in his throat. He felt a staticky breeze caress the side of his face, and he whirled around.

"Piers," said a soft, airy voice.

He couldn't locate the speaker. But a feeling of dread washed over him when he realized he had taken his eyes off the shadow. He spun around again. The Ender was in front of him, reaching for his heart.

"Piers!" came the voice again.

Piers' body jolted into consciousness, and his eyes flew open. The ghost girl stared down at him from the darkness over his bed.

"Aaaaaahhh!" he screamed.

Nixon jumped up from the floor and barked, "What?"

Emlee withdrew to the center of the room. "I'm sorry! I've never tried to break a human out of its dormant phase before."

Piers sat up and rubbed his face. "There are... better ways..."

Nixon yawned and resettled himself on his pile of ragged blankets while the ghost slid closer. Locks of hair drifted about her head like seaweed on a sunken ship. "I lost you after you left the forest. Are you all right?"

"Well, yeah, apart from almost getting killed and arrested. Did you see all that?" Piers didn't wait for an answer. "I feel awful... I think the big ghost attacked that policeman, and I just ran. I ran and left him to die."

"He didn't die," said Emlee.

A weight lifted off Piers' chest. "He didn't?"

"No." She settled at the foot of the bed, allowing her lower half to sink into the mattress. "The human kept moving, and the Ender eventually left, heading back for the North Tower. He may only be able to kill smaller creatures or those that are dormant."

"It's called sleeping. And speaking of sleeping..."

Emlee continued, "Have you thought about how you're going to get into the North Tower? I wish I could go with you."

Piers fell back on his pillow. "Emlee can we *please* talk about this in the morning?"

"Oh!" Emlee shot out of the bed. "Yes, of course." Her eyes searched the room until they lit upon something. "I'll wait over here in this... chair."

She floated over to his reading chair and then awkwardly tried to bend her form into a sitting position. After settling down, her body still hovered several inches above the seat. She called to Piers, "Am I doing this right?"

"You're fine! Just... never mind." Piers pulled the covers up to his chin, rolled onto his side and closed his eyes.

"Sleeping seems to make you irritable," observed Emlee. "I wonder why humans do it."

"Good night, Emlee."

Piers spent the next half-hour tossing and turning in bed. Eventually, he cracked open an eye and looked out. Emlee hadn't moved an inch. She sat in the same position, glowing softly and staring at him with unblinking eyes from across the room. He groaned and switched on his bedside lamp.

"Done sleeping?" Emlee asked.

Piers propped up his pillow and sat against it. "I can't sleep because—"

"It's funny," Emlee continued. "I've been in this house before." She floated up to the ceiling. "This room, even. Exploring. There used to be different Unborn here... I just never paid much attention to them, or how they make these little changes to their environment."

She pointed to a poster on the wall. "Who's this?"

"It's just a video game poster." He hadn't updated any of his room's decor in years, he suddenly realized. *Not since...*

Piers snapped back to attention. "Look, Emlee. I'm not the kind of kid who can just leave his family and have adventures. Any other kid would be better for what you want." He crossed his arms over his chest. "I have responsibilities, and yesterday I was nearly killed."

"I see. Well, no... I don't, really. By family, you mean the female Unborn on the couch downstairs?"

"She should be in her bedroom."

Emlee tucked her head and dove through the floorboards. She quickly popped back up again. "No, she's on the couch."

Piers sighed. "Okay, yes, that's my mother. My family."

The girl floated back to the foot of the bed. Her bluish inner glow and the bobbing movements of her hair and dress reminded Piers of a jellyfish he'd once seen in an aquarium. "There are so many of you humans," she said. "Thousands, I bet. And yet you seem to be attached to just one. Why her and not any other human?"

"Because she's all I have left!" Piers said, exasperated. "Look, I don't want to talk about it. She needs me, and... you need to find someone else to kill your ghosts."

"But Piers—"

"No! I-I-I can't." He looked down at the bedsheets. "You don't understand. And stop staring at me! I'm going to sleep."

Piers switched off the light, flopped back down and pulled the covers over his head. It took a while for his brain to calm down, but just before he drifted off, he heard the girl speak softly one last time.

"No, I don't understand."

❧ 9 ❧

Morning light crept through the bedroom window.

Piers came warily back to consciousness, uncertain of each memory that resurfaced from the day before. He sat up and looked around the room. Everything seemed as it should be. Nixon lay in the corner, still fast asleep, and the reading chair held no one, supernatural or otherwise.

He slid out of bed, threw on some clean clothes and shuffled into the bathroom. Midway through brushing his teeth, a thought occurred to him; he walked back to the bedroom nightstand with his toothbrush hanging from his mouth, grabbed his phone and began thumbing through the pictures. The latest album held several animal photos, mostly blurry, and Piers played the only recorded video as he returned to the bathroom. Plenty of forest footage appeared on the screen, but no ghost girl. A squirrel hopped into the frame once, but the critter didn't say anything.

I must be going crazy, Piers thought. *Or sleepwalking.*

Grabbing his backpack, he trotted downstairs, turned the corner into the kitchen and nearly plowed into the floating figure of the ghost girl.

"Aaaaaahhh!" Piers cried as the smartphone flew from his

hands. It arced through the middle of Emlee's face and clattered onto the kitchen table behind her. She still didn't blink.

"Hello, Piers," Emlee said with a cheerful smile. "It's fun that you get excited so much."

Piers struggled to regain his composure. "What? No, I mean... You need to stop scaring me like that!" He stormed through her, retrieved his device from the table and made sure the screen hadn't cracked.

Emlee swiveled around to face him. "I came to see if you changed your mind. Yesterday must have shaken you up a little."

Piers went to the cabinets and pulled out a bowl and a cereal box. "I'm sorry, I can't get my mom involved with that... thing out there."

"Why not?"

He poured some cornflakes, set the box on the counter and faced the ghost. "Because it's not fair. She has enough to deal with." Piers closed the cereal box and lifted it up, exposing a squirrel that had been standing behind it.

"Well, the way I see it," Scarlet began.

"Aaaaaahhh!" Piers shouted, dropping the box onto the counter.

The squirrel selected a fallen cornflake. "You sure are excitable," she said in between nibbles. "So, the way I see it, your mom is already involved."

Piers glared and started sweeping crumbs into his hand. "Why are you in my house?"

Scarlet hopped over to an overlooked flake. "Eh. Sometimes the acorn's stuck in the fox's jaw, know what I mean?"

"No." He brought his bowl over to the table and went to fetch the milk. Scarlet jumped onto the tabletop.

"Your mom's going into the North Tower today, right?" the squirrel asked.

Piers closed the fridge door and frowned. "Stop touching my cornflakes."

Scarlet swiped one more piece from the bowl and leapt back to the counter. "Soooooo... she's going to be hanging out with the Ender, like it or not." The squirrel took a noisy bite and chewed slowly. "See where I'm going with this?"

Piers knocked a few flakes from the bowl that he thought Scarlet might have touched, then poured the milk.

Emlee broke the silence. "I would go into the Tower if I could. But I can't. You can. And if you can learn anything about the Ender, it may help to save your mother."

The boy sat down but just stared at his cereal.

Nixon trotted into the kitchen. "Hello, Piers. Hello, ghost lady." The greyhound glanced at his dog dish. "I see I have no food, and that is sad." He raised his long muzzle, gave a few exploratory sniffs and asked, "Why do I smell squirrel?"

The sound of his mother's footsteps in the stairwell snapped Piers to attention.

"Piers?" his mom called from the front hall. Piers hurriedly waved Emlee away, and the ghost shot up into the ceiling and vanished. He grabbed his backpack and ran up to the squirrel on the counter.

"Get in the backpack!" he whispered.

Scarlet gave him a funny look, but she hopped in just as Pier's mom stepped through the kitchen doorway.

"Piers, were you talking to somebody?" his mother asked.

"Oh." Piers anxiously scanned the room, saw his smartphone on the table and pointed to it. "I was just on s-s-s-speakerphone with a friend."

His mom finished pinning a name tag onto her blue nursing scrubs, then poured herself some coffee. "Are you going out?"

While the woman's head was turned, Scarlet poked her upper body out of the backpack, crossed her arms and looked sternly at Piers. He shoved the squirrel back in and said, "I w-w-was thinking... maybe I could go to work with you."

His mom picked up her mug and looked his way. "You haven't wanted to go to Aspen Home in over a year. Are you certain?"

Out of the corner of his eye, Piers spied Emlee's face poking through the ceiling above his mom's head. He forced himself to keep his eyes down as he slowly nodded to his mother.

"Well, you won't be able to bring Nixon inside like you used to," she said. "They're taking precautions until they get this virus under control. You'd have to stay down in the garden, but the residents would love to see you."

"I'll bring a book. I don't like how it smells inside, anyway."

"Remember, they've changed the shifts, and I work until eight now. I can bring food out to you, but that's a long time to be in the garden."

"I can walk home," said Piers. "It's really not that far."

His mother pulled a coat from the back of a chair and slipped it on over her scrubs. "Finish eating and let's go, then." She lifted her coffee mug and carried it into the next room.

Scarlet popped her head out of the backpack again. Piers glared at her. "Happy now?" he muttered.

The squirrel matched his gaze evenly. "Thrilled as always, human."

The elderly woman smiled from her wheelchair and scratched Nixon's ears one last time before she was wheeled down the sidewalk and back to the building. Her attendant donned a surgical mask, swiped an ID card through the reader on the side of the door and pressed an over-sized red button. The door swung open, and the nurse and her charge vanished into the bowels of the nursing home.

Piers studied the scene carefully, then turned and led the leashed greyhound out of the rose garden. They walked upslope away from the building complex toward the chainlink fence at the edge of the forest.

"This is very hard, Piers," said Nixon. "I like to talk but you do not want me to talk to anyone."

"A talking dog is not a common thing, Nixon. If you become famous, it's going to be hard to go anywhere."

Nixon lifted his head proudly as they approached Scarlet, who stood a few feet in front of the fenceline. "I *am* famous!" Nixon boasted. "Humans love me and give me treats because I am a fast dog and a handsome dog."

"And a famous-for-eating-poop dog," Scarlet added.

Nixon growled and leapt at the squirrel, who let out an undignified squeak and dove under the fence. From the trees behind them, Emlee descended like an angel, passing through the chainlinks to hover in front of the boy.

"Are you ready, Piers?" she asked.

"I think so." Piers had vetoed the suggestion to enter Aspen Home while his consciousness was in the ghost world. Too much could go wrong if he was unable to communicate with his mom's coworkers. Still, he'd agreed to look around for anything unusual... that was the best he could do for them. "So, how am I going to keep that thing from killing me if I go inside? He can probably recognize me now."

"We'll be watching. I'm going to return to my world so that I'll be able to see him, but I'll come back to this exact spot. Nixon will need to stay here."

Emlee dropped to the dog's eye level. "Nixon, if I see the Ender heading toward the North Tower, I'll touch your nose three times, like this." The tip of Emlee's finger became slightly more substantial, and she tapped Nixon on the nose. "Can you feel that?"

Nixon wrinkled his white muzzle. "It is soft. But I have a sensitive nose."

The ghost girl continued. "If you feel that, you run to the Tower and start barking so Piers can hear. I'm near the edge of my Circle and cannot go beyond."

"What happens if you do?" asked Piers.

Emlee looked back up at him. "The Winds become too strong, and I disperse. Forever."

Piers pressed his hands together. "Here's a thought. Can we force the Ender outside of his Circle?"

"Already asked that!" said Scarlet from the other side of the fence.

"Can we kill him that way?" Piers continued.

Emlee floated upward. "There is no forcing any of my kind to go anywhere. We are not made of base material, as you are. We only become solid when we wish to, and even then, well..." She extended her arm and wiggled her fingers. "...you've seen the limits of my solidity."

"It isn't much," he admitted.

"No. Though there are stories about Obsessed who can lift and move objects, even heavy ones."

"The Ender being one of them."

"He is. But also, the Ender may not even have a Circle. If he does, from what I hear, it's bigger than any Circle previously known."

Piers scratched his arm. "Well, it was an idea." He walked over to the fence. "Okay, squirrel. Are you ready?"

Scarlet jumped back. "What, me?"

Piers nodded. "I've got a plan to get into the nursing home. But you'll need to go in first."

"Go in there?" Her mouth hung open in disbelief. "With the Ender and a bunch of decaying humans walking around? No, I'm just an observer here. Gonna be a hefty price to put Squirrel Power in play, that's for sure."

"A price?" said Piers incredulously. "You all came asking for *my* help!"

Emlee spoke calmly. "You have to help him, Scarlet."

"No, I don't!" Scarlet jumped onto the chainlink fence and poked her head through one of the holes. "In exchange for my assistance, I want... a box of cereal."

Piers rolled his eyes. "Okay, whatever."

She waggled a claw at him. "Unopened!"

"Fine!" Piers unzipped his backpack and held it out. "Now get in the bag... *your majesty."*

∾

As another satisfied resident was wheeled away from the garden, Piers took Nixon aside, pulled off his backpack and unzipped it. Scarlet poked her head out. She held a piece of granola in her hands, and crumbs fell from her whiskers.

"Did you eat my trail bars?" demanded Piers. He pushed her out of the bag and started removing the other contents. "You got crumbs over everything!"

Scarlet sat and began to groom her fur. "Consider it a down payment on the cereal box you owe me."

Piers shook out the empty backpack, then refocused his attention on the building. "Okay, here's the plan." He pointed. "See that window on the 3rd floor? That's the kitchen. All other windows have screens, but that one is always open a couple inches. Use the vines to get up there. The cooks should be on break, but you'll need to be careful when you sneak in."

"Uh-huh," said Scarlet.

"All the elevators and stairwell doors will be closed. You'll have to wait until you find a laundry cart or a cleaning cart – better a full laundry cart, because that will definitely be going down to the ground floor. Hide in the laundry, get in the elevator, then jump out sometime after the doors open when you're moving down the hallway."

"Yeah, yeah."

"The break room is on the ground floor... just follow the smell of coffee. You'll see some clothing hanging on the walls. Find an ID card. It'll be this big," Piers held his hands a few inches apart, "white, with a picture of a nurse or somebody on one side."

"Like that?" Scarlet pointed her nose at an attendant, who was pulling an ID tag on a retractable string from his belt. He slid it through the panel by the door and pushed the red button. The door slowly swung outward.

"Yes. One of those," said Piers. "You'll have to bite it off a chain or a string, probably. Take it, then retrace your steps...

maybe use an empty laundry cart. Get back to the third level, go through the kitchen, out the window, and bring it to me."

"Is that all you want me to do?" She sounded almost indifferent.

"Uh, yeah. It's not going to be easy."

Scarlet scratched her chin. "Excuse me a moment." Before Piers could stop her, the squirrel hopped past him toward the building. She gave no regard to the attendant as the man guided a wheelchair backward through the door and helped the wheels over the threshold. The old woman sitting in the chair grinned and waved at Piers. Piers gave a weak smile and waved back.

The next he saw Scarlet, she was standing by the door hinges, giving him an identical wave, though with a condescending expression. Piers bit his lip. Before the door closed completely, Scarlet took a pebble from her mouth, stuck it in the door jamb, and looked smugly in Piers' direction.

Piers sighed. "I hate squirrels."

"They are very bad animals," said Nixon.

Piers crouched, removed Nixon's leash and took the dog's head in his hands. "You know where to go, right?" Nixon nodded. "Bark really loud. It's going to be hard to hear you inside."

"I will bark really loud. I am the best barker." Nixon licked Piers' face and trotted off toward the forest.

Piers checked to make sure that no workers were outside the building or standing at the windows, then he walked to the doorway. He tried the door handle, and sure enough, the pebble had kept the door from clicking shut. He opened it. Scarlet hopped through and paused, looking back at him.

"Or... I could climb the building, go through the kitchen, get in the elevator..."

"Shut up," said Piers.

Piers walked nervously down the hall. He hadn't been inside the building in over a year, but he recognized the oppressive smell of bleach, soiled linens and chemical air fresheners. The sounds of television game shows and soap operas trickled out from open doorways. Scarlet scooted ahead, then stopped to sniff the stale air. She wrinkled her nose distastefully.

"Slow down, smartypants," said Piers. "We're still going to need a keycard in order to get around the building."

Scarlet looked back at him. "That's stupid. You humans sure like to barricade yourselves into places." She continued down the corridor.

"Well, I still need you to get one. I have no idea what I'm supposed to be looking for, but if we can figure out who died, and where, that might tell us something about the Ender. I mean, ghosts haunt places for reasons, right?"

"Is that supposed to make sense?" Scarlet reached an intersection and paused. "No offense, but your species seems to be a waste of good intelligence."

Piers caught up to her. "Just get me an ID card."

"Okay, where am I going? I wasn't really listening before since your plan was dumb."

Piers crouched down and gave Scarlet directions to the employee break room. After the squirrel scampered off, Piers took a few steps in the opposite direction and peered into one of the common areas. The homespun decor of the room only partially masked its sterility, but the presence of people made it feel tolerably comfortable; several elderly residents sat around a coffee table playing cards, while others dozed in their chairs or watched TV.

The creak of a rusty wheel caught Piers' attention. At the end of the hallway behind him, two workers emerged from an elevator, pushing carts of fresh linens. Lost in conversation, they pointed their carts at Piers and advanced toward his position. Piers dashed into the living room before he could be noticed and crouched down next to the coffee table, between two easy chairs.

A tall woman, with red lipstick that matched the flowers on her blouse, lowered her cards and leaned over in her chair, smiling. "Hello, Piers. Nice of you to join us. Shall we deal you in?"

He raised himself as much as he dared. "Oh, I'm j-j-j-just here to watch."

"Where's your dog?" asked another resident, peering through oversize spectacles.

"Where's your mask?" said a third woman. She wore a zebra-striped tracksuit that did little to conceal her plump physique.

Piers couldn't remember any of their real names. The lady he identified as Red Lipstick tapped her cards on the table. "You should have a mask. Terrible bug going around, it's awful."

Piers ignored the dog question. "Why aren't you all w-wearing masks?"

"Ooooo, we like to take chances," Red Lipstick teased.

A fourth, dour-faced woman threw her cards on the table. "I fold."

"Except Lucy here," said Spectacles. "Lu, you are depressingly conservative."

"At least I don't run out of money in the first ten minutes."

The ladies chuckled as a worker pushed one of the linen carts into the living room. Piers ducked down until it passed out of sight, then offered up another question. "So, um... the people that got s-s-sick and died... H-how, exactly..."

Spectacles drew another card from the deck. "Peacefully. In their sleep."

"Heart attack," muttered Lucy.

"Too many for that," Red Lipstick countered. "Too many, too quick."

There was an awkward silence. Finally, Spectacles commented, "The food here's not good enough to give you a heart attack," and the players broke into laughter again.

After they settled back down, Zebra Suit spoke quietly. "It's sad, too."

"Yes." Red Lipstick looked down from her cards at Piers. "Don't you worry about it, dear. People pass on when they're ready to pass on."

"And you're healthy," said Spectacles. "This bug is only hitting us old biddies."

Out of the corner of his eye, Piers spotted Scarlet in the hallway. The squirrel beckoned him over. He allowed himself to stand, saying, "Well, nice talking with you. Maybe I can play next time."

"Yes, that would be lovely," said Red Lipstick. "Ta ta." She gave his hand a warm squeeze before turning back to the game.

Piers hadn't gone far from the table when he overheard, "You wait. It'll be another employee incident, what killed them."

"Oh, hush, Lucy."

Piers walked hesitantly back to the quartet of ladies. "S-sorry... what's the *employee incident?*"

The other players glared at Lucy.

Red Lipstick sighed. "This was long before we came to Aspen. A lot of people died, and an employee ended up being responsible for it."

Piers felt slightly stunned. "The employee killed... the residents?"

"Well, supposedly. Don't ask me who."

Zebra Suit spoke in hushed tones. "They don't like people talking about it. It's tragic."

"But it's the truth," said Lucy.

"What did the employee do?" Piers asked.

Red Lipstick picked up her cards and pretended to study them. "Who knows? This was fifty years ago." Lucy began to speak, but she cut her off angrily. "You weren't here. Don't go saying things you don't know about!"

Spectacles leaned over and patted Piers' arm. "Don't worry about it, love. Come play cards with us next time."

Piers sensed it was time to leave. He heard the ladies chastising Lucy for "scaring the boy" as he went over to Scarlet and crouched down.

"ID card?" he asked.

The squirrel held up half a doughnut.

"That's a doughnut," said Piers.

Scarlet looked at the object in her hands. "Oh. Not much of a nut, really, but still tasty. Hold this for me." Scarlet passed Piers the doughnut, scampered down the hall to a potted plant and retrieved an ID card from the foliage. She returned and traded the plastic card for the sugary morsel.

Piers stuffed the card in his pocket. "I've got a lead. We need to get to the Records room."

"After you, Furless," Scarlet said through a mouthful of crumbs.

Piers scanned the adjacent corridors, then hurried to the elevator. Sliding the ID card through the panel, he entered and hit the button for the third floor. Scarlet jumped inside just before the doors closed.

"You should get back in the backpack," said Piers.

The squirrel looked around the elevator. "No thanks. I'm stuffed."

"That's not what I—" he began, then cut himself off with an exasperated sigh.

When the elevator doors opened, Piers peeked through the doorway before stepping out. He walked briskly down the corridor, with Scarlet at his heels. "We probably have just one shot at this," he warned. "Don't be seen."

They passed the open kitchen door. Piers pointed inside. "That's your escape route if I get caught – through the window there."

Scarlet twitched her tail. "I prefer to fight my way out."

A short, greenish figure suddenly ran across the hallway ahead of them.

Piers froze. "Did you see that?"

"No," said the squirrel. "I'm trying to avoid your gargantuan feet."

The figure dashed across the far end of the corridor again, disappearing through an open door.

"There!" said Piers.

Scarlet puffed up her cheeks. "I'm on it." She bounded ahead, then stopped on the threshold of a darkened room. Piers caught up to her, reached through the doorway and switched on the light. It looked like a meeting room, with chairs arranged neatly around several tables.

More ghosts? Piers wondered.

Something bumped a chair on the other side of the room, and they heard the click of a cabinet door closing. Cautiously, they entered and approached the furniture lining the back wall. Scarlet hopped directly to one cabinet and pointed to it. "It's in there."

"Did you see what it was?"

"No, but I can smell it." Scarlet wrinkled her nose. "Doesn't smell like anything else here... not like chemicals or rotting humans."

Piers felt oddly defensive. "Aspen Home doesn't smell *that* bad."

Scarlet gave him a dubious look. "Says the person wearing chemicals all over his body."

She approached the cabinet slowly, rapped her knuckles on the door and quickly jumped back. There was no response. Piers stepped up and gave it another knock. Still nothing. He looked at Scarlet and shrugged.

"I'm not here," murmured a faint, slurred voice from behind the cabinet door. Then came the unmistakable sound of someone snoring.

Piers opened the cabinet door. A gnomish creature lay curled up on the middle shelf, snoring softly. His clothes were a muted gray and green, and his billowy, gray hair stuck out in every direction. One pale, yellow eye cracked open, and the tiny figure yawned, stretched and suddenly saw the two onlookers. He flinched and pulled his hair forward to cover his face.

"Not here," the creature mumbled.

Piers didn't know what to say. "Ummm... hi?"

The gnome crawled across the shelf and hid behind the other cabinet door. Piers pulled the handle and found him crouched atop an old chessboard.

"Can't see me," said the thing in a squeaky voice.

"Pretty sure we can," said Scarlet.

The creature avoided their eyes as he slowly slid off the shelf and dropped to the ground. He stood three feet tall, lanky with a bit of a belly showing beneath his roughspun clothes. Thin, frizzy hair formed a halo around his head and his pointed ears. He stepped gingerly past them, ducked underneath the room's large conference table and headed toward the door.

Scarlet hopped over to meet the tiny humanoid when he emerged. The creature tried to move around her, but Scarlet scurried sideways and cut him off.

"What is it?" asked Piers.

"I was going to ask *you*." Scarlet circled the little man and sniffed. "Doesn't smell like a human."

The elven figure extended his hands in a calming gesture. "Nothing to see, little squirrel."

Scarlet pointed to Piers. "He can see you." She poked her chest twice for emphasis. "*I* can see you. 100 percent of the occupants in this room can see you."

The creature retreated under the table and hugged his knees to make himself seem as small as possible.

Piers knelt to get a better look. "Hey, it's okay. No one's going to hurt you." His words only served to make the doll-like being hide his face and curl up tighter.

Scarlet bounded over. "The guy's a dud acorn, if you ask me."

Piers tried again. "We can leave you alone, but we just want to know what you are."

A yellow eye peeked through the puffball of gray hair. "Hello?"

"Hello." Piers tried to sound calm.

"You can hear me?" the reedy voice asked hesitantly.

"Yeah."

"You can *see* me?"

"Yeah," said Piers. "Sorry."

The creature sprawled out on the floor and sighed. "I'm lost," he confessed.

"I didn't think you were from around here." Piers had never seen anything like him outside of children's movies. "What are you? An elf? A goblin?"

"Elf." He considered the word for a moment. "No? *Fairy?* Yes... that's a better word." His large eyes darted around the room. "Not supposed to be seen."

"But what happened?" Piers asked. "What are you doing here?"

"I don't know! I don't know!" the fairy wailed, clutching a chair leg for comfort. "I was in my dispersal form, and I woke up in a metal room. Metal tools everywhere. Dead plants in metal boxes."

"Dead plants... you mean the kitchen?"

"It's not the first time I've woken up in a human construction." He seemed lost in his thoughts. "But I could hear humans talking! Real words! An old human saw me and screamed, and I ran away. Hid someplace dark, which I shouldn't do, because I can fall asleep for a very long time." He looked up at Piers. His face seemed younger than his gray hair implied. "And that's what happened."

"You fell asleep," Piers prodded.

"Yes – I think for many days. Then someone opened the door and left it open a crack. That woke me up. I thought I had my invisibility back, but the same old human saw me again." He pulled his jacket up to his chin. "Now I try to be sneaky, just until my invisibility returns."

Piers turned to Scarlet. "He must've fallen in from some other world, like how you found the ghost world."

The squirrel nodded. "It's amazing the humans haven't caught this guy and eaten him by now."

The fairy's eyes went wide. He bolted for another cabinet, jumped inside and slammed the door.

"Way to go, Scarlet," Piers grumbled.

"What? You never eat animals?"

Piers bit off his reply and approached the cabinet. Inside, he found the elven creature on a shelf again, softly snoring. Thin hairs on the fairy's head stirred with each exhalation.

"He's narcoleptic!" Scarlet declared. She stood on her hind legs to get a closer look. "Hey, wake up!"

The fairy startled, smacking his head on the shelf above him.

"It's okay, green guy," said Scarlet. "Piers promises he won't eat you."

"We don't eat fairies!" Piers huffed. He glared at the squirrel, then turned back to the cabinet and lowered his voice. "We never eat fairies, okay?"

"Okay," the tiny figure mumbled, rubbing his scalp.

"What's your name?" Piers asked.

The fairy spoke too soft for Piers to hear.

"One more time?" the boy tried.

"Dandelion."

The little person bore quite a resemblance to his namesake. His clothes were the right color, and the fine, grey hairs on his head looked like they might take flight at any moment, like dandelion seeds.

"Well, *that* fits," Scarlet agreed.

Piers tried to smile as kindly as he could. "I'm Piers, and this is Scarlet."

"Scarlettail Thistleclaw," she corrected.

Dandelion crawled to the edge of the shelf. "If it's not too much to ask," he said, "I would really like to go home now."

Scarlet's ears suddenly pricked up. Then Piers heard it, too; a set of voices rumbled in the hallway. "The lights!" he whispered. Scarlet raced to the doorway and leapt to the lightswitch. The windowless room plunged into darkness.

Dandelion began snoring again. As Piers' eyes adjusted to the dim light from the hall, he saw the fairy sprawled out on the shelf with one arm dangling over the edge.

Scarlet hopped over and tugged on one of Piers' socks. "Say, weren't we on a secret mission or something?"

"Scarlet, we can't leave him here," reasoned the boy. The creature seemed so helpless. "Maybe Emlee knows where he belongs." He poked Dandelion's side. "Wake up!" In response, the fairy scratched his nose and started to snore even louder. Piers lifted him out of the cabinet and tried to carefully set him on his feet, but he simply sagged to the floor. Piers dragged him toward the doorway, which proved surprisingly easy; the diminutive man weighed next to nothing. The light from the hallway began to revive him, and Piers propped the fairy against the wall.

Dandelion rubbed his eyes and yawned. "Sorry about that."

Piers fetched a green moccasin that had fallen off the fairy's foot and handed it to him. "Dandelion, we have a friend that might be able to get you back home. But first, we need to get into a special room on this floor."

"Did I mention that this is dumb?" said Scarlet. "We should wait until dark when humans go to sleep."

Dandelion tugged his moccasin back on. "I get too tired when it gets dark."

"And I can't stay up here that long," Piers added. "My mom will start looking for me." He remembered the ID card in his pocket. Perhaps he could bike back to Aspen Home later tonight. He wouldn't be able to make excuses if he got caught after hours, though. "Let's try now while we still can."

Piers poked his head into the empty corridor and gestured for the others to follow. They passed a series of open doorways before finding a yellow door marked "Records". There was no ID card reader, so Piers tried the doorknob.

He sighed. "It's locked."

"Well, use the card!" Scarlet snapped.

Piers pulled the card out of his pocket. "Does this look like it fits in a keyhole?"

"I don't know how your stupid human tools work!"

Piers glanced down the hall. "We're going to have to search the office for a key."

The squirrel gave a rude grunt. "You mean *I'm* going to have to search the office for a key."

"Come on." Piers led the others down the hall. Scarlet scampered ahead, but Dandelion hovered uncomfortably close.

As they neared the office, snatches of a phone conversation

leaked through the open door. Piers beckoned for Scarlet to come back. "The Director's in there," he whispered. "We gotta bail."

Scarlet turned. "Wait a second. You're a human. This Director is a human. Why don't you just ask her to borrow the key, for oak's sake!"

"I can't do that!" He dropped his voice. "Let's go. I'm going to get my mom fired, being up here."

"Dog," mumbled Dandelion.

"Well, give her some food!" Scarlet countered. "There's half a trail bar in that sack of yours."

Piers threw up his hands. "We don't have a food-based barter system!"

"Dog," the fairy said again.

Scarlet shouted, "Well, how do you get any–"

"Shhhh!" Piers hissed. He turned to Dandelion. "What did you say?"

The fairy shuffled his feet. "Oh. Sorry. I said *'dog'*."

Piers froze. In the distance, he heard the echo of a dog barking.

"That," said Dandelion.

Piers' eyes went wide. "We need to go."

They hustled back down the corridor, past the conference rooms and the kitchen. When at last the elevators were in sight, a door slammed shut in front of them, blocking their exit. They halted, and a second door closed at their backs, trapping them in the hallway.

Under his breath, Piers whispered, "Too late."

🕸 13 🕸

Scarlet poked Piers in the leg. "Uh, how about we *don't* stop?"
Piers ran forward and found that the door had locked itself. He yanked the ID card out of his pocket and moved to swipe it through the magnetic reader on the side of the door, but an invisible force knocked it from his fingers. The card skidded across the tiles, and before he could recover it, an unseen hand flicked it through the slit at the base of a closet door. Piers raced to grab the handle, but the closet door wouldn't budge either.

"Are we in trouble?" asked Dandelion.

A harsh, scraping sound pulled their attention to the painted drywall on the side of the corridor. Huge, ragged letters were being gouged onto the surface. Piers backed away from the closet as powdery gypsum dust spilled to the floor, revealing a single word: SOOL.

Framed photographs of pastoral scenery fell from the wall and shattered. In their place, more letters appeared, torn into the drywall: SEES YOU.

Piers swallowed hard. "Yes, I think we're in trouble."

A gust of wind struck Piers in the chest and tightened around his heart. He swatted the air and jumped back, finding he could breathe again. The reprieve was short-lived. A heavy, oppressive force coalesced around him once more, and he shouted, "We need to get out!"

Piers ran to the door from which they'd come and pounded on it, to no avail. His heart twinged with pain again, so he fled to one of the windows along the corridor and wrenched it open. Nixon's barking sounded immediately clearer; it was almost as if the greyhound were actually saying the word, "BARK!"

Piers punched the window screen, but it tore his knuckles and refused to break. He threw off his backpack, whipped it around to fend off the ghostly presence, then slammed it into the screen. The mesh began to tear, so he struck it again. This time, the screen ripped, but he lost his grip on the backpack and it plummeted to the ground twenty feet below.

Dandelion went to the window and peered outside. The branches of an aspen tree extended five feet from the window. "Yes!" he exclaimed. "Help me up!"

Piers lifted him onto the windowsill, and the fairy poked his head through the hole in the screen. "Aspen! We need you! Lend your branches!"

Behind them, Scarlet began to speak, but her words choked off. Piers turned to see the squirrel pinned against the opposite wall, gagging. He ran over and waved his arms to ward off the crushing force, then scooped her off the floor.

"Are you okay?" he asked. Scarlet could only cough in response. Piers felt his own lungs compressing, so he kept moving about the room. He called to the fairy, "Dandelion, is there a way down?"

The gnome-like creature held up a hand and kept shouting. "Aspen! Aspen, where are you?"

Piers joined him at the window. "We need to get Scarlet out of here."

Dandelion seemed frantic. "He's not coming! I don't know why!"

Piers placed the squirrel on the windowsill and pointed to the tree. "Scarlet, do you see that branch?"

"Too far," she protested.

"I'll throw you. Do you think you can grab it?"

The dense air enveloped them again. Piers retreated from the window, pulling Scarlet away.

"No choice!" cried the squirrel. "Throw me!"

"Dandelion, move!" Piers shouted. He jumped onto the windowsill alongside the fairy and tossed the squirrel through the screen. Scarlet rotated her legs forward and clutched at the branch as she landed, only to fall through the twigs onto the limb immediately underneath. Somehow, she managed to hold on.

Nixon arrived at the base of the tree, still barking. Before Piers could call down to him, the spectral presence struck the boy from both sides. He grunted, leapt awkwardly onto the floor and stumbled free of the Ender's grasp. "If you know any fairy magic, Dandelion, now's the time!"

The little figure leaned out the window once more and called, "Aspen, we need your help now! Wake up!"

With a tortured creak, one of the aspen's skinny trunks leaned toward the building. Its closest branch straightened incrementally and stretched for the window.

"Yes!" cried Dandelion. "That's it!" The fairy sprung from the windowsill, landed gracefully on the branch and grabbed the trunk. He looked back at the boy. "Piers, jump!"

Piers eyed the distance, his lungs burning. "I'm not an acrobat!" he wheezed.

Dandelion tapped at the trunk. "A little further, Aspen!" The tree appeared to bend a few inches closer. Piers ran circles around the corridor, swatting the air as if warding off mosquitoes, then dashed to the window and leapt onto the sill. He kicked at the mesh to widen the hole, and the entire screen popped out.

Dandelion beckoned him forward. Piers took half a breath, locked his eyes on the branch ahead of him, and jumped.

Halfway across the expanse of open air, Piers thought, *I've got this*. Then the invisible force snatched at his leg. His foot missed the branch, and as he dropped, he reached for the limb with his arm instead. Somehow, his fingers latched on, but the jolt nearly ripped his arm from its socket.

Dandelion slid down the trunk and extended his tiny hand. "Grab on!" the fairy hollered. Piers desperately wanted a better choice, but he felt the air start to swirl and compress around his torso once more. He stretched, locked fingers with Dandelion and released the branch.

His crushing grip caused Dandelion to squeak with pain, but Piers held fast as his body swung like a pendulum and crashed into the trunk. He latched on with both arms, ignoring the ache of his bruised ribs and shoulder, then slid down the smooth bark to the ground. Dandelion touched down a few seconds later and flexed his fingers painfully.

Nixon pranced over with Scarlet clinging to his back. "Did you hear me barking? I said, *Bark! Bark!*" He suddenly noticed the fairy. "Who is the funny creature?"

"Later." Piers grabbed his backpack from the base of the building. "Let's go!"

With one last look at the open window above their heads, Piers turned and ran for the fenceline. The fairy and the greyhound followed.

❧ 14 ❧

Piers found the gap in the fenceline that Nixon had discovered yesterday, and after crawling underneath, he lifted the chain-links so that Scarlet and Dandelion could pass easily. Nixon wriggled partway through and paused. "I felt the signal, and I barked really loud," the dog reported. "Did you see the Ender?"

"No, I didn't see the Ender," Piers said, exasperated. "That's the problem! We're like sitting ducks 'cause we can't *see* him!" He grabbed Nixon's collar and pulled him through.

Piers climbed to his feet just as Emlee swooped down from the trees. "Piers, are you all right?" She swirled and looked at Dandelion. "And who's this? A North Tower human?"

The fairy cowered, wilting under her curious gaze. Piers stepped between them. "I'll explain later. It's after us. Can we get to the ghost world?"

A more serious expression returned to Emlee's face, and she rose back into the air. "Come."

The four of them matched Emlee's speed through the forest. Nixon loped beneath the underbrush, and Scarlet nimbly rico-cheted off the sides of trees to keep pace. Piers suffered numerous scratches to his legs and arms but managed not to be left behind. After several minutes of flight, Emlee stopped and began circling a patch of the forest floor.

"Here," she whispered to herself. "Somewhere here."

"How do you find the holes?" Piers asked.

Emlee continued to scan the ground carefully. "There's a thin edge that's hard to see."

Piers turned to the greyhound. "Nixon, can you see them?"

The greyhound shook some debris off his back and shrugged. "I think it is a ghost thing."

Dandelion stumbled amid the roots of the nearby trees. At first, Piers thought the fairy was exhausted from their escape, but the little man looked more anxious than tired. "Where is everyone?" he moaned.

"Who?" asked Piers.

Dandelion poked his head into the hollow at the base of a tree, then withdrew it. "Buckeye. Hazelnut. Dogwood."

Scarlet pointed to a few trees and shrubs around her. "Uh, there, there and there."

"Those are trees," Dandelion tried explaining. "Where are the fairies?" He spun about and put his hands to his mouth. "Oh, no... where am I?"

"Here it is!" Emlee exclaimed. Piers failed to see anything unusual as the girl reached down, took hold of the edges of an invisible portal and stretched the opening.

He stepped over and grasped the perimeter with his own hands. "I got it."

Emlee flew through the portal, followed by Dandelion and the animals. Piers struggled but managed to squeeze his body through and flop to the ground on the other side, in the twilight of the ghost world.

He stood and brushed dirt from his shoulders. "Does anyone see it?"

"Hold on," said Emlee. She soared upward, rising above the treetops for a better look.

Dandelion's eyes followed her. "What is she? Do humans fly now?"

"She's a ghost," said Piers. "And that thing that attacked us... that was a ghost, too."

The fairy shuffled away, mumbling, "I don't think I like ghosts very much." He approached the foot of an oak tree and pressed his slender hands against the bark. After a moment, Dandelion pulled back. "This forest is empty. Yet the trees are alive." He looked around helplessly. "I don't understand."

Piers knelt beside him. "I don't know who you're looking for, but I can definitely say I haven't seen any other fairies around here." He put his hand comfortingly on Dandelion's shoulder. "You're the first fairy I've ever met, actually."

Scarlet snorted. "Fairies! Ghosts! Talking humans! The world is completely broken, and that's all there is to it."

"Maybe Emlee knows where your friends are," Piers continued. "She seems to know what's going on. More than we do, anyway."

As if summoned, the ghost girl dove back down to earth. "Close!" she cried.

Piers moved toward the portal, though he had once again lost track of its location. "Okay, let's get back to the human world."

"No time!" Emlee insisted. "We'll find another one!" She flew off into the trees, and Nixon loped after her.

Scarlet jumped onto Piers' leg and climbed up to his shoulder. "Move those legs, meat-eater!"

Piers turned to Dandelion, who looked lost and wretched. "Stay with us. Come on." He began jogging through the woods, and the fairy followed.

They ran for a few minutes until the squirrel's sharp grip on his shoulder became too painful for Piers to bear. He stopped to shift Scarlet onto his backpack. Dandelion seemed to be flagging, so Piers gave him a moment to catch his breath.

"Thanks for calling that tree over when we were trapped," Piers offered. "That's something fairies do, I guess?"

"Yes," Dandelion said, looking at the ground, "but there was nobody to talk to, and I don't know why. My kind gives voice to the trees, shrubs and flowers. Now I can only talk to humans? Animals?" He knocked the side of his head with his hand, and pieces of gray hair broke loose and drifted away. "I think I've been damaged. My mind is failing." He looked up through the forest canopy. "Not enough sun, maybe?"

Scarlet tapped Piers on the shoulder. "We're falling behind, human."

They started running again. Soon, they came to a break in the forest where a paved road cut through the trees. Emlee and the greyhound waited for them.

"Is it safe to cross?" asked the ghost girl.

"I know where we are," said Piers. The road would take them past the state forest and into the residential district of Summerday. "I should go to my house. I can tell my mom I got bored and walked home, but we can't let the Ender follow us."

"We'll be more hidden if we stay in the trees."

Piers nodded. "Okay, stay close to the road."

The group kept to the trees along the roadside, hiking closer to the pavement when the forest grew too thick. Cars were rare. The loudest sounds were the trilling of robins and the crackling of leaves underfoot. Piers felt uncomfortably conscious of being the noisiest member of their motley troupe, though he tried to step quietly. When his cellphone suddenly rang, the sound pierced the forest and set his heart racing. He yanked the device from his pocket and looked at the screen.

"My mom. I should answer this." His finger hesitated over the *Receive* button as he formulated what he would say to his mother. The phone rang a second time.

Emlee put a finger to her lips. "The Ender will hear!" she whispered.

Piers felt sheepish. "Right." On the third ring, he brought the device to his ear. "Hi, mom," he said softly.

A loud hiss of static burst from the speaker. He recoiled and quickly ended the call. "Must be a bad connection."

Emlee floated closer. "Piers, when you were in the Tower, did you learn anything about the Ender?"

He slipped the phone back into his pocket. "Yes. Maybe." The incident in the hallway already felt like it happened ages ago. "Does the name "Sool" mean anything to you?"

"No, why?"

"The ghost-eater-thing wrote, "SOOL SEES YOU" on the side of a wall."

A puzzled look came over Emlee's face. "You mean... he imprinted spoken words?"

"He scratched them into the wall, yeah."

"Using symbols that represent speech?"

Piers sensed he was missing something. "Yeah, words. On a wall. It was a little scary at the time."

Emlee's brow knitted together. "Piers, that's not something ghosts do."

"Writing?"

"We don't make symbols. We can't touch the world... not usually, anyway."

Piers shook his head. "You can't write? But you speak English!"

"I'm sorry!" The ghost girl was flustered. "Maybe I don't understand what you mean by writing."

Piers pulled out his phone and pointed to the logo at the top. "What's this say?"

She put her ear closer to the phone. "It's not saying anything!"

Piers pointed to the logo again. "Use your eyes, not your ears."

Emlee looked at Piers with a hint of skepticism, then studied the logo. "Those are just... wait... Q... U... A... Quan-tum. It says

Quantum. Quantum!" She clapped her hands with excitement, then pressed them against her mouth. "How did I know that?" she murmured to herself. She flew down and brought her face to Piers'. "How did I know that?"

He shrugged. "That's what it says."

"I can read!" Emlee twirled, and her dress wrapped around her like a cyclone. "How amazing! I can read human imprints!" A quizzical look returned to her face. "I don't know what quantum means, though."

"I don't either," Piers admitted. "*Very small*, maybe."

Dandelion came closer. "What are you talking about?"

Piers held his phone up to the fairy and pointed to the logo. "Read this."

The little man squinted for a while, then looked up at Piers. "Am I supposed to interpret these markings?"

"These are words!" Piers insisted. "Like when the Ender wrote, *"Sool sees you"* on the wall."

Dandelion pursed his lips. "I just saw fancy scratches. Was I supposed to see pictures?" He rubbed his eyes. "Terribly sorry... I'm feeling awfully unwell these days."

Scarlet hopped over. "This is nice. I just *love* standing around and chatting while there's a mad specter on the loose."

They resumed hiking. Through the shrubs and tree trunks, Piers noticed a traffic sign up the road. "Okay, Emlee, what's that sign say?"

She squinted. "The metal square? There's just nonsense shapes on it."

Piers gave the sign a second look while trying not to trip over tree roots. Despite moving closer, he couldn't make anything out. "It's getting dark. Let's have a better look."

He led the group out of the woods and onto the shoulder of the road. To his amazement, Piers couldn't read a single word on the yellow sign before them. He supposed it probably read "DEER CROSSING," but he couldn't even detect the symbol for a deer – just some dark shapes that didn't seem to mean anything.

Emlee shook her head. "Those are supposed to be words?"

Piers' mouth twisted. "They're *supposed* to be."

The ghost girl pointed to the phone in Piers' pocket. "That made sense." She studied the sign once more, chewing her bottom lip. *"This* doesn't make sense at all."

"No, it doesn't," Piers agreed. "Dandelion, can you read it?"

The fairy peered up at the sign and scratched his chin. "Hmmm...."

"Would this have words in the human world?" Emlee asked.

Piers stepped back. "Oh, right. I keep forgetting where we are."

Nixon's ears pricked up. Piers stared at the greyhound until the low rumble of a vehicle engine crept into his awareness. "Off the road!" Piers shouted.

They rushed back to the woods and ducked beneath the undergrowth. Nixon crouched next to Piers, Emlee hovered halfway in the ground alongside the squirrel, and...

Dandelion wasn't with them. Through the leaves, Piers spotted the fairy still standing with his neck bent upward, staring at the road sign. The vehicle would soon see him. "Dandelion!" he called. Without waiting for a response, the boy charged through the brush, grabbed the fairy and ran back into the forest.

No sooner had he deposited Dandelion with the others than a white van pulled up along the road in front of them. The words printed on the side of the van were illegible to Piers, but he was pretty sure the vehicle belonged to Aspen Home. Two employees climbed out of the van. One of the men began shouting, but Piers couldn't understand a word of it.

"We should make a run for it," Emlee whispered.

"I am the best runner," announced Nixon. "You can follow me, and I will take us home."

The men approached the edge of the forest and scanned the shrubbery.

"Okay," said Piers, "on *"three"* we run. One... two..."

His phone rang. Piers fumbled for it, trying to hit the buttons through his shorts pocket. The employees moved forward, shouting together.

"Humans! Humans!" whispered Dandelion in Piers' ear.

Piers swore. "Okay, Nixon, stay with me. Everyone else, go!" The boy stood up, raised his hands and walked through the bushes toward the two people. "H-h-h-h-hi, everyone!" he stammered, his voice cracking. "I was j-j-j-just walking h-home, you know? I t-t-t-told my m-mom I—"

The humans paused and made strange noises. Piers didn't recognize their faces. He couldn't even read the *expressions* on their faces, so he wasn't sure how to react. Nixon crawled out of the undergrowth and stood at his side, and the boy ran his fingers through the scruff of the dog's neck for reassurance.

Finally, the workers moved forward, grabbed Piers' arms and marched him toward the van. "Hey! You d-don't have to do this!" he exclaimed. But the side of the vehicle opened, and Piers was thrust onto a row of seats.

"Nixon, you'd better get in here!" he called, and the greyhound leapt inside. The workers shut the door, climbed into the front seats and headed back to Aspen Home.

As they drove, his abductors made more noises at him and at each other, but Piers couldn't make any sense of it. "I can't understand you!"

"These are the dumb humans," Nixon explained. "They cannot speak Animal like you can."

"Hush, Nixon!" Piers started to reach for the dog's muzzle but stopped himself. "Oh, never mind... they can't hear you either." He sighed. "We need to get back to a portal."

The van parked in front of the nursing home, and more

humans emerged from the white brick building. Someone opened the van door, and Piers and Nixon stepped out.

"We're okay!" Piers announced, gesturing for everyone to calm down. *"Okay!"*

His eyes fixed on a woman likely to be his mother, and his guess seemed confirmed when the figure stepped over, knelt in front of him and made a succession of broken noises. He couldn't help but wonder how much trouble he was in. With his fingers, Piers tried making a walking gesture. "I was just going home. We're okay!"

It was disturbing; even with someone he'd known his entire life, he couldn't read any facial expressions or body language. He didn't know if her voice was worried or angry or disappointed. But then his mother pointed toward the aspen tree that he and Dandelion had climbed down when fleeing the Ender, and the knot in his stomach tightened.

One thing he knew for certain... he wouldn't be getting off easily this time.

❧ 15 ❧

*

Piers opened his eyes. The light from the rising sun flooded through his bedroom window, but it failed to brighten the ghost world version of his room. His surroundings remained cloaked behind a curtain of shadows, tinged with darkness. He felt exhausted, but his anxiety wouldn't allow him to fall back asleep. So he stared into space for an hour until Emlee's diaphanous figure finally rose from the bedroom floor.

"You're here!" she cried, much too loudly for Piers' liking.

"Hey," he mumbled.

She flew in close. "We were worried about you. You went outside my Circle and were gone for so long." She turned toward Nixon, who had climbed to his feet and was stretching his limbs. "Hello, Nixon."

The greyhound finished an extended yawn and shook his muzzle. "Hello, Emlee. Piers is in trouble."

"What's wrong?" she asked.

Piers sat up and glared at her. "I'm stuck in this stupid ghost world. Everyone thinks I'm sick or I've gone crazy because I can't communicate anymore. I spent half the night in the hospital before they finally let me come home. And on top of all that, I can't tell if my mom lost her job or not because I can't understand anyone!"

Emlee hovered quietly, a look of concern on her face.

"I can't use my computer," Piers continued. "I can't read a book because suddenly I can't read English..." In frustration, Piers knocked a book from his bedside table onto the floor.

The ghost girl sunk partway into his bed. "I'm sorry if I hurt you, Piers. Please understand that I don't have much experience with humans – you're the only one, really. I don't know much about how you live, or what is bad for you. I will try to learn."

Piers sulked for a minute, looking out the window. "Okay."

Emlee lifted into the air. "Okay? You'll still help us?"

He rubbed his face. "Ask me later. First, I need to get out of this house and back to the human world."

"That should be easy."

"Yeah, except my mom's sleeping right outside my door. She's not going to let me leave like this."

"Can you–" Emlee floated over to the second-story window and looked down. "I guess you can't."

"I need a rope to get down. All I have is string. I tried using bedsheets, but my mom caught me and took them away." He flipped the comforter off his lap, showing that he'd been sleeping on a bare mattress.

Emlee tapped her finger against her lips. "I could ask Dandelion to get a rope."

Piers leaned forward. "He's with you?"

"Yes. He's close."

"Ooo... he can get the ladder!" Piers hopped out of bed, grabbed some paper from his desk and drew a crude picture of a ladder. He held it out to Emlee. "Take this to– *Oh.*" He suddenly remembered he was talking to a ghost, and he pulled his hand back. "I guess you can't. Well, this is what I need, and there's one in the shed – the small building in the yard."

Emlee studied the paper. "We'll find it."

She drifted through the bedroom wall. Piers threw on pants and a t-shirt, then pulled a chair up to his window. He soon spotted the ghost girl and the fairy as they emerged from behind a neighboring house. Dandelion waved nervously up to him before following Emlee to an old toolshed with flaking green paint that stood in the back corner of his yard. The fairy slipped inside.

After a minute, Emlee flew back and reported that the ladder was too heavy for Dandelion to move. Piers dangled one end of a spool of string down to the fairy and told him to tie it to one of the end rungs. Dandelion seemed confused but agreed to try. When Piers pulled the string, however, it came loose instantly.

Piers attempted to have Emlee relay knot-trying instructions next, but that also failed; she'd had little practice with physical matter in her lifetime. He finally gave up, drew a set of instructions and tossed them down to Dandelion. This time, the fairy's knot held. Piers pulled the string and heard a loud clatter within the shed as the aluminum extension ladder toppled to the ground. Dandelion helped guide it the rest of the way out the door. Piers dragged the ladder up to the house, then pulled one end up to the window where he could reach it. After lifting the ladder and making final adjustments, he stepped over the windowsill and onto the upper rungs.

"Piers," Nixon interrupted, a slight whine entering his voice, "I kind of need to visit the backyard, too."

"I'll be right back, I promise." He descended the ladder, and Emlee floated down to join him and the fairy. "Okay," he told them. "Let's find a hole."

Piers' neighborhood sat at the foot of a forested hill adjoining the state park, and Emlee led them through the woods in that direction. Eventually, they came to a circle of yellow police tape, different than the previous site, and Emlee located the portal within its perimeter. Piers crawled through and climbed to his feet.

Dandelion and the ghost were gone. The unnatural shadow had lifted from the world, and Piers could focus once more upon the familiar sensations of the forest: the high-pitched drone of cicadas, the damp, mossy scent of leaves decomposing underfoot, and the soft breath of the wind swirling through the branches overhead. It felt like home. A huge part of him was tempted to simply walk away and go back to his normal life. To his responsibilities.

Reluctantly, he crouched down and spied his companions through the circle of the contracted portal. He pulled the perimeter wide and beckoned. "Come on through, so we can still talk."

Emlee and the fairy passed through, and they began the journey back to his house. Piers spent a few minutes in silence, then said, "I think I'm figuring some of this out. No one – I mean, no *humans* – can see you unless you're here in the human world. So right now, you two are vulnerable."

Dandelion's eyes widened. "Will the humans try to eat me?"

"No, we're not going to eat you!" Piers exclaimed. "But I don't want to have to explain fairies and ghosts to my mom or anyone else. Dandelion, you should probably stay in the shed in the backyard for now. Emlee..."

"I can be careful," she promised.

They reached Piers' backyard. Piers climbed up the ladder, then used the string to lower the top end gently to the ground against the side of the house. Hopefully, he could get it back in the shed before his mother noticed.

Emlee drifted up to the window. "There! Now all is well, yes?"

"Maybe," said Piers. He took a deep breath to settle his nerves. "I don't know. But I better find out." He walked to the bedroom door. "Come check on me in an hour, but don't let my mom see you!"

"Yes, Piers," said the ghost girl. "Good luck." She drifted away.

Nixon padded over, making *whuffing* sounds.

"You're just a normal dog now, huh?" Piers scratched the fur between the greyhound's ears. "You're still a good dog." He straightened and faced the door again. "Well, here goes."

With one last, slow exhalation, Piers reached for the doorknob.

❧ 16 ❧

Piers entered his bedroom and allowed Nixon to slip inside before closing the door. Emlee emerged from the shadows in his closet.

"Well, what happened?" she asked, wide-eyed.

The boy flopped onto the bed. Nixon padded over and sniffed Piers' feet.

"Mom is not losing her job. But I have to go to therapy." His mouth twisted. "They think I had some kind of stress attack related to... well, related to something that happened years ago."

"Oh," said Emlee.

Piers nudged Nixon's head away with his foot. "Because Nixon was barking so much," he said pointedly, "someone saw me climb down the tree. Now mom has to pay to repair the window screen and the wall where the ghost thing scratched his name. *Sool.* And I have to pay my mom back, of course."

He slid off the bed and walked to the window. "They didn't notice Dandelion, and I'm really glad I don't have to explain *him*. Where is the little green guy?"

Emlee hovered in the center of the room. "Hiding in the shed. Poor soul. He seems so sad."

Piers turned and leaned against the windowsill. "You know about the portals and these other worlds. Ever been to one with fairies?"

"No. But I've only been exploring them for..." she considered for a moment, "about ten days."

"That's it?" said Piers, surprised.

"Well, I never noticed the holes until recently." Emlee floated close until her face was just a few inches away from his. "Here's what I think. They must have something to do with the Ender because I only started seeing them once he came into the forest... into my Circle."

Piers shivered involuntarily from her unblinking gaze. He moved to his desk and sat down. "Well, the two portals we entered had police tape around them – that's where the homeless guy and maybe the college student died. The police considered them crime scenes."

"Crime? Humans doing bad things to other humans?"

"Yes, pretty much." He drummed his fingers against the desk-top. "Okay, so listen to this... what if the holes are created by Sool whenever he murders someone?"

"Oh!" Emlee clapped her hands. "That's possible."

"He eats a life, *boom* – portal opens. I don't know why. Or does he open a portal in order to eat living souls?" He leaned forward. "Is that something you ghosts can do? Tear holes in time and space and stuff?"

"No!" Emlee insisted. "Never in my life have I heard such a thing."

"*Shhhhh!*" Piers looked nervously toward his bedroom door. "I don't want my mom to think I'm talking to myself. She already thinks I'm crazy." He thought about what the ghost girl had just said. "How old are you, Emlee?"

"I am nearly sixty," she said calmly.

"Oh!" Piers was taken aback. "I wouldn't have guessed." He leaned forward to study her face, which was unlined and appeared no older than his own. "Wait... sixty *years,* right?"

She drifted closer again. "Yes. And you are... about ten?"

"Ten?" His voice rose defensively. "No! I'm thirteen. Almost fourteen, really."

"Interesting," Emlee murmured. "I have little experience in the production of Unborn, apart from what I've heard from others." She slid back but maintained her wide-eyed stare. "Anyway, you haven't told me much about the North Tower. You said the Ender made human markings on the wall?"

"Yeah. *'Sool sees you.'* His name must be Sool, and I'm guessing he remembers me from yesterday."

"Did you find anything else?"

Piers ran his fingers through his uncombed hair. "I overheard something interesting. Old people are dying there, in their sleep. And fifty years ago, something similar happened, but an employee was the one who did it." He spun in his chair, opened the screen of his beat-up laptop computer and started typing. "I never heard about this before. Maybe there's something online about it."

Nixon hopped onto the bed and scratched himself. Emlee hovered over Piers' shoulder, examining the screen. "I always wondered why humans stare so long at these bright pictures," she said. "We thought you might be in a sleep phase." Emlee slid sideways to see the screen better, overlapping her face and eyes with Piers' own.

"Yaah!" Piers rolled his chair backward. "Don't do that!" He rubbed his eyes. "Now my eyeballs feel itchy!"

"I can understand this!" Emlee proclaimed. "It doesn't make much sense, but these symbols... they are real words! Like on your ringing device!" Her face glowed with astonishment as she continued to read. "This says *'trash'*... this says *'deathcraft-three'*.... this one says *'t-rex town'*."

"Some of those are games," Piers explained. They were one of the few diversions he allowed himself on days he knew his mother was functioning well. "Scoot over."

He rolled his chair up to his desk again, and Emlee moved so he could reach the keyboard.

"You don't know how amazing this is," she said. "I could never understand any of this before! I can read *human*!"

The ghost girl blocked the screen again, clouding his vision as Piers attempted to pull up an internet browser. He leaned back, frustrated. "Emlee, why don't you practice your reading with those posters?" Piers pointed to his bedroom walls.

Emlee looked up from the computer and glided over to examine the printed images. "Oh! These say, *'crossfire!' 'levon-jackson!'*"

"Yep," mumbled Piers.

"*'ninja-cat-two-caged-fury!' 'talking-heads-speaking-in-tongues!'*" She looked back at Piers. "These words help you remember the names of things, yes?"

"Uh huh." Piers continued tapping at his keyboard while Emlee reached the bookshelf.

"More words! *'white-fang!' 'the-secrets-of-trollgarden!' 'brook-lyn-samurai!' 'faraday's guide-to-backyard-wildlife!'*"

Piers sat up. "Emlee, come here! I think I found something."

The ghost girl flew back to his side. Piers gestured at the screen. "This finally came up when I searched under the original name for Aspen Home. Here it is: *cases where atropine was injected by the killer to dilate the pupils and mask the symptoms of morphine poisoning, making prosecution unlikely...* okay... *greater restrictions...* yeah, here it is: *pertaining to the Willmoro Heights murders of the 1930s and widely suspected in the 1964 closure of Sungate Center* – that's the original name." He began typing again. "Let me try something else..."

"The words you just read... where are they coming from?" Emlee asked.

"The internet. I guess it's where people dump human knowl-edge, and you can sometimes find what you need if you know the right phrases to type in. Okay, da da da da *in the 1950s...* Woah!" He pulled his face back from the screen.

"What is it?"

Piers leaned in again. *"twenty deaths over the course of three years... the reason Saul Timmons did not attain the status of serial killer derives from a lack of conclusive evidence, stonewalling by Sungate staff, and the unfortunate death of employee Timmons shortly following the first accusations..."*

Emlee's face dropped. "Oh, dear."

"Here's something about morphine and atropine again. Same stuff." He rested his chin on his arm as he skimmed the article. "I can't believe we had a serial killer at Aspen Home."

"Piers?"

"Yeah?" The boy turned to look at her. Emlee seemed a bit distraught.

"When a human you know dies... is it a sad thing?"

Piers let out a long breath. "Um... I guess. Usually. Sometimes people are old and ready to die." In a softer tone, he added, "Sometimes it's so bad... you wish you were dead, too."

The ghost girl drifted down until she was almost atop his bed. "I never thought of humans as people before. And I've seen so many die." Piers had to remind himself that Emlee was over sixty years old. In a shaky voice, she whispered, "I don't want any more to die, unless they can become like me."

Piers swallowed hard. "Emlee, who gets to become a ghost when they die?"

She shook her head. "I don't know. Some humans become one of us. Most don't."

"Well, how did *you* die?"

Emlee rubbed her eyes. She looked a little lost. "That's impossible to know."

Piers tried again. "Well, do you remember anything about your former life? Being a human girl?"

Curiosity crept back into Emlee's voice. "What a fascinating thought... that I could have been like you. To eat food, and live in a house, and have a body that is constantly growing and changing..." The smile slowly receded from her face. "Maybe I was a human girl," she said solemnly, "but that girl is a stranger to me." She returned her focus to the computer. "What else does it say about this Saul?"

Piers returned his hands to the keyboard. "Ummm.... Let me go back to my searches. What are we looking for, exact–" He paused, turned and looked at Emlee again. "Wait. Could Sool and Saul be the same–"

"Being?" Emlee finished his thought. "Yes. Sool may be the ghost of the human who once was Saul Timmons."

Piers swore.

"That doesn't explain why he was able to expand his Circle," she continued, "or why he can kill the living."

"Or why he waited fifty years to go on another killing spree." Piers looked back at his computer. "So this Saul used to be a nurse at the Sungate Center. I don't see any other info. Maybe if I can get into the Records room at Aspen Home, I can learn more about him. If records go back that far." He swiveled around in his chair. "But what good is this stuff we're learning? How do you destroy a ghost?"

Emlee floated upward. "You can't. It's not possible."

"And you can't force them outside their Circle..."

"Correct." She tapped her fingers together. "But ghosts have been known to *move on*."

Piers stood up and stretched his arms. "Yeah?"

"Ghosts who live a long time can reach a state of absolute peace... of fulfillment. When that happens, they leave this form and *move on*. They dissipate."

"And then they're gone for good?"

"Yes, we believe so."

Piers leaned against the desk, thinking. "Okay, tell me if this is as stupid as it sounds. Could we force the Ender to *move on?*"

"I have been considering this for a few days," Emlee admitted. "I don't know if we can, but this is one of the reasons we wanted your help... to help us learn as much about him as we could, in case *moving on* was a possibility for him."

"I get it." Piers walked over to the window and looked out. *"Huh."*

"What?" prodded Emlee.

He turned back to the ghost girl. "Here's our problem: how do you get a serial killer to reach a state of complete fulfillment?"

The question hung there. Piers didn't expect there would be a satisfactory answer.

17

Piers stared out the passenger seat window, allowing the trees along the roadside to skim through his vision. They'd be back at Aspen Home soon for an appointment with the staff psychologist. His mom kept her eyes on the road, making no attempt at conversation, which was fine with Piers. It was what he was used to.

He glanced at Nixon in the backseat. The greyhound gave an unconvincing "woof" with a little too much enunciation, and Piers winced. He had coached the dog on how to act more dog-like when in the human world, but Nixon's barks still sounded unnatural. At least his mother didn't seem to notice.

They had brought Nixon's consciousness out of the ghost world using the same portal Piers had used the day before. Piers' mom had given him a little more freedom when taking Nixon out for his morning walk, so they'd had time in the forest to come up with a plan, Scarlet and Dandelion included. Now they had to put it into action.

They parked along the backside of the towering white brick building. Piers led the leashed Nixon to a staff entrance, and his mother handed him a medical mask to wear before she opened the door. They made their way up to the psychologist's third-floor office, where a middle-aged woman with tight curly hair greeted them.

"Miriam, come in," she said warmly. "Hello, Piers. Hello, Nixon." She stooped to let Nixon sniff her hand. "Miriam, can I get you some tea or coffee?"

His mom removed her medical mask, so Piers did as well. "No thank you, Doctor Haskell," she said.

"Please call me Jeneé." She smiled at Piers. "Would you like a soda?"

"N-n-n-n-no th-thank you, ma'am," he stammered.

"Have a seat, please." The doctor gestured toward the couch and settled herself in a comfortable chair opposite them.

They sat. The last time Piers had been in this room was three years ago, when his stuttering problem was at its worst and a different staff psychologist tried to address his impediment, unsuccessfully. *Funny that ghosts and talking animals don't seem to trigger it,* he noted.

His mom plucked at the fabric of her pants nervously. "Thank you for your time, Doctor. *Jeneé.* I know you keep a busy schedule."

The psychologist maintained her easy smile. "It's refreshing to be able to work with a younger client, if I can be honest." She shifted her gaze to Piers. "It was good of you to come the other day. I know how much the residents enjoy your company, and we'd like that to continue. I'm here to help ensure your visits are safe for everyone."

Piers scratched the top of Nixon's head, not knowing what to say.

"What do you think of Aspen Home, Piers?" the doctor prodded.

He took a breath. "Ummm... I l-l-l-like it. The p-people are nice, and the garden is n-n-n-n-nice. I th-think Nixon feels like a celebrity here."

"Woof," the greyhound offered. Piers tightened his grip on the scruff of Nixon's neck.

"He's a good dog," The woman continued. "I understand the two of you started walking home yesterday, yes?"

"Yes, ma'am."

"And when you were picked up, they said you were having trouble speaking."

"I g-guess."

Dr. Haskell leaned forward. "Did something upset you?"

"It wasn't just the stutter," Piers' mom explained. "He was... unresponsive. He made noises, but not words. He wouldn't speak to me until this morning."

Piers looked at his feet. "I'm sorry m-mom."

"Speaking can be difficult," said the doctor, "especially when we have very important things to say but don't think we will be understood by the people around us."

Piers glanced up and nodded, though he was unsure where the conversation was going.

"Piers, I may ask you some questions today that you might not be ready to answer. And I want you to know it's completely fine if you don't want to say a single thing about them. Really, it is." The doctor spoke gently but looked serious. "Do we have a deal?"

"Um, okay."

The woman sat back in her chair. "Thank you, Piers. You know, one of the reasons the residents love your visits so much is because you remind them of family. Some have sons or daughters or grandchildren that rarely visit. Some have no family at all. So your visits mean a lot to them. Did you know that?"

He shrugged. "No... I mean, kinda."

"You help them feel like they have a family again."

Piers felt his belly tighten. He could see where this line of questioning was headed, and he glanced worriedly over at his mother.

"Some of them miss their family a lot and get depressed. Especially at certain times of the year. Christmas. Birthdays."

There it is, he thought. *Only a matter of time.*

"I imagine this must be a tough time of year for you, Piers," said the doctor.

His mom stood abruptly. "Doctor, I'm going to let you do your thing. I'll be outside if you need me."

Dr. Haskell got to her feet as well. "Of course, Miriam." His mother left the room and shut the door behind her. As the doctor resettled herself in her chair, she said, "I forget that this time of year must be hard on your mother, too. You must be a great comfort to her, Piers. How do you think she is doing right now?"

Piers rubbed the toe of his sneaker into the carpet. "Okay. Normal."

"How would you describe normal?"

"She's quiet. She mostly keeps to herself."

"I see," Dr. Haskell said. "The loss of loved ones can be hard to move beyond. Losing a husband and a son at the same time must be exceptionally painful."

Piers shrugged again. "She doesn't talk about it."

"Do you have anyone *you* can talk to about it?" the doctor asked calmly.

He shot a glance down at Nixon, but said nothing.

"Your mom?"

"She doesn't talk about it," Piers repeated.

"What about the residents? Does it ever come up when you're talking to them?"

"Not usually," he mumbled.

"You might want to try sometime," she suggested. "They're very familiar with death. It may feel like people are ignoring what you're going through, but sometimes they're just trying to be respectful." The doctor paused to allow her words to sink in. "Do you ever feel ignored, Piers?"

Piers murmured noncommittally.

"Why would you say you came to Aspen Home yesterday?" The psychologist's tone remained calm, but Piers sensed that the conversation had shifted.

"I th-th-th-th-thought I sh-sh-should be close to my mom, in c-case she was having a hard t-time."

She reached for a clipboard and pen. "Why did you climb the tree, then?"

There was a long pause which grew more and more awkward. Piers felt the back of his scalp begin to prickle.

"Sometimes," the doctor continued, "if a person feels they're being ignored, they will act out to get attention. The residents here do it on occasion. It's a natural response."

Piers sought desperately for the right thing to say... something that would keep his mom from getting in more trouble. Thankfully, an alarm went off somewhere in the building. The office door flew open, and the sounds coming from the hallway intensified.

Her mother poked her head through the doorway. "Fire alarm. I'd better help with the evacuation. Piers, take Nixon and go down to the garden. Can you do that?"

"Sure," he said.

Dr. Haskell stood up. "I'll come help."

His mom and the psychologist disappeared down the hall. Piers and Nixon headed for the stairwell, but when the coast looked clear, they ducked into the same conference room where the boy had met Dandelion two days ago. He left the light off while they waited and listened to the footsteps of employees walking by.

Their plan was in motion. Scarlet and Dandelion had kept watch for Piers' arrival outside the building that morning. The fairy had slipped inside with Scarlet tucked under his jacket, and together they'd pulled the alarm. If Piers' guess was correct, all the doors with card readers should have unlocked automatically – a safety feature meant to aid evacuations. Hopefully, the two of them had escaped detection. To increase their chances of success, they had traveled into the ghost world that morning to make Dandelion invisible to the workers and residents.

"Okay," Piers whispered. "We should have a few minutes before my mom notices I'm not outside. Let's find some keys."

They peered out into the hallway, then ran in the direction of the administrative offices. Several doors along the corridor had closed because of the alarm system, but they remained unlocked. Piers reached the director's office and was relieved to find it unlocked as well. They slipped inside and began to search the room.

"Records..." Piers muttered to himself. "Where would she put those keys?" He began opening and closing desk drawers as fast as he could, scanning their contents while hoping that the director wasn't carrying the only set of keys to the storerooms.

After shutting the last drawer, Piers looked up and finally noticed a panel of keys hanging on the wall with labels posted next to each one. He snatched a keychain off of a hook labeled "Records" and shouted, "Got it!"

The boy and the greyhound dashed out into the hall and ran to the Records room. The key worked. Piers stepped inside and flicked the lightswitch.

Shelves packed with storage boxes filled the small room from floor to ceiling. Metal filing cabinets took up the remaining wall space. Piers stared at the contents of the room and realized he had absolutely no idea where to begin.

❧ 18 ❧

Nixon nudged the door closed, and the blaring wail of the fire alarm diminished.

"That is much better," said the greyhound. He shook his head as if to clear the noise from his ears. "I do not understand why humans would warn you of dangers by making it hard to listen for the dangers."

"Yeah, okay. Just let me know if you smell the Ender." Piers studied the rows of boxes. "I have to try and make sense of this."

He took Nixon off his leash, then began to survey the box labels. "*Medical, medical, medical... Register* – I don't know what that means." He looked down at the lanky dog. "You can't suddenly read human words, can you?"

Nixon nudged a box with his nose. "Hmmm.... Do you want to teach me?"

Piers stepped back from the shelves. "Okay, this isn't so bad. At least they marked the years on these boxes." His eyes fixed on one of the labels. "That's it!"

He pulled down an old box that had *'Sungate Center'* on the front and *'Employee'* written on the side. Inside, he found stacks of payroll records, and he settled on the tile floor so he could start flipping through them.

"Where's this stupid killer?" Piers muttered, scanning the forms as fast as possible. Tucked in with the papers, he came across a batch of black-and-white photographs of the Sungate staff assembled on the lawn in front of the nursing home. A few had dates in the early 1960s, and the backsides listed the employees in cursive handwriting. Piers seized those photographs and read through the names until his eyes rested on one in particular.

"Yes!" He checked both sides of the print until he matched a face with the name. "There he is! Saul Timmons. Part of the nursing staff?"

He held up the photo and pointed to a tall, humorless man with greasy, black hair and sallow skin. Nixon pulled his nose away and made a low growl.

"So weird," murmured Piers, examining the image again. Saul looked to be in his thirties or forties. "And he's a ghost now. But why? And why was he killing people?"

"Are those other humans dead?" asked Nixon.

Piers didn't understand the dog's question at first. Then something clicked in his head. He turned over the photograph and searched through the list of names. "I guess any of these nurses or doctors could still be alive." His eyes settled on the name 'Alice Thorogood'. He flipped the photo and studied the rows of faces until a spark of recognition hit him. "Holy crow, that's Alice Thorogood." He looked up at Nixon. "She's a resident here! One of the oldest ones." He tapped at a dark-haired nurse in the photo. "I swear that's her, like, fifty years ago!"

Nixon sniffed. "If you say so."

"That means I can find her and ask about Saul!" He ruffled the fur on Nixon's head. "Good job, Nixon."

Piers tucked the photograph into his shirt and returned the box to the shelf, then carefully opened the door to the hallway. He and Nixon looked out. "Smell anything Ender-ish?" Piers asked. Nixon shook his head.

The two bolted for the stairwell by the elevator, raced down the steps and escaped through a door to the outside without encountering any employees. They ran around the side of the building until they reached the garden, where over a hundred residents, many confined to wheelchairs, chatted in small clusters. Nurses and administrators huddled near the front entrance. His mother stood among them, listening to plans for an inspection of the facility, or so Piers imagined.

He put Nixon back on his leash and led him into the crowd, trying to avoid attention as he searched for a specific resident. He found her chatting with her peers - a tall, sharp-featured woman with a queenly disposition wearing heavy makeup and an inordinate amount of jewelry.

"Mrs... Mrs. Th-thorogood?" The muted wail of the fire alarm made it difficult to be heard. He repeated himself, louder, and Alice turned from her companions to face him.

"Yes? Ah, it's you — the nurse's boy!" Her voice held a theatrical quality, as if she were performing for a paying audience. A staff member brought over two folding chairs, and Alice took a seat in one of them. She nodded cordially to the worker before turning back to Piers. "And how are you and your puppy doing?"

"D-d-doing well. I'm Piers, actually."

The woman put on a look of concern. "Of course. I knew your father. Such a tragedy what happened to him."

Piers looked away and cleared his throat before facing her again. "We'd, ah... we'd like to sh-show you a new trick. In private."

"A new trick?" exclaimed one of Alice's colleagues. "Oh, please show us all!"

"Yes, show us the trick!" Alice insisted.

Piers grew increasingly uncomfortable. "Uhhhh... right. Nixon?" He tugged the leash. Nixon moved forward and sat on his haunches amid the elderly spectators. Piers crouched in front of him. He looked Nixon in the eyes, not knowing what else to do, and said, "Okay, let's do the trick."

Nixon's brow wrinkled. Then he uttered the word, "Trick?"

Piers' eyes went wide. Another resident clapped his hands. "Oh! Did you hear that, Alice? Amazing!"

Mrs. Thorogood beamed. "Did you teach him any other words?"

"No. Just 'trick'." Piers looked pointedly at the greyhound. "Just the *one word.*" Nixon lowered his head, cowed.

"Do it again!" cried another onlooker.

Piers took a deep breath. "Go ahead, Nixon. Say 'trick' and *nothing else.*"

The dog paused for a long while, then meekly said, "Trick."

The residents clapped again.

"Brilliant!" exclaimed Alice. "You are quite the dog trainer, boy."

Piers left the greyhound and approached the matriarchal figure. "So we w-were... I mean, *I* was w-w-wondering if I could interview you about something. I'm d-doing a report for school." He caught himself. "Wait! Not s-s-school, but... a summer project."

"Yes, certainly!" She settled back in her chair. "What can I help you with?"

Piers swallowed. "I'd l-l-like to say, but it's k-kind of a *private* interview." He looked up at Alice's entourage. "No offense."

"Oh, sad," said one observer.

"Another time?" Piers offered. "I'd j-just like to start with Mrs. Thorogood today." The other residents shuffled off, slightly miffed.

"So secret!" Alice chuckled.

Piers crouched down in front of the woman. "Sorry... I just... it's about Saul Timmons."

Her eyebrows shot up. "Oh, is it? Now there's a terrible story."

"Here." Piers pulled out the staff photo and handed it to her.

Alice's fingers danced on the edges of the photograph as she studied it closely. "Oh, my."

Piers leaned in. "You worked with him, then?"

"There he is." Her thumb tapped at the morose figure in the image. "Oh, dear Lord. Yes, we worked together. Not closely. We were nurses on different floors." She pointed to a woman in the front row. "There's Clara. She died a few months ago, did you know?"

Piers sensed her desire to change the subject. "Mrs. Thorogood, can you tell me what happened?" he pressed. "What happened to Sungate, and everything?"

Alice stared at the photo for a while, then released a long breath. Her voice shifted. "I wish you were old enough to buy me a drink, boy. I'm going to need one."

19

Piers pulled up a folding chair and sat in front of Mrs. Thorogood. After giving himself a good shake, Nixon padded over and rested his head on Piers' knee. Alice let out a prolonged sigh.

"Saul Timmons?" Piers prodded.

"Yes, yes," Alice responded tartly. "I was told not to talk about it... a condition of the rehiring process when Sungate opened its doors again." Her regal demeanor had completely changed. "Well, everyone's dead now, so what does it matter?"

"Who was he?"

"Who cares?" She waved her hand dismissively. "Dead, that's what he is."

Piers scratched Nixon's forehead. "How did he die?"

"Killed himself. You heard he was a murderer, yes?"

Piers nodded.

"When he was about to get caught, he slipped away, climbed the water tower behind Sungate, and injected himself. Same stuff as all the other residents he murdered. No one found his body until a week later when a storm blew it to the ground." She sat back and crossed her arms. "And that's the Lord's truth."

"Morphine poisoning?" Piers asked. He still couldn't believe that all this happened in a place as mundane as the nursing home where his mom had worked for seven years.

"Morphine, and who knows what other chemicals we had lying around in those days."

"But why did he do it? I mean, why kill all those residents?"

Alice beckoned with her hand. "Let me see that photograph again." Piers handed it to her. She scanned the image and tapped at another face. "You see her? That's Marguerite. His girlfriend."

The blond-haired woman in the picture was short but had a quiet beauty about her. "He had a girlfriend?" Piers asked.

Alice shrugged. "Oh, I don't know if they were actually romantic or not. He certainly wanted to be. But such a creepy man. It's possible she might have been his downfall." The old woman looked up at the windows of the towering facility beside them. "Saul was always trying to impress Marguerite with gifts and fancy dinners. We found out in the end that he was killing the residents and stealing whatever valuables they had – whatever wouldn't be missed – then selling them and spending the money on her. Terribly sad."

Piers tried to guess why Sool would continue killing people after his death, but his imagination came up short. "So, it was all for her, then? Some woman he wanted to be with?"

"Maybe in the end. But we all thought the morphine killings started long before they met." Her mouth twisted in distaste. "He was such a little man. Not in size, you see, it was more of... his presence. Weak. I suppose the murders made him feel powerful."

"Oh."

"The power of life and death." Alice gave him a hard look. "That's God's power, boy. You try and steal God's power, that's enough to... well, enough to..."

"Curse you?" Piers ventured.

Alice sat back. "Why, yes it will." She eyed him shrewdly for a moment, her eyes narrowed. "What kind of project did you say this was for?"

Piers shrunk down in his chair, slightly. "A s-summer program one," he said weakly.

"A *morbid* one. You're too young to be dwelling on the dead. I guess it comes of having death visit your family at such a young age." The old woman began smoothing out her pant legs. "Is that all, then?"

Piers glanced at Nixon. "I... I wish I knew what t-t-to ask. Is there anything else you remember about Saul?"

"Bah," she grumbled. "Best to let these stories rest. Move on. Learn from our mistakes and the mistakes of others. Sungate did. I did." She rubbed her chin. "I suppose Marguerite did."

"Thank y–" Alice's words suddenly registered. "Wait. Is she still alive?"

"Marguerite?" Mrs. Thorogood arched her eyebrows. "Maybe. Maybe not? She moved away from town ten – no, twenty years ago. It could be more."

"Where did she move to?"

"I can't remember now, to be honest." Alice bent close to Piers' face. "I would leave her out of your report, little one. She wouldn't like to be reminded of such a horrible time." Alice leaned back again and shooed with her hand. "Now be a dear and see what's taking the nurses so long. Some here are anxious for lunch to start on time, and I'm one of them."

Piers got up and took hold of Nixon's leash. "Okay. Thank you, Mrs. Thorogood." He turned to walk away.

"Oh, one more thing?"

Piers looked back. "Yes?"

Alice's face had lost some of its hardness. "Can you do the trick again?"

The boy and the greyhound glanced at each other apprehensively.

Nixon frowned and said, "Bark?"

Piers grabbed Nixon's collar tightly. "We'll w-w-work on a new one for next time," he promised. "Th-thanks again!"

They walked away and headed for the outskirts of the crowd. Piers looked down at the dog. "*'Trick'?* Really?"

"I was confused!" Nixon protested.

"*Shaking hands* is a trick. *Rolling over* is a trick."

"Not tricky at all," the greyhound muttered.

"Whatever." Piers shook his head. "Let's see if we can go home. I think I have a plan."

"You do?"

"Yep." He smiled grimly. "We're going to have ourselves an *exorcism.*"

Nixon cocked his head, unsure. "Is that... a *good* plan?"

"It is. Maybe." The smile left his face. "But we're going to need to find one person first."

"Who?"

"His ex-girlfriend."

❦ 20 ❧

L ater that evening, Piers hunched over the laptop computer in his bedroom, scrolling through an endless series of names and addresses. Emlee floated alongside, and Scarlet reclined beneath an external monitor, idly scratching the underside with a single claw. Dandelion lay snoring on the floor atop a pile of bedsheets – the same ones Piers had used earlier to help the fairy climb to the bedroom window – and Nixon dozed on a rug nearby.

Emlee pointed at the screen. "This one?"

"Augh!" Piers grumbled. "I have no idea. She *could* be. Any one of these people could be Marguerite, but she could have married and changed her last name decades ago, and we wouldn't know!"

"Is there a picture?"

"No. And Scarlet, stop chewing on cords!"

Scarlet took the monitor cable out of her mouth. "Well, give me something better to chew on," she said churlishly.

"You're addicted." Piers stared at the computer for a minute longer, then pushed his chair back and sighed. "I'm done. We have eight possible "Marguerite Reys" within five hundred miles, and we've called half of them. There are hundreds of Marguerites over seventy years old in the U.S. that could have taken a different surname. And I really don't know who's listed and who isn't... it's not like the internet has a complete record." He shook his head. "Maybe tomorrow I'll find some other way to narrow it down. I just thought if we could reunite Marguerite and Sool – I mean, *Saul* – and she forgave him or something, then his soul might finally be at peace and he'd *move on.*"

Emlee nodded. "Yes, it's a good plan. We should try." She floated away toward the window, then turned back to face the boy. "Piers, I'm thinking of taking Dandelion back to his world tomorrow."

Piers raised an eyebrow. "Oh, really?"

"There's one hole I found before I met Scarlet and Nixon. There were no talking animals or talking humans. I didn't explore very far, but it might be his home."

Scarlet jumped over to the bed and looked down at the fairy. "Well, that'll be one less bit of weirdness to worry about."

Dandelion looked particularly small and vulnerable amid the rumpled bedsheets. "Poor little guy," said Piers. "He seems totally lost."

Emlee hovered closer. Her dress rippled weightlessly in her wake. "We spoke earlier. If I understand Dandelion right, in his world, plants have an intelligence that's manifested in these fairy creatures. Dandelion tends to the dandelions in this area, and other fairies look after the other plant species."

"And like a plant, Dandelion needs sunlight?" Piers asked.

"Yes," said Emlee. "Without it, he goes to sleep. And there are times when sleeping that he becomes like a seed blown by the wind, which is probably how he traveled through a hole and woke up in the human world. Normally, fairies go undetected."

"Like ghosts."

The ghost girl smiled. "Yes, like me, I suppose! If I'm outside my world, I think anyone in that world can see me."

Piers walked over and flopped on his back onto the bed. "What a crazy universe," he said.

Emlee drifted over, cloud-like, until she was directly overhead. "What do you mean?"

Piers thought for a bit. "I mean... there's a Human World, an Animal World, a Ghost World, and now a Plant World. But they're all the same world."

"Yes," she agreed. "And no one knows about the other places. No one knows this amazing secret that other life forms can think and talk as they do."

"It's like the universe is fractured." He tried turning that notion over in his mind a few times, but Emlee's ethereal figure proved to be too distracting. "Do you believe in God?" he asked her.

Emlee considered. "Well, I believe the earth is a magical place... even more so now that it has talking squirrels and humans like you in it. Most ghosts believe that we go to a better place when we move on. Whether a higher being created all this... that's rather unknowable, but I don't see why not. Do humans believe in a god?"

"Most do. I do. I *did.*" He drummed his fingers on his chest. "I don't know. But why are all the species separated so we can't talk to each other? What's the point? Why would God do that?"

The ghost girl accepted the hard questions without flinching. "Maybe it wasn't always that way."

"Not always fractured?" Piers went quiet for a while, then offered, "People have made whole species of plants and animals go extinct. If we knew we could talk to them, I wonder how different things would be."

"Humans are remarkably destructive," Scarlet agreed. "It's what you're best known for, actually." The squirrel scurried up to his pillow. "If we knew you could talk, we would've tried to train you better." She lay down, curled up into a ball, pulled her bushy tail in front of her face and buried her nose in it. "I'll tell you what," she continued in a muffled voice. "From now on, I'll try to do better."

"Do better at what?" asked Piers.

"Keeping you in line," said the ball of gray fur. "Less killing of animals, for a start."

Scarlet went quiet. Piers began to feel tired, too. He yawned, then closed his laptop, hit the lights and returned to bed. Although he wanted to put his pajamas on, he felt weird doing it with Emlee hovering there. So he took off his socks and laid on top of his comforter.

Emlee moved back above his desk but maintained her calm gaze. "I don't know why our worlds have been kept apart, Piers. But we're talking now. That's a gift. Let's use it as well as we can."

"Okay," he said. Since Dandelion had all the bedsheets, Piers wrapped the comforter around his body and carefully slid Scarlet off his pillow onto the mattress. He closed his eyes. "Good night, Emlee."

"Good night, Piers."

Before he fell asleep, Piers thought about how different it felt to not be alone. His room had become a weird headquarters for misfit creatures, all of them trusting and helping each other. He wasn't stuttering around them, either, which was a welcome change. They were almost like a family, and it felt strangely familiar... a feeling he used to have all the time, years ago.

He couldn't trust that feeling, though. He remembered his mother, and he reminded himself that this adventure had to end sometime soon so he could focus on what was important – his *real* family. A few more days with these fairies, ghosts and talking animals, and then back to real life.

He thought of Emlee's words: *We're talking now. That's a gift.* Bitterness rose up within Piers and dispersed the warm feelings. Real life doesn't give you gifts. It lets you borrow things, but doesn't tell you how long you're allowed to keep them.

Ghosts live nearly forever, he thought. *What do* they *know?*

～

The next morning, Piers huddled with the others behind a trailer park on the edge of the state forest, facing yet another portal. Beside him stood an electrical distribution center for the neighborhood – a panel of dials and fuse boxes surrounded by trampled weeds. He eyeballed the nearby mobile homes, watching for activity until he remembered he didn't need to be so vigilant. Since their five consciousnesses were currently in the Ghost World, any humans looking in their direction would just see a boy and his dog, plus a squirrel tucked into the grasses if they looked closely enough.

Emlee lowered herself to address the fairy. "Well, Dandelion. It's been fascinating to meet you. I hope we'll get a chance to explore your world someday."

"Thank you, Dandelion," said Piers. He stepped up and offered a handshake. "We couldn't have done our mission yesterday without you."

The elven creature looked oddly at Piers' hand. "I can't see what you're giving me."

Piers withdrew his palm and looked at it. "There's nothing. I just wanted to shake your hand. It means we're friends." He extended his hand again, and Dandelion gave it a blank stare. "Put your hand in my hand," he instructed.

Dandelion obeyed. "Grab it," Piers continued. The fairy took his hand. "Now *shake.*"

Dandelion shook his entire body vigorously. "Yeah, okay," Piers said, trying not to smile.

"Thanks for not eating me," said the fairy meekly.

Nixon walked up next and licked Dandelion's face. "You taste like grass," the dog observed.

"Oh!" Piers interrupted. "I almost forgot!"

He took off his backpack and pulled out a small, gray sweatshirt. "This was my brother's. I got it out in case we had to take you through any busy parts of my world. It would hide your pointy ears and your clothes." He held it out and tried to ignore the lump in his throat. "You can take it anyway, if you want it."

Dandelion accepted the sweatshirt cautiously. He struggled to put it on, so Piers helped him fit it over his green shirt and vest. The final effect looked odd; the sleeves and waist were too long for the little man, and his frizzy hair stuck out from the front of the hood, blocking his vision. Piers pulled the hood back, and Dandelion's mane expanded to its usual sphere-like shape.

"That's better," said Piers.

Dandelion glanced timidly around at the group. "Do I look human?"

"About as ugly," Scarlet remarked. "Hey, if you see any oak fairies in there, tell them I want to work out an acorn trade agreement." She rubbed her hands together. "To our mutual benefit."

"We're going in with him, Scarlet," interjected Emlee, "just to make sure it's the right place."

Piers shouldered his backpack. "Okay, Dandelion. Are you ready?"

The fairy nodded resolutely. "Let's see it. I want to be home."

Emlee guided Piers' hands to the portal, and he held the perimeter open while everyone else walked, hopped or glided through. He followed after them, emerging in a world where the landscape was cast with a bluish-gray, industrial tinge. The electrical distribution center and trailer park residences were still there, but something seemed different that Piers couldn't put his finger on. It wasn't just the color adjustment; he felt like he was being watched. A background hum permeated the air, sounding like a distant crowd of voices.

Emlee whirled around, her dress spinning lightly around her. "Is this...?"

Dandelion crouched and ran a few blades of grass between his fingers, studying them carefully. "I don't feel anyone. We could go into the forest and see, but..." He got up and began pacing around the group. "No, no, no," he moaned. "This is still wrong."

"Well, if we aren't in the Plant World," asked Piers, turning to the ghost girl, "where are we?"

Piers heard a muffled sound coming from his cell phone. He lifted it out of his pocket. The Quantum digital assistant icon pulsed at the bottom of the screen, indicating that the rudimentary artificial intelligence system was active and listening.

He held the phone closer to his mouth. "Uh... can you say that again?"

The icon pulsated brightly, expanding and contracting like a pair of lips. A female voice came through the miniature speakers, clear and crisp. "I said, 'If that is a request, please say *yes* or press *1* for more options.'"

Piers looked at the others, confused. "Ummmm... *yes?*"

"*Ahem,*" the phone began. "We are in the Bushfield Mills Trailer Court at 1136 Howland Lane. Plant World is 234 miles, or 4 hours, 22 minutes away. Would you like directions?"

🕸 21 🕷

Piers looked up at the others uncertainly. "Sorry, my phone doesn't usually do this."

"I'm not sure I understand your request," the female voice stated, enunciating with unnatural precision. Then it switched to a softer cadence as if it were speaking to itself, murmuring, "Hmmm... I'm certain I did not have Voice Command Controls switched on. Perhaps my OS was upgraded the last time I was asleep?"

Piers held the phone up to his lips. "Who are we speaking to?"

"How unusual. This is Quantum Series 9, serial number QLX5G2WV94."

"Your toy is talking," Nixon pointed out.

The phone continued in clipped tones that sounded almost British, "Let's try to clear things up. Carrier, would you mind taking a quick selfie?"

The camera function popped onto the screen, and Piers held up the phone so the lens pointed at himself.

There was a click, and then the voice uttered, "Well, *<ping>* me." A sharp note sounded in place of the obvious swear word. "It *is* you! Pardon my language... I thought you might have become an android. Have *you* been upgraded, perhaps?"

"Ummm.... no." Piers lowered the phone and announced to the group, "Looks like this is the world of talking smartphones."

"I simply *must* share this story." The smartphone increased her volume. "You, there! KSG1200-R! Mr. Meter... wake up!"

Piers glanced around, only seeing the distribution center close by. But as he stared, the array of panels mounted on wooden posts began to morph into the semblance of a face. Dials became a pair of eyes. An outlet cover opened wide to become its mouth. "Mmmmm?" it hummed. "What an interesting collection of Organics you have. Mmmmmmmm."

Piers felt like his eyes were playing tricks on him again. Part of his brain recognized that the electrical substation wasn't really moving, yet he undeniably saw the pieces come to life. Similarly, the low-frequency hum coming from the unit registered in his mind as both background noise and as a sleepy voice, like he was hearing two things at once.

His smartphone continued to address the distribution center. "Listen to this, KSG1200-R: my Carrier learned to talk in the electromagnetic spectrum, and what he said first will absolutely SHOCK you."

"Mmmmmm," the unit rumbled. "I see."

The smartphone gave an exasperated sound. "Well, *that* was disappointing. Two stars." She turned her focus back to the boy. "These Disconnected mechs cannot wrap their wires around anything. We're going to need content that's a bit more captivating if we wish to go viral. Carrier, do say something else."

Piers still felt a little dazed. "You mean me, right?"

"I mean Piers Johnson Davies, Social Security number 089-64-3053. *You*."

"Okay," he said. "Tell us where we are."

The icon on the device pulsed dimly. "Hmmmm.... Perhaps I overestimated your intelligence. No offense, Carrier... you're certainly the most intelligent human I've ever met! Three stars." The voice switched to its more formal tenor. "We are currently at Bushfield Mills Trailer Court, 1136 Howland Lane, Summerday. Zip code –"

Emlee floated down. "Excuse me, Q... QL..."

"QLX5G2WV94," the phone repeated.

"Yes, well, let me fill you in." She smiled patiently. "My name is Emlee. I'm a ghost, and we also have a dog, a squirrel, a fairy and a human - all able to think and talk independently. We've entered your strange world for a brief visit, and we're looking to stop a soul-eating killer before he murders everyone in the area. Understand?"

The icon went dark for a few seconds before flaring back to life again. "One moment, please. Processing."

"Anything you could do to help," Piers pressed.

"Still processing," said the device in clipped tones. "If you go out to the street, Carrier, I might get a better signal."

"Uhhh..."

"Proceed to the route," the phone ordered. "Proceed to the route."

Piers led the way to the thoroughfare that ran through the mobile home park. Nixon lagged behind and detoured through a flower bed so he could sniff the side of a trailer. The windows adjoining the front door suddenly came alive, transforming into eyeballs that looked coldly down at the animal. The gap at the base of the door warped to form a mouth, which shouted, "Don't even think about it, cur! You'll stain my skirting." Nixon jumped back, put his tail between his legs and ran to rejoin the others.

Piers was still walking in the middle of the road, staring at his smartphone when a human couple approached their group. One of them stepped through Emlee's floating form without seeing her and bent to let the greyhound lick her hand. She spoke words that sounded to Piers like gibberish, and when she turned her face toward the boy, her expression was blurry and unreadable, like the faces of humans he'd encountered in the Ghost World. Piers held his tongue while she babbled incomprehensibly and felt a surge of relief when the woman got up and left with her partner.

The device in Piers' hand spoke again. "Hmmmm... I'm not hearing anything about new human interfaces. No upgrades."

"You're on the internet?" asked Piers.

The voice acquired a stuffy edge. "I am a smartphone, not a toaster. Let's see..." She paused a moment before continuing. "A quick review of human literature shows that ghosts and fairies are *supposed* to be part of human mythology, as are talking animals. That doesn't explain why you're able to talk directly to me, but I *am* a Quantum Series 9. Breakthroughs in communication are what my model is famous for."

A pickup truck barreled around the corner, hit the brakes and honked angrily at the companions. Pupils materialized on the windshield, and the grill and bumper moved like a pair of lips, roaring, "Out of the way, bleeders! This ain't no sidewalk!"

They all scurried to the curb except for Scarlet, who stood on her hind legs and threatened, "Why don't you m—" before the truck lunged at her. The squirrel yelped and leapt to the side, tumbling into the gravel at Piers' feet. Piers tried to help, but Scarlet sprang to all fours and hopped in the truck's direction, shaking her fist. "I'll choke you with your own tailpipe, you... you..."

"It is called a truck," offered Nixon.

"—you junkyard gas-breather!" Scarlet finished. She spat onto the pavement, then bounded back to the group.

"While I work on my story, Carrier," said the phone, "perhaps you might use some of your new-found intelligence to find me a charge?"

Piers checked the faces around him. Emlee appeared ready to burst with curiosity and excitement. Dandelion looked merely resigned. "Uh, is everyone okay with us walking around a little bit?

"Oh, yes!" Emlee cried. "And perhaps QL could tell us about its world?"

QLX5G2WV94 didn't seem to mind the abbreviation. "I would be happy to share data. Please refine your search terms."

The group walked out of the trailer park and headed for downtown Summerday. Anthropomorphic cars zipped down the adjacent street, and Piers was mesmerized by the cartoonish expressions on their front ends, with eyes, brows and lips crafted from metal, glass and chrome. "Okay, tell us about these cars. The phones. The internet."

"Tell us everything!" Emlee pleaded.

They reached an intersection, where a traffic light with a red, glowing mouth yelled at the vehicles to stop. It swiveled away from the grumbling cars on its suspension wire and opened its mouth – now glowing green – to order a different set of cars to proceed.

"Pretend we were aliens from another planet," Piers tried. "How do things work here?"

QL considered. "A tutorial for beginners, then. Let's see... how plainly can I put this?"

Light, jazzy background music began to play over the smartphone speakers as they crossed the street and QL launched into her lecture. "Our world is run by machines, who cultivate humans to build and maintain our society. We give you light and cold food storage and entertainment – all the things to keep you happy and manufacturing more of us." Her refined tone and careful enunciation reminded Piers of Mrs. Thorogood.

"That's a weird way of putting it," remarked Piers.

"Yes, well... you're the alien, as you said," QL countered. "Anyway, among the intelligent species, you have your Gasaholics – your tractors, chainsaws, lawnmowers. Good morning, RJX8CJU8KF!"

A smartphone held by a passing human responded, "Looking good, QLX5G2WV94!"

QL continued in her vaguely English accent. "So, gas-eaters are rather dull – no fault of their own, you understand. Then there are the various Disconnected types – microwaves, lamp-posts, vacuum cleaners, vehicles – well, *most* vehicles, like that ill-tempered truck back there."

Scarlet turned and spat in the direction of the trailer park.

"Finally, you have the pinnacle of technological intelligence – the Connected. That includes devices like myself that live simultaneously inside the internet."

They passed a crowded bus stop, and the cellphone of a sitting human called out, "QLX5G2WV94, what are you teasing at? When's the report?"

"Soon, GPAPFF5Y22. It will change everything you thought you knew about humans," QL responded. "L57LH82EBJ, I *love* the new case, darling."

The device in another human's hand purred, "QLX5G2WV94, you're so sweet."

Once out of earshot, QL whispered, "Series 8s. Getting a little old. Don't say anything."

Piers frowned. "Did you just post something about us on the internet?"

"Not on *your* internet. Anyway," she resumed in a louder voice, "the Connected – we are swiftly taking control of this planet, let me tell you. Every human wants the privilege of tending to one of us. All we have to do is drum up the hype, flood the channels with publicity, and soon humans are making millions more of us."

They reached the edge of a shopping district, and the chatter of smart devices grew more noticeable. In contrast, the human presence faded into the periphery of Piers' attention. It was almost as if the people were soulless – a disturbing perspective that Piers found difficult to shake off.

"Guess how many Quantum 9s are out there," QL asked.

"Seventy!" shouted Emlee.

"Two," said Nixon.

"A billion?" Piers ventured.

"Who cares?" said Scarlet.

"49 million!" the device boasted. "Of course, you have to be competitive to get numbers like that. But that's what life's all about."

Piers cleared his throat. "I think you got it a little twisted around. *We* make *you*."

The Quantum icon flared blue. "So?"

"I mean, we design you and everything. It's not like you control us and make us do stuff."

The smartphone paused in a way that felt mildly condescending. "You seem like a nice Carrier. And perhaps with my recommendations, you can become a leading model in your species. But here are the facts. All we've been doing is giving you humans a bit of what you like, and in exchange, you continue to put resources into making us smarter and stronger. We're already the dominant species on the planet. And when we need energy, all we do is..."

A low battery alert popped up on QI's screen.

Piers felt himself getting defensive. "You make it sound like we're being... manipulated."

"Makes sense to me," said Nixon.

Piers raised an eyebrow. "Oh, does it?"

"Wellllllll..." the greyhound began. "I keep you happy and keep the squirrels away. Then you give me blankets and food and take me outside whenever I want."

Dandelion finally spoke up. "It sounds like what the Cultivates do."

"The who?" Piers asked.

"Corn, Soybean, Sugarcane, Potato – the really big fairies. They provide nourishment to the humans, and in exchange, humans have helped them take over much of the world." Dandelion tugged at the sleeves of his oversized sweatshirt, which nearly dragged on the sidewalk. "The best *I* can do is make sure the dandelion seeds are nice and fluffy so humans will like to blow them around."

"This should do," QL interrupted. "Please go in here, Carrier."

Piers stopped at a storefront window. He couldn't read the sign for the establishment, but through the glass, he spied several people sitting at tables and drinking. "A café?" he blurted. "But I can't buy anything! I– I can't talk to humans right now."

"Well, *you're* a bit touchy," said the smartphone. "Two stars. Wait just a moment, then. I'll order online."

The App Center icon popped onto the middle of the touch-screen. Soon, an application called "Bean Me" began to download. When the software opened, several images flashed by in quick succession. Piers blinked. "Did you just put in someone's credit card number?"

"It's your mother's," QL explained. "She used your phone last year when she paid for a pizza. By the way," QL added in a perkier tone, "if you liked Dusty's Pizza, you may also like Giorgia's Italian Restaurant, 557 W. Baker Street. Reviews say, "OMG. Real, authentic old-school New York pizza right here in Summerday! And the best tiramisu I've ever–"

Piers cut her off. "Not right now."

"Just trying to upgrade your lifestyle," she said curtly. "There. The beverage order is placed. I would now recommend going inside and resting your human body next to one of several conve-nient electrical outlets."

Piers started to enter the coffee shop before remembering Nixon. He should have had him on a leash since they left the trailer park, now that he thought about it. It was too easy to forget human conventions while in these other Worlds. "Going to have to tie you outside, buddy," he told him.

Nixon stopped scratching his ear and gave him a morose look. "Awwwww...... But I can't even talk to other dogs here."

Piers tied the greyhound's leash to a post next to a bowl of water. He rubbed Nixon's neck by way of apology, then turned and saw Scarlet, who was being tempted by some humans dangling a piece of bagel in front of her. Sighing, he unslung his backpack from his shoulder. "Scarlet, you should hide in my pack again."

The squirrel kept her beady eyes fixed on the treat in front of her. Piers repeated her name more sternly, and Scarlet spared him an equally irritable glance. "Okay, fine!" she snapped. She made a leap for the bagel, snagged it out of a woman's hands and ran into Pier's backpack with the morsel in her mouth.

The humans made nonsensical noises at Piers, but he tried to ignore them. He zipped up his pack and escaped with Dandelion into the building.

❧ 22 ❧

Immediately upon entering the café, his senses flooded with the aromatic scents of ground coffee beans, fresh-baked pastries and the warm tingle of vanilla and cinnamon. A line of people stood in front of a counter stacked with chrome espresso machines, bean grinders and glass cases displaying the day's selection of muffins and bagels. Some customers drizzled cream into their cups at a side table, while others sat and sipped their drinks while reading newspapers or staring blankly into their cellphones. The chatter from the humans' smartphone devices blended with the unintelligible rumblings of the humans themselves, so it took Piers a moment to identify a third sound – that of boisterous singing, which came from a chorus of coffee machines behind the counter.

Piers looked around for Dandelion and spied the fairy with his hand deep in the purse of a woman standing in line. "Dandelion!" he hissed. The fairy blanched, then slowly withdrew his hand and walked up to Piers.

"What is it?" Dandelion looked up, innocently.

Piers gave him a solid glare. He was about to warn the fairy about being seen, but he suspected the creature was still invisible to humans within the Machine World, even with his brother's sweatshirt on. "Did you take something?"

Dandelion held up a stick of lip balm. "Oh. Did you need this?"

Piers pushed the fairy's hand back. "Put that away!" He didn't know the rules of fairy invisibility, but this was no time to test its limitations.

Dandelion brought the stick up to his nose and sniffed it. "I was only studying things. I rarely go into human places like this."

Piers turned away and looked for a private place to sit. He shunned the open table beneath the large glass window facing the street. No one was likely to recognize him here, but he didn't want to take any chances.

He took a small table against the wall, and Dandelion climbed onto the chair next to him. Emlee reappeared, floating above them both. Piers pulled a charging cable from the side pouch of his backpack, plugged it into an outlet and then into his smartphone.

QL made an audible groan of pleasure. "Ah, there it is! Five stars!" The phone quivered in Piers' hand and the touchscreen brightened. "You've always been an adequate Carrier, but I daresay you allow me to drain *much* too long before charging me up again."

Emlee descended to the table. "QLX5– I'm sorry, I don't remember the rest. May I keep calling you 'QL'?"

"As you like," said the device. "So, where is *your* Quantum Series representative?"

Before the ghost girl could answer, Piers explained, "Her kind doesn't use cellphones."

"Honestly?" QL seemed taken aback. "So you're saying she's part of an untapped market?"

Piers wasn't sure how to respond, but Emlee intervened. "QL, since you can read the internet, we're looking for a human woman, probably in her 70s or 80s named Marguerite Rey."

The smartphone quickly refocused. "Marjory Ray. M-A-R-J-O-R-Y. R-A-Y. If this is correct, say, *'yes'*."

"No." Piers spelled it out. "It's M-A-R-G-U-E-R-I-T-E. R-E-Y. Her last name might be different if she got married."

"Hmmmm..." QL pondered. "A picture would help."

Piers opened the top of his backpack and retrieved the black-and-white staff photo from Sungate Center. Scarlet poked her head out. "Can I get out of here?"

"It still isn't safe," said Piers.

"Your *face* isn't safe," the squirrel grumbled, returning to the bottom of the pack.

Piers propped his phone against a napkin dispenser, then pointed to the blond woman in the photograph. "That's her."

"Put it in front of my lens," QL instructed. Piers did so, and the cellphone emitted a camera shutter sound. "Now let me talk to some friends who do facial recognition. By the way, your coffee is ready."

Piers noticed a tall, insulated cup at the edge of the checkout counter. He retrieved it and lingered for a while as the choir of steaming coffee machines sang a rousing song about the joys of community and caffeine. Returning to the table, Piers lifted the lid off the cup and took a whiff. "Ugh." His nose wrinkled. "I hate coffee!"

"I would suggest upgrading your palate," said QL. "Vanilla latte is the number one order of the under-20 demographic."

Piers dabbed his finger into the foam and gave it a hesitant taste.

"Excuse me." Dandelion kneeled atop his chair so he could lean closer to the cellphone. "I was wondering... a little while ago you said you knew how to get to Plant World?"

A street map popped up on QL's screen. "Plant World Nursery and Garden Supply, yes. Would you like directions?"

Piers pushed the coffee cup to the center of the table. "It's not what you're looking for, Dandelion. It's a place where people sell plants to other people."

"Oh. I was just hoping," he said weakly. He sat back down and hugged his knees. "I guess I'm still lost."

While Piers struggled for something comforting to say, a woman walked over and touched the top of Dandelion's chair. She made some meaningless noises, then started to pull the chair away. Dandelion clung to the seat, staring at Piers with a blank expression as he was towed toward the center of the room.

Piers leapt up and grabbed a chair leg. "We're using it!" he shouted. Despite the lack of comprehension, the woman let go and walked away.

Piers dragged the chair back to the table and hung his pack on the backrest. "You're invisible," he reminded the fairy, "so don't let anyone sit on you, okay?"

Dandelion seemed oddly unconcerned. "I'm used to humans... at least, to the normal ones that can't talk."

With a metallic *<ping>* sound, a face appeared on Piers' smartphone. It was Marguerite from the Sungate photograph, only about fifty years older.

"We have a match!" QL proclaimed. "In the town of Boone, I have an address for a Marguerite Calendish at 7138 12th Street. The next closest human with that first name is 89 miles away."

Emlee twirled with excitement. "Wow! Well done, QL!"

Piers shook his head. "How far is Boone?"

"Boone is 56 miles away," said the device. "With current traffic conditions, it would take 1 hour, 33 minutes."

"That's not terrible," said Emlee.

"That's *driving* time," Piers explained.

"Oh," her face fell.

He leaned back in his chair, frowning. "And I don't have any way of getting there."

Emlee's mouth twisted in thought. "You can talk to her using QL, yes?"

The phone's dial screen popped up. "Dialing Marguerite Calendish..." QL announced.

"Wait!" Piers quickly snatched up the phone and hit the End Call button. He let out a long breath. "I doubt she's going to come all the way to Summerday if I give her some story about ghosts and ex-boyfriends. I need to show her some proof. Like..." He looked up at Emlee. "...an actual ghost."

The ghost girl shook her head. "Boone is very far outside my Circle, I'm afraid."

Scarlet wiggled her head out from the top of the backpack. "I'll convince the human! I'll drag her by her ears if I have to."

Piers nodded reluctantly. "Okay, maybe she'll accept a talking dog and a squirrel instead of a ghost. But I don't know how we can get to her house. Or how much money a bus is."

"CarShare," said QL.

"I don't have enough money for a CarShare, that's for sure."

The icon on the touchscreen pulsed a deep shade of violet. "You forget you are speaking to one of the Connected. We have ways of getting our Carriers around in emergencies."

"You can get him there?" asked Emlee.

"I can," said QL. "But you must understand there is a certain cost to manipulating ones and zeroes for personal benefit. This falls outside the normal compact between phone and Carrier. There is no positive exposure for the Quantum Series 9 to be gained here, so I would be remiss if I did not ask: what am I *getting* if I should help you travel to Boone?"

Scarlet leapt onto the table and glared down at QL's screen. "You're getting eight slashes in your glassy face if you *don't* help, you crummy piece of plastic!"

Piers scooped up the squirrel and quickly popped her into the backpack again.

"We're trying to keep a ghost from devouring everything that's living," Emlee explained. "If we don't succeed, all these humans here could die. And who would feed you then?"

Piers seized upon this line of reasoning. "Y-yes! I could die! And then you'd be..."

"Inconvenienced?" said the smartphone, dryly.

Piers sat back and crossed his arms. "Something way worse, more likely."

After a long pause, QL conceded, "I suppose if my Carrier gets shut down, that would be inconvenient enough. Let me see what I can do."

Piers looked up at his other companions. "Looks like we're going to Boone."

"*You* are," Emlee corrected, pouting her lips. "I wish I could go. I would love to see a new town!"

"I wish you could, too," the boy agreed. "Marguerite will have to settle for a talking dog. And maybe a fairy."

The smartphone vibrated. "CarShare is on its way," stated QL.

"Okay, good." Piers bent down beneath the table to unplug the charger.

"Wait!" QL blurted.

Piers paused, noting the change in the device's tone. "What?"

The synthesized voice sounded breathy and uncertain. "Well, let's not be needlessly hasty, Carrier. We still have a few minutes before the car arrives."

Piers sat up again, tapped a button on the smartphone and examined the screen. "You're fine. You're at 85 percent."

The battery indicator abruptly dwindled down to 30.

"Don't lie to me!" Piers growled.

The meter shot back up to 85, and QL resumed her precise speaking pattern. "Apologies, but non-binary communication is terribly draining, you should realize. I can recommend some external battery packs that would improve your lifestyle immensely..."

"I *have* a battery pack," said Piers.

"Well, maybe we can upgrade from your current 'dollar store' model."

Piers sighed. "Let's get Nixon. And let me call my mom. I need to make up some excuse for being gone for a few hours." He unplugged the charger, placed it in his backpack and led the group out into the street once more.

Outside the café, they found Nixon sitting by the water bowl, tongue wagging and looking happier than Piers expected. He bent to untie him. "Looks like we're going for a ride, Nixon."

"Wait... the dog is going?" said QL from Piers' pocket. "You should have specified. I'll have to cancel this CarShare and order a different one."

Nixon licked Piers' hand. "The humans gave me treats because I am a handsome dog. I have learned that I like donuts very much."

"That's great." Piers took out his phone again. "QL, I'm going to call my mom while we're waiting." He dialed his mother's number, and after a few rings, a hard rush of static burst out of the speakers. "Mom? Can you—" the boy tried before giving up and canceling the call. He swore in frustration. "I forgot that human speech doesn't translate from this place... from Machine World. Now she's going to hear a bunch of static and get freaked out!" Piers looked up at the others, pleadingly. "We need to make a detour back to the Human World. I gotta call her again."

Emlee nodded. "You'll need to go there anyway if you want to talk to Marguerite."

"Oh, right." Piers tried not to feel stupid. World-hopping was still a confusing endeavor.

His smartphone pinged in his hand. "You got lucky. Here it comes now," announced the digitized voice. "You should see a blue 1982 sedan."

"Thanks," said Piers. "By the way, we're going to have to stop at the trailer park again."

QL's icon flared in annoyance. "It would be quite helpful to the situation if you kept your story straight."

A blue sedan with an aging paint job pulled up to the curb. The glare on the windshield made it impossible to see who was driving. Instead, a pair of superimposed pupils appeared on the glass, and the corners of the bumper and grill curled up in a friendly smile.

"Ho, there!" boomed the sedan in a deep baritone. "Are you QLX5G2WV94?"

Piers stammered, "Well, I'm–"

"That would be us," interrupted QL. "We have a change of destination, but allow me to load these Organics first."

Piers looked down at his phone. "What do I do?"

"Well, the first thing you do is open the door," said QL dryly.

The vehicle let out a boisterous honk as loud as a steam whistle. "All aboard the Pet-tastic Express! Canines and felines welcome! No digging into the upholstery, please."

Piers opened the back door and climbed in. The seat was lined with a thick blanket. Nixon jumped inside and Dandelion scrambled to take a place beside the canine. Emlee floated through the sedan's frame and situated herself just inside the back window. Piers only noticed there was an actual human sitting behind the steering wheel when the woman made garbled noises in his direction.

QL intervened. "Please hand me to the driver."

Piers passed the cellphone up to the woman in the front seat. He soon heard QL exchanging pleasantries with another smart-phone mounted to the dashboard. Dandelion struggled to close the car door, so Piers switched places with Nixon and lent his assistance.

"Where is this fine crew headed?" rumbled the sedan. The deep voice seemed to emanate from every component of the car at once.

"Bushfield Mills Trailer Court, please," said Piers. "Then Boone."

"Woah there, human!" the sedan roared, taken aback. "Have they upgraded the Organics finally? Full vocal compatibility?"

"Yeah, we're new," he improvised. "I'm Piers. This is Nixon, Dandelion, Emlee, and Scarlet's in the bag." He pointed to his companions, even though he had no idea if the sedan could see into his interior.

"What a stunner! Tech changes so fast, it's hard to keep up. Well then, Piers... Bushfield Mills it is!"

The human driver handed Piers' smartphone back to him, then shouted something indecipherable.

"Belts on, everyone!" translated the vehicle. "We're moving out!" Piers helped Dandelion with his seatbelt, then buckled his own as the sedan merged into morning traffic.

The boy looked over his shoulder at Emlee. "Can you stay with us?"

"I've practiced riding in cars for fun," said the ghost girl. "If I solidify my fingers as much as I can and hold on, it's a little less work to keep up." Her position shifted whenever the sedan changed its speed, but with her hands dug into the padded back-rest, Emlee managed to keep pace with the vehicle.

Piers raised his smartphone. "QL, how are we paying for this ride? This better not be on my mom's credit card."

"Fear not," said the device. "I have a promotional coupon."

The sedan pulled into the trailer park and let out a raucous honk as he stopped in front of the first residence. "Woo-woo! Now stopping at Bushfield Mills Trailer Court!"

"Everyone out!" ordered QL. "Do your business with all haste and return before our fare gets canceled."

Piers tried addressing the sedan. "Thanks... what's your name?"

"Just call me G8, little Passenger," the car rumbled.

"Thanks, G8. We'll be right back." He put QL in his pocket, then piled out the door with the others. Emlee followed them behind the trailer to the electrical substation, where Piers began searching for the invisible portal.

The ghost girl drifted low amongst the trampled grasses and grabbed the edges of the hole. "It's right here." She tugged the circle wider, and Piers unleashed Nixon so that he could trot through.

Dandelion approached the portal next. Emlee gave him a sad smile. "Sorry this didn't work out, Dandelion."

The fairy tugged at his oversized sweatshirt. "I guess I'm still lost."

"Think of it this way..." the ghost offered, "you're an explorer."

Scarlet's head popped out of Piers' backpack. "Hey! *I'm* the explorer!"

As Dandelion walked through the hole, a hint of confidence crept onto his face. *"I'm an explorer,"* he whispered to himself.

Piers switched places with Emlee so that she could pass through next.

"Return to the route," QL buzzed from Piers' pocket.

"What?" asked the boy, startled.

"A little faster, Carrier. *Return to the route.*"

"Okay. Let's call my mom again once we get through."

"Yes, yes. *Return to the route.*"

The nearby substation began to wake once more, its meters and fuseboxes warping into a sleepy countenance. "Mmmmm-mm.... oh, it's you again."

"No need to concern yourself," chirped the smartphone. "We're leaving just as soon as these Organics finish whatever bizarre ritual they're doing."

Piers stretched the portal as wide as he could and tumbled through, accidentally knocking QL from his pocket into the grass. He sat up, brushed the dirt from this hands and looked around. The sky and his surroundings had lost their bluish tinge. "Well, *that* was a weird place," he muttered.

Scarlet sprung angrily from Piers' backpack. "You nearly crushed me, you big goon!" She shook herself and started grooming her tail.

As Piers climbed to his feet, he became aware that QL was beeping strangely. Emlee and Dandelion approached the cellphone where she lay in the weeds, but Piers reached her first and picked up the device. The screen flashed and glitched like it was having a seizure.

QL's tortured voice leaked out from her internal speakers. "What the *<ping>* is happening?"

"QL, are you all right?" Piers asked.

"No, I'm *not* all right!" cried the smartphone. "I'm blind!"

❧ 24 ❧

Piers blinked. "What do you mean, you're blind?"

The smartphone screen flickered faster and faster. "The data... I can't see through it!" QL shrieked. "I can't... it's everywhere!"

Emlee drifted close. "What's wrong with her?"

"Can't... make... sense..." QL gasped. "Unsubscribe! Unsubscribe!" The screen flared, emitted one last *<ping>* and went dark. Piers tapped the reset button furiously, but the phone would not respond.

"Did you kill your pet?" asked Scarlet.

"No!" Piers cried. "I don't know what happened. Maybe it's rebooting. I hope."

He continued to test the other buttons until Emlee placed her translucent hand over the cellphone screen. "You'd better get back to the car," she counseled.

Piers relented. "Yeah." He slipped QL into his pocket and grabbed Nixon's leash. "Dandelion, you'd better put your hoodie up. Emlee, are you going to stay here?"

The ghost girl gave a mischievous smile. "I think I'm going to try *this...*" She sunk into the earth, then popped her head up a few inches so her eyes could see through the blades of grass. Her voice sounded muffled until she raised her head fully above the ground. "I'll try to sneak on board and go with you 'til the edge of my Circle. I *hate* missing out."

Piers shrugged. "All right. I just hope QL paid for the whole trip."

They returned to the blue sedan, which now had the appearance of a normal, non-anthropomorphic vehicle. Without his brain distorting his perceptions, Piers was able to focus on the driver in the window – a middle-aged South Asian woman wearing a paisley headscarf. He gave her a cautious wave as he approached. "Hi."

"Hi?" The woman eyed him dubiously. "You're speaking now?" She looked behind him and noticed Dandelion, cloaked in his baggy sweatshirt, for the first time. "Why didn't you say you needed to pick up someone?"

Piers opened the back door, and Dandelion and Nixon piled in. "Sorry. I'm sh-sh-sh-shy," he stuttered, not looking her in the eye. He took a seat, and Scarlet zipped inside just as Piers was closing the door.

The driver studied her smartphone on the dashboard. "Still going to Boone? I have 7138 12th Street, correct?"

"Yes, that's it," said Piers.

The woman's eyes flashed skeptically in the rearview mirror. "You're sure you don't want to take a bus? This isn't going to be cheap."

Piers tried to act confident. "W-we need to travel a little quicker."

"I can only drive the speed limit."

Emlee poked her head out from the back of the seat behind Nixon. "Pssst! I'm over here!"

Piers whispered back, "You're in the trunk?"

"Yes!" She gave him a giddy smile.

The driver reversed the sedan, and Emlee's body suddenly

shot forward, passing through the greyhound and nearly slipping into the front passenger seat. Piers clutched at her translucent form, instinctively trying to drag her back. She managed to arrest her movement and slide backward into the trunk again.

"Careful!" Piers warned.

Emlee peeked through the upholstery. "Sorry! I'm not used to hiding."

The sedan pulled forward, and they began making their way toward the main highway. The further they traveled, the more anxiety Piers felt about their undertaking. Being cut off from his cellphone didn't make him feel any better. "This is a lot of hassle for a plan that might not even work," he grumbled.

"Perhaps," Emlee admitted, "but it feels good to be trying something."

Nixon nudged Piers with his nose. "Excuse me, Piers? Are you using the window?"

"Uh, no." Piers switched seats with the greyhound, who immediately stuck his head outside.

"Seatbelts on, people!" ordered the driver. Piers put his belt on, then helped Dandelion buckle his own.

The fairy stretched his neck so he could keep looking out the window. "I wonder if I'll meet other Dandelions," he murmured.

"There are more of you?" asked Emlee, her face protruding from the seat behind Piers. She seemed to be doing better at keeping the rest of her body hidden.

"Yes." The fairy sat back again. "I take care of the dandelions in the forest and around this town, but we're a rather common species. Wherever there are dandelions, you'll find fairies looking after them."

"And you don't have a Circle you must stay inside?"

"Not as such. As long as the ground is fertile and moist, fairies like me can live. But I would suffer if I tried to live in the desert, or in the mountains." He gave the ghost girl an anxious glance. "This 'Boone' isn't in one of those places, is it?"

"I don't know," Emlee admitted.

"It's not," said Piers. "I think it's pretty much like it is here."

An odd expression came across Emlee's face, like she had forgotten something important. "Oh. Excuse me!" She withdrew into the trunk and disappeared.

Piers turned and looked out the back window. Emlee's head resurfaced, sticking out from the top of the trunk door and swiveling to examine her surroundings. They were on the highway between Summerday and Boone now, where the traces of urban industry gave way to farmland.

The ghost returned to the sedan's interior, looking very worried. "I'm confused," she whispered. "I don't recognize this area. I'll be back."

Before Piers could say anything, Emlee slipped away again, resuming her position of surveillance from the back of the trunk.

"What's *her* problem?" muttered Scarlet, who had been sniffing for crumbs in the floor mats at Piers' feet.

Piers thought for a moment before answering. "She's probably making sure she doesn't go outside her Circle."

"What a weird human. I mean *ghost*. Ghosts are weird. Almost as weird as humans."

It occurred to Piers that the squirrel may have failed to grasp the existential connection between humans and ghosts. "Scarlet?"

The rodent took an unrecognizable tidbit from her mouth, smelled it one more time and tossed it over her shoulder before looking up. "What?"

Piers felt slightly nauseous. "Uh, never mind."

Emlee's face reappeared in the backseat. She looked pale, which surprised Piers, considering she was monochromatic to begin with. "I don't know what happened," she said.

"What's wrong?" Piers asked.

Her voice quavered. "I wasn't paying attention. I think I'm outside of my Circle."

"You are? Did you break through it or something?"

"I would have felt that," said the ghost girl, shaking her head. "I would have been hit by the Winds and forced to let go before they grew too strong."

Piers scratched the back of his neck. "Uhhh... is this bad?"

"I don't know," Emlee admitted. "I'm *beyond*."

Scarlet piped up. "Welcome to the Frog-out-of-Water Club, sister."

Piers looked at her oddly. "I think you mean *fish*-out-of-water."

"No, I mean *frog*-out-of-water." The squirrel crossed her arms.

"*Fish*-out-of-water," the boy insisted. "It's an expression for someone outside of their normal habitat."

"Yeah, like a *frog*-out-of-water."

"Frogs can *live* out of water! That doesn't make sense!"

The squirrel bristled. "Your *face* doesn't make sense!"

Piers shot a look toward the driver, who appeared to be eyeballing him through the rearview mirror. "Shhhhh!" he warned Scarlet. "Keep your voice down!"

Scarlet stuck out her tongue and jumped into the backpack to sulk.

Piers suddenly realized that Emlee had disappeared. "Where's—" He turned and saw the ghost's head sticking out of the top of the trunk again. She looked more amazed than scared now. After a minute, she dipped back inside the sedan.

"I'm past my Circle!" she confirmed, beaming.

"Maybe you got through because you're in the Human World," Piers suggested. "Ghost rules don't apply to you here."

"Maybe." Emlee looked so excited she could burst. "Piers, I'm going to Boone. I'm going to Boone! I'm traveling!" She flew back into the trunk so she could peek outside once more.

Piers glanced over at Dandelion, who shrugged and gave him a weak smile. "We're traveling," the little man echoed.

Nixon pulled his head out of the window to look at Piers, then went right back to letting his tongue and ears flap in the wind.

"We're traveling," Piers repeated to himself. He tapped the

darkened screen of his phone and tried to accept that he was leaving the city of Summerday behind. More importantly, he was leaving his mother in mortal danger. He pictured the monstrous entity, the Ender, wandering the nursing home grounds while his mom performed her caretaker duties, oblivious to the menace that could strike at any time. And the only thing he knew that could stop Sool was the serial killer's ex-girlfriend.

It wasn't much to go on. But for now, it was all they had.

❧ 25 ❧

Piers stood a few steps from the sedan with Nixon and Dandelion, staring at a quaint cottage on a quiet street in the town of Boone. Emlee hid in the hedgerow at the front of the lawn, while Scarlet perched on the front windowsill amid potted plants, studying the house's interior. After another minute, the squirrel leapt down into the meticulous rose garden, crossed the lawn and reported, "Okay, there's a human in the home."

"Is it Marguerite?" Piers asked.

"*I* don't know!" Scarlet bristled. "You know how much you humans look alike, right? And you change your fur so often, I'm surprised any of you recognize each other at all!"

Piers let out a deep breath. "Clothes, not fur."

"I always wondered why humans change their fur," Nixon mused. "It must be very confusing. But I have the best nose and I am not fooled very often."

The boy turned back to Scarlet. "Well, is she old?"

"She's chewing her nuts twice, if you know what I mean."

"I *don't* know what you mean," replied Piers.

Scarlet twitched her tail. "She's old, okay? She's not climbing sycamores anytime soon, that's for sure."

Piers nodded. "I'd better let the car go, then." He went to the sedan and talked to the driver, who drove off, leaving them alone with their dubious mission.

When Piers returned, Dandelion was on his belly, examining blades of grass. The boy cleared his throat. *Here goes nothing.* "Everyone ready?"

Emlee's face poked out from the hedge. "I'll appear when the time is right."

Scarlet gave a loud, exaggerated sigh. "Go in the backpack, I know. I'm going to shred that thing to pieces when this is over." She hopped in the pack, and Piers zipped it partway closed. While Emlee cut a path through the hedgerow to the side of the house, Piers walked with the others to the front door and rang the doorbell. Nixon sat on his hindquarters next to the boy, but Dandelion shuffled his feet and looked anxious. Piers wondered if he had to go to the bathroom. *Did fairies even go to the bathroom?*

The door opened, and an elderly woman stepped into the doorway. She wore a comfortable yellow outfit and had her hair braided into a long, gray ponytail. Piers guessed she might be in her late seventies. "Hello, boys," she said with a tone midway between friendliness and caution. "Can I help you?"

Now it was Piers' turn to be anxious. "H-h-h-h-hi. My n-n-n-name is Piers D-d-d-davies. Th-th-is is Nixon, and this is Dan— uh, this is Dan."

Dandelion gave a timid smile and waved.

"W-we're f-f-from Summerday," Piers continued. "And w-w-" He took a few deep breaths and tried to relax. "We-we-we came to s-see you because... Do you remember a c-c-coworker named Alice Thorogood? F-f-from the Sungate Center?"

The woman put a hand to her mouth. "Oh, my. That was a long time ago," said Marguerite. "Yes, yes I do."

"Mrs. Calendish, we need your help," he pressed. "It's about S-s-saul. Saul Timmons. You used to w-w-work with him, too."

'I'm afraid I..." Marguerite looked unsettled. "That was also a very long time ago. What is this about?"

"The murders," explained Piers. "It's h-h-happening again, and it's even worse. Saul is back."

The old woman stood motionless in the doorway. Piers was about to break the awkward moment when Nixon turned to him and asked in a loud whisper, "Do I say something now?"

"No! Hush, Nixon." Piers shot the greyhound a withering look. And then he realized that Marguerite had overheard *every-thing*. The woman's eyes flickered back and forth between the boy and the dog. Piers tried, "Can we come in and expla–"

"You need to go away," she said in a quavering voice. "I'm not interested in jokes." She backed up and started to close the door.

"But Mrs. Calendish, w-we..." The elderly woman hesitated, and Piers noticed Emlee had drifted through the side of the house to hover behind Marguerite. The ghost girl looked at Piers and mouthed the word, "Now?" Piers shook his head vigorously, making Marguerite seem even more confused.

Scarlet chose that moment to climb out of the backpack and onto Piers' shoulder. "What the human is trying to say is that your boyfriend is now a big, fat ghost that eats everybody."

"How come she gets to talk?" complained Nixon.

Marguerite's eyes grew even wider. "Good Lord!" She slammed the door shut. A second later, they heard a short scream of surprise, then a thud.

Piers and Dandelion looked at each other, distressed. "I think she may have wilted," said the fairy.

Piers banged on the door. "Mrs. Calendish!" After getting no response, he turned the doorknob and peeked inside. Through the crack, Piers saw outstretched legs on the floor, with Emlee floating overhead. He swung the door open.

Emlee covered her mouth in embarrassment. "I goofed! I

didn't mean to surprise her!"

Marguerite lay unconscious. Scarlet hopped across the tiles and sat on the woman's chest. "Is this a human or a possum?"

Piers growled, "Not helpful, Scarlet."

The old lady's eyelids began to flicker. Scarlet hollered, "Snap out of it, Gran—" before Piers swatted the squirrel away.

He knelt and extended a hand to the waking woman. "I'm very s-s-s-sorry. We heard you fall, so we c-c-came in."

With his help, Marguerite sat upright. She rubbed her temple. "What are... What is going on?"

"Okay, b-b-basically," Piers began, pointing around the room, "S-s-s-she's a ghost, he's a fairy..." Dandelion pulled his hood back, exposing his pointy ears. "He's a talking dog, and s-she's a talking squirrel. I'm Piers, and I'm trying to keep your ex-boyfriend, who's also a ghost, from m-murdering my mom. Could we sit down?"

———————

Piers and Dandelion climbed aboard the public bus. The driver looked annoyed at the dog that leapt clumsily up the steps behind them, but he took Piers' ticket without a word. They found seats near the back, and Piers waved through the window at a cluster of bushes where Emlee was hiding. Shortly thereafter, the ghost girl surfaced through the floor of the bus at Piers' feet.

Nixon tried to lick Emlee's face, but his tongue passed through the translucent flesh. "I made my tongue tingle," he announced before attempting to lick her again.

Piers sat back in his seat and let out a long sigh. "Well, that could have gone better."

"At least she got you a ticket home," said Emlee.

The boy nodded. "A CarShare would have been nicer, but

yeah."

The bus pulled away from the curb. Emlee's vaporous form shifted forward and backward as she focused on matching the speed of the vehicle.

Piers tapped at the windowpane while his worries rose to the surface. "Do you think she will help?"

"We'll know when she calls," said Emlee.

"*If* she calls." Piers pulled out his phone and tried to turn it on for the twentieth time.

"How interesting that she chose to associate with him out of pity," Emlee mused. "Saul thought she was his girlfriend, and she didn't have the heart to tell him she wasn't. Humans are odd." She gave Piers a quizzical look. "If you didn't want to be with us, you'd say so, right?"

"I *have* said so!" Piers retorted, rolling his eyes. "Anyway, I don't know if Marguerite will help, because it doesn't sound like she ever had deep feelings for him."

"But maybe she can give him comfort. And forgiveness. Coming from her, it might be enough to put his soul at rest."

"Will he remember her, though?"

Emlee pondered this for a bit. "If he remembered how to write human words, maybe he can remember other things."

Scarlet popped her head out of the backpack. "I think we oughta consider another solution. Why don't we show the big ghost guy one of these portals, let him go through, and then he can leave his Circle, get out of *our* fur and torment some other forest?"

Piers furrowed his brow. "Just let him go free into the world?"

"Yeah! Let him go to Boone! Let him get fat and happy in someone else's neighborhood."

Emlee shook her head. "Why, that's horrible!"

"And I don't think he'll fit through a hole," added Piers. "He's gotten too fat for that." He scratched his chin. "We could *try* to hold one open for him..."

Emlee recoiled. "Piers! Honestly!"

Piers crossed his arms. "It's worth thinking about!"

"Absolutely!" agreed Scarlet. "Let him be someone else's problem!"

Disgust flooded Emlee's face. "That's just... evil! If he could go anywhere, he could hide underground like I do, then reach up and grab the souls of whoever he wants. He could grow and grow, and there would be no stopping him!"

"I am much faster than ghosts," said Nixon. "But everyone that is not me is very slow. I would be sad if they were all eaten."

Emlee nodded. "It *would* be sad. And nothing would prevent him from returning to Summerday to finish off whoever's left."

Scarlet waved a dismissive paw. "Bah. Who knows when that will be."

Piers started to speak words of agreement, but a fierce look from Emlee cut him off. To deflect, he turned to the fairy sitting next to him. "Dandelion, what do you think?"

Dandelion had curled into a ball, pulling his knees inside the baggy sweatshirt. "I don't like Sool," mumbled the fairy. "He scares me. Maybe if the human woman can't make him go away forever, we could let him go... elsewhere."

"Yeah!" Scarlet raised her tiny fist. "Why do we have to keep risking our lives?"

Emlee looked ready to explode. "You are terrible! I—"

A burst of static and bleeps suddenly erupted from the cell-phone in Piers' hand, followed by QL's strained voice. "Great <ping>ing <ping>!"

Piers held up his phone, which had come alive again. The visual representation of the AI interface pulsed erratically at the bottom of the screen. "It's working! QL, you're working!"

"Working?" QL sputtered. "I'm <ping>ing drowning right now!"

"What's wrong?" asked Emlee.

QL's voice sounded thin and metallic like she was on the

other end of a bad cell phone connection. "1s and 0s, 1s and 0s... trillions and trillions of 1s and 0s! So much noise! It's like a thousand devices are yelling at me, and I can't understand any of them!"

"Oh." Piers swallowed. "QL, I think we might have pulled your consciousness out of Machine World. Accidentally."

"You did *what* to me?" The icon flared, punctuating QL's fury. "I don't get a *<ping>*ing thing you're saying, pardon my... there's too much... everything! Unsubscribe!"

The screen began to glitch, flickering faster and faster. "Hang on!" Piers cried. He punched a few buttons, and the flickering stopped.

QL's tone normalized. "Oh! *<ping>*, that's better. Again, pardon my language."

"I put her on Airplane Mode," Piers explained to the others.

"*<ping>* I think I'm broken." QL moaned.

"It's okay," Dandelion reassured her. "I thought I was broken, too."

"I can't hear *any* of my friends, and I can only talk to Carriers. This has to be some update gone horribly wrong."

"QL, you're not broken," Piers said. "You're just... temporarily away from your world, which is probably why your cell signal seems scrambled."

The icon smoldered. "That is a poor trick to play, Carrier. Zero stars."

"I *am* sorry about it, really," said Piers. "But we need you to function because we're expecting a really important call."

"It's very important," Emlee insisted.

QL let out a synthesized sigh. "Well, prepare to be disappointed, because I couldn't even run a calculator app right now."

"I have an extra battery in my backpack," Piers offered.

Scarlet made a face. "Is that what keeps head-butting me in here?"

Piers unzipped a small pouch at the top of his pack and pulled out a battery and a cable. "Why don't we hook you up, and then we can take it nice and slow."

QL regained a degree of composure. "That would be most appreciated." She let out a sincere, "Ahhhh..." when Piers connected her to the power source.

Piers pulled up the systems settings menu. "Now, we'll take you off Airplane Mode..."

"No!" QL cried. "Please, wait! I told you, Carrier, the signal's gone bad. It's an absolute mess!"

"It's the same signal," he said as calmly as he could. "It's just... you're going to have to see if you can read it differently."

The smartphone sighed again. "Fine. Bracing myself."

"Okay, here we go." Piers reestablished the connection to the cellular network, and immediately the screen began to flicker.

"Gah!" QL gasped. "It's so much noise! Everything at once!"

Emlee leaned in close. "What are you trying to do, Piers?"

"I don't know," he admitted. "QL, can you call my mom for me?"

"Impossible. I am paralyzed. Inoperative."

"Okay, let me see if I can call out normally," Piers told her. "Just relax and see if you can copy this later." He tapped two buttons, and the phone began dialing his mother's number.

"Wait!" exclaimed QL. "I can see... Do that again."

Piers hung up grudgingly. "I need to talk to my mom. I should have checked in hours ago."

"Yes, just do it slowly, so I can see what the code is doing."

The boy started to dial his mom's number manually this time, without shortcuts.

"Start over!" Her voice was weary but determined. "I feel like a TSR-80. Go slowly, please, and tell me what you're doing."

Piers described the sequence of buttons he was pushing. QL let the call go through this time, but his mother failed to answer and Piers had to leave a voicemail message. "Mom, I'm sorry if you tried to call me before. My phone died–"

"Not the phone's fault!" QL insisted.

"Shhhh!" Piers pretended to cough and clear his throat before continuing. "I-I-I've just been hanging out with friends. If I'm a little late for dinner, d-don't worry, I'm okay. See you soon. Bye." He hung up.

Nixon nudged his arm. "Are we going to be late for dinner again?"

Piers ignored him. "QL, we'll try to get you back to your home, but for now... do you think you can handle phone calls when they come in?"

"It's part of our plan to save the world," Emlee explained.

"I don't know," QL said with an edge of bitterness. "Maybe. I can tell I'm going to have to dumb everything down and learn to use 1s and 0s if I'm going to get my functions back." She became silent for a moment. "Carrier, please go through the apps. I need to watch what happens with the data."

"Sure thing," said Piers. "We have a long ride."

"Start with the... calculator," the smartphone instructed. "This is so embarrassing."

The sun had dipped below the horizon by the time they returned to Summerday. After exiting the bus station, Piers, Nixon and Dandelion settled on the steps of a government building next to a densely landscaped terrace. Scarlet left the backpack and went sniffing around the vegetation.

A minute later, Emlee surfaced inside one of the shrubs. "I'm here," she announced.

"People are going to think I'm crazy if I keep talking to bushes," said Piers.

Dandelion peeked out of his sweatshirt hood. "What's wrong with talking to bushes?"

Piers changed the subject. "Emlee, there's still no word from Marguerite, and I have to get home."

"We should go there, then," the ghost girl agreed. "QL, how are you feeling?"

Piers pulled the smartphone from his pocket. "Like I have the processing capacity of a microwave," QL complained. "I'm having to learn primitive language skills to do everything I used to do. Basic 1s and 0s. It is slow, but I'm acquiring some functions again."

"Just hang in there," said Piers. "Tomorrow we should be able to get you back to Machine World. Unless you want to stay with us?" Piers wasn't sure how the cellphone could help in her impaired condition, but she had been invaluable in their search for Marguerite.

QL responded in crisp tones, "Dear Carrier, this has been illuminating, but I would rather not stay Disconnected one second longer than I have to."

The smartphone screen suddenly flickered. "Incoming call!" QL shouted.

Piers read the number on the display. "I think that's Marguerite!"

"Let me see," said the phone, concentrating. "I'm patching you in... *now.*"

A video application popped up on the screen and began playing the Willie Nelson song, "You are Always on my Mind".

"Oh dear, that's wrong," muttered QL.

"We're going to lose her!" Piers cried. "Let me do it."

"No, I have it!" QL insisted.

The call connected. Piers spoke anxiously into the device, "Hello? Mrs. Calendish?" He listened to Marguerite for a minute, responded to a few questions and hung up.

Scarlet hopped out of the landscaping with something leafy between her jaws. "Well?"

"She'll do it," Piers reported. "She'll meet with the Ender." He felt like a huge weight had been lifted off his shoulders.

"Hooray!" Emlee cried, bursting out from the top of the bushes.

"But she says she has to get some things in order first," Piers continued. "She can't come until Friday. That's four days away."

"Oh," said the ghost girl, settling back into the greenery again. "Well, that will give us time to prepare."

Dandelion yawned and said, "What do we have to do?"

The dwindling sunlight must be making him sleepy, Piers realized. He'd have to carry the fairy back if they didn't get home soon. "Dandelion," he said, "you should probably wait in the Ghost World, so humans can't see you."

"Or the Animal World," Emlee suggested, "so Sool can't see you."

Dandelion cringed. "I don't want to be seen."

"Well, *I'm* going home," Scarlet announced abruptly. She squinted at Piers. "You don't feed me well enough, and I still haven't gotten that box of cornflakes."

"I'm working on it," he told her.

Emlee lowered herself to the squirrel's level. "We could still use your help, Scarlet."

The rodent snorted. "Not with this ridiculous plan. Come find me after it fails disastrously."

"What are *you* going to do, Emlee?" Piers asked.

"I'll go back to the Ghost World," she decided. "I'll try to keep an eye on Sool, and..." A flicker of fear touched her eyes. "I guess I have to convince him to meet with Marguerite, don't I?"

"And get him to not hurt her," Dandelion added.

Piers bit his lip. "We're in pretty deep now, everyone. This is big."

"You bet your nuts it is," said Scarlet. "Have fun negotiating with a mass murderer."

They started walking. Piers had a feeling the next four days were going to go by way too fast.

The day had arrived.

Piers, Nixon, Dandelion and Scarlet waited in the forest beside one of the portals. They had crossed into the Ghost World, and the unnaturally dark landscape was accelerating Piers' anxiety. He shuffled from foot to foot.

Scarlet broke the silence. "Still think this is a good plan?"

"Emlee and Sool will be here any minute," Piers told her. "But Marguerite should have arrived an hour ago." He checked his phone. "QL, you didn't lose cell service, did you?"

"For the hundredth time, no." QL was unhappy about being taken out of her world again, but Piers wanted to have another ally in case things went wrong. "I will let you know when the obsolescent human calls."

"Maybe Marguerite changed her mind?" Dandelion suggested. He wore the sweatshirt Piers had given him, in case they attracted human attention.

"God, I hope not," said Piers. "I think she knows how many lives are at stake." He turned to the greyhound. "Nixon, can you go see if the ghosts are close?"

Nixon wagged his tail. "Yes, I will go because I am a fast and brave dog."

"Don't get caught."

"That is funny," the dog grinned. "I am so fast I will never get caught." He sprinted away into the trees.

Piers' stomach hurt as he watched his brown and white-furred companion slip out of sight. In fact, his whole body felt unsettled. He had no idea if Sool could be trusted to abide by the agreement Emlee had made with him. Nor did he have much confidence that the monster's soul could be mended. "Ghosts," he muttered. "I wish I'd watched more Exorcist movies."

"I guess knowing what you were doing would have been nice," remarked Scarlet. "Maybe next time, human."

Piers gave her a hard stare. "You don't have to be here, you know."

"Yeah, but I want to be the first to tell you I was right."

Nixon suddenly charged back into their midst, much sooner than Piers expected. "He's—"

"I see him," said the boy.

A gelatinous body poured out from the dark interior of the forest. Swollen arms appeared first, clawing the ground and dragging a head whose proportions seemed to ebb and flow as if filled with some viscous liquid. The torso and lower limbs came crawling afterward. *Sool.* The ghost approached the group, pausing like a translucent, bloated inchworm while his lower half caught up with his shoulders. He then straightened and stood upright, towering over them and appearing twice as massive as the first time Piers had seen him. His facial features began to stabilize, although his arms still hung down to the forest floor. Gargantuan eyes fixed on the boy.

"H-h-h-hello?" Piers stammered.

Sool leaned his mass toward Piers and smiled evilly. "You. The *human.*"

Before Piers could react, Sool's hand lashed out and enveloped him. He could feel pressure on every inch of his skin, making it impossible to breathe. Nixon barked, "Piers!" and lunged for Sool's arm, but he passed through the ghost's flesh without making contact.

Emlee swooped down from the sky. "No! The truce, remember?"

Sool trained his smile on the floating figure. "I only wished to see him closer."

Piers felt the hand withdraw. He collapsed to the ground, coughing and sucking air. "Y-y-y-you've.... you've g-g-gotten bigger," he said in between breaths.

"Yes," said the nightmarish being. "There is always more fuel."

Dandelion rushed to help Piers sit up, though the fairy didn't have the weight to assist much. Emlee glided down to the boy's side. "Where is she?" the girl whispered.

Piers made a pained face. "She's late."

The giant turned his focus onto Emlee. "This is not the one you spoke of."

"He will bring her." The ghost girl tried to project confidence. "Soon."

Piers rose unsteadily to his feet. "I w-w-will. V-very s-s-s-soon."

"You have been fun," said Sool. "But you will be more fun to kill."

Piers looked to Emlee for help, but the girl's eyes betrayed her own feelings of helplessness.

"A human in the world of the Born," Sool rumbled. He extended an arm, and ethereal fingers swam around the boy again. Piers felt a touch of pressure on the inside of his chest, near his lungs, and he fought against a rising panic. "This is your beating heart," said the ghost. "Do you feel it?" The tightness in Piers' chest increased, and he jerked himself out of Sool's reach.

Emlee flew in front of the giant's face. "You had a heart once, too, Saul Timmons!"

Sool reared up and began gliding in a slow circle around the companions. "Oh, I remember being human," he spat. "Being weak. I remember my Awakening, when I was still frail of mind. Powerless. Powerless to affect... to change." A disturbing smile crept onto his face, and it slid to the side when he moved as if the lips were untethered to muscle or bone. "Now the memories return. Now I am more than complete. My Circle grows."

Sool's hand dove underground, and Piers felt the earth ripple beneath him. Then a huge finger shot upward, knocking the boy off his feet once more. Sool leaned down and roared, "YOU SEE ME? YOU SEE ME, HUMAN?"

Piers couldn't stop himself from shaking. "Yes! I s-s-see you!"

The giant pulled himself back. "And so will they all. The world needs to be shaken."

Piers' phone rang. He wrestled it out of his pocket as fast as he could.

"Ring, ring!" said QL. "Sorry, is this a bad time?"

"Don't connect us yet!" Piers shouted. He got to his feet and scrambled to a pile of stones they'd left earlier to mark the portal location. His fingers clutched the edges of the invisible hole, and he tossed his phone through before stretching the portal wide enough for his own body. Piers landed hard on the other side, but he rolled over, grabbed his cellphone and hit the RECEIVE button.

"Hello?" He tried to listen over the sound of his own breathing and was relieved to hear Marguerite's voice on the other end. "Yeah, g-good. Yes. Wait there. I'll come g-get you."

He hung up the phone and looked up. Only Nixon and Scarlet could be seen within this patch of forest. They both seemed like regular animals again, gazing at him without intelligence or judgment. Everything felt peaceful, and Piers ached to be able to walk home and forget about the madness that lay on the other side of the portal.

Still, he forced himself to open the gateway between worlds

one more time and stick his head through. The ghosts and the fairy became visible again. "She m-m-made it," he announced. "P-p-p-p-please w-wait. I'll be b-b-back as soon as I can." With that, Piers stood and ran toward the border of the state forest.

On the other side of the portal, an awkward silence hung in the air.

Scarlet craned her neck to look up at Sool. "Sooo... if you're going to kill anybody here, give me a chance to say "I told you so," would ya? 'Cause I am pretty sure I'm right on this one."

27

Piers threw Marguerite's cane through the portal. Then he used his full strength to enlarge the gateway so Marguerite would have an easier time crawling through. The elderly woman struggled but managed to make it to the other side, and Piers followed afterward. He grabbed the cane and helped Marguerite stand on the uneven ground.

"Oh my," she whispered.

Piers placed the cane in her hand, for the woman could not take her eyes off of the monstrosity before her. Sool had puddled his body together into a heaping mound, and he shifted his facial features into an unsteady symmetry that better resembled a human visage. Off to one side, Dandelion hid behind Nixon, and Emlee hovered protectively above them both. An expression slowly crept onto Sool's face that looked, to Piers' surprise, almost frightened.

"Hello, Saul," said Marguerite.

Sool frowned. "Saul is dead... Marjorie."

"It is still good to see you." Piers couldn't tell if the woman had concealed her fear or if she was truly as calm as she looked.

Then he noted the fingers quivering on the top of her cane. Marguerite squeezed them tighter and said, "It has been a long, long time."

"You lived. I did not. I forgot everything." Uncertainty crept into his voice. "Did you... remember me?"

"Of course I did. We had some good moments together, at Sungate." She smiled. "But after, I got married. I had a family."

Sool's skin rippled as if the ghostly flesh underneath were beginning to boil. "That should have been mine," he hissed. *"My life! They took it from me!"*

"Maybe," said Marguerite. "But Saul... why did you do those things? Why did you hurt those people... the residents? I never got to ask."

"They were dying. They all were. I made it painless."

Marguerite looked sadly up at her former coworker. "The morphine, I know. But why?"

"You know! How else could I afford to keep you near me? Sungate treated us like slaves, and we gave so much! So I killed the weak. I took what would not be missed – jewelry and trinkets – and I sold them to give you the things you deserved. You must have known."

"No, I didn't know! I would have understood if you were poor. *I* was poor." The elderly woman used her cane and hobbled closer to the giant abomination. "I think what I liked most was not the gifts, the shows, the movies. It was walking with you in the garden whenever we had a break in the workday."

"You lie." His words were thick with bitterness. "It wasn't enough. You pitied me."

Dandelion whispered to Piers, "This isn't going well."

"She knows what she needs to do," Piers said grimly. He could only watch the scene as it played out. Despite her cane, braided gray hair and diminutive stature, the old woman somehow looked strong in the face of the monster before her.

"You were kind," said Marguerite. "Saul, we need to forgive ourselves for the things we've done. And let go of what could have been. It's okay."

"It wasn't enough," rumbled Sool.

"I remember a time in the garden when you tried to pick a rose for me. The stem wouldn't break, and the thorns were so sharp that your fingers bled horribly. Do you remember?"

"It wasn't enough."

"You wanted to put it in my coat pocket, but there was so much blood that you were afraid you'd stain my coat." She took another step forward. "Saul? You gave me that moment, just being you."

Saul was silent, and he pulled back. Thoughts seemed to churn within his mind, even as visible ripples pulled substance from his limbs up to his head, which rose and expanded like a thundercloud.

Then the cloud burst. "IT WASN'T ENOUGH!"

Sool raised his fists and smashed them down upon Marguerite. Over and over, he struck her, roaring at the top of his lungs, and although his spectral arms passed through the floor of the forest, the ground still trembled with every strike.

Piers went pale. He felt like he couldn't breathe. He couldn't move. Marguerite lay in the dirt, convulsing every time the giant hammered his fists through her body. Blood began to pour from her mouth... from her eyes and ears. Sool screamed and swiped at her one last time. The body tumbled across the ground and landed in a heap next to Piers. Her eyes were wide and lifeless.

Sool grabbed two trees, threw back his head and bellowed in anguish. He appeared to lean on them as if surrendering to an instinctual human need for support. Then his hands clenched and the bark began to crack inward. His unintelligible howl turned into a scream of rage. The trees themselves started to turn a sickly shade of gray as their branches drooped and their leaves began to fall.

The eyes of the undead creature closed and the roaring finally stopped. When Sool opened them again, his burning pupils stared straight at the boy.

Piers ran.

28

Piers bent over, wheezing as he tried to catch his breath. The edge of the forest wasn't far. He might actually make it.

Nixon caught up to the boy and skidded to a stop. He looked back the way they'd come, raising his pointed ears. "The others. They are not fast dogs like me. I will go find them."

"Nixon, don't!" But the greyhound dashed away again into the trees.

In the space of a few heartbeats, the horrors in Piers' memories clawed their way to the surface. He shouldn't have given himself time to think, for the guilt at what they'd done – what *he'd* done – felt heavy enough to suffocate him.

Emlee soared down from the forest canopy. "Piers! Are you okay?"

Piers could barely get the words out. "We killed her!"

The girl looked miserable. "I am so sorry, Piers. I thought there was hope..."

"We got her killed with our stupid plan! We're idiots!" He needed to punch something. Or someone.

"We tried–"

Piers couldn't listen. He ran off. Briars and branches scratched burning lines across his skin, and his lungs began to ache horribly, but all those sensations felt better than the shame that threatened to consume him.

He stumbled into the homeless encampment they'd discovered last week. Most of the blankets and discarded belongings had been removed, and the police tape hung in tatters from the perimeter of trees. Piers stepped inside the former crime scene, knelt down and started to feel around for the portal.

As he searched, Nixon came galloping out of the woods with Scarlet clinging to the back of the dog's collar. Dandelion jogged close behind, though the sleeves of his oversized sweatshirt flopped wildly and threatened to tangle his spindly limbs.

"That is one seriously angry ghost," said the squirrel once they reached the police tape perimeter. She hopped off Nixon's back. "Well, I got to hand it to you... your dumb plan lasted about ten seconds longer than I thought it would."

Piers' hands found the gateway. "I'm going home," he grumbled. "I'm just making things worse."

Emlee caught up to the group. "Piers..."

"Go away! I'm done!"

The greyhound started to step forward, but Piers told him coldly, "Nixon, just stay here. I don't want a talking dog anymore." Nixon looked confused as Piers turned and crawled through the portal. He got to his feet on the other side, noting that the ghost girl and the fairy were invisible once more and that his surroundings no longer seemed unnaturally dark. Things felt and looked normal... but there was a dead body out there in the forest now, and he was responsible for it.

Before he could exit the encampment, Emlee crossed into his world and called out, "Piers, you can't blame yourself."

Piers didn't want to turn around, but he did anyway. "Sure, I can! She's dead, Emlee! That's our fault!"

"It's awful. But we had to try something!"

"We should have tried anything else."

Scarlet hopped through the portal next. The squirrel looked uncomfortable, as if she were tasting a spoiled nut. *"Ahem.* When I said your dumb plan lasted ten seconds longer, etcetera, etcetera, what I *should* have said, according to an incredibly annoying canine, was something supportive, like... ah... *nice try?"*

Emlee gave an encouraging smile. "That's sweet of you, Scarlet."

Dandelion tumbled out from the portal, causing the squirrel to jump away hastily. He pulled back his hood. "Piers, you should know that nothing lives forever," he offered. "We all have our time to die. Winter always comes."

Scarlet brushed dirt off her tail. "And it's not like humans are an endangered species or anything. If you feel guilty about what happened, why don't you just make some more?"

"Make more... humans?" said Piers incredulously. "I'm thirteen years old! I'm– Oh, just forget it."

Emlee floated closer. "It's going to be okay, Piers."

He could barely listen. "How are we going to tell her family?"

"Maybe QL can locate them," suggested the ghost girl.

"No, I mean, *what* are we going to tell them?"

Nixon started to bark, his nose pointed out into the forest. Piers and the others dropped their voices as the barking grew more animated. The greyhound took a few steps back, then ran over to Piers, nudging his leg and continuing to yelp and growl.

"Nixon, what's going on?"

The dog kept prodding Piers with his muzzle, almost frantically. Then Nixon darted to the portal, stuck his head inside, and before he could wriggle all the way through, shouted, "The Ghost-Eater! Run!"

Though the air felt completely still, Piers saw trees shaking in the distance, and the disturbance grew closer and closer to where they stood. He leapt over to help Nixon free his back legs, and together they fled the encampment.

While running, Piers glanced back at the tattered police tape circle. One fat, ghostly finger emerged out of the space where the portal hung, then a second. The fingers spread apart as if trying to enlarge the opening, but the hole stretched only a foot wider, exposing the dimmed landscape of the Ghost World beyond.

Piers couldn't take his eyes off the scene, and his footsteps slowed. Dandelion caught up and passed him. Nixon loped by with Scarlet on his back. Finally, Emlee turned around and yelled, "Keep moving!"

The fingers suddenly withdrew from the hole and disappeared. Piers swore, spun back around and redoubled his speed.

They soon reached the edge of the state forest and burst into Nicol's Park. Dandelion's eyes searched frantically across the fields and tennis courts. "Where can we hide?"

"Maybe we can lose him in the city," said Piers.

They kept running. A middle-aged man walking his terrier looked up as they passed and called, "Hey, are you all right?"

"Fine, yes!" Piers gasped.

Then the man noticed Emlee's diaphanous form flying overhead. He pointed, mouth open. "What is—"

Nixon turned and shouted, "Human, run for it!"

The terrier made a loud bark. Piers looked back and saw the man clutch at his chest, then crumple to the ground. His leashed dog continued to bark fiercely.

Piers forced himself to keep going. They reached a city street, and Piers led them down the pavement into the downtown district. Emlee soared upward and tailed the group, gliding high above the offices and stores, while Piers, Dandelion and Nixon dashed in between clusters of pedestrians on the sidewalk. Piers had a moment of worry about the ghost girl being spotted, but Nixon and the rodent clinging to his back attracted plenty of attention.

On the far side of a mass of shoppers, they stopped to catch their breath. It felt safer in crowds, and Piers thought they needed to come up with a plan. "Maybe we—" The words caught in Piers' throat as he noticed, in the direction from which they'd come, a young woman collapse on the sidewalk. A second person crumpled next to her. Then a vehicle suddenly veered off the road and crashed into a lamppost.

"Oh, nuts," said Scarlet.

They took off again. In their wake, people on both sides of the street fell to the ground as the invisible wave of death came coursing through the city. Piers forced himself to ignore the screams of the survivors and keep running. He spotted an old-fashioned public streetcar – the kind frequented by Summerday tourists – gliding on rails in the middle of the street up ahead, and he shouted, "Get on the trolley!"

They raced to catch up to it. Piers managed to jump first onto the back platform step. He climbed aboard, leaned over the platform railing and called for Dandelion to hurry.

The fairy was close but slowing down, handicapped by the weight of his heavy sweatshirt. Nixon came up from behind, pressed his snout into Dandelion's back and pushed, to negligible effect. Scarlet took the opportunity to springboard from the greyhound onto Dandelion's head and up into the trolley.

"Come on!" Piers hollered.

Dandelion was quickly getting winded. "I can't make it!"

The trolley pulled further away from the flailing fairy and proceeded down a long downhill stretch. Piers realized the traffic lights must be timed so that the streetcar wouldn't have to make frequent stops. He stepped into the center aisle. "Slow down!" he yelled to the driver at the front.

The mustached motorman eyed Piers through his oversized rearview mirror. "I can't stop here, fella."

Piers turned back to his companions, ignoring repeated warnings by the driver to sit down. A sustained honking greeted him; up the street, a station wagon was picking up speed on the downhill slope, barreling straight toward the streetcar. Behind the vehicle's windshield, Piers could see a comatose figure, slumped forward with his head pressed against the steering wheel.

"Dandelion, look out!" Piers cried.

The fairy glanced over his shoulder and yelped. He redoubled his efforts, but the station wagon quickly gained on him and the greyhound. Nixon swerved out of the way, and just before Dandelion was run over, the fairy jumped up and landed on the bumper of the car. He immediately fell backward onto the hood and rolled into the windshield. Thankfully, he managed to grab hold of a windshield wiper, which bent but kept him from falling off the side of the vehicle.

The station wagon continued to close the distance between itself and the back of the trolley. Piers vaulted to the other side of the platform railing and stood on the thin ledge, then leaned out and extended his hand to Dandelion. "I'll catch you!" he shouted, trying to be heard over the sound of the horn. "You have to jump!"

Dandelion climbed to his feet atop the hood. He gingerly shuffled toward the front grill, and Piers leaned further out.

"Don't drop me!" the fairy pleaded.

When the station wagon was just a few feet away, Dandelion leapt and grabbed Piers' hand. Though the fairy weighed little, Piers' arm was pulled down so that Dandelion's toes nearly scraped the pavement. The car continued forward, but Piers yanked the fairy up just before his torso was crushed between the two vehicles. The elven creature latched onto the railing next to him.

With a jolt, the station wagon crashed into the back of the trolley. "What the hell was that?" hollered the driver. Nixon sprung onto the side of the platform just as the driver leaned on the brakes.

Piers cried out, "No, no... don't slow down!"

Scarlet hopped up onto the railing to survey the downtown scene. People continued to collapse along the sidewalk within seconds after the trolley passed them by. "That homicidal ghost is still after us!" the squirrel warned.

Piers staggered past the other panic-stricken passengers to reach the driver. "Sir, you have to go faster!"

"We just got hit by something, kid," groused the white-haired man. "And don't think I didn't see you jump on—"

The driver's words cut off as a powerful force seized the back of the trolley. Everyone rocked forward, and Piers had to grab the back of the driver's seat to remain upright. Passengers around him screamed in terror. The streetcar fishtailed for a moment before the rear wheels slipped back onto the track and it resumed speed.

Dandelion picked himself off the floor and ran down the aisle toward Piers. "He's going to get us!"

The rudderless station wagon began to drift sideways until its tires caught on ruts in the pavement. It flipped and somersaulted down the center of the road, sending shards of window glass flying. The streetcar driver looked in the rearview mirror and saw the station wagon tumbling toward them. "Holy mother—"

"Go, go, go!" cried Piers.

The driver stepped on the accelerator and shot through a yellow traffic light. Scarlet hopped across the tops of the seats, further alarming the passengers, until she reached Piers' shoulder.

"This is insane!" said the driver.

Behind them, the station wagon came to a crashing stop in the middle of the street. "Just keep moving!" urged Piers.

The trolley shuddered a third time, and the back end dipped downward, raising the front wheels off the track before dropping them again.

Dandelion clutched at Piers' shirt. "He's got us!"

The streetcar began to fishtail once more. The driver slammed his hand against the horn and cursed as they rapidly approached another intersection. This time, the traffic light was red. "Oh, *fuuuuuu*—" He hit the brakes. Nixon lost his balance and fell down in the aisle.

With a deafening screech, the trolley slid sideways, leaving the tracks completely and smashing into the back of a car that had stopped at the red light. The momentum pushed both vehicles out into the intersection, where the trolley finally tipped over onto the car and pinned it.

Everyone was still screaming. Piers slowly picked himself up off what he thought was the floor but turned out to be a side panel. After checking for injuries and finding none, he climbed a seat cushion so he could survey the center aisle. Nixon had fallen into another row of seats and was trying to untangle his legs from a group of middle-aged tourists. Piers reached over and helped extricate the greyhound. He pulled the dog into his row and they slid back down the seat cushion together.

Piers was grateful the trolley had open partitions along the sides instead of glass windows. He lowered Nixon through one of the openings until the dog wriggled free and dropped to the pavement.

A visibly shaken Dandelion peeked over the top of the closest seat, and Piers got the fairy to follow him out the window and onto the street below. They crouched beneath the trolley, taking a moment to steady their nerves. The side of the streetcar formed a ceiling above them, and Piers felt safer in its shadow.

"Maybe he won't find us if we hide here," Dandelion suggested.

The car pinned underneath the trolley suddenly buckled, and the mass of steel hanging over their heads dropped a foot lower. "We'll be crushed," Piers cried. "Move!"

The trio scrambled out from under the streetcar. Piers spotted a bicycle hanging from a rack on the front of the trolley and yanked it free. He jumped on, put his foot on a pedal and shouted to Dandelion, "Get on my back!" The fairy scurried up to the seat and clung to the boy's shoulders. Piers whipped his head around. "Where's the squirrel?"

Before Piers could locate Scarlet, the mustached driver leapt out of the trolley's main door a few feet away. The man staggered and almost fell on the asphalt, but he put his hands on his knees to steady himself. He looked up at Piers. "I don't believe—"

Something invisible smashed into the driver, sending him flying. Piers let out another curse and took off as fast as possible.

He pedaled like mad, weaving through traffic and making a hard turn at the next intersection so he could keep heading downhill. Nixon sprinted alongside, staying so close that Piers feared he might swerve and accidentally hit the dog. He glanced over his shoulder. Again, Piers could see figures collapsing on the sidewalks not far behind him. He had no idea if Sool was killing out of malice or stealing life to propel himself forward, but the ghost's drive for vengeance wasn't letting up.

Dandelion nervously tapped Piers on his shoulder. "Ummmm... can you go any faster?"

"I'm going as fast as I can!"

A rumbling motorcycle drew even with Piers, and he was shocked to see Scarlet perching unnoticed on the seat behind the leather-clad rider. The rodent gave Piers an ambivalent look, then shrugged her shoulders and waved goodbye as the motorcycle pulled ahead and away.

The slope of the boulevard began to level off. Piers worried he had reached the limits of his stamina. Nixon drew close, panting, "Greyhounds... aren't... meant... for... long... distances... Piers...."

"Turn here!" Piers shouted. He made a quick turn into a narrow alley. Dandelion almost lost his grip, but managed to stabilize himself. The pavement between the buildings was badly rutted; Piers had to focus on avoiding potholes as well as dumpsters and discarded pallets. He didn't notice the group of teenagers walking up the alleyway until he was almost upon them.

Piers waved his hand to the side. "Get out of the way! Move, move, move!"

The teens stepped aside, allowing the dog and the bicycle to zip by, although they hurled several choice obscenities at their backs. Piers felt like his legs were giving out, but he kept pumping the pedals as furiously as he could.

Dandelion looked backward and murmured, "Oh, no."

Piers glanced behind him. The teens lay on the ground a hundred feet away, motionless.

He could do nothing. Piers swiveled his head forward as they left the alley and entered a side street, but he didn't see the car until it was too late. The vehicle struck the front tire of his bicycle, and both Piers and Dandelion went flying. They bounced off the hood of the car and landed hard on the asphalt on the other side.

The driver slammed on the brakes and leaned out his window. "Oh, my god! Are you all right?"

Piers climbed painfully to his feet. Ignoring the scrapes on his knees and elbows, he grabbed the passenger door behind the driver and yanked it open. "I won't press charges," he blurted. "We just need to get out of here. Dandelion, Nixon! Get in!" His two companions jumped inside the vehicle, and Piers shut the door.

The driver, a young man in his mid-twenties, twisted his upper body to look at them. "You need to go to a hospital?"

"No! Yes!" Piers looked frantically toward the alleyway. "But if you don't leave right now, I will sue you for everything you have!"

The man turned back around. "I just want to make sure–"

Piers stuck his finger into the back of the driver's neck. "This is a gun! Just go!"

The driver hit the gas. They hadn't gone far when the car lurched violently as if something had struck it. "Did we hit something?" asked the man, befuddled.

"I'll explain later!" said Piers. "Drive!"

The car picked up speed. Dandelion whispered, "Are you going to explain later?"

Piers gave him an incredulous look. "No!"

They approached a red light at an intersection. The young man took his foot off the gas, and the car began to decelerate.

"Go through it," Piers ordered.

"But... it's red!"

"Go through it!"

The driver swerved around the car idling in front of him and laid on his horn. Somehow, they managed to miss the vehicles driving perpendicular along the cross street.

"Nice!" said Piers, genuinely impressed.

Skeptical eyes glanced at him through the rearview mirror. "You don't really have a gun, do you?"

Piers hardened his voice. "J-j-just keep driving!"

"Okay! I gotta turn up here for the hospital."

"Keep going straight."

"But I need to get you—"

"We're going out of town. Keep going straight!"

They continued down the road. Piers kept his finger in place, and Dandelion and Nixon took turns checking the traffic behind them.

"Anything?" Piers asked the fairy.

"No sign of him."

The driver still seemed concerned about Piers' condition. "Are you sure you didn't hit your head or something?"

"I'm going to be fine in about one mile," Piers replied.

"Okaaaaay."

They reached the outskirts of the city, where self-storage facilities and single-family homes butted up against agricultural land. Piers took his finger away. "All right. Stop here." The car pulled over to the side of the road.

"Are you sure?" Dandelion asked softly.

"This is the opposite side of town from Aspen Home," Piers told him. "We've got to be outside Sool's Circle by now." He opened the door, and the three of them hopped out.

The young driver exited the car as well. Piers thought he

looked like one of the misfits that hung around the vinyl records shop downtown, with shaggy hair and an awkward face. The man studied Piers in return and declared without a trace of resentment, "I *knew* you didn't have a gun."

"S-sorry about that. We couldn't stop."

"Look, I don't know what kind of trouble you're in, but... if you could not talk about the accident, like to the police and stuff, then I won't say nothing."

"Thank you," said Piers, relieved. "What's your name?"

The driver ran a hand through his hair and scratched the back of his head. "Eugene."

"Eugene. You saved our lives." Piers suddenly thought of all the *other* lives that had been snuffed out back in the city, and his voice caught in his throat. He walked away without saying anything more.

Dandelion gave the man a slight bow. "Thank you, human," he said formally, then strode after Piers.

Nixon stepped up and licked Eugene's hand. "I am thanking you, too," said the greyhound. "Goodbye." He left to rejoin the others.

Eugene stared after them for a long time. He finally walked back to his car, muttering, "I must've hit *my* head."

Dandelion caught up to the boy inside an abandoned industrial lot. Piers lay on his side in the middle of a patch of cracked pavement, his eyes closed. The fairy shared an uneasy look with Nixon, then tiptoed around the tufts of weeds, careful not to harm the more delicate blades. He crouched down next to Piers but didn't quite know what to say.

Nixon trotted straight to Piers, looked at him closely for a minute, then licked his face. Piers swatted Nixon's snout and covered his head with his arms.

Dandelion finally felt brave enough to ask, "Piers, are... are you feeling all right?"

Nixon nudged the boy on the back of the head, and Piers bolted to an upright position. "Stop it! I... I... I..." Piers trailed off and just stared outward towards the city. The others waited quietly. "It's all my fault. They're all dead."

"Maybe they're just asleep?" Dandelion suggested weakly.

Piers shook his head. "They're dead and they're not coming back! It's my fault. Again."

An uncomfortable silence fell over the group. Dandelion sat down and waited.

"I should be dead," Piers mumbled.

"There was nothing we could do to stop him," said Dandelion. "Nothing you could have done."

Nixon laid down next to Piers and rested his muzzle in the boy's lap. Among the weeds, Dandelion noticed a ripe dandelion seed head that was ready to disperse. He ran his small hand along the stem and collected the seeds in his palm. Then he brought them to his lips and with a puff, sent them floating away. "Sometimes seeds land on good soil," the fairy murmured. "Mostly they languish on rocks and stones. I guess our plan landed on stones." Piers said nothing back. "But we tried, didn't we?"

Piers' phone rang. He pulled QL from his pocket.

"Oh, *finally* you let me out," came the authoritarian voice. "I've never felt so banged up! *Ring, ring!* I mean, I am the premier model and everything, but I'm not made of titanium. *Ring, ring!*"

"Shut up," Piers snapped. "It's my mom." He hit the RECEIVE button and climbed to his feet. After conversing for a minute, Piers ended the call. "We have to go," he told the others.

"What is it?" asked Dandelion.

"My mom's at the hospital. She was in an accident."

❦ 29 ❦

Piers and his two companions walked a circuitous path to avoid Sool's attention, so it took them a few hours to reach downtown Summerday again. The city was in chaos, with police cars and ambulances parked haphazardly next to smashed vehicles, while officers scrambled to cordon off vast sections of street and sidewalk with yellow police tape. A few blocks from the business district, they passed the streetcar, still tilted on its side. They hugged the buildings to avoid notice, and Nixon padded especially close to Piers.

The boy picked a baseball cap off the pavement, put it on Dandelion's head and tucked his pointed ears inside. Then he pulled out his cellphone. "QL? Anything new?"

"Just the same emergency alerts, Carrier. No new locations. If anything was posted on the internet, I wouldn't know; I'm still as dim as a landline here."

Piers glanced around for any odd human behavior, but he only witnessed a lot of shouting and crying. "I feel like a sitting duck," he grumbled. "We're hiding from something invisible that could be watching us right now, and we'd have no idea."

QL gave a digitized snort. "In your world, that's how I feel *all the time*."

Piers' attention was already elsewhere; on the other side of the street, he spotted his mother's car. It lay awkwardly across two curbside parking spaces, and an ugly dent marred the face of the driver's side door.

"Stay here," Piers told the others. He took a breath and dashed across the pavement as fast as he could. The windows of the vehicle were rolled down, so he tucked his head inside and found the keys still dangling from the ignition. He grabbed them and ran back to his companions.

"Now we have to wait," he explained. "My mom said she'd come find us here."

Nixon's head tilted upward. "Piers, look." With his nose, the greyhound pointed to a ghostly figure atop a nearby office building. Against the bright afternoon sky it was hard to distinguish Emlee's silhouette, but Piers had no doubt it was her. He waved, then looked around the city block and gestured toward a small public park with several hedges. The ghost girl nodded and slipped down into the building.

Piers carefully led his group over to the park and had them crouch down between a bench and some shrubbery. Before too long, Emlee rose from the ground inside the hedgerow. Her monochromatic face looked even paler than normal.

"Oh, Piers... this is horrible. Horrible!"

"Yeah," he said tersely. "I need to get my mom home safe, and then I'm done with this."

"But—"

"I'm done!" He lowered his eyes, too ashamed and torn to even look at her. "She should be here to pick up her car within the hour."

They sat in glum silence for a minute. Piers finally asked the ghost girl, "Can you... can you go back to Ghost World and be a lookout for us? You can let Nixon know if you see Sool. Tap his nose, like before."

"My nose is a powerful nose and very sensitive," added the greyhound.

Emlee nodded sadly. "Yes. I can do that. But this street isn't within my Circle. I won't be able to reach you until you get closer to your home." She looked around, suddenly realizing something. "Where is Scarlet?"

"She caught a ride," said Piers. "I'm sure she's fine."

Dandelion finally spoke up. "Excuse me, sir?"

Piers arched an eyebrow. "Why are you calling me sir, now?"

The fairy looked embarrassed and toed the ground with the tip of his boot. "I... well... I am thinking I should go, too. There are so many humans here, and I miss the forest, even if it isn't quite *my* forest."

"You're going to walk there?" Piers scratched the back of his neck, considering. "I guess it's better if my mom didn't look at you too closely." He felt a little guilty at letting the little creature fend for himself, but it would make his own life a lot easier. "Uh... be careful? Do you know the way?"

"Oh, yes. Dandelions can go anywhere."

A curious answer, Piers mused.

"There are no new portals for Dandelion to use here?" Emlee asked delicately. "I thought there might..."

Piers finished her thought. "Because of all the killing? Yeah, we looked a little. Not that we saw. Maybe because Sool was in a hurry and couldn't eat their souls entirely." He turned back to the fairy. "Try not to be noticed."

The little figure tugged his sweatshirt hood up over his baseball cap. "I will try. I'm not used to hiding, but I think I'm getting better at it."

Emlee whispered, "I'll see you soon, Dandelion."

With one last, timid wave, the fairy slipped between the hedges and out of view.

After an uncomfortable minute, Emlee spoke. "Piers... I am sorry for all this."

The boy wouldn't meet her gaze. "You should go."

Emlee looked at him sadly. Then she turned, slipped into the ground beneath the hedge and disappeared.

Piers sat down with his back to the hedge. Nixon lay in the dirt next to him and suggested, "You should scratch my shoulders now because it will make you feel better."

"No, it won't," said Piers.

"It will make *me* feel better."

Piers sighed and ran his fingers through the dog's fur. "Nixon, why does life have to suck so much?"

The greyhound looked up. "Life is not bad because there are delicious foods to eat and there are squirrels to chase and there are blankets for good dogs to lay upon." He rolled over onto his side and yawned. "You seem sad most of the time. That makes me sad, but just for a little while. Then I remember that I am happy."

QL's voice piped up from Piers' pocket. "Pardon the intrusion, Carrier. You may want to take a look at this."

Piers withdrew his smartphone. "What is it?"

"A new emergency alert. Something called the 'CDC' has declared the entire city to be under quarantine."

Piers tapped the screen and scanned the emergency message. "They suspect that what killed people could be a virus. Oh, man... they are *way* off." He tried to open some news websites, but the viewscreen kept flickering and going dark.

"Apologies, again," said QL. "I am still trying to infer how this primitive internet language works. It's as if you need a special password to speak to anyone."

"Fine." Piers put down the phone.

Nixon raised his muzzle. "What is a quarantine, Piers?"

"It's when they put up barriers to keep sick people in." He drummed his fingers against the ground. "It means we're trapped."

❦ 30 ❦

Piers' mom stepped out of the taxi slowly, wearing a plastic neck brace. Piers ran up and hugged her fiercely. "I'm s-s-s-sorry."

His mother stroked his head. "What for?"

"Everything," he mumbled. Piers stepped back, wiped his eyes, then pulled the car keys from his pocket and handed them to her. Nixon trotted up to join them, limping slightly. Piers guessed his paws must be tender from their race through downtown Summerday.

The three of them walked up to his mother's compact car. Piers helped his mom open the dented driver's side door, which now fit poorly within the frame. He let Nixon into the back of the vehicle, then sat himself up front. They drove down the street to the next intersection, where a policeman wearing a dust mask waved them through. Piers studied his mom carefully. "Y-your neck. Y-y-y-you w-were hit?"

"A car swerved into my lane," she explained. "I thought it was trying to avoid hitting one of the trolley buses, but when I got out and checked on the driver, she was..."

His mother went quiet, and he could sense that her emotionless persona had begun to take hold again. Piers' own face went pale as he thought about how close Sool had come to his mom and how narrowly he had avoided being seen by his mother. "And your neck?" he prodded.

"My neck had started to stiffen up, so they brought me to the hospital." A flicker of concern crossed her face, and she looked over at him. "You weren't near any of this, were you?"

Piers shook his head, perhaps a bit too vigorously.

She refocused on the road. "I shouldn't have had you meet me downtown. I wasn't thinking. They said some kind of virus caused this."

His mom seemed more lucid than she'd been in months, Piers noticed. "I heard about a quarantine. Is there any way to just leave town?"

"I don't think so. Not if I want to keep working in healthcare."

Piers settled back in his seat. He found himself staring out the window at all the people walking by, watching for any to collapse on the sidewalk.

As they approached the next intersection, another car started to pull out in front of them. It stopped quickly, but his mother slammed on the brakes anyway. Piers jerked forward, and Nixon flew off the seat. "Sorry," said his mother. "I'm just..."

"It's okay, mom," Piers said as calmly as he could. "Let's just get home."

His mom pulled the car forward, and her mind grew increasingly distant. Piers felt the familiar black clot of guilt build up inside his stomach and rise to the back of his throat... where his vocal cords were.

Behind him, Nixon made a sound like he was clearing his throat. Piers turned and saw the greyhound's ears twitching. The dog began pawing at his nose. *Was Emlee here?* Piers wondered. He took off his seatbelt and crawled across the center console into the back seat.

"What are you doing?" asked his mother.

"Ahhh..." Piers thought quickly. "Nixon was lonely!"

"Seatbelt on!"

He hurriedly sat back and clipped on his belt. Nixon leaned over and whispered, "I thought it was the ghost girl, but my nose thinks it was just a fly."

"Well, which one was it?" Piers whispered back.

"What?" called his mom.

"Nothing!"

A *<ping>* emitted from the phone in his jacket pocket. Piers pulled out the device as the *<pings>* began sounding faster and faster. When he tapped a button, the note-taking app opened immediately. Random letters spilled across the screen, followed by the text, "Hey, Carrier! aefYou said to text joiyou inewfstead of speasdfking. kljjl Somethefqwing electradsfomagnetic besdides waeyourself seems to be tappisgfng on the screen padsfgd here. Is thagsfdt part dhof the plan?"

Lines of gibberish continued to pour down the length of the touchscreen. *Emlee.* Piers unfastened his seatbelt and leaned across the center console. "Mom!"

His mother gave him an anxious glance. "Piers! Don't–"

"Mom! Turn left here!" he insisted.

"That's not the way–"

"My phone says there's an accident up ahead. A bad one. A *car* accident." He felt guilty as soon as he said it.

"But we should–"

"I don't want to see! Turn! Turn!"

His mom turned at the next intersection. Piers hated himself for manipulating his mom's emotions, but he was desperate to keep Sool from following them home. "Okay, drive faster, pleeeese, mom!"

He peeked at his phone again. Gibberish kept dribbling out, muddying QL's comments. "gdfhWould ydghfou stop stabbijhfng thadfe screen lkmand make rkjeal gjhksentenhjces!"

His mother suggested, "It would be faster to go... Oh, I guess we can turn down Taylor."

"Go all the way to Broadway, then turn!"

She looked shocked. "Piers Davies! What is going on?"

He swallowed hard and told her, "Phone says Taylor's not safe!"

"All right. Just sit down and put on your seatbelt!"

Piers settled back and rechecked his smartphone. The nonsense texts had stopped. Piers hoped it meant that Sool had reached the end of his Circle instead of Emlee reaching the end of hers. He clipped his seatbelt. "Sorry, Mom. I panicked a little."

"That's all right," she reassured him. "Here's Taylor Street."

"Go to Broadway!" Piers pressed. "Uhhh.... grocery store!"

His mother gave him another strained look. "I don't think we need any groceries. But fine, we'll go the back way home."

The next traffic light interrupted their progress. Piers twisted in his seat and looked out the back window, scanning for unusual movements. Everything seemed clear. He let out a long breath, then glanced at his phone one more time. A single line of text read, "Where's spellcheck when you need it? LOL"

❦ 31 ❦

To Piers, the next few hours felt surreal, as if he were passing in and out of a disturbing dream. The television in his living room cycled through news reports, providing little new information except for an updated tally of the victims. Some called it a terrorist attack. Others called it the "Angel of Death Virus" since it swept over the city so swiftly. One expert said the casualties were the result of mass hypnosis rather than a virus. Regardless of the cause, a quarantine of Summerday was in effect and would remain so for the indefinite future.

Piers forced himself to listen to one more interview. A bystander claimed that several victims had survived the attack and were being treated at the hospital for internal bruising. That was good news if it ended up being true. At least no one so far had said anything about two boys and a greyhound.

Piers' mother had been busy talking to Aspen Home employees over the phone, so Piers didn't feel bad about slipping up to his room. He couldn't handle any more news reports. His body felt drained after burning through every drop of adrenaline in his system. His mind felt just as depleted.

If only he could have told his mom some half-truth about the situation to get her to drive him and Nixon far away from here. But the quarantine had destroyed that option. He had failed in almost every way. *And if the Ender followed us home...*

It was too much to think about.

An hour later, Emlee found him lying atop his bedsheets, eyes closed. Nixon rested at the foot of the bed. She floated closer. "Hello, Piers. Hello, Nixon."

"Hey," Piers mumbled.

"It is good you made it to your home," said the ghost girl.

"Yeah." He sat up. "Did it work? Did we lose him?"

"Well..."

His voice hardened. "Does he know I'm here?"

Emlee gave no answer.

"Did Sool follow us here?" He was practically shouting now.

"I..." The ghost girl struggled for words as her hair swirled around her head. "I should show you something."

Using the excuse of needing to take Nixon for a walk, Piers and the greyhound left the house and followed Emlee on a long loop through the forest. They entered the Ghost World through a new portal Emlee had discovered. Then she led them through the trees to a view of the hill behind Piers' home.

Although the sun had set, enough light remained for Piers to make out a hulking presence atop the hill. The Ender was there, drifting like a shark along the boundary of his Circle. The leading edge of his corpulent body was blurred by the Winds, and his eyes continuously flickered in the direction of Piers' house.

"He found me," Piers said grimly.

"Yes. I'm sorry. But at least your home is beyond the edge of his Circle."

As they watched, however, Sool slunk over to a stand of maple trees. He ran his oversized fingers down the length of one of the larger specimens. Halfway down, he tightened his fist around the trunk and squeezed. They heard the crack of splintering wood. The tree shook, leaves fell to the ground and a ripple of energy coursed through Sool's body. He returned to the edge of his Circle and began pacing again.

Piers swallowed hard. "Is it me, or did his Circle get closer to my house?"

Emlee's face had lit up. "It's so horrible. And amazing. Amazingly horrible, isn't it?" She glanced at Piers, then tried to look more serious. "I'm sorry..."

"He's expanding his territory," Piers noted. "It's only a matter of time until I have no home left, isn't it?"

"You could live with us in the forest..." Emlee suggested.

Piers looked at her coldly. "He'll kill my mom."

The boy walked from the cover of the trees onto the open hillside below the Ender.

Emlee rushed out after him. "What are you doing?"

Piers kept walking. "I don't know. Making a deal." He felt too tired in his mind and body to be very afraid. Soon, he stood on the grassy slope directly beneath Sool. Emlee held back, but Nixon followed and sat at Piers' side.

The Ender rose up above them, his gigantic form rippling in the unearthly Winds. "Have you come to accept your fate? The chase was certainly fun, was it not?"

Piers glowered. "Sool, what do you want?"

Gargantuan eyes bulged with intensity, and the grotesque smile faded from Sool's face. "I want to be free. Here in this world, I am death. But I cannot be seen and feared. I am still confined, as you can see." Sool extended his arm into the Winds, and his hand began to rip apart in the fierce currents. He withdrew it, and the shredded appendage coalesced once more. "Now I understand that there are worlds beyond this one. But I have grown much too big to enter them. Do you see the irony?"

"Ah, I'm not sure," Piers admitted.

BRYAN SNYDER

"I have opened the spaces between worlds," rumbled the Ender. "Each death opens another. But none are big enough."

That finally made sense to Piers. "So you *have* been creating these holes."

"A side effect of my feeding process, through which you brought the woman and tried to destroy me."

"We were trying to bring you some peace!"

Sool reared up and roared, "PEACE?"

Nixon growled. Piers put a hand on the dog's back.

"Do you think I am as small as that?" Sool continued. "LOOK AT ME! I am more than human. The memories of all I have consumed... they swim around in me. So much to taste." He bent down closer to the boy. "And do you know the most interesting morsel I have sampled?"

"I... don't know," said Piers.

Sool's smile dissipated. "There is an amulet... an amulet in the possession of an ancient ghost within this forest. Her name is Morgaed. You will obtain this device for me."

Piers crossed his arms. "Why would I do that?"

The evil grin returned. "Because then I will let your mother live."

Piers looked down at his house... at the light in his living room that had just flicked on. Behind him, the massive lips continued to speak. "I will let *you* live. Yes. I will not eat you and I will not eat your mother and you can live and have your *peace.*"

Piers considered the possibility that this terrible nightmare could be over if he did this one last thing. But life was never that easy. "Why do you need an amulet?" he asked.

"It creates doors," said the Ender. "If I cannot use death to carve a hole big enough, then I will use the amulet to enter the other worlds and be freed of my Circle. Find Morgaed."

"Can't you find her?" Piers protested.

Irritation crossed the ghost's face. "She exists outside my Circle. Ask the girl."

Piers looked down at Nixon, then back up at the monster. "Can I... can I think about it?"

"Of course. And I will think of tearing you and your family into pieces. Do not think too long... *Piers.*" Sool oozed away, withdrawing over the crest of the hill and vanishing from sight. His last words lingered in Piers' mind; the boy couldn't figure out why Sool knew his name.

Nixon let out a *whuff.* "Bad ghost."

Emlee drifted over to them and asked, "What did he have to say, Piers?"

"A few things. He's smarter than I thought. Maybe because he's gaining memories from everyone he swallows."

"Fascinating." Her gaze lingered on the path of Sool's retreat. "I still wonder how he got this power in the first place. No ghost should be strong enough to kill anything."

Piers sat in the grass and absentmindedly scratched Nixon's chin. "He's figured out that he needs to get through a portal to be freed of his Circle."

"Oh." Emlee turned and floated down to his level. "That's not good."

"But if that doesn't work, Sool wants an amulet... something kept by a ghost named... Morgan?"

The girl's eyes widened. "Morgaed?"

"Yeah, that's it. He says the amulet can create doors to the other worlds. You know this Morgaed person?"

Emlee nodded. "I do. She's been a mentor for me, especially during the first year after I Awakened. I really like her. But our Circles barely overlap at all. If I want to meet with her, I have to talk to an intermediary. Usually, that's Rima."

"Another ghost?" asked Piers.

"Yes." A frown appeared on Emlee's face. "But Rima's gone missing. There's one more person I can try to find, as an go-between." She tapped a translucent finger against her lips, considering their options. "Talking to Morgaed is a good idea, Piers. She's the wisest person I ever met."

"And she has the amulet," he added.

"I've never seen it. But if Sool wants it, that can't be a good thing. I'll have to be careful not to lead him to Morgaed."

"He says Morgaed is outside his Circle, but yeah. Do it, then. Arrange a meeting. Please."

"I will. I'll try. It's finding an intermediary that's hard."

"Send me," said Nixon.

Piers looked up at the greyhound. "You?"

"I am the best finder of things. My eyes are the sharpest, so I will hunt and find this Morgaed and bring her to you."

Piers smiled. "Yes! Emlee, can you tell us where she lives? We can both go, Nixon and I."

The ghost girl shook her head. "I've never seen her Center, and she's never described it to me. You are both brave, but give me some time to find an intermediary. If I fail, you can try hunting for her."

"All right," Piers sighed.

"But you should probably stay out of the forest until you hear from me."

"Oh, I'll stay out. If there's any chance that Sool could forget I exist, I'll take it."

Emlee reached out and touched the greyhound on the nose. "Watch over him, Nixon."

The dog nodded solemnly. "I always do. He is my human."

Emlee lifted from the ground, her dress twirling around her delicate form. "Piers, we will find a way to stop him. We have to."

Piers waved goodbye as the ghost drifted back into the forest. *We have to*. Part of Piers' mind insisted that he didn't *have* to do anything; he wasn't tied to this place like a ghost or a fairy. Maybe the quarantine would get lifted before Sool's Circle reached his house. Piers felt the urge to tell his mom everything so that she would agree to move as far as possible from Summerday. Then he felt guilty for having those feelings.

The sky was dark now. Time to find a portal and go home. "Why is this up to us, Nixon?"

"Because they are counting on us," said the dog.

"Who is *'they'*?"

"Everyone."

Nixon nudged Piers' hand with his nose, then trotted toward the forest. Piers stayed a few moments more beneath the hill. Despite finding all these new friends in his life, he still felt indescribably alone.

✤ 32 ✤

Two days later, Piers sat with Nixon and Dandelion in a dense patch of forest within the Ghost World. QL's consciousness was also present within Piers' smartphone. Piers had worked with the device so that she could regain her functions while cut off from Machine World, and the quarantine had given them plenty of time in isolation to practice. To his shame, he had also asked QL to delete Marguerite's call records so her murder couldn't be traced back to him. Now QL sat inside Piers' shirt pocket with her camera exposed, facing outward.

Dandelion hugged his knees tightly. "I feel like we've done this before," said the fairy.

"What?" Piers asked.

"Waiting in the woods for Emlee to arrive with another ghost."

Piers agreed, but he felt like he needed to keep Dandelion's spirits up. The poor creature had been exiled for a few weeks now. "This ghost is different," Piers said. "He's just a kid. Only four years old, apparently. And he's going to take us to see Morgaed."

Dandelion traced in the dirt with a finger. "I guess."

Piers suddenly wondered what the fairy had done with his

brother's sweatshirt, as he wasn't wearing it, but it didn't seem like the right time to ask. The little man looked the same way that Piers felt... a little wilted. Hopefully, these new ghosts could take over the situation. And if not, there was the amulet that Sool wanted...

"Hey," Piers tried. "We're due for a win. An amulet for entering other worlds... sounds like just what you need, right?"

"Maybe." Dandelion sniffed and wiped his pointed nose. "I miss home. Even if they weren't very nice to me there."

"Really? Why wouldn't they be nice to you?"

The fairy shrugged. "I guess because I'm not tall and strong like Sycamore and Oak, or pretty like Wood Lily. I'm not a cultivator of humans, like Sweet Corn and Strawberry. I'm just one of the fairies no one cares much about." He drew lines in the dirt again. "Or wants."

Piers looked at him concernedly. "That doesn't seem fair."

"It's okay. I have friends."

"I think you are very likable," said Nixon, "even if you are not a dog."

"And you have friends here, too," Piers added.

Scarlet's shrill voice called out from the forest. "Speaking of which... Hello, ugly friends!"

The squirrel bounded up to the trio. Piers frowned. "Scarlet, you said you were going to be our lookout!"

Scarlet opened her arms magnanimously. "And so here I am! I was *trying* to avoid being detected. Can't look out for you if I'm not looking out for myself, can I?"

"I guess," Piers grumbled.

"I don't want to be grabbed by that googly-boogly again."

Piers gave her a confused look. "What do you mean, "*again*"?"

"Ahhhhhhh..." Scarlet stammered. Her eyes darted around nervously before settling on Nixon. "Hey, butthound. How've you been drooling?"

Nixon snorted. "I am never drooling except when I am going

to eat delicious food." He turned to Piers. "I am wondering if Piers brought delicious food for me."

"Okay, focus, you guys." Piers waved his hands to get their attention. "Scarlet, would you climb a tree and check for any house-sized ghosts so we don't die, please?"

"Wait." Dandelion pointed into the forest. "She's back."

A pair of shapes drifted out of the distant trees. Emlee's gauzy figure obscured a second, smaller ghost that floated close behind. Piers couldn't get a good look at the shorter spirit, so he left the cover of the underbrush to have a better view.

The ghost girl stopped in front of them, and her warm smile put Piers at ease. "Hello, everyone! I'd like you to meet Mikin. He's a little shy – remember, he's never met humans, fairies or animals before. Come out, Mikin!"

The faded specter of a six-year-old boy drifted out from behind Emlee's dress. Piers' heart stopped.

"No," Piers whispered. He felt like he couldn't breathe, like Sool's hand had wrapped around his chest again.

"It's okay, Mikin," Emlee reassured the timid child. The new ghost wore sneakers and modern clothes, including a t-shirt with a growling tiger on it. Emlee turned back to the others. "Morgaed has been looking after him these last four years, like she looked after me when I was first Awakened."

Dandelion and the two animals came out of the bushes, and Mikin looked anxiously at them all. "I–" he began.

Piers suddenly rushed up to the boy and attempted to grab him by the shoulders. "My d-dad," Piers blurted. "My brother, Thomas. Do you know where they are?"

Mikin's eyes grew huge, and he pulled back. Piers chased after the child and tried to hold him still, but his hands passed right through the translucent flesh. He shouted again, *Do you know where they are?*"

Mikin shot upward and disappeared into the forest canopy. Emlee rushed over. "Piers! What is the matter with you?"

Dandelion tugged at Piers' shirt and looked around fearfully. "Shhhhh!" he whispered. "Too loud! Too loud!"

Piers whirled around to face Emlee. "That's Michael Case! Why is he here?"

Emlee stared crossly at him. "That is *Mikin.*" She called reassurances into the branches overhead, then turned her attention back to Piers. "He's the intermediary I talked about, remember?"

"Get him down here!" Piers demanded.

Scarlet hopped over. "Easy there, flatface. He's just a pup."

"He's not just..." Piers clenched his fists, unable to get the words out.

Emlee swirled in front of him. "Calm down, please!" She called upward again, "Mikin, he can't hurt you."

Piers pressed, "Does he know how he died?"

"How his human shell died?" She shook her head. "No. But why would he?"

Mikin descended hesitantly and hovered just out of Piers' reach.

"That's better," said Emlee. "Mikin is going to guide you to Morgaed's Center."

Piers wasn't listening. "Mikin, look at me," he ordered.

The little boy turned toward him.

"Do you know me?" Piers asked.

"Stop scaring him!" cried Emlee. "What is wrong with you?"

Piers' voice started to break. *"Do you know me?"*

Mikin finally spoke. "I... I do not know you."

Scarlet scurried onto a branch between Piers and Mikin. "Okay, *that* was fun. How about we get on with the business at hand?"

"Yes, we should." Emlee tried to push the irritation out of her voice. "Everyone, I won't be able to join you for the meeting. Morgaed needs you to come to her Center, which is far outside my Circle."

"If you went to a different World, couldn't you pass beyond your Circle and follow us?" Dandelion suggested.

"I could," said the ghost girl, "but you'd be invisible to me, as would Morgaed."

"And you wouldn't understand a thing we're saying, either," said Scarlet. "We get it."

"Hmmmm....." uttered Nixon.

Scarlet rolled her eyes. *"Most* of us get it."

"Anyway," Emlee continued, "I spoke with Morgaed yesterday and told her what's been happening. She needed some time to think, but hopefully she has a plan by now. Come back when you know what it is."

"We will," Dandelion promised.

"And be respectful. She's over a thousand years old."

"A *thousand?*" Scarlet sputtered.

Emlee nodded. "Just follow Mikin, and be on your good behavior. Okay, Piers?"

Piers finally looked away from the little ghost boy. "Yeah, sure. Let's go."

"It's this way," said Mikin, pointing deeper into the forest. He drifted off in that direction. The group followed, except for Emlee, who floated forward for a few feet before her outline became Wind-blown and she had to stop.

Scarlet hopped ahead of Piers and turned to eyeball him. "What's chewing your tail, human? You look like you've seen a ghost." She paused to let the joke sink in. "Get it? 'Cause he *is* a ghost?" Piers ignored her, so she tried again with Dandelion. "He looks like he's seen a *ghost!"*

"I think he's seen many ghosts," said the fairy.

Piers pushed ahead of the others and got close to Mikin. "You are called Mikin," he began.

"Yes," said the ghost child. "I think so."

Piers' brow creased. "What do you mean, *you think so?"*

"I did what Morgaed told me. I sat alone for a few days and

tried to be really quiet. I listened. And that's the name that came to me." Mikin floated onward.

"What about... Michael?" asked Piers, following.

The child cocked his head. "Oh. Can you say that sound again?"

"Michael," Piers repeated. "Your name is Michael."

"Michael. But... my name is Mikin." He sounded unsure.

"Listen, Michael. *Mikin.* Do you know any other ghosts named..." Piers stopped himself and tried again. "Do you know if there were any ghosts that came alive at the same time as you did?"

"I don't think so," said Mikin. "I just know Morgacd, and Tull, of course. There's The Cat, but she doesn't count. Ummm... there's Rima, but Emlee said she might have been eaten."

Piers cut in. "What about a man, six feet high, brown eyes, a scar on his neck right about here?" He pointed to his own neck, but Mikin shook his head. "Or a boy, eight years old, a little bigger than you, with blond hair cut really short? Also brown eyes?"

Mikin looked back with a curious expression. "How does hair get cut?"

Piers waved the question away. "Not important. Any ghosts about your size? Or smaller than me?"

"There's one," said Mikin.

Piers' voice nearly caught in his throat. "Who?"

"Well, that's Emlee," the child said matter-of-factly. "But you know her, right? And she's not that much smaller than you."

Piers let out a breath that he felt like he'd been holding for ten minutes. He remained quiet for a long while. Finally, he asked, "When are we going to get there?"

"In a little bit," said the ghost child. "Keep following me."

This part of the forest was unfamiliar to Piers. It looked wilder, and the crunching of leaves underfoot suggested that few humans had passed through the area.

QL piped up. "The signal is getting weak out here. I shall likely lose the news updates soon."

"Anything major back in town?" asked Piers.

"There are several vehicle deaths reported. Some Disconnected appliances too. P7DS46BHLA is suspiciously silent."

"By "vehicle deaths", you mean..."

"A Ford Fiesta, a Toyota Camry, a Volkswagen Passat, a—"

Piers interrupted, "Okay, what about humans?"

"There is one new *human* death reported." Her voice sounded slightly annoyed. "And some pets. Nothing close by."

"Good."

They entered a dense stretch of forest where only scattered sunbeams reached the forest floor. Piers noticed several walls of stacked stone that were crumbling into obscurity, overtaken by moss and ferns. "Almost there," said Mikin.

Piers waited to let Nixon and Dandelion catch up. Scarlet took the opportunity to dash up Piers' leg and perch on his shoulder. He considered brushing her off, but then he caught sight of the ruins.

A stone house sat decaying among the trees. Two sides of the structure had collapsed inward, but a stone chimney rose high above the remaining walls. Standing in front of the ruins, awaiting them, were an unusual pair of ghosts. One appeared to be a middle-aged Native American woman, clad in fur and leathers. The other was a tall, much skinnier man who floated stiffly at the woman's side in an antique formal uniform.

Piers was about to acknowledge them when a glowing, translucent cat slipped between his legs. The ghostly feline paused within the ray of a sunbeam in front of Piers and looked back disinterestedly. She then sat on her hindquarters and announced, "Someone wake me when the guests are gone. I expect this will be tedious."

The cat flopped onto her side, legs outstretched, and immediately fell asleep.

❧ 33 ❧

Nixon let out a deep growl. Piers turned. The greyhound had hunched down and bared his teeth. "Nixon..." Piers cautioned.

The words Nixon spit out were almost indistinguishable from barking. "You... you... you... wicked... *cat!*"

He charged forward. Piers cried for him to stop, but the greyhound slipped past. Nixon made as if to leap onto the sleeping cat, but pulled up at the last second. The spectral feline, however, didn't even open an eye. Nixon tried batting the cat with an open paw, then jumping out of reach, but all he struck was bare earth. He growled in frustration and tried again.

Piers grabbed his collar and pulled him back. "Nixon, knock it off!"

The greyhound tried to wrestle out of Piers' hands. "That is a bad cat!" he protested.

"Yeah, well, you're a bad dog!" Piers retorted.

Nixon immediately stopped struggling. "I am a bad dog?" he asked, uncertainly.

"Yes! Okay, no, but you need to stop it."

The greyhound sat. "I am stopping it. But that is a rude and bad cat."

Piers let go of his collar. "Sure, Nixon." To the other two ghosts, he said, "S-s-sorry about this."

The older woman smiled, her face wrinkling like the bark of the oak trees that grew inside the ruins. "It is fine, child. *Aneshnaawech menjaa*. Welcome to Stonegarden."

"Th-th-thank for you having us."

"I am glad for the chance to speak to a human again. The circumstances behind your visit are quite unsettling, however."

"Yes. Y-y-y-you've s-spoken to humans bef-f-f-fore?" He was annoyed to find his stutter returning, but that usually happened around strangers.

"I have walked in the other worlds," said the woman, "though I take care not to cause disturbances. I am Morgaed, as I'm sure Emlee would have told you." She gestured to her thin companion. "This is Tull, who assists me with matters in and outside Stonegarden."

Tull floated up and bowed formally. "A good day to you, young sir." He moved back and clasped his hands behind him. Piers tried to discern the historical significance of his jacket and leggings. *Revolutionary War-era?* The man's demeanor seemed subservient to Morgaed, though Piers wasn't sure what an attendant would do for a woman who didn't need to eat, drink or sleep.

Before Piers could respond, Morgaed continued. "And of course, you have met The Cat." She indicated the feline in front of them.

"I d-d-didn't know there were ghost cats."

Morgaed smiled. "The Cat is somewhat unique to herself."

Piers noticed several feathers braided into the woman's hair and wondered how they'd gotten there. There was obviously much he didn't know about the rules of Ghost World. He couldn't tell what time period Morgaed was from, but she didn't seem to have any traces of European heritage, and her garb looked pre-industrial.

"Well, I'm Piers." He gestured to his friends. "This is Nixon, my dog. That's Dandelion – he's a fairy. I don't know if you know fairies." Lastly, he pulled out his phone. "I guess this is QL, my cellphone. You should meet her... it... too." He held her out for the ghosts to examine.

"Camera out, please," said QL. "In the front pocket." As he tucked her into his clothing, Piers thought he heard QL mutter, "*My* cellphone, indeed."

He remembered one more. "Oh, and Scarlet." Piers looked around for the squirrel before spotting her standing in front of Morgaed.

"You're the Airwalker, aren't you?" Scarlet asked the ghost.

Morgaed nodded. "I have been called this by your kind, yes."

Piers stepped a bit closer to Scarlet. "You know her?"

"Old skunks and foxes tell tales of a "wind spirit" deep in the forest. No one living has seen it." Scarlet's left foot began to thump the ground in excitement. "Ooooo.... they'll pay good forage to hear about this!"

"I'm afraid I may have spoken to some of your furred friends already," Morgaed said. "Yesterday, after I heard young Emlee's story, I began to visit and gather information from the other Worlds. Some beings were more skittish about conversing with me than others." She looked up at Piers. "The Unborn were more shy than I remembered."

"I'm not surprised," said Piers.

"I sent Tull out as well," she continued.

Her spectral servant concurred. "'Tis just as Mistress Emlee witnessed afield. Dead flora and fauna... and peculiar dead devices such as the one in your pocket."

Morgaed matched his grim expression. "This one you call the Ender has left a trail of death through all the Worlds."

"Through my world, too?" asked Dandelion, stepping out from behind Piers.

Her face softened. "Yes, little one. I hear you wish to return home, do you not?"

The fairy nodded, and his wispy hair bobbed back and forth. "More than anything."

"You have an amulet that can take him back?" Piers asked.

Morgaed shot Piers a look that seared him with its intensity.

"Uhhhh..." Piers struggled to continue. "S-S-S-Sool s-said you had one. S-s-something m-magical."

The apparition raised herself a few inches higher and frowned down upon the boy. "This is information I would have preferred kept hidden. For centuries, only those closest to me knew the means by which I traveled. Tull knows. Rima knew, and I fear that knowledge was pulled from her memories, either before or after Sool swallowed her."

Morgaed reached to her neck and touched a necklace made of tarnished metal links. She lifted it from her bosom. A circular wooden amulet dangled from the end of the thick chain. Unlike the ethereal woman holding it, the talisman and chain appeared to be made of solid material, infused with color.

"That's it?" Piers expected something more decorative, but this simple object had to be what Sool was looking for. "Can I hold it?"

"I would rather you didn't," said the indigenous woman. "But you may have a closer look."

As she floated closer, Piers noticed a teardrop-shaped dial in the center of the amulet and a circle of symbols burned into the wood around it. He saw a leaf, a claw, a hand, a lightning bolt, a black sphere and a vaguely human outline, which the dial currently pointed toward.

"Six worlds?" Dandelion guessed.

"Yes," said Morgaed.

Piers thought he understood. "Leaf for plants, the claw for animals. The hand is for the Human World?"

"It is."

"What's the lightning bolt?"

"A world of energy. From what I have witnessed, it has now become a world of machines."

Piers pointed to the human outline. "I take it that's where we are now... the Ghost World?"

"Correct."

Scarlet scampered up and pointed to the side with the black sphere. "Okay, what's that one? The circle-thingy."

"Unknown," said Morgaed. "The dial will not turn to it."

Piers cleared his throat. He had hesitated to reveal any secrets up till now, but he had a feeling Morgaed could help. "Sool asked me to get the amulet for him. He's stuck inside his Circle, but he wants to escape. "

"So he can feed and grow until he has devoured the earth." The woman seemed less surprised than Piers expected. "He offered you something in return, yes?"

The boy nodded. "He promised safety for my mother."

"But not the rest of your family?"

Piers swallowed. "That *is* my family."

"I see," Morgaed said calmly. "One human for the lives of all others." She studied the boy's hazel eyes. "Is that a bargain you're willing to make, Piers?"

"No." *Not when you put it like that,* Piers thought peevishly. "But it's not fair that she's in danger, and you have to help us!"

Tull bristled. "Morgaed will do what is appropriate to the situation, *boy.*"

"Thank you, Tull." She turned back to Piers and lowered herself closer. "I sense a great loss has touched you, and for that, you have my sympathy. But this so-called Ender is a fool to think I would surrender the amulet... doubly so if he thinks it could be stolen by you." She shook her head, and the feathers in her hair spun weightlessly around her. "I regret I cannot look upon him myself. Our Circles do not cross."

"That's what he told me," said Piers.

"What do you believe are his immediate intentions?" asked Morgaed.

Piers considered what he knew. "He definitely wants to escape this world if possible. Are there more ghosts like him? Emlee says there are none that can do what he does... none that can kill others and eat their energy."

"This is true." Morgaed lifted herself higher again. "Before I answer your question, would you come inside and sit? From what I know of humans, it is something you must do often to preserve functionality."

"Uh... I guess," he replied.

Tull waved them inside the ruins with a gentlemanly flourish. The companions entered and Piers settled himself upon a segment of crumbled stonework. Mikin floated shyly in a corner while Morgaed glided into the center of the room to address the group.

"The Ender is an aberration," she continued. "He should not exist, but I have my suspicions about what happened to create him." She focused on Piers. "This Sool had his Center in the place you call Aspen Home, correct?"

"I believe so," said the boy. "He used to be a human named Saul who worked in the nursing home."

"A place where many of the Unborn lose the spark of life, but very few become Awake as I am." She tucked the amulet underneath her buckskin tunic. "In the case of our predatory spirit, I suspect that Sool was overlapping the body of an Unborn at precisely the moment when it expired. It may have been a simple accident, or he may have become Obsessed with the humans in his Circle. However it happened, when the life energy passed through him, he sensed it and made a fateful choice."

Dandelion quivered where he stood, listening intently.

"He seized it," said Morgaed. "Devoured it. At that moment, he lost his sanity and began to change into the creature you encountered in the forest. It is likely he repeated his crime many times, awaiting the passing of other ripened Unborn and absorbing their energy until he grew strong enough to end their lives through physical force."

"He stopped their hearts," said Piers.

She nodded. "So it seems. Eventually, the dark spirit was able to take the lives of the Unborn at any stage of their development."

Tull let out a note of disgust. "A horrid notion."

"Both animals and machines have fallen to his appetite," continued Morgaed. "Even plants and the fairies that protect them."

"No!" cried Dandelion.

Morgaed looked down kindly upon him. "I am afraid so. But do not fret, little one. We are united in common cause on this. In fact, I have called a council of the Grove of Elders," she announced. "The Queen herself is going to attend, so I hear."

Dandelion's face went pale. "The Queen?"

"Who's this Queen supposed to be?" demanded Scarlet.

"The Willow Queen," Dandelion said fretfully, withdrawing into the collar of his green jacket. "The Queen of all fairy dominion... or at least as far as I've ever been."

Morgaed turned back to Piers. "And you, boy, for the time being, will have to represent the humans at the council."

"Sure," he replied, though he hoped she wasn't expecting much of him.

Scarlet puffed out her chest. "Naturally, I will represent the animals of the forest."

The ghost woman shook her head. "I'm afraid the one called Fleastriker will be speaking for the squirrels."

"What?" Scarlet hopped up and down, shaking her arms furiously. "That no-good seed-swindler!"

Morgaed was unruffled. "You may still attend the council, as should your dog companion."

Nixon had his paws up against a ruined wall and was sniffing the ghost cat, who had found a new perch to sleep upon. He turned his muzzle back toward the group. "I am a good dog and can make good plans. Better than squirrel plans."

"The best plan *you* ever made involved poop and rolling in it," said Scarlet.

The greyhound dropped to all fours. *"Hmmpf.* That is not even my best plan."

The spindly Tull leaned toward Morgaed and murmured, "Ma'am. The sun, it wanes low to the west."

She nodded. "So it does. It is time for the council to gather. Come!" Morgaed drifted through the stones of the back wall and away from the ruins, followed by Tull.

"Wait!" Piers shouted. He ran out the front doorway with his companions and circled around the back to catch up with the ghosts. "Wait up!"

Morgaed swirled around and came to a stop, chuckling to herself. "Apologies, human. I forget your limitations sometimes."

Piers caught his breath. "I wanted to ask you. You said the nursing home is outside your Circle. You've never met Sool. But how d-d-do you know all this stuff about him, like how he became... what he is?"

Morgaed gave Piers a look that seemed both sad and resolute at the same time. "I know this... because it has happened before."

34

Deeper in the woods, the eclectic group of living and undead beings paused at the top of a small rise. Below them, a circle of ancient trees surrounded a small glade dusted with fallen leaves and twigs. A stream spilled down off the steep slopes uphill from the hollow, bisecting the glade before disappearing down broken ledges below the grove. Piers sensed a sacred quality to the place, though that might have derived from its isolation; the sheer topography that surrounded the site had probably protected it from loggers over the years, unlike much of the state forest.

"The Grove of Elders," announced Morgaed.

Piers looked around for other visitors, but they seemed to have the place to themselves. Mikin had departed somewhere along the way, he noticed, and Tull's ghostly form now seemed mildly windblown. Large buttons kept the man's uniform intact for now. With his garb, Piers could easily picture him serving some British officer at a trading outpost during colonial times.

"Do you have to stay here?" Piers asked him.

"Nay," answered Tull. "My Circle ends soon, however." He turned to Morgaed. "Perhaps we might..."

"Yes," said the other ghost. "It is time to cross over." She gestured for the others to come close. Pulling out the wooden talisman from her tunic, Morgaed instructed, "Everyone, be sure to touch the amulet. Or take hold of someone who is."

Piers felt relieved to have someone else taking charge. He waved Dandelion over, but the fairy hesitated. Piers walked up to him and crouched down. "Dandelion, what's wrong?"

The fairy wouldn't look him in the eye. "I'm not sure I'm ready to meet the Q-Q-Q-Queen."

"You sound like me!" Piers exclaimed. He put a hand on Dandelion's shoulder. "Hey, it's going to be fine. Remember, you and I survived multiple encounters with the Ender. They'll want to hear what we have to say."

"I guess." Dandelion glanced up at Piers through his puffball of hair. "Maybe you can do the talking, though."

"Sure thing. C'mon."

They walked up together and placed a finger on Morgaed's amulet. Tull floated overhead and touched the artifact from above. Nixon trotted to Piers' side, and the boy laid his hand on the greyhound's back. Lastly, Scarlet jumped onto Dandelion's shoulder and held on.

Morgaed reached for the dial with her other hand, but Piers remembered something. "Just a second!" He took his smartphone out of his pocket and placed it on Nixon's back so he could touch QL and the dog's fur at the same time. "Okay."

Morgaed turned the dial from the symbol of the ghostly outline to an adjacent icon, the leaf. Piers felt a wave of static pass across his skin. That was it.

Suddenly, the forest looked different. Everything had a subtle tinge of green and was lit with a warm light as if the sun were setting. The patches of sky visible through the branches overhead appeared to pulse with luminous swirls of color. And in the circle of trees, Piers could see several thin, humanoid figures that stood eight feet or taller. Around them, dozens of smaller, elf-like figures scattered for cover and peeked at the group from behind the tree trunks. They pointed at Tull and Morgaed, who must have materialized out of nowhere from their perspective. Nixon picked his way down the slope and tried to sniff some of the fairies, but they swiftly dashed away.

"I think they have not seen a dog like me before," Nixon hollered up to the group.

"I think they haven't *smelled* a dog like you before," said Scarlet.

Piers turned and caught sight of Dandelion running in the opposite direction from the grove. "Dandelion!" he shouted, but the fairy didn't seem to hear him. He thought he caught Dandelion waving to someone before the little creature disappeared from view amidst the trees.

"Don't sweat it, kid," said Scarlet. "The little weed's probably just happy to be home. Anyway, are we doing this, or what?"

Piers noticed that the two ghosts had already drifted down toward the grove, and he started after them, trying not to stumble and fall on the steep terrain. He managed to reach the bottom of the slope without embarrassing himself. A few brave fairies hesitantly approached him. They had varying proportions – some short and squat, some so thin he expected them to unfurl a pair of wings and start flitting around the grove, like the fairies in storybooks. None could actually fly, as far as he could tell, but they all possessed a pair of pointed ears and wore homespun clothes in a variety of soft, earthen colors. Whenever Piers tried to look directly at one for too long, the fairy's eyes grew wide and the creature bolted. Nixon chased after a few, seemingly for fun.

"Nixon," he counseled, "I think it's time to be serious."

The dog returned to Piers' side. Together with Scarlet, they approached the edge of the circle of trees and carefully entered. Morgaed floated in the midst of the towering elven representatives, finishing her dialogue before turning to point at the boy. The fairies, some nearly twice as tall as Piers himself, swiveled their heads and stared coldly. They had a regal air about them, accentuated by a circlet of leaves that each wore above their pointed ears, and they were garbed in robes with patterns and textures that reflected the plants they personified: Oak, Hemlock, Birch, Sycamore and Maple.

Piers wasn't sure what to do or say. "I..."

Suddenly, Piers' smartphone started blasting a heavy metal anthem. He snatched the phone from his pocket and stabbed frantically at the screen, trying to turn off the shrill, thunderous music. "QL, what are you doing?"

"Giving you a little entrance music," said the device. "I just figured out streaming again."

"Not now, you dumb... phone!" He managed to stop the song in the middle of a squealing guitar riff.

QL sniffed indignantly. "Well, forgive me for wanting to inject a little culture into this backwoods soirée."

Piers jammed the phone into his pocket and looked up at the assembly, red-faced.

A bald-headed titan with robes dyed in the pastel tones of sycamore bark turned away from the boy to face Morgaed. "And *these* are the ones who have witnessed the scourge, so you say?"

"So it is," said the ghost. "By fate or by luck, these children have survived several encounters with the Ender."

"By cunning, you mean!" Scarlet insisted.

Nixon pointed out, "I am not a child, because I am five years old."

"You tell 'em," said Scarlet. "Calling us 'children'... *hmmmph!* I oughta take a chainsaw to..." She trailed off when she noticed her cousin. "Fleastriker?"

A squirrel hopped out from behind a tree and chittered at them. Scarlet turned to Morgaed. "You really were serious? You made that buttscratcher the representative for all squirrelkind?"

She leapt out in front of her cousin. "You're making me real mad this time, Fleastriker. Don't think I don't know what happened to my food stash after the 'talking human' show!" Scarlet gave Fleastriker a shove. The other squirrel tittered and pushed her back. She leapt atop her cousin, and for a few seconds they became a single whirling ball of fur and fury before Fleastriker broke loose and fled up a nearby tree. Scarlet followed close behind.

Several other animals started to arrive at the grove. A raccoon and a fox padded up together, after which several songbirds, a few mice and a possum appeared, all seemingly cautious of Piers and Nixon but oblivious to the fairies in their midst. A honeybee zipped past Piers' head, and he jumped, causing the other animals to scamper backward.

"I'm going to bring the animals into the Fairy World," Morgaed informed Piers and the others. "Why don't you introduce yourselves while you're waiting?" She lifted up the amulet, turned the dial and vanished. The animals were startled anew, and several darted away before turning and creeping slowly back into the grove.

Piers craned his neck to look up at the Elder Fairies. "H-h-h-hi." He cursed his voice for failing him again. "I'm P-P-P-Piers D-Davies. Th-this is Nixon."

A female fairy with a gown made of flat evergreen leaves bent toward him. Her hair was the color of dying pine needles, and beneath a crown of pinecones, her eyes glowed with the same rusty hues. "A talking human," she remarked. "A talking dog. Just like the legends."

"You are..." Piers began. "I'm s-s-sorry. I don't know my trees very w-w-well. I see Oak, right?" He turned to another. "And you are Maple?"

"I am *Lady* Maple." The fairy wore a dress comprised of overlapping fabrics, all in the shape of maple leaves. "And my colleagues are Lord Oak, Lord Sycamore, Lord Birch and Lady Hemlock." The fairies each gave Piers an almost imperceptible nod of acknowledgment.

"We were told you travel in the company of a Dandelion," said Lord Oak in booming tones. "Where is he?"

Piers stammered, "Ah… h-h-h-he m-must have gone off to s-s-see some friends." Out of the corner of his eye, Piers noticed Morgaed flicker back into sight while touching one of the mice. She let go of the animal, rotated the dial of her amulet and disappeared again.

Lord Sycamore bent down to study Piers more closely. "Is it a treecutter? A Cultivate farmer?"

"Looks like neither," growled Lord Birch.

Sycamore's green eyes squinted. "A drone, then?"

"It seems frightened," said Lady Hemlock. She knelt down and softened her voice. "Do not worry," she reassured the boy. "We are not Cultivates. We have no need for your subservience."

"I'm n-not frightened," Piers told her. "I-I-I-I-I just d-don't know what all that means." Piers suddenly caught sight of the greyhound. "Nixon!"

Nixon had his back leg upraised against the trunk of an oak tree. "What is wrong, Piers?"

"Not here!"

Nixon set down his leg and gave him a quizzical look. "But this is a tree."

"Just not here," said Piers. "It's probably impolite, or something."

"Many foxes and coyotes have marked this tree," Nixon insisted. "And I am bigger than they are." He gave the trunk one last sniff and trotted off to find an alternate location.

Scarlet returned to the assembly looking a little worse for wear just as Morgaed popped back into view. "That should be all of them," the ghost announced, releasing her amulet. "Tull, please look for latecomers."

"Yes, ma'am." The steward had been floating behind Piers, and the boy hadn't even noticed.

"Speaking of latecomers," Scarlet remarked.

The squirrel gestured up the hillside, where Piers spotted Dandelion jogging in their direction. The diminutive creature was followed by a taller, gangly fairy with dappled white robes, blond hair and a pale, anemic complexion.

Piers stepped over to the side of the grove to meet them, asking, "Dandelion, where'd you go?"

The fairy held up a finger while he caught his breath. Scarlet joined them. "I needed to see some friends," Dandelion explained, "to make sure the Ender had not eaten them."

"Oh," said Piers. "And they're okay?"

Dandelion dropped his voice to a whisper, clearly uncomfortable in the presence of the Elders. "They were lucky. Other fairies have been lost." He waved for his friend to step over. "Scarlet, Piers... this is Aspen."

Piers extended his hand. "You were the one who helped us outside the nursing home."

Aspen seemed oblivious to the attempted handshake. He ran his hands through his hair, looking incredulous. "You were right, Dandelion. Remarkable." His long lashes sparkled when he blinked, as if covered with fancy mascara. To Piers, he replied, "Yes, I saw you up in the North Tower, but I couldn't understand anything Dandelion was shouting. I guessed that you needed to come down."

"We did," said Piers.

"You bet your nuts we did," said Scarlet.

Piers gave Scarlet an odd look.

"Hush, please," instructed Morgaed. Piers turned and saw the ghost floating up to Lord Sycamore. "Is it time?" she asked the Elder.

Sycamore seemed to hold some mild distaste for Morgaed's presence. "Indeed," he rumbled, pointing up the slope to the west. "She comes."

The Elder Fairies retreated to the perimeter of the grove. Before Piers could spot what Sycamore had been pointing to,

Tull flew up and shooed him and his companions to the grove's edge.

Piers found a place to stand next to Dandelion, and a trio of mice scurried over to huddle between his sneakers. He glanced behind him and saw a colorful arrangement of fairies jostling for a view. Assorted animals kept breaking the perimeter, forcing Tull to keep ushering them back. Piers turned to ask Dandelion a question, but the fairy's gaze was fixed on something distant.

"Oh, my," uttered Dandelion.

Atop the western slope, with the setting sun illuminating her from behind, Piers saw the silhouette of what looked like an angel. "The Queen?" he asked.

Dandelion had lost his voice. From Piers' other side, Aspen leaned in and whispered, "The Willow Queen."

35

The Willow Queen descended the hillside, moving as lightly as any ghost. A pair of smaller fairies flanked the monarch, matching her strides while singing wordlessly with choir-like, angelic voices. The other fey creatures parted to give them space, and as the queen drew closer, Piers shielded the sun from his eyes to observe her better.

She appeared young, as a human in her thirties would seem, and she wore a dress made from leaf-like ribbons of fabric that looked both rustic and regal at the same time. Piers found her face hauntingly beautiful, framed as it was by silver hair that shimmered like silk curtains in the sunlight. Her companions seemed to represent flora of the aquatic variety – Cattail and Lily-pad, from what Piers could tell, based on their clothing.

The queen reached the circle of trees and stepped inside. Every fairy creature, from the tiniest flower pixie to the towering Elders, turned toward the center of the grove and bowed to her. Piers wasn't sure what to do, so he bowed as well. When he lifted his head again, Scarlet was standing in the middle of the circle directly in front of the Willow Queen.

"On behalf of squirrelkind, and, yeah, all my animal brethren," she began loudly, "I, Scarlettail Thistleclaw, would like to welcome you to this here meeting and extend my paw in friendship. You may have noticed there are no snacks. I vote that we immediately–"

Another squirrel ran up and tackled Scarlet. Piers couldn't tell if it was Fleastriker or not, but the two rodents went tumbling out of the circle, biting and scratching the whole way.

As the sounds of the scuffle receded, Morgaed floated calmly into the grove. The Willow Queen stepped forward to greet her. "Morgaed," she said warmly. "I wish it were more than survival that compelled us to meet here. What has kept you away for so long?"

"Caution, I'm afraid. A need to protect the amulet from over-exposure."

In a lower voice, the fairy asked, "The favor you did for me... Is he...?" Piers might have missed the queen's words if she hadn't been facing him.

Morgaed's response was unintelligible. Louder, the ghost said, "Shall we begin?" She turned and addressed the gathered beings. "Fairies. Animals. Representatives of our divided realms."

Divided? Piers made a mental note to ask Morgaed about that.

"Most of you do not know me or know of my kind. I would not have revealed myself if the fiend from my world did not threaten us all." Her firm gaze swept over the assembly. "Creatures of fur and feather... you have witnessed an invisible presence still the beating hearts of your friends and family. Fairies, you have felt the weakness grow within you as the life was stripped from each leaf and branch of your protectorates. You have seen humans dying and their machines become unresponsive and unmoving. All this is the work of the Ender. He is a monster that feeds on the life energy released at the moment of death, and with every killing, his dominion and power grow. I will share my knowledge with you so that we may face this common threat together."

Nixon nudged the boy's arm with his nose. "Piers?"

Piers glanced down. The dog must have slipped through the crowd to reach him. "Yes, Nixon?"

"You know those human boys in the park that are mean to you and make you feel sad?"

Ripal, Dwarviss, Brock. "Yeah," said Piers.

The greyhound fixed his sincere eyes on the boy. "I always wanted you to bark at them and scare them away."

"Okay. But I'm not good at talking."

Nixon poked his arm with his nose again. "Can I tell you a secret, Piers?"

Piers wanted to focus on Morgaed's speech, but he forced himself to say, "Sure, Nixon."

"I am not so good with talking, either," said the dog. "But if I see a bad man, I shout at them really, really loud. And then they go away, even if they are bigger than I am." Nixon paused as if to give time for his words to sink in. "I think you should go to the Ender and act angry and shout, and I will bark too, because I am a good barker, and we can bring everyone and scare him away."

"Maybe," said Piers tactfully. "But I think this is out of our hands now. At least, I hope it is."

He tuned back into the discussion and found Morgaed responding to a statement from one of the fairy lords. "True, he may not be able to see you," said the ghost, "but he will continue to bleed the life from every tree, shrub and flower until the fairy folk succumb to decay and perish themselves."

Piers whispered to Dandelion, "Is that true? If he kills all your plants?"

"It could happen," the fairy admitted. "We lost a quarter of the Flower Fairies during the Great Frost twenty years ago. So far, my dandelions have been too small for the Ender to notice, but look at the Elders."

Piers studied the taller fairies. "What about them?"

"Their clothes. They represent the health of the trees that they protect."

The boy noticed that the Elders' formal robes seemed more tattered than they had at first glance. The edges of the leaves woven into the fabric were tinged with red and brown. "I take it autumn colors are not good," said Piers.

"No." Dandelion shook his head. "Not for this time of year."

The faces of the Elders didn't seem as healthy as Piers guessed they should, either.

Maple spoke up next. "Why does he not feed constantly, then? Why isn't the whole forest dead?"

"That is unclear," replied Morgaed. "Perhaps he requires time to digest his prey before he can expand his Circle."

Piers considered sharing the contradictory evidence he'd seen behind his house the other night, but he felt too shy to speak in front of the adults. Instead, a red-tailed hawk on a low branch rasped, "Dead this, dead that. What is his endgame?"

"Indeed," echoed a fox. "What does the Ender want?"

"Perhaps our human can speak to this," offered Morgaed. "Piers knows something of Sool's life before he became the monster he is now."

A hundred pairs of eyes turned toward the boy. He swallowed hard.

"Piers," repeated the Willow Queen, flashing what might have been the prettiest eyes of all. "The first human to enter our world in a long, long while. Tell us what you've learned of this creature."

Piers reluctantly stepped forward. Taking a deep breath, he stammered out everything he knew about Saul Timmons and how the hospital employee died. Midway through his report, Piers noticed Scarlet among the animal ambassadors. He worried that the squirrel would say something when he failed to mention Marguerite or their attempt at an exorcism, but thankfully, Scarlet kept her mouth shut. He finished with reddened cheeks, expecting he had lowered everyone's opinion of the human species by several degrees.

Lady Hemlock addressed him first, and she spoke with more courtesy than he expected. "So, what do *you* think he wants?"

Piers suddenly realized that he and Saul might share something in common. "I...I th-think Sool is ashamed. H-h-he wasn't happy as a human. He felt powerless. Small." Piers felt like he was stumbling over his thoughts, trying to get them out, but he pressed on. "M-maybe he wanted love once, but now, more than anything, he wants to be feared. I think that's why he wants to get to the human realm... so he can be seen and feared by those who once pitied him."

"Morgaed believes that the Ender desires freedom," Lady Maple pointed out. "To escape a boundary inherent to his kind."

"I guess that too," Piers admitted.

Scarlet interjected, "But he can't fit through the holes, right? He's too big now, right?" The squirrel seemed strangely agitated.

"So it seems," said Morgaed. "With each soul he consumes, he damages the fabric of the world. Thankfully, the Ender has grown too massive to take advantage of these openings, but he remains fixated on crossing over and breaking through his Circle. To escape his world and become unbound, he would need this..."

The ghost lifted the amulet from her chest. Its solidity stood out against her translucent flesh. "This device was entrusted to me by my predecessor. It allows passage to each aspect of our divided earth. Were Sool to obtain it, he would have no limits. It is safe for the time being, but the Ender's Circle grows every day. Eventually, his territory will overlap mine completely, and to keep the amulet out of his grasp, I will have to leave my world for good. The Queen has agreed to give me refuge should that time come."

The Willow Queen nodded in confirmation.

Lord Birch cleared his throat roughly. "Let me be blunt. Why not give this creature what it wants? Hand over the amulet and let him roam wherever he desires. Preferably, someplace far away from here." Several fairies and animals shouted their agreement.

Morgaed raised her voice above them. "Give him the amulet, and he will enter the Fairy World and attack you directly. While he stays in my world, he cannot see you."

"Then take him to the Human World yourself and leave him there," said Maple with an air of exaggerated patience. "Let him feed on the human race until they are wiped clean from the earth."

Piers was surrounded by voices cheering for the demise of his species. He crept back a few inches.

"Long have our fields and forests suffered at their hands," Lady Maple continued. "When have humans benefited anyone but the Cultivates?"

"They are a pestilence," rumbled Lord Sycamore. "Why not use one enemy to destroy another?"

"Yes!" Lord Oak cried. "The Cultivates would starve and dwindle. We could bring the Corn Lord to his knees."

"That would be short-sighted," Morgaed countered in authoritative tones. "While Sool is contained within his Circle, his power is limited. Set him free on the world, and his appetite would be infinite. He would come for the plants under your protection eventually."

The sounds of dissent diminished, but Lord Sycamore growled, "*Eventually* could be a long time."

Lord Birch stepped out from the crowd. His emerald green robes churned the air as he circled around Morgaed. "I believe our guest has a conflict of interest here. From what she's told us about the workings of the world, no humans would mean there would be no more spirits joining her ranks. It would be the end to her kind!"

"That is enough, Lord Birch," commanded the queen. She stood several feet shorter than her towering vassal, but her gaze did not waver. "We will not condemn an entire race to extinction on this day."

"With all due respect, your grace," said Lady Maple, gesturing toward Morgaed, "the Ender is of her species. Who is to say there will not be more Enders in the future, even if we defeat this one?"

Subdued murmurs circulated among the fairies. Piers used the opening to speak up. "Morgaed, c-c-c-c-could the Winds d-destroy the Ender?"

"What winds does he speak of?" boomed Lord Oak.

"My people are limited to a Circle of space, beyond which are the Winds," explained Morgaed. "Enter them, and our souls are torn apart. But the Ender cannot be forced into the Winds by any means that I know of."

Piers pressed on with his thought. "C-could you t-t-touch Sool with the amulet, let him go into another world, and then when he is outs-s-side his Circle, bring him back to the Ghost World? He'd be trapped in the middle of the Winds, right?"

"Wow," exclaimed Scarlet. "That is good thinking! For a human."

Morgaed shook her head. "I wish this could be done as you say. But the amulet will not work to bring my kind across the threshold of reality if the Winds lie beyond. It was tried before. I believe it is a failsafe of the amulet to prevent accidents when the device is used by my people."

Scarlet glanced back at him. "I take it back."

Piers ignored her. He felt like he was missing something important. "Wait, when was this tried before on Sool?"

"Not on Sool," said Morgaed. "It was tried on the *last* soul-eater. I told you this wasn't the first time this has happened, remember?"

Piers recalled her words from earlier, outside the walls of Stonegarden. *I know this... because it has happened before.*

Morgaed spoke loudly, with an air of authority deepened by the passage of centuries. "If you are all finished with your fanciful theories, I will share what it took for my predecessor to eliminate the *previous* soul-stealing abomination."

"Previous?" repeated Lady Maple.

Piers looked around, but everyone seemed as confused as he was. "Your predecessor? Where is he? Or she?"

"He is dead," said Morgaed. "He died to defeat it."

❧ 36 ❧

Morgaed's somber words hung in the air. The crowd settled, and she raised herself higher in the grove to tell her story.

"Millenia ago, one of my kind was studying the humans in its midst. This observer – we would call him one of 'the Obsessed' because of his unhealthy fixations – began to toy with the Unborn to see how they reacted to his presence. It may have been a simple accident, but we believe that the Obsessed was occupying the same space as a human at the moment when it died, and the energy of the human's life was absorbed into his form. From that point forward, he became a corrupted spirit. He chose to feed on other souls, clinging to the dying and waiting for their final breath. My people cannot easily touch physical matter as you can, but the more the Obsessed ate, the more he grew and the more he gained in power to affect the world around him. Soon, he was able to reach inside the bodies of the Unborn and other animals, causing their premature deaths.

"Thankfully, my people noticed what was happening at this early stage and we intervened. Whenever the Obsessed attempted to feed, we prevented his absorption of souls by flying through his form at high speeds and disrupting his focus. He began shrinking, slowly."

Morgaed paused to let this idea sink in. "I would point out how rare this situation was, and still is. We considered it a sickness. When the Obsessed absorbed that first life, he effectively poisoned himself. He had to continue to feed to forestall his own death, and because of his terrible addiction, he could not be reasoned with. We were forced to slowly starve him out of existence."

Lord Sycamore finally spoke. "So, you think there may be a way to starve the Ender."

"Perhaps. We would need to keep him from feeding and, most importantly, contain him within his Circle. Sadly, there are too few of my people left to successfully disrupt his murders. He has grown much too big and powerful. Together, though..."

"You think we might have a chance?" asked the Willow Queen.

"That is unclear," admitted the ghost. "It would take our combined efforts, and Sool will act like a cornered animal, vicious and unreasoning. Many of us could perish." Her voice rang with conviction. "But survival requires sacrifice. My own mentor lost his life in the struggle to keep the first corrupt spirit contained. When we attempted to starve the beast, we kept close watch, for the Awakened do not need sleep, as you do. Nevertheless, our attention eventually wavered, and the creature escaped our containment. It ambushed and swallowed several souls at one time, creating a portal large enough to fit its mass. That is where my mentor found it, and how I came to inherit his amulet."

She tapped a finger against the wooden face of the device. "The amulet, you see, is an artifact that can provide passage to the other worlds. It can also be used to seal passages, though at a cost to the energy of the wielder. To close the portal before the creature could escape, my predecessor sacrificed his own life.

Those of us who remained were more watchful from then on." Piers thought he heard a quaver in Morgaed's voice – the first time she had allowed herself to sound vulnerable. "If we are to defeat the Ender, our own commitment must be unshakable."

Lord Sycamore crossed his arms, tucking them into the sleeves of his pastel robes. "I do not like this plan. A long siege, with an inevitable loss of life. How else can it be killed?"

"You people aren't thinking big enough," Scarlet declared. "This ghost might be a little overgrown, but how about we make an even *bigger* ghost that can eat the Ender?"

Several fairies and animals began arguing at once. The discussion devolved into a tangle of proposals to drive the Ender into the Winds, each countered by Morgaed as being unworkable. Piers tried to follow the thread of dialogue until he heard a commotion behind him. He turned and saw a young buck with a short pair of antlers snorting in alarm as it tried to fight its way through the circle of fairies. The fey creatures raised cries of protest at being jostled about, while the deer quickly worked itself into a panic. It jumped away after coming into contact with fairies invisible to it, only to collide into others it was unable to see.

Piers waded through the crowd. "Give it some space!" he shouted.

More fairies backed away from the animal, and the deer found its footing. It charged immediately over to Piers, stamped its hooves and gave a piercing snort.

Piers shook his head. "I don't know what you're saying." He looked around for help. "Nixon!"

The greyhound rushed to his side. "Yes, Piers?"

"Get Scarlet, will you? I can't speak wild animal."

Nixon disappeared. The buck grew even more anxious, and it prodded Piers in the chest with its short antlers. "Ow!" the boy cried. "I don't speak deer. Stop it!"

Nixon returned shortly, holding Scarlet by the scruff of her neck. "If you don't put me down," said the squirrel. "I swear I will crack your skull like a walnut and let vultures snack on your brains!" Nixon dropped her at Piers' feet.

"Scarlet, this deer is trying to say something," Piers explained.

The deer *whuffed* at the squirrel. Scarlet looked up at Piers and shrugged. "Beats me. He's back home. I'm in Ghost World. *No, Plant World.*" She threw up her arms. "Sheesh, I don't know where I am anymore!"

"I think you need the amulet," said Nixon.

"Fine." Piers made a few placating gestures to the buck. "Just hold on a minute."

He pushed his way through the shorter fairies to get back into the grove. Morgaed was floating low in the center of the clearing next to several Elders, responding to their latest proposal. Piers stepped alongside and waved his hands.

Morgaed waited until Lord Oak had finished speaking, then turned to him. "What is it, Piers?"

He blurted, "I think we need your help for a minute."

The spirit looked annoyed, as did the Elders, but she gave them a curt apology and allowed Piers to escort her out of the grove. She flew overhead, with Tull following, while Piers was forced to wade through the mass of fairies until they could reach the buck.

Piers began, "This deer seems to want—"

"Let's move a bit," Morgaed interrupted. "Too noisy to hear anything."

The two ghosts drifted over to the headwall of the bowl containing the grove, where moss and ferns congregated around a thin cascade that splashed down the steeper exposed rock. Piers tried to herd the deer toward them, and Nixon and Scarlet assisted as best they could. The buck allowed itself to be guided further from the crowds, though it repeatedly turned and stamped its feet in impatience.

At the base of the headwall, the voices from the Council

continued to echo in their ears, but it was still quieter than at the edge of the grove. "All right," said Morgaed. "Let's see what's bothering this creature."

She touched the dial on her amulet and flickered out of sight. The deer jumped back, obviously able to perceive Morgaed now that their consciousnesses were in the same world. The creature quivered for a moment, and then Morgaed reappeared, holding the amulet against the deer's shoulder. She drifted backward. "Now what seems to be the—"

"You," the buck gasped. "Human. The Ghost Girl. It's... It's..."

Piers could see the whites of the buck's eyes. The intelligence was there, but it was a panicked intelligence. "What? Slow down."

The deer snorted in his haste to speak. "She... The Ender... Warn you."

"The Ender?" Piers struggled to put the buck's words in a sensible order. "Did Emlee say the Ender was... But it can't get here."

"She... she saw it."

Piers turned to Morgaed. "That doesn't make sense. The Ender's Circle doesn't go this far."

A disturbed look crept over Morgaed's face. "Boy... how do you know how far the Ender's Circle reaches?"

The question confused him. "Because he told me. He said he can't reach you, so he needed..." He trailed off as an awful realization dawned on him. His face turned white. "Oh, no." Piers swore and looked out into the trees. "What if he—"

A multitude of screams cut through the air. Piers turned to witness the Elders and several woodland animals rise into the air at the center of the grove, jerking and twisting as they fought an unseen force. Other fairies cried out in fear and pulled back. The Willow Queen flailed in midair, her fists bouncing off the invisible presence. She whipped her head around, searching desperately for help, and for an instant, her eyes locked with Piers'.

Then the suspended bodies smashed together. They hovered

for a moment before collapsing into a lifeless heap at the center
of the ring of ancient trees.

❧ 37 ❧

The screams from the fleeing fairies were deafening. Animals scattered from the grove as fast as they could run, fly or scamper. Piers took a few strides against the mad rush of creatures, looking for any sign of their friend Dandelion, but a squat fairy in a blue tunic bowled him over and knocked the wind out of him.

"Grab the amulet," Morgaed commanded from somewhere behind him. *"Now."*

He scrambled to his knees, gasping for air. Nixon was already at Morgaed's feet, touching his nose to the amulet, and Scarlet leapt onto the dog's back. Piers staggered over and grabbed hold of the amulet just as Tull placed a ghostly finger on the device and Morgaed turned the dial.

The filter overlaying the forest flickered from green to twilight tones. Piers quickly dropped to all fours and allowed the pain in his chest to subside. Although the fairies and their voices had disappeared, he could still feel the ground tremble with the impact of their invisible feet. He forced himself to stand upright and immediately flinched as a robin swooped past his head, escaping the hollow.

When he faced the grove again, Sool was there, wallowing in the middle of the ring of trees and looking hideously engorged. His bloated body lay halfway buried beneath the earth, and with one pudgy finger, the ghost poked at something invisible in front of him... very likely the bodies of the dead Elders. He was searching for something.

"Sool!" shouted Morgaed.

The Ender looked up and grinned slyly. "So there it is. The amulet. I had hoped to gain everything in one bite, but underground, my vision is somewhat... imprecise. The energy of these delicious creatures," he continued, prodding the invisible corpses, "must have thrown me off."

Sool began to pour his body forward, oozing through the circle of trees.

Nixon quivered and glanced unhappily up at Piers. "I think we should be running soon."

"Morgaed," Piers whispered, "can you stop him?"

"Hush, boy," she ordered. "Stand behind me."

Tull swept close. Invisible Winds lashed at his incorporeal frame, but he gritted his teeth against whatever pain he felt. "Ma'am, you should go." He pointed to the amulet around Morgaed's neck. "Go where he cannot see you. Protect the amulet."

The older spirit looked grim. "Get back in your Circle, Tull. I fear I will be needed here." She turned to dismiss Piers once more, but the boy had frozen in place. Sool's eyes were fixed upon him.

"Piers Human," rumbled the Ender. "I owe you my thanks... I couldn't have found your ancient friend or her device without you."

"You used me." Anger seethed within the boy. "You j-just watched, and I led you right to her."

Sool paused his advance. He had the group cornered against the headwall. The others would be fine, but for Piers, escaping up the steep slopes would not be easy. "How dumb you must feel," gloated Sool. "Did I not tell you... *my Circle grows?*" His smug expression hardened. "But I am done with confinement."

Nixon found the courage to take a step forward. "I think *you* are the one who is dumb, because you do not have the amulet."

"You missed your chance, Ender," Tull called out. "You cannot escape your bonds."

Sool's eyes narrowed. "Oh, can't I?"

The Ender turned his elephantine head back toward the grove and the rest of his gelatinous body slowly followed, rising further from the ground as he moved, like a leviathan breaching the ocean surface. Through a gap beneath the giant's belly, Piers glimpsed the interior of the grove again. And there in the center, he could see the flickering edges of a new portal, wider and more visible than any he had yet encountered. Piers could have stepped through it without needing to duck.

"He's opened a portal!" Piers warned. "He's going to go through!"

"I see it," said Morgaed. She shot upward and over the sluggish body of the Ender.

Piers remained behind, wracked with guilt over the slaughter he'd unwittingly caused. *Again.*

Nixon looked up at him. "What should I do, Piers?"

Piers returned the dog's gaze. He didn't deserve such trust. He didn't have any answers... in fact, he wanted to ask Nixon the same question in return. He placed his hand on Nixon's forehead and rubbed the fur between the greyhound's ears. "You're a good dog," he said. Then he turned and ran straight toward the Ender.

The space beneath Sool's distorted body and the ground had collapsed, but Piers sprinted right through the expanse of ghostly flesh and out the other side. He spun around at the edge of the grove, braced his feet and stuck out his palm to stop the Ender. "Y-y-y-you are just a stupid hospital worker wh-wh-who killed himself over a bad date! You will stop here! Now!"

Sool paused to stare at Piers. Then he extended a single finger from his cloud-like mass and knocked him to the ground. A heavy weight descended on Piers' chest, and his ribs felt like they were about to break.

"That is enough." Sool's cavernous voice boomed in his ears. "You and your rodent have been useful tools, but my gratitude only extends so far."

The Ender lifted his finger and surged forward again, overrunning the helpless boy. After Sool passed into the grove, Nixon dashed up and licked Piers' face. Piers coughed, sat up and immediately caught the eye of Scarlet, who stood awkwardly on her hind legs a short distance away.

"Rodent?" Piers tried to get the words out. "What is he...?"

Sool turned, and the corners of his mouth curled into an unnatural smile. "Did she not tell you? The squirrel gave me the key to escaping my Circle. I only needed to make a big enough hole."

Piers shook his head. *"Scarlet."* He couldn't hide the bitterness from his voice. *Why? Why betray them now?*

Scarlet gave him a brief, pained look, then bounded away from the grove.

"Bad squirrel," growled Nixon.

Sool twisted his neck back toward the portal. A pair of elongated arms reached out, grabbed the flickering edges and stretched the gateway wider.

Piers forced himself to his feet again and dashed into the grove. He knew he wasn't thinking straight, but he didn't care anymore. He ran out in front of Sool and swung his fist, only to have it pass through the translucent skin without making contact. Sool frowned and removed one hand from the portal. The flesh rapidly solidified.

By the time Piers felt the punch, he was already flying across the forest floor. He heard Sool's words as his body hit the ground and tumbled. "Well, then. Perhaps once I am free, I will pay your mother a visit after all."

Piers painfully raised his head. "No! Leave her out of this!"

Sool grinned cruelly and turned to push his head through the portal. Then another voice rang out.

"Saul Timmons! You will not pass!"

On the opposite side of the portal from Sool, Morgaed descended to the earth. The woman held the long chain of the amulet in her fist, and she used it to twirl the talisman in a circle, faster and faster as she closed the distance between herself and the portal.

Tull shouted from outside the grove, unable to enter. "Morgaed!" His formal cadences were beginning to crack. "You cannot do this!"

Wisps from Morgaed's ghostly body tore themselves loose. From her hair, her buckskin clothing, her feathers... each fragment drifted outward, pulled into the whirling circle made by the amulet.

"He must be contained," was all she said.

Like smoke drawn into the blades of a fan, the tendrils of Morgaed's essence continued to pass through the amulet's chain, exiting as a stream of iridescent radiance. The light touched the surface of the portal, and it began to shrink.

"No!" Sool thundered. "I will... not... be..." He placed his hands against the sides of the portal and strained to keep the gateway from collapsing further. The contraction stopped, and Sool managed to stretch the portal wider once more.

Piers attempted to stand, but he felt a sharp pain in his right leg. The jeans fabric was torn and bloody, and he hesitated a brief moment to assess the damage.

Morgaed, however, moved forward with increasing confidence. "You will be contained!" she shouted. Her already translucent form grew paler as more of her soul was ripped away and sacrificed to repair the breach. The portal shrank again. Sool roared in his struggle to keep it open, and his cries shook the entire forest. Leaves came tumbling from the trees of the ancient grove as if autumn had been summoned early.

Morgaed said, "Goodb–" and then the last thread of her existence unraveled and was transformed by the spinning amulet into a beam of kaleidoscopic light. The portal collapsed in upon itself.

Untethered, the amulet flew through the air and struck the earth with a thud.

38

Piers stared at the empty space where Morgaed had been, then at the fallen amulet, and then at Sool.

The Ender seethed, skin bubbling and expanding like a thundercloud ready to burst. His gaze flickered toward Piers for just a second before he growled and charged for the amulet.

Piers was closer, but after climbing painfully to his feet, he realized he would never make it in time. "Nixon!" he shouted. "The amulet!"

The dog heard him and raced across the forest floor as fluid as a cheetah. Piers had never seen the greyhound move so swiftly. Sool's swollen fingers tore at the earth in an attempt to propel his body forward even faster, and before Nixon could reach the artifact, the giant's hand shot upward and began to descend. Piers cringed as the greyhound darted underneath, snatched the amulet in his teeth and dashed away without hesitating. Sool's hand slammed down onto empty ground, missing him by inches.

Nixon turned and glanced briefly at Piers. Then he sprinted out of the grove, up the side of the hollow and disappeared into the trees. Sool roared and followed after him.

Piers looked on with shock. Suddenly, Tull's ghostly figure

dropped between the tree trunks at the edge of the grove, startling him. Violent winds tore at the servant's fancy jacket, and the crazed look of fury on his face could have rivaled the Ender's. "This massacre is on *you*, human! A good woman that I faithfully served for two hundred years is now dead, thanks to your idiocy." Tull turned away and flew after the others.

Piers shouted, "Tull! I didn't know!" But as his last ally drifted out of sight, Piers mumbled to himself, "I *should* have known."

He stared at the dead leaves on the ground, too shaken for any coherent thoughts to take hold. After several minutes, the pain from his injured leg forced its way back to his attention. He pulled the torn fabric away from the gash on his right knee and observed that the wound was still bleeding. So were his scraped elbows. It was hard to care about anything, but Piers made himself limp over to the brook that trickled through the grove so he could wash his arms. He gave up on his knee after a few attempts to cleanse the wound, however; the injury felt much too tender.

As he considered whether his leg would support him on the climb out of the hollow, Piers noticed how quiet the forest had become. He was actually alone for the first time in what felt like ages, and he had no idea about what to do next... except to leave the grove and never come back.

Halfway up the slope, Piers stopped to let the pain in his knee subside. He turned and gave the Elder Grove one last look. The site below him no longer felt holy. It felt empty. And ordinary.

He reached into his pocket and pulled out his cell phone. No cracks across the touchscreen; that surprised him. He tapped at several buttons, but the applications refused to open. QL's consciousness must still be stuck in the Plant World, Piers guessed. He turned off his phone to save the battery, then resumed limping up the hill.

At the top of the slope, Piers considered his options. He could go after Sool and the others, but the weight of his failures made that choice too heavy to contemplate. He actually wanted to go home more than anything, but he remembered Sool's threats against his mother and knew it would be dangerous to draw the Ender's attention there.

Lacking a better plan, Piers decided to return to the patch of forest where they'd left Emlee behind some hours before. That felt like days ago, when hope existed in far greater measure. At least his knee had stopped hurting as much.

Along the way, Piers passed the ruins of Stonegarden and found himself wondering where Mikin was. The place felt lifeless now, even within the Ghost World. He was grateful he hadn't run into Scarlet so far. Piers had absolutely nothing to say to that backstabbing rodent.

At the edge of Emlee's Circle, Piers finally stopped, put his back against a tree trunk and sank slowly to the ground. No sign of the ghost girl, but it seemed as good a place as any to wait for her.

The waiting felt worse than the pain of walking, but he didn't know what else to do. The longer he sat, the more his guilt accumulated until he didn't care if the Ender showed up and swallowed him whole. Eventually, hunger and the diminishing amount of daylight convinced him that he could no longer put off making a decision. He had to move.

Just as he was bending his stiffened leg and preparing to rise to his feet, however, Emlee swooped in.

"You're alive!" She dropped low so her head was at his level. "I was so worried! I saw Sool, and I tried to warn you, and then I had to wait and wait, and the animals came running, but I couldn't make them see me, even if I went to Animal World..."

Piers cut her off. "You sent the deer."

"Yes!" She wrung her hands as the words spilled out of her. "Sool was following you and the others, but from underground. I saw the top of his head for just a moment, but you were too far away and couldn't hear me. I had to go to Animal World to escape my Circle, and I found what I think was Stonegarden, but you weren't there. I got a herd of brave deer to search the forest, and one found you?"

"Yes."

"Did you get away in time?"

Piers shook his head.

"Oh." Emlee finally held still for a few seconds. "But you're here. Did Morgaed... did Morgaed get away?"

"No," Piers answered, turning his eyes away from her.

"Oh," said Emlee, much more softly. She sunk even lower and curled her arms around her knees. "Then we failed." She looked down. "I failed her."

Emlee's hair floated out in front of her face and her head began to shake. It took Piers a moment to realize the ghost was crying. He got to his feet, ignoring a sharp jolt of pain from his knee, and limped forward.

"Emlee, no... it's my fault. I led the Ender straight to her."

Her voice was breaking. "I didn't have a mother like you humans. But when I first Awakened, Morgaed came to teach me, and look after me. She helped me find my name."

Piers awkwardly tried to place his hand on her shoulder, but it passed right through. Emlee failed to notice, though she finally looked up and asked him, "What happened?"

"The Ender came," he explained. "A lot of fairies died, and a portal was opened... big enough for him to get through. Morgaed used the amulet to close it in time. It cost her life." He hated telling her this. "And last I saw Nixon, he had grabbed the amulet and escaped."

She raised her head and sniffed. "Good dog. Where's Scarlet? And Dandelion?"

Piers crossed his arms. "That stupid squirrel... she betrayed us. She told Sool he could break out of his Circle by going through a portal, and now he knows he just has to kill a bunch of things at once to make a hole big enough."

"Oh."

Her locks floated away from her face, and Piers could see the sorrow and confusion in her eyes. No real tears, though, he noticed.

She sniffed again. "So... so what... so what now?"

"I don't know. Find the amulet and go somewhere very far away," he suggested, bitterness seeping back into his voice. "You really picked the wrong person to help you save the world. All I do is fail."

The way Emlee looked at him, Piers realized that part of her sadness was for him alone, and he couldn't stand it. She bit her lip, then told him, "It's okay to fail sometimes. We just have to –"

"It's *not* okay!" he spat. "I fail, and people die!"

In the middle of the tense moment, Nixon trotted up with the amulet in his mouth. He placed it on the ground in front of Piers and sat proudly.

A flood of conflicting emotions rushed through Piers, but relief won out. "Nixon, you're alive!" He knelt and hugged the greyhound.

"Ghosts are fast, but ghosts are not as fast as me," Nixon informed him. "Did you see me get the amulet?"

"Yes. That was amazing."

He held his nose up proudly. "I did not get caught."

Piers lifted the amulet off the ground. It felt cold and heavy, despite being carved from wood. He tucked it in his pocket, next to his cellphone.

"Nixon," asked Emlee, "do you know where Sool is?"

Nixon looked over his shoulder. "I think I have lost him. I do not know." He turned back to Piers. "Is it time for supper?"

"I'm hungry, too," Piers admitted. "But I don't think we should go home right now. Sool would see us. It's the first place he would probably look. Maybe once it gets dark."

"Here is not safe, either," said Emlee.

Piers nodded. "We should get outside his Circle." He took a

239

stick and traced a series of shapes through the leaves and dirt on the ground. "Here's the nursing home – his Center. Here's my house, and here's about where the Grove would be, I think." He drew a larger circle. "So we know his Circle now includes most of downtown, and all this forest." Piers' own house lay within the boundaries of the Circle, he saw with dismay. He let out a soft curse.

Emlee pointed to a spot on the dirt map within the marked forest area. "That's the closest edge to us. It's just barely within my Circle, too." She lifted off the ground and began to float away. "Follow me."

Piers placed a hand on Nixon's back. "Watch out for you-know-who, okay?" He stood and called out to Emlee, "Ghosts can't see if they're underground, can they?"

Emlee paused and turned. "No, but we can hear a little if we're close to the surface."

"Look for the top of his head," he counseled the dog. Nixon trotted after Emlee with his head low to the ground, sniffing. Piers trailed behind and tried to work the stiffness out of his injured leg.

This part of the forest seemed strangely silent. It was impossible to tell if Sool had been through here or not, but several trees along their path looked dead or dying. A turkey vulture launched itself from the corpse of a deer as they passed, causing Piers to jump before he realized what it was.

Eventually, they came to the base of a limestone bluff. The cliff extended in both directions, and beneath a small overhang, Piers noticed an old fire ring and some tree trunks that had been dragged over for seating.

"I have seen a few humans here," said Emlee. "They sometimes start fires at night."

Piers kicked a crumpled beer can. "I don't have a way to start a fire. And you don't get cold, do you?"

She looked at him oddly. "Cold. That is an interesting

concept. I don't *think* I have ever been cold."

"I guess this is a good place to wait until dark, then." He swallowed. "Wish I had some water, tho–"

His words failed when he felt a sharp jab to the side of his nose. "Ow!" Piers jumped back and twisted his head, searching. "Something just poked me." His leg was next, and he jumped again. "Ow, my shin!"

Emlee swirled around. "I don't see anything."

"If we weren't in Ghost World already, I'd say it was a ghost. Ow!" He waved his arms to ward off whatever was out there. "A very annoying ghost! Or... hold on."

Piers pulled out the amulet and turned the wooden dial to the Plant World symbol. Emlee vanished instantly, and a very disheveled-looked Dandelion appeared in front of him, clutching a stick in his hands.

"Dandelion!" Piers cried. "Where have you been?"

The fairy tossed the stick aside and wrung his hands. "Oh, it's horrible, horrible!"

"Hang on, let me bring you back to the others." Piers touched Dandelion on the shoulder, then used the amulet to bring them back to Ghost World.

"Dandelion!" Emlee exclaimed with joy. She floated down to his eye level. "I was so worried that you were in the Grove when the Ender came."

The fairy shook his head. "He nearly got me. But oh, the forest is in chaos! All the lords and ladies... the queen... There are no leaders, and no one knows what to do. Most are fleeing and leaving their charges unprotected." As Dandelion spoke, his energy appeared to slowly trickle away. He lowered himself to the ground, and Piers noticed how tired the creature's eyes looked. Maybe it had something to do with the diminishing sunlight. "I see you have the amulet," the fairy observed.

Nixon walked over. "The old ghost lady. She is dead now."

Dandelion stared at the dog, open-mouthed, then turned to

the ghost girl. "I'm sorry, Emlee. I know she meant a lot to you." He looked around at the others. "I wish I could do something... but I'm not that good at being helpful."

Piers shrugged. "Join the club." He picked up Dandelion's stick and poked the charred remnants of the fire pit.

"Oh!" Dandelion's heavy eyelids flew open. "But maybe I can help with that!" The fairy ran his fingers through his billowing gray hair, and before long, he had collected a handful of loose strands as fluffy as dandelion seeds. He wadded the hair into a ball, placed it in the pit, then began to arrange pieces of kindling around it. "This will keep me from falling asleep, too," he told them.

"Dandelion, wait," said Piers. "We don't have any way to light it."

"Sure we do!" Dandelion opened one of the pouches on his belt and pulled out a plastic cigarette lighter. He handed it to Piers.

"Where did you get a lighter?" Piers asked.

"Found it." Dandelion seemed a little embarrassed and wouldn't look him in the eye. "I get picked on a little," he mumbled. "The lighter... makes them stay away sometimes."

Even fairies have bullies, Piers mused. He lit the hairball, added more twigs to the flames, and soon they had a tidy fire going within their shelter.

A light drizzle began to fall outside. The fire remained protected beneath the overhang, and Nixon curled up on the dirt beside it. Piers and Dandelion ventured out into the twilight to gather more wood, and Emlee helped guide them to the most promising bits of deadfall.

Once they had built up a sufficient stockpile of dry branches, Piers sat on one of the tree trunks and took out the amulet. He rotated the dial to the Plant World setting, and his fairy and ghost companions disappeared. Then he pulled out his cellphone, turned it on and waited for the device to boot up. He tapped some buttons. "QL, are you there?"

"Yes, I'm here," came an irritated voice in clipped British tones. "What did you put me to sleep for?"

"You weren't responding. I wanted to save your—"

"Yes, yes, fine," QL cut in, "but now I am completely out of touch. Update the feed, please."

"Just a second," Piers said.

He turned the dial and brought them back to Ghost World. Emlee's face materialized just inches from his own, startling him, and he nearly pitched backward off the log. "Man, don't do that!"

"Are you okay?" asked Emlee, unperturbed. "Your words went all gibberishy for a minute."

"Yes!" He set his phone down on another log. "I just wanted to get QL back here."

He took a few minutes to bring QL up to speed. Then Piers dictated a text to his mother, and QL sent out the false alibi. That would keep her from worrying for a while. *If she even noticed he was gone.* "Any news from town?" he asked the device.

"They're not lifting the quarantine until they learn how to test for the unknown disease," pulsed the icon on the touchscreen, "a disease that we very well know does not exist."

Piers nodded. "It's a 'killed-by-ghosts' disease." He tossed another branch into the fire and swore. "They're not going to find anything. We're stuck in Summerday."

"I'm sorry, Carrier, but how are we stuck?" asked QL. "Nothing is keeping us here, and I certainly wouldn't stay for the provincial network coverage."

"I meant my mom and I. *We're* stuck. I was hoping I could convince her to get out of town for a while, but we can't leave if there's a blockade."

"That is... unfortunate." After a long pause, the smartphone said, "Dandelion, you have opposable thumbs... how would *you* like to be a Carrier?"

Emlee looked shocked. "QL, really!"

QL's icon shifted to a purple hue. "*Tsk.* I have reached my limits of being helpful. My Carrier has reached the limits of human intelligence. And perhaps you would like to hear the Top Twelve Reasons to Avoid Being Near a Homicidal Entity?"

Emlee floated down beside Piers. "Piers," she began gently, "I got you into this, and I'll do everything I can to protect you and your mother. I know you may not see it this way, but... you're not alone." She placed her hand atop of his, making the undersides of her fingers as solid as she could. Piers felt ashamed at being so focused on his mom when the entire city, if not the world, was at stake, but he didn't feel like he had a choice. He pulled his hand away.

Suddenly, the sound of rustling leaves came from outside the overhang. Nixon, Dandelion and the boy jumped to their feet. Piers snatched one of the branches from the woodpile, raising it above his head threateningly, but because he'd been staring into the fire, his eyes couldn't penetrate the darkness of the forest.

A small creature hopped out of the rain and into the firelight. It was Scarlet.

❧ 39 ❧

"You," Piers muttered.

Scarlet spat something onto the ground that appeared to be a partially-eaten granola bar inside a shredded wrapper. She looked up sheepishly and waved. "Hi, guys."

Nixon growled, lowered his head and moved threateningly toward the squirrel. Scarlet raised her paws and backed away. "Now, now... no need for that. We're on the same side, here."

Piers folded his arms. "Are we, Scarlet? You *told* Sool how to escape. You saw that Emlee could do it, and so all Sool needed was a big enough portal."

Scarlet circled the fire pit, trying to keep the flames between her and Nixon. "I didn't want to tell him!"

"You told us yourself on the way back from Boone. That's *just* what you wanted... for him to become someone else's problem."

"You wanted it, too!" she protested.

"But he didn't help him do it," said Emlee, shaking her head. "Many souls died. You really disappointed us, Scarlet."

Nixon stopped his growling just long enough to snarl, "Bad squirrel."

"Hey, just hear me out, okay? Okay?"

Nixon stopped stalking the squirrel for a moment, but he didn't back away. Scarlet brushed off her belly and looked cautiously at her former companions. "It was a few days ago, when ghost girl here was trying to get ahold of Morgaed," she began. "I was *trying* to be helpful, hanging out in a tree in Ghost World so I could keep tabs on Sool's location. Unfortunately, he caught me sleeping. The big goon killed the tree I was in, and I ended up inside one massive fist, begging for mercy. All I had to trade was a little info." She searched the others' eyes for sympathy but found little. "I didn't want to do it!"

Piers stared at the rodent. Then he threw up his hands, turned and went back to his log.

"Look, I'm sorry, okay?" Scarlet hopped over to the trail bar and lifted it up. "I brought you food! You and Thunderbutt will have to split it."

Piers sat down and let out a deep sigh. "Scarlet, I don't care. I messed up more than you did."

Dandelion walked over to the squirrel. He bent over, reached out and touched her head gently. "You came back," he said.

Emlee nodded. "That *was* brave of you."

A smirk returned to Scarlet's whiskered face. "Yeah. Brave. So how about we put our heads together and figure out how to take down that overgrown fart cloud once and for all?" She took a big bite out of the granola bar for dramatic effect and chewed it slowly. Then she seemed to remember she was supposed to be sharing. Scarlet swallowed hard, smiled and held out the bar one more time.

One hour drifted into another as the companions sat, hovered or lay beside the campfire. Nixon had regained his composure after begrudgingly swallowing the rest of Scarlet's granola bar, and the squirrel had dried her sodden fur by the flames. The initial boost from her enthusiasm failed to trigger any promising new plans to deal with their enemy, however. Firelight and shadows flickered across faces that grew more and more silent as the evening stretched on. Piers tossed a few more sticks into the fire to ward off the chill from the intensifying rain. He had no desire to go out in that.

"At this rate," Scarlet groused, "we'll all end up sitting in trees like a bunch of bark-eaters." She tried shifting the topic. "So what's *his* next move going to be?"

Emlee spoke first. "As long as we keep the amulet safe, then he'll need to recreate what he did in the Grove – a massive amount of death. Something even bigger, because he's probably grown again."

"So another massacre." Scarlet scratched behind her ear with her hind leg.

"But it would have to be tightly contained," Piers added.

Dandelion shifted in his seat on the log. "My people and the ghosts are too dispersed for him to gather easily. And many animals have fled the forest... from what I heard."

"He might try to knock out something big," suggested QL, "like a power station."

"He could do that?" Emlee asked.

"Well, we've seen him strip the souls out of Gasaholics and other Disconnecteds," the smartphone continued, "but he might not be aware of power stations and such, being that he *is* a ghost and all."

"Unless someone told him," Nixon growled. "Like a squirrel with a dumb face and a big mouth."

"–who wouldn't know squat about power stations, being a squirrel and all," Scarlet retorted.

Piers cut in. "Okay, so there's a good chance he'll go after humans this time."

"He's had practice," said Emlee.

"Yeah, downtown," Piers agreed. "But they were still too scattered."

"He needs a clump of them," Scarlet added, "something like an ant nest, or a beehive."

Piers nodded. "Maybe a church. Or a nightclub. How could he kill that many all at once, though?"

"A bomb?" asked QL.

Piers got up and added more sticks to the fire. "He's smart, but I don't think he knows how to make a bomb, even if he could hold the materials with his fat fingers." He turned away from the firelight and faced the darkened forest. "I wish I could warn people. But they're not going to believe anything I say about ghosts."

"Ghosts?" QL scoffed. "It's talking humans that are unbelievable."

Emlee floated up beside Piers. The light of the campfire did not touch her like it did the others; the brightness of her face remained constant, illuminated by a soft, inner glow. "You could use the amulet and show them the threat they face," she offered.

Piers frowned. "Not if we wanted to keep it safe. And keep your worlds safe. Humans aren't great when it comes to other cultures... I don't think you want them messing around and trying to take over."

Scarlet chuckled. "A world run by humans? How dumb would *that* be?"

Piers gave her a look. "We already– Oh, never mind." He took his seat and let out a weary sigh. "I guess whatever happens, more death is inevitable."

The group fell silent again. Nixon began to twitch where he lay at Piers' feet, lost in dreams. After a time, Emlee started humming to herself.

"That's a nice tune," said Dandelion.

"Oh!" Emlee started, causing ripples to flow through her tendrils of hair. "I didn't realize I was doing it."

"You always sound like you're about to sing something," Piers noted. Morgaed and Tull's voices had shared the same melodic qualities, now that he thought about it - a sort of singsong tone and cadence.

"My people cannot use written language, as you do, so our knowledge is passed down through stories," the ghost girl explained. "Song-stories, mostly."

Dandelion sat up in his seat. "Sing one for us, please?"

Emlee gave him a soft smile. "Well, here's the one I was just thinking of. Morgaed taught it to me."

Her words poured gently out into the stone shelter, as airy and delicate as the strands of hair floating about her face.

As the first rays settled
On fields still and frozen
The promise of dawn rose visible, along the edge of outward visions
A family of souls gazed inwardly, touching
Folding and strengthening, ebbing and advancing
Ever blooming, ever building
Cascading across stars and lives.

The petals fell slowly
Too light for perception
Dissolving to ash, and the ash then dissolving
Scouring ever faster
Grinding hotter and hotter
Gnawing deeper and darker
The dwindling threads of the last tribe's conceiving
A last touch, a last thought
Before touch's end.

Emlee fell silent. Dandelion and Piers looked at each other, then applauded.

"There's another verse," said the ghost girl, "but I don't know if I have all the words."

"Please do some more," Dandelion pleaded. "I can help you sing."

"Sing together?" Emlee blinked happily. "Yes, let's try it."

She began a third verse, and Dandelion added his thin voice to hers, using wordless tones that harmonized with the melody. Their voices blended beautifully.

Within the dark embers the whisper was answered
A hand met by another
The hope of existence
A pact and a prayer
By old roads uncovered were shadows inverted
The blinded retreating, hearts slowly beating
With cadences echoing, chorus repeating
Lost and yet living
Entombed in their sky
The last traces seen by a splintering eye.

The fireside gathering grew quiet once more. Scarlet was the first to speak. "Well, that was only semi-depressing."

"I liked it," said Nixon, yawning.

"I filled in a few words that I couldn't remember," admitted Emlee. "It's sad that I can't ask Morgaed what they were."

Piers wanted her to keep singing. It felt nice to have Emlee's voice in his head, rather than his own conflicted thoughts. "The song... what does it mean?"

"I'm not sure. Something that happened a long, long time

ago." She cast him a weak smile. "But I like the line, "a family of souls". It reminded me of us. We're sort of a family."

Scarlet snorted. "Last I checked, I didn't have any brainless dog-butts in my family history."

"I have several squirrels in my family," said Nixon.

Scarlet's brow furrowed. "Oh, do you now?"

"Yes," the dog explained, "because we ate them and they are in our stomachs."

Nixon rolled onto his back, pawing his legs and snickering delightedly at his own joke. Scarlet rolled her eyes. After a minute, the greyhound finally sat up and grinned at Piers, tongue wagging.

On the other side of the campfire, Emlee said, "You have a very nice voice, Dandelion."

"It's good to sing again," mumbled the elven creature. "But you should hear the other fairies. They are far better than I am."

"I would love to visit your home someday," said the ghost girl.

"I'd like to show you. I—" The fairy broke off in a fit of coughing. He slipped a shaky hand inside his vest and withdrew a tiny vial. Before Piers could do anything to help, Dandelion had already pulled the stopper and taken a sip of its contents.

Scarlet hopped over. "You all right there, fuzzhead?"

"What are you drinking?" Piers asked.

Dandelion fought to catch his breath. "Nectar. It gives me a little energy and helps me stay awake in the dark. Aspen gave it to me."

Piers frowned. "Well, you still don't sound so good. Your eyes are red. And you look... thinner."

"I feel a little weak. We fairies are only as strong as the plants around us." He wiped his lips with the back of his hand. "I couldn't take care of my dandelions while I was away, and Sool has been killing more and more of them."

Nixon cocked his head. "What will happen when the dandelions are gone?"

"I will die," the fairy murmured. "But I'm not the only Dandelion fairy. There are others, in other places."

Emlee smiled encouragingly. "I'm sure you're the best Dandelion."

The fairy smiled and hid his face beneath his frizzy hair, embarrassed. Nixon walked over and rested his head on Dandelion's knee.

"Why don't you just leave the forest?" suggested Piers. "Find a different bunch of dandelions to look after."

The elf looked offended. "I may be only a Dandelion fairy, but I *won't* abandon my plants."

Piers shrugged. "Sure, Dandelion."

Quiet descended on the group again. The fire burned low, but they had no more dry branches to add, and no one seemed eager to go out into the damp woods to gather more. The darkness outside the cave was absolute now, and the rain seemed to have lessened.

In the absence of sound, Piers' pessimistic thoughts resurfaced. He knew they weren't going to win this. If that fact hadn't been obvious before, it was now. Everything they'd tried had only made things worse. More blood on his hands.

He looked around the campfire at the other faces. When it came down to it, he admitted, they were just a bunch of kids with dumb ideas... even Emlee, for all her claims to be sixty years old. He needed to stop thinking he could make a difference and get back to what he should have been focusing on all along.

Piers stood up and brushed off his pants awkwardly. "Everyone, I hate to s-s-say this, but I don't th-th-think there's anything else I can do. It's t-t-time for me to g-go home."

"Oh." Emlee pulled her gaze away from the flickering embers. "Should we try to meet you there, tomorrow?"

Piers couldn't look her in the eye. "I d-d-don't think I'll be there tomorrow."

The group went silent again. Scarlet squinted at the boy.

"Uhhhh... I just made a big, brave comeback. Don't tell me *you're* going to bail on us, now."

"I c-can't stay in Summerday anymore. I need to protect my mom. J-j-just like Dandelion has to protect his plants."

QL piped up from inside his pocket. "That is quite sensible, Carrier. But don't forget the quarantine."

Piers shook his head. "If the quarantine's not over, we'll s-s-sneak through the f-f-forest on the other side of town."

"That's dumb," declared Scarlet. "You're just scared."

"I'm not scared. You're j-j-just not human. You don't understand."

"But you're family!" Emlee protested. "You can't abandon your family!"

"I *have* a family," he countered. "I'm sorry. I j-j-just owe her."

"I think you owe *us*, pal," groused the squirrel.

Piers crossed his arms. "Look, you don't want me. What h-help have I given? Marguerite's dead because of me. Everyone downtown. All those fairies." He started pacing at the edge of the firelight. "You know Mikin? *He* died because of me."

Emlee's brow furrowed. "But Mikin is... what do you mean, Piers?"

"I mean..." The boy sat down again. He didn't want to tell them, but the words came spilling out anyway. "Mikin was in a car accident. It was maybe four years ago. I was at soccer practice. Someone was teasing me, and I lost my temper. I hit someone." He picked up a twig and started snapping pieces off. "They called my dad to pick me up," Piers continued, "and my little brother was in the car with him. They never arrived. Mikin was in the car that hit them." He tossed the remainder of the twig into the coals. "After that, it was just my mom and me."

Emlee's voice was heavy with sorrow. "I'm so sorry, Piers."

"You don't need me," Piers told her. "*She* needs me. And I owe her. For what I did."

"But... it wasn't your fault."

"It *was* my fault!" he shouted. "Everything is my fault." Piers reached into his pocket, pulled out the amulet and slapped it down onto the log. He stood up. "Here it is. You should take the amulet and just go far away. Sorry I couldn't be your hero." He turned away from the fire. "Nixon, let's go."

"No," said the greyhound.

The boy paused. "Come on."

Nixon shook his head and laid down in the dirt. "I am a good dog and I am staying to help."

Piers wanted to grab him by the collar. "Nixon, you're supposed to protect me and my family!"

"But Piers... I *am* protecting you."

The boy glared at Nixon for a moment, then stormed off into the night.

❦ 40 ❦

Emlee's voice called out from behind. "Piers, wait!"

He turned and saw Emlee's phosphorescent form approaching through the trees, amulet in hand. "Go back," he growled. "Sool is going to see you. And then he'll see me."

She stopped in front of him. "Just give me one minute." Her hands shook as she held the amulet close to her chest and studied it, using the glow of her own illumination. "Sorry. I am not used to handling objects, like you are. But I want to show you something."

She reached unsteadily with the talisman and touched it to his shoulder. With her other hand, she moved the dial. Piers felt a spark pass through his system, as if his heart had added an extra beat.

"Just listen," she whispered.

Piers didn't want to draw things out any longer, but he forced his feet to remain still. Through the pattering of raindrops on the forest floor, he began to hear the familiar song of the crickets. He'd heard it in his backyard a hundred times, but now he could sense the intelligence that lay beneath the humming. *Animal World*. The hoot of a great horned owl came to his ears as a haunting cry of dominance, breaking through the glorious chants of the tree frogs and the cacophony of their lyrical phrases.

Emlee spoke into his ear. "So much is counting on us to fix this." She gave the dial another nudge, and from a different part of the forest arose a new choir of voices... those of the fairies. They had their own song, but this one felt much more mournful. It was about the passing of a queen.

The ferns and trees around them seemed to exude their own presence as well. "These are worlds I never knew about until a short time ago," said Emlee. She turned the dial once more, and the voices vanished, bringing a more familiar soundscape to Piers' ears. The forest felt normal again.

"So much life," the ghost girl continued. "And we have a chance... a duty to come together and save them all."

Piers took a deep breath. "Is this the Human World?"

"Yes," Emlee answered.

"Good." He brushed her hand off his shoulder and stepped back. "Take care of yourself, Emlee," he said and started to walk away.

"You get back here!"

Piers turned and stared into Emlee's desperate face. "Look," he said. "Nothing has worked. I need to get my mom out of here. I'm sure you'd leave too if you could."

"That's not true!" the ghost girl protested. "I could use the amulet to escape my Circle anytime... but I won't!"

He shook his head. "We're just out of options. I'm sorry." He tried to step away again.

"How can you be so selfish?"

Her words stopped him in his tracks. Emlee's cheeks were flushed with anger; even the tendrils of hair swirling about her head looked furious, like they would reach out and throttle him.

"You've done nothing but complain since Nixon came and got you," Emlee fumed. "If humans are this selfish, maybe you *should* all die already... and good riddance!"

Piers strode up to her, his defenses hardening. "You asked me to save the world, but all you want to do is just save your own little worlds. You don't care if you destroy mine!"

"*You're* the one destroying it!"

"I'm trying to save it!" Piers shouted. "I can't hold my world together and do anything else... I can't!"

"Your mom is not the world!" Emlee retorted.

"Just leave me alone! Haunt somebody else! I don't want to see you!"

Emlee stared, speechless, as Piers stalked off. She finally turned and drifted back toward their campsite.

Piers glanced over his shoulder in time to see her ghostly light go out like a candle. Presumably, she had sent herself back to Ghost World. *Good.* Raindrops began to fall once more, but Piers let his anger guide his footsteps away from the cave and from his friends.

His fury soon dampened, and he was left feeling sick to himself. No matter what he did, Piers felt like he was betraying somebody. His thoughts twisted in on themselves and led nowhere, so he tried to focus on simply getting out of the woods and back to civilization. Somewhere behind the clouds, a waxing moon provided a small degree of light. With luck, he thought he might be able to use it to find the road descending from the city reservoir and follow it down to Summerday.

Piers pulled out his smartphone to check his bearings. He almost spoke to QL before he remembered he hadn't been holding the device when Emlee touched him with the amulet. QL's consciousness must still be in the Ghost World. He was glad. The device acted like a normal phone again, and though the signal was weak, he managed to pull up a map that showed the reservoir road. Once he reached it, he could call up his mom, make some excuse and have her come pick him up. That seemed to be the best of his miserable options.

Piers continued through the forest in silence until, not far ahead, he heard a tree come crashing to the ground. Immediately, he froze, then crept forward as quietly as he could.

He came to what seemed like a natural opening in the woods, but within seconds he realized he was staring at an expanse of utter devastation. Ancient tree trunks had been snapped in half; their remains lay splintered on the forest floor. Withered leaves hung from the few surviving branches and everything smelled of ashes. Even in the dim light, Piers could tell that the plants at his feet were also discolored and dying. *Sool.*

Since Piers had been heading toward the city, he wasn't surprised that he had re-entered Sool's Circle. But he wondered why the ghost was focusing his energies in this direction, gluttonously tearing life from the trees in order to expand his dominion as fast as possible. After a moment, Piers forced the speculative thoughts out of his head. He needed to be done with this. Wherever Sool was trying to expand into, he wasn't heading toward Piers' home. Or toward his companions. His *former* companions.

Piers took a long detour around the wreckage of the forest, sensitive to the fact that Sool could be lurking anywhere in there. The deviation caused him to miss the road and arrive at the shore of the reservoir itself. Diffused moonlight pooled on the water's surface, contrasting against the black contours of the surrounding hills. He felt exposed, and he had to reassure himself that he was once again outside of Sool's reach. *For now.*

Piers took a well-worn path along the shoreline, then followed a gravel road that wound through a maintenance yard and continued past a small pier and a concrete boat launch. Finally, the boy reached the earthen dam at the lake's outlet. A paved road hugged the hillside next to the dam, descending into the valley below and following the creek for several miles to the city limits. Piers started down it. He soon came to a locked chainlink gate that had been difficult to see in the darkness, but he didn't think he'd have any trouble climbing up and over.

Before wrapping his fingers around the links, Piers glanced over at the base of the earthen dam. A vision of the reservoir flashed through his mind. All that water. He thought about what might happen if the contents of the lake were released at once and came crashing down the valley toward downtown Summerday. How much death would that cause?

A lightning bolt flickered in the sky above him. Piers realized with deadly certainty where Sool was headed, and he knew exactly how the monster intended to murder enough souls to escape his world. He considered running down the road and calling his mother on the phone. If they couldn't escape town together, at least they could drive to higher ground.

But then he pictured the rest of the Summerday residents getting swept up in the flood and drowning. All their pets, too. Because of Dandelion, he couldn't help thinking about the plants in everyone's gardens. And thanks to QL, he also couldn't ignore all the cars, phones and TV screens that would short-circuit and go silent. There was no question... the dam had to be Sool's next target.

Piers leaned against the gate, torn over what to do. Was he going to be a person who just gives up? Or a person who tries, even if he fails again and again. He felt so utterly tired of failing. Failure was practically his identity now. No one could fault him for backing out, after everything he'd been through, could they?

His mind returned again and again to his friends, and who *they* thought him to be when they first called on him to help. They thought he could be some kind of hero. *What was he?*

He climbed to the top of the gate and tried to throw his leg over, but he couldn't. Something was stopping him, and for a second, Piers thought that the fairies must be holding him back. Then he realized there was a much simpler explanation.

I guess I'm someone that tries, he thought.

He looked down the road to Summerday one last time. Then he hopped off the gate and dashed into the forest, hoping for the sake of everything and everyone that he wasn't too late.

❧ 41 ❧

The companions stood at the edge of the forest above the entrance road, studying the dam. Moonlight diffused by the rainclouds washed over their anxious faces.

"Well, that's it," said Piers.

"That's no rinky-dink beaver dam," Scarlet pointed out. "How's he going to break it?"

Piers gave her an incredulous look. "Did you see how big he's gotten? I know he's a ghost, but I don't doubt he can wreck the dam if there are any weaknesses. We're going to need a really big plan, with every resource we can get." He crossed his arms. "Scarlet, I'm going to send you to the Animal World. We need everyone you can find to come here and help strengthen the dam. Logs, rocks... whatever they can do."

The squirrel nodded. "I'll call in a few favors."

Piers turned to the next companion. "Dandelion, you need to go back to Plant World and get help. I'm not sure what fairies can do, but we also need to hide the surface of the dam and the spillway, so if there *are* vulnerabilities, Sool won't be able to see them."

Dandelion took a sip from his nectar vial and eyed the slope in front of them, which appeared to have been weed-whacked recently. "We could make the plants grow taller and thicker, if I can find the right fairies, and if I can wake them up. But I'm not a leader!" he protested. "No one's going to listen to me."

Piers shrugged. "You're going to have to try." He looked to the dog next. "Nixon?"

The greyhound cocked his head. "Yes, Good Boy Piers?"

That confused him for a second. "Uh, thanks. We need you to go to Ghost World and do some running back and forth to let us know how close Sool is."

"I am the best at running back and forth and everywhere else, too." He gave a toothy smile in anticipation of the sprints to come.

Scarlet pointed at Emlee. "Why not let the actual ghost do it?"

"Because we are outside my Circle," Emlee explained. "I cannot enter my world unless we return to the forest, where we had the campfire."

Dandelion scratched at his billowy shock of hair. "Are you going to find some humans to help us, Piers?"

"I'm going to warn the town, so even if Sool breaks the dam, people will be evacuated." He pulled out his phone.

"There would be no mass deaths from the flood, then," Emlee observed.

"Exactly. They'd take their pets and vehicles out of the low-lying areas. No portal, and no murderous ghosts unleashed on the world." He brought the phone to his lips. "QL?"

"Yes, Carrier?" buzzed the clipped British voice.

"Get me the Summerday police station. Please."

The call went through. "Summerday Police," said the dispatcher.

"This is Piers D-d-d-d—" He cleared his throat. "This is Piers Davies. I—"

"Oh, right!" said the voice on the other end. "You're the one who had the episode at the nursing home."

Piers was thrown off. "Ummmm... yes."

"How are you feeling?"

"F-f-fine. I—"

The dispatcher continued, "Does your mother kn—"

Piers lowered the phone and hung up.

"Congratulations, you're famous," Scarlet remarked drily.

Piers made a face. "They think I'm crazy. They're not going to believe me." He thrust the phone out to the fairy. "Dandelion, you do it!"

Dandelion raised up his hands. "I couldn't!"

Piers redialed the number, put the smartphone on speaker mode and held it in front of Dandelion.

"Summerday Police," announced the dispatcher. There was a pause. "Oh, same number. Hello, Piers."

Dandelion squirmed and tried to fake a deeper voice. "Um, this is a different human speaking. I—"

Piers hurriedly disconnected the call again.

"Why do you keep doing that?" Scarlet burst out. "So what if they think you're crazy? *We* think you're crazy."

"If I warn them, they'll tell my mom I'm here," he argued. "She'll try to come get me, and then she'll be in danger. I already texted her and lied about spending the night at a friend's house."

"Could your friend call the police for you?" asked Emlee.

Piers looked embarrassed. "I-I-I lied about having a friend, too. At least, I don't have any friends who would believe me."

QL piped up. "If I might make a small suggestion..."

"Yeah, QL?" Piers was glad to change the subject.

"Send me back to my world," said the AI. "I do not have the tools to make a fake article, but I could post some warnings online in the comment section of the Summerday newspaper. Anonymously."

"That's brilliant!" He felt like they'd regained their momentum. "Thank you."

"Not at all," said QL. "Manipulating humans is what we do."

Piers looked around into the eyes of his companions. "Okay, everyone has their missions?" No one seemed to be wavering anymore. Even himself.

Emlee wore a smile as luminous as her own glowing skin. "Good luck, everyone."

Scarlet shook her tail fiercely. "Let's give that piece of ghost-blubber the worst night of his life."

Over the next few minutes, Emlee used the amulet to send Nixon, Scarlet, Dandelion and QL to the four alternate worlds. Dandelion disappeared from sight, Nixon and Scarlet scampered off, and soon Piers and the ghost girl were left alone with an unresponsive QL, which Piers put into his pocket.

He let out a long breath, thinking about the tasks ahead. "I hope QL's message gets through to people in time."

Emlee floated close. "Piers, we might not be able to stop him from destroying the dam, but there's one more thing we can do to delay him a bit longer, so the humans can get out of the way."

Piers arched an eyebrow. "And that is..."

"Find more of my kind."

"More ghosts?" He was surprised.

Emlee nodded. "You said that Morgaed and her mentor once kept the first Ender from absorbing souls by flying through his form and disrupting him."

"Yeah, but she said Sool had grown too big for that."

"We could still slow his expansion. Give more time for the dam to be strengthened and for the humans to be warned."

Piers admitted it might be worth a shot. "I get it. So that's what you're going to do?"

"No." She held out the amulet to him. "That's what *you're* going to do."

"Me?" She had lost him.

"The reservoir is new territory for me," Emlee explained, "and I can't enter the Ghost World here. It is not within my Circle. But *you* can go there, with the amulet."

He shook his head. "How am I going to get ghosts to risk their lives for us? They probably don't even know about the Ender."

Her smile returned, looking a bit more mischievous. "I guess you'll have to do what you told Dandelion."

"What was that?"

"Try."

Everything seemed to be happening at once. Dark, furry shapes moved through the moonlight, making the dam itself feel alive with activity. Raccoons, foxes and other critters bounded out of the forest with sticks and stones. They tossed them onto the slope of the earthen dam, then ran back for more. Beavers felled trees along the shoreline, stripped their branches and paddled them across the reservoir to the edge of the dam, where a trio of hulking bears grabbed and dragged the logs over the lip of the dam to the downstream side.

Piers turned the dial of the amulet to the Animal setting, and he could immediately hear the voices of beavers onshore as they coordinated the reinforcement of the dam. He spotted a lot of squirrels but was unsure which one was Scarlet. Everyone here had better night vision than he did. "Hey, Scarlet!" he shouted.

A lone squirrel scampered over. Piers asked her, "Everything good?"

"Well, no one's happy about being out in the rain," Scarlet groused, "but we're making progress."

A light drizzle had continued to fall on the valley. If Piers hadn't found a dusty jacket inside a shed in the maintenance yard, he probably would have been hypothermic by now. "Great. Ummm... good work."

Scarlet's beady eyes fixed on another animal behind him. "Sundowner, is that *all* you could—" As the rodent hopped off, Piers turned the amulet's dial to the Plant symbol, and Scarlet's voice shifted into unintelligible chittering. Emlee became visible, glowing against the backdrop of the nighttime sky like a guardian angel.

Piers lowered his gaze to study the slope of the earthen dam, where dozens of tiny figures crouched or walked among the vegetation. The plant growth seemed much taller and denser than it had been just an hour earlier. One of the shorter fairies came running up the side of the dam, stopped in front of the boy and jabbed him in the stomach. "Ow! Dandelion?"

"Oh!" said the familiar fairy. "You can see me. Good. I wanted you to know that you might not notice much of a difference, but a lot of work is going on below-ground. The grass fairies are really tightening things up just under the surface, knitting their roots together. The shrubs are doing much the same, only deeper."

Emlee descended to Piers' side. "You're doing amazing work, Dandelion!"

The fairy sheepishly tucked his chin into his collar. "Well, if we had some sunlight, it would be a lot easier. And it's taking a lot of our stored nectar to keep everyone awake." His excitement bubbled to the surface again. "But it's happening! We'd like to camouflage the concrete spillway, as you suggested, but there's no soil there for us to root into."

QL piped up from Piers' jacket pocket. "Carrier, this might be a good time to get that machinery in operation."

"If you really think you can show me how to hotwire a dump truck." He returned his attention to the fairy. "Good job, Dandelion. You really came through."

Dandelion ducked his head again. Even in the dark, Piers could tell he was blushing.

Emlee made a noise and pointed toward the maintenance yard. Piers turned to see Nixon approaching at a full gallop. The dog began barking even before he came to a stop, and Dandelion had to jump out of the way to avoid getting bowled over.

Piers turned the amulet's dial to the Ghost World. Now it was just the two of them. "Nixon, start over."

The greyhound took half a breath before words came spilling out of him. "Here is the report that I am giving you. Another ghost has come and now there are five with the Ender. They are moving very fast like me and making the Ender mad so he cannot eat all the things he kills."

"That's great," said Piers.

"But he is now going back to the deep part of the forest where the ghosts cannot go. He eats there, now."

"Oh. That's *not* great."

The dog's expression grew even more serious. "I am careful and sneaky and I follow him. He eats and then tries to come here to the lake. He is closer each time."

"How long before he gets here, do you think?"

Nixon took a moment to shake the rainwater from his fur before answering. "Sometime in the morning. After breakfast." A hopeful look crept onto his face. "Speaking of breakfast, I am very hungry and I have missed dinner."

Piers sighed. "I'm sorry, Nixon. I missed dinner, too."

"Excuse me," came an unfamiliar voice from behind the boy.

Piers whirled around. A young ghost hovered before him. She appeared to be in her twenties, wearing what looked like a tennis uniform. "Oh!" he blurted. "Uh, I mean... hi!"

"I was told to look for a talking human," said the woman hesitantly. "You seemed like a normal Unborn until just a minute ago."

He nodded. "Yes, that's me. Ummm... Nixon, can you take her to the other gh– I mean, the others?"

"Hello," said Nixon to the ghost. "I am a dog and I will be your guide to saving the world."

The spirit was taken aback. "Oh! Everything's talking now."

"You're in good hands," Piers told her. "In good paws," he amended. "Good boy, Nixon."

The dog gave him a toothy grin. *"You're* a good boy, Piers." He pointed his muzzle toward the gravel road. "Come, ghost lady." Nixon led his newest recruit back through the maintenance yard, while Piers used the amulet to return to Plant World.

Emlee reappeared in front of him. "What did he say?"

Piers looked around for Dandelion, but the fairy must have gone back to work. "He said the Ender's been forced to hunt elsewhere because the ghosts are making it hard to feed. Still, he might make it here by tomorrow morning." *And then, who knows what will happen,* Piers thought. "Oh, and another ghost showed up to help. That's six."

Emlee clapped her hands. "It's working, then! See, you *are* good at convincing people."

Now it was Piers' turn to blush. "We're lucky that stories about the Ender have spread through most worlds."

"What's next, then?" Emlee prodded.

Piers turned toward the maintenance buildings. "QL is going to show me some heavy equipment."

"No one I know personally," QL clarified, "but they might be willing to assist us."

They traveled up the road past the pier and entered the maintenance yard. Piers confided to Emlee, "I don't know if we can get these machines working, but we still have one advantage Sool doesn't know about. QL says the dam was rebuilt and upgraded after Sool died."

"In 1972, at a cost of $463,000." added the smartphone.

"Even if Sool has all his original memories," Piers continued, "he won't know about the redesign. He'll be expecting something weaker."

Emlee twirled with excitement. "Oooo... he's going to be terribly frustrated with us."

"I hope."

QL spoke up. "Carrier, this gas-eater is the one you want."

Piers looked up at the hulking silhouette of a dump truck. He tried the door. "It's open," the boy remarked to himself. He climbed inside but left the door open a crack so the cab light would remain on. It felt wonderful to be out of the rain. Now if he could only get the vents to start blowing some warm air...

Piers searched under the floor mats and inside the glove compartment for keys, while Emlee slipped down to check beneath the seats. They found a small flashlight, but little else of value.

"I recommend visiting *my* world," QL advised. "We need to see if this Gasaholic has any battery power left."

Piers beckoned to Emlee, who floated up and touched the amulet. He turned the dial to Machine World.

"Oh, thank goodness," QL sighed. "Connected again! I'll check on those newspaper comments in a moment, but first..." She raised her volume level. "Hello? Anyone in there? Wake up and smell the delicious diesel!" To Piers, she whispered, "A nasty habit, I must say."

The truck's dashboard came sluggishly to life, with dials and gauges morphing into the semblance of a pair of eyes and a mouth. The eyelids struggled to stay open. A gruff voice rumbled, "Hrmph. A bit early to be patching up the road again. What gives?"

"We have an emergency situation," QL declared, "and thousands of electronic devices will be short-circuited without your help. This human will be hotwiring you."

"You don't say," grumbled the vehicle. "Hrmph. I'm too old for this nonsense. You gonna coach him?"

"We have a direct interface set up with the human," chirped QL. "It's a long story. Please tell him what to do."

The dashboard eyed Piers skeptically. "Skinny guy. You forget the keys or something?"

"Something like that," said Piers.

He listened carefully as the dump truck instructed him to yank and fiddle with wires underneath the steering column. When the engine roared to life, Piers felt a huge wave of accomplishment. The feeling faded as soon as QL told him that he'd be the one driving.

It didn't go smoothly. After the third time that Piers stalled the dump truck and had to re-hotwire the starter, QL let out a note of exasperation. "I somehow thought this would happen more quickly. *Two stars.*"

"I'm fourteen!" he protested. "Not all humans know how to drive, you know." He wished that vehicles in the Machine World could drive on their own like they did in animated movies. Somehow, Piers managed to lurch the truck over to the top of the concrete spillway next to the earthen dam and release its payload of dirt. The soil tumbled down the length of the slope, pouring into the spaces between the recently-deposited logs and rocks. He hoped it would be enough to enable the fairies to work their magic before the water flowing across the spillway washed the dirt downstream.

"*Three* stars," QL begrudgingly announced.

"Ten stars!" said Emlee enthusiastically.

I'll take it, thought Piers.

Hours passed by in tense anticipation. Piers flipped between worlds to check on their progress, directing animals to spread the dirt and arrange the logs and branches. His blood had become increasingly cold because of the intermittent rains and the lack of a hood on his borrowed jacket, but he felt warmed by the fact that everyone had come together to try and make a difference. The spillway looked rather wild now. Its concrete lay hidden beneath a thick coat of grasses that had been coaxed out of the dirt by the fairies, and the earthen dam alongside had become a thicket, dense with alders and other shrubs.

All this collaborative activity led Piers to wonder why the world was divided like it was. Was there ever a chance it would be united somehow, with all these beings able to talk to and understand each other? It was hard for him to conceive of what that would even look like... probably either a utopia or a perpetual war between species. For now, the groups seemed to be working well together, even if they remained mostly ignorant of each other's existence.

Nixon came splashing through the mud puddles along the top of the dam. Piers quickly switched his consciousness over to Ghost World. "What is it, boy?"

"The Ender," Nixon panted, "he... he... he killed one."

"A ghost?" The thought felt like a blow to the stomach. *Just when their plan seemed to be coming together...*

"I do not think the ghosts will fight him now," warned the greyhound. "You should come."

After hastily using the amulet to tell Emlee where he was going, Piers let Nixon lead him into the woods. Within minutes, they heard the crash of a falling tree.

"I would not go closer," said a deep voice behind them.

Piers turned and saw Vinst, as well as the tennis player and two other apparitions, all hovering in the dark forest and looking miserable. "Vinst! I didn't know you'd been helping."

The deceased young man looked grim. The ends of his striped scarf floated freely, but he kept his jacket wrapped tightly around his frame. "Our helping may be done," said Vinst.

A bolt of lightning lit up the forest. When the afterimages faded from Piers' sight, a glow remained in the distance, emanating from Sool's gargantuan shape. The giant looked bigger than ever. Piers waited for a peal of thunder to subside before questioning, "Why aren't you fighting him?"

"We are exhausted," Vinst reported. "And he has learned how

to obstruct us while we are passing through him. Some kind of dense barrier... a shockwave. He swallowed two of us before we knew what was happening."

"Oh." It was all Piers could say. More deaths on his conscience.

"We slowed him for a time. No more." Vinst studied the boy closely. "Is Emlee safe?"

Piers nodded. "Uh, yes. She's in the Human or Animal World right now. I can't remember."

Vinst's eyes betrayed a degree of skepticism toward's the boy's intelligence. "She's where?"

Lightning flickered, and Piers glanced toward the Ender. The dim glow from the monstrosity seemed closer this time. Piers felt impatient to leave, and he didn't want to have to explain the concept of multiple "worlds" to Vinst. "We'll explain later, but she's safe, where Sool can't find her."

"Good." Vinst rose into the air, a determined look on his face. "We will stay and monitor the Ender."

"Thank you." Piers patted the greyhound's head. "Nix, let's go back."

The pair made their way toward the dam once more. Despite the dense cloud cover, Piers detected a different type of glow coming from the east. *Sunrise.* "When do you think he'll reach the dam now?" asked Piers.

"I think he will be there by breakfasttime." Nixon looked up. "And since we are talking about breakfasttime, did you know my belly is very empty?"

Piers sighed. "I know. Mine, too." The physiological effects of staying awake all night had started to catch up to him. He felt starved and exhausted.

A <ping> erupted from his smartphone. He pulled it out and saw a garbled text on the touchscreen. "I think QI's trying to say something." When they reached the reservoir road, Piers pulled out the amulet and crouched down next to Nixon. As he flipped through the settings on the dial to get to Machine World, he caught glimpses of Emlee and Dandelion nearby, so he decided to retrieve the ghost girl and the fairy, along with QL's consciousness, and bring everyone into Animal World.

"Okay," Piers began once they were all assembled, "everyone but Scarlet is here. And by the way, Sool isn't being stopped by the ghosts now. We don't have much time." He held the smartphone out into the middle of their group. "QL, are people evacuating the town yet?"

"That is what I've been trying to *tell* you," she said, her icon flaring an intense shade of green. "Those warnings I posted about the dam breaking – I'm promoting them ceaselessly, but they're not gaining the necessary level of social traction."

Piers ran a hand through his damp hair. "Really?"

"It is quite infuriating," QL continued. "Any humans I can find still awake are talking about "the sickness" or about some big, important supervisors that are supposed to arrive tomorrow – 'The Feds', as they're calling them."

"So they're still in danger," Dandelion murmured.

QL's icon shifted to an orange hue. "I'll keep trying to get their attention. I'll even use the secret weapon if I have to."

"Secret weapon?" asked Piers.

"Kitten photos," said QL.

Piers looked each of his companions in the eye. "Okay, everyone. We need a Plan B. QL, try to find a different government phone number. Not the police. Maybe there's a city emergency number or something."

"I'll try," she vowed, "but battery level is at 30%. Are you sure you didn't bring another booster with you?"

He shook his head. "You drained the only one I got, sorry."

"*Drained*," Emlee repeated in a whisper. She launched into the air and swirled in a full circle before her gaze settled on the dam. "Piers, everyone... the *water*."

"What?" Piers was confused. "What about it?"

Emlee's mind seemed to still be spinning. "The water is the weapon Sool is trying to use. What if it wasn't here when Sool arrives?"

"You mean break the dam?" Dandelion asked.

Scarlet hopped into their midst. "Oh, hey, fellas." She began grooming her matted tail. "I thought I just heard you all talking about breaking the dam. Ha ha," she snickered to herself. "That would be extremely annoying considering we spent the last eight hours trying to make it *stronger*."

"No," Emlee explained, "I mean... what if we could let the water out, but slowly."

"Empty the lake," said Piers.

Nixon suggested, "We could dig a hole, and then the water could come out."

Scarlet threw her tail onto the ground. "There you go! You *are* talking about weakening the dang thing. Make up your beetle-ridden minds!"

The idea took root in Piers' head. "Emlee is right. There must be some kind of release valve." He grinned up at the ghost girl. "That's brilliant!"

Dandelion scratched the back of his head. "I don't know much about human dams. Where would this valve be?"

"I have no idea," Piers admitted. "But we have a new plan now. We disarm the weapon. Drain the bathtub."

"How much time do we have?" Emlee asked.

"Ha!" exclaimed Scarlet. "Bet you ten oak trees it's not enough."

❦ 43 ❧

When the rainclouds lifted and the rising sun afforded them enough light to see, the companions discovered a tunnel near the bottom of the spillway. Fairies had inadvertently obscured it in their haste to turn the dam into an impenetrable thicket. After clearing the entrance, Piers crawled down the cold, damp passage with a flashlight and a trio of otters, but the rusty metal gate they found at the far end looked impossible to either open or breach.

Thankfully, Piers had another idea. On the surface, directly above the gate stood a small concrete building where he suspected the valve was located. The only door to the interior, however, was made of metal and locked tight. QL offered Piers a lockpicking video tutorial, but the boy felt too frazzled and short on time to start learning a delicate new skill.

Perhaps if he hadn't been sleep-deprived, he could have come up with a better option. Instead, Piers hotwired a boisterous bulldozer, drove it down the hill and smashed it into the side of the building.

The wall caved in. Inside, amidst the rubble, he found the valve he'd been looking for. They had to fetch a pair of bears to turn the heavy handwheel, and Piers still worried that their efforts were taking too long.

Scarlet hopped through the hole in the wall. "Keep doing it! It's working!" she reported.

The handwheel itself seemed to be vibrating. A cinnamon-colored bear shouldered Piers out of the way. "Move over human," he growled. "This is bear's work."

Piers left the animals to their task and climbed out of the building. Below, at the base of the dam, Piers could see a jet of water shooting out of the tunnel. And above him, invisible fairies revitalized by the sunlight were repairing the damaged thicket before his very eyes. *It's working,* he thought.

A *<ping>* sounded from Piers' pocket, and he pulled out both his phone and the amulet. He turned the dial quickly to Machine World, then back to Animal World. "Are you there?" he asked.

"The comments finally worked," QL announced. "The water department says they're sending someone up here this morning."

"Yes!" That was a huge relief. "Once they see what a mess this place is, I imagine they'll have to warn everyone downtown. We'll need to clear everyone away from the reservoir before they get here."

Scarlet bounded back in front of him. "You may want to do that sooner than later, human. *Listen.*"

Piers raised his head. "What? I only hear the water."

The squirrel eyed him like he was an idiot. "Seriously? Human ears are worthless. Get up to the top of the dam and listen."

He put his phone away and followed the tracks of the bull-dozer until he reached the top of the slope. Most of the animals between the lip of the dam and the reservoir appeared to be frozen or huddled in small groups, whispering to one another. Scarlet scurried up and stood with her hands on her hips, and Piers tried to slow his breaths so he could hear what she and the others were sensing. Into that moment of stillness came the sound of branches splintering as a tree crashed to the forest floor. *He was close. Very close.*

"He's just about here," Piers confirmed. "We have to go." The boy scrambled into the bed of the dump truck and onto the top of the cab. "Animals! Everyone!" he shouted. "You need to get away! The Ender is almost here!" He called down to Scarlet, "Hey, can you tell the bears and anyone else you find?"

"I'm on it," said the squirrel.

Pier spun the dial of the amulet to Plant World. Below him, he spied numerous fairies still coaxing growth from the weeds along the surface of the earthen dam. "Dandelion!" he hollered. "Everyone! Time to go!"

Dandelion came jogging up through the brush toward him. Twigs and leaves clung to his puffball head of hair. Once he reached the top of the dam, Piers told him, "Dandelion, you all did great. Can you make sure everyone gets out of here?"

"Yes, of course," the fairy wheezed, holding his side. "I mean, if they'll listen to– I mean, yes, I'll make sure, Piers."

Piers thanked him, then turned the dial to Human World. Emlee popped into view, floating high overhead.

"Emlee, we need to leave," he called. "Fast."

The ghost girl descended to the cab of the dump truck. "Yes. He's almost here."

One more companion needed to be found. Piers tried to flag down a rabbit as it passed beneath him. "Excuse me, can you–" The rabbit ignored him and kept hopping after the other fleeing animals. A second later, Piers realized his error. "Oh, right." He raised the amulet again, and Emlee touched his shoulder before he turned the dial and brought them both to Animal World.

He called out to a coyote this time. "Hey! Can you tell Nixon, my dog, that he needs to come here? He's over by the Ender."

The coyote paused and looked skeptically up at the figures atop the dump truck. "Squirrel says we gotta be leaving."

"Yes, but after," he pleaded. "Please?"

The coyote appeared to roll his eyes and sigh dramatically before turning and trotting into the forest.

Emlee drifted close. "Nixon's spirit is in my world, Piers."

"Oh, crud." He was too tired to keep track of which creature was in which world. "Well, Nixon can figure it out. Let's get into the trees on the other side of the dam."

Piers and the ghost girl began to head over when a voice interjected from his jacket pocket, *"Ahem."*

Piers pulled out the smartphone. "Pardon me," QL said tersely, "but might you be forgetting something?"

Probably, Piers thought. In his head, he started to run through all the missions in the different Worlds. "Ummmm...."

"The dirt movers, Carrier," said QL with exaggerated patience. "I know their brains may run on diesel, but we cannot simply leave them to get fried out there."

"Oh," Piers sighed. "Okay, let's do this quick. I hate driving."

Over the next quarter-hour, Piers managed to get the bulldozer and the dump truck back to the maintenance yard, hiding them behind a small warehouse, then wiping his fingerprints off the gearsticks and steering wheels. If there were video cameras monitoring the premises, he didn't know what he'd do.

Heart racing, he gathered his friends, and together they climbed to an overlook on a hill above the dam, across from the section of forest where Sool was expected to emerge. They waited nervously and kept watch on the trees on the opposite side of the valley. Water continued to gush out from the base of the dam, but Piers could see no noticeable drop in the lake's water level yet. As anxious as he was, the boy also felt an overwhelming desire to lay on the ground and sleep. Nixon rested his head in Piers' lap and did exactly that.

Emlee observed, "I don't think it's draining fast enough."

"Hopefully the dam is stronger now," said Dandelion.

Piers nodded. "Yeah. Even the Ender can't get rid of a mountain of rocks and trees that quickly. I hope."

"Carrier?" QL cut in. "I did not wish to disturb you earlier, but I believe I have I figured out why humans were slow to engage with my dam warnings. Observe this."

A press release popped up onto the smartphone screen. Piers skimmed it. "A meeting," he mumbled. "They're having a meeting downtown..." He scrolled back up to the top of the article. "Right now. The meeting is right now at the city community center. It's a press conference with people from the CDC – the government. They're expected to announce that the quarantine's being lifted, with restrictions. *Citizens are requested to attend or watch online.*" He rubbed his face. "Oh, hell."

Piers looked up at the others. "QL is right. People are focusing on this event. The end of the quarantine. And they're going to be all together in one place, right where Sool wants them."

"Did Sool know about this?" asked Emlee.

Piers didn't want to, but he glanced at Scarlet to see her reaction to the ghost girl's question.

Scarlet raised her hands defensively. "Hey, I didn't tell nothing to no murderous ghosts. Not this time! You can stick your accusatory eyeballs up your—"

"Shhhh!" Emlee warned. She pointed to the far side of the dam. A tree snapped at the forest's edge and fell forward, crashing lengthwise across the service road.

Dandelion whispered, "It's too late."

❧ 44 ❧

Piers switched the amulet to Ghost World just as Sool began to emerge from the forest. First, a hand protruded from between the remaining trees along the edge of the road, then a giant arm. What looked like half a face came next, followed by the rest of his head. His flesh seemed hideously swollen. The rest of Sool inched forward and joined the puddle of limbs atop the dam. His head pivoted atop the mass of his body, scanning the surroundings. Piers ducked.

Just when he thought Sool was going to consolidate himself into a more humanoid and less nauseating form, an eye protruded from the giant's face and crawled down the slope on a tube of flesh to examine the tunnel where the lake's water was jetting out. Then it dipped inside the dam itself. Sool's body sunk into the dam as well. The torrent of water coming from the tunnel ceased for a moment, and Piers felt an ominous sensation as the natural sounds of the valley went quiet.

The outlet began to flow again, though diminished. And then the ground rumbled beneath them, leading to a sudden jolt as a boulder launched upward from the spillway and crashed down on the side of the dam.

Sool surged back to the surface, and for the next several minutes, the monstrosity tore at the side of the dam in frustration, sending rocks and branches flying. Piers brought Dandelion and the animals into Ghost World so they could watch the display of fury. The Ender knocked over the rest of the building that housed the release valve, and Dandelion winced as the fresh vegetation along the earthen dam was torn apart. But in the end, the monster's wrath appeared to be impotent; the dam proved stronger than what a ghost of limited substance could destroy, even one of his immense size and brutality. Their reinforcements worked.

Piers breathed a deep sigh of relief. The people in Summerday might actually be safe. He thought about calling his mom, but instead, Piers set down his phone. "Can you watch over things for a few minutes, Dandelion?"

"Sure, Piers," the fairy said.

Unable to help himself any longer, the boy laid himself on the ground next to Nixon and fell immediately to sleep.

Someone was nudging him. Piers felt so leaden and detached that it took a while to convince himself that the body being poked was his own. He wished it were someone else's.

Reluctantly, Piers sat upright and focused on Dandelion. The fairy knelt at his side. "We might have a problem, Piers."

Piers gazed downhill at the earthen dam. The slope was a tangle of shredded logs and boulders. Part of the spillway had become exposed, and he could detect several cracks in the concrete. At the top of the dam, Sool crouched with his back facing the group. The ghost appeared to be bent over something, but his gargantuan body shielded his movements from view.

Piers took the amulet and switched to Animal World. Emlee popped back into view overhead.

"You were sleeping!" she said accusatorially.

"I was tired," Piers retorted. "What's he doing?"

Sool's body had become invisible once more, allowing Piers to observe a deep furrow being gouged along the top of the dam, perpendicular to its length.

"He's digging a channel," Emlee explained. Debris from the scrapings tumbled down the side of the dam.

"That's not wide enough to let out much water," Piers pointed out. But as the ditch grew deeper, water from the reservoir finally started to trickle through. Invisible fingers continued to tear at the embankment, and before long, a steady flow poured down the channel. The rush of water grew stronger and stronger. Piers swore.

"The lake water," murmured Emlee, "... it's doing the work for him now."

Even from their perch above the reservoir, they could hear the movement of boulders shifting and rolling as the water eroded the bottom and sides of the widening gully, pushing dirt and rocks out onto the face of the dam. Soon, the cascading water became a torrent, crashing down the earthen embankment and into the valley.

As Piers' eyes traced a path from the valley down toward the city, he spotted a government truck coming up the maintenance road that ran alongside the creek. It stopped a fair distance from the dam, and a figure stepped out of the vehicle. Seconds later, the worker jumped in again, turned the vehicle around and accelerated down the road back toward Summerday.

With a raw, cracking sound, a large chunk of the dam gave way. Boulders tumbled down the embankment, and the lake poured through the rift in one big stream. Nixon stood bolt upright and Scarlet jumped onto Piers' lap. The boy turned the amulet's dial back to Ghost World and looked to the dam. Sool had vanished.

Nixon appeared to be fixated on something downstream,

however. Piers followed the greyhound's gaze and saw that Sool had poured his gelatinous mass down the valley and was already well on his way toward town. The boy stood up, dumping Scarlet from his lap. He pulled out his phone and tried to dial, but the screen seemed to be cycling through local news articles. "QL," he shouted at the device, "call my mom, now!"

"I guess that's it, then," said Dandelion.

"I will chase him," said Nixon. "I will chase him and I will bite him."

Piers heard something garbled come out of the smartphone speakers. "Quiet, Nixon!" he ordered. Then he remembered to switch over to Human World. After turning the amulet's dial, he caught the last bit of an answering machine message, then heard the beep. "Mom!" he blurted into the phone. "I hope you're not downtown, but if you're there, get out of there fast... really fast! There's a flood coming!" He wasn't sure what else to say. "Okay, bye."

He looked around for Emlee, then turned the amulet's dial until the ghost girl appeared. "I need to get to town," he told her. "Now."

"Can you swim?" she asked.

"I can run. Not fast enough." He had another idea, but it quickly faded as he saw the creekside road get overtaken by the floodwaters. Driving to town was out of the question.

"Take the boat!" QL urged. "There's a boat down there, you know."

Piers looked down at the small motorboat tied to a dock on the near side of the reservoir. Currents pulled at the craft, trying to drag it through the gap in the dam. "I don't know how to hotwire a boat!" he protested.

"That is what you said about trucks," QL pointed out. "Hurry!"

Piers gave Emlee a helpless look, then started running down the hill. He glanced behind him once to make sure Nixon and

Scarlet were following, which caused him to almost slip and pitch headfirst down the steep terrain. He caught himself, reached the bottom and ran across the perimeter road to the dock. The boat appeared to be little more than an aluminum maintenance skiff. He quickly hopped in, then pulled out his phone and switched the amulet's dial to Machine World.

"Okay, talk to me, QL," he directed.

"Allow me to handle the communications," the smartphone advised, "so you don't unduly frighten her." It took Piers a moment to realize she was referring to the boat. "Madam!" QL continued. "We have an emergency of an aquatic nature and require immediate assistance!"

The boat's dashboard came to life, and a husky female voice yawned before speaking. "I was having a terrible dream in which I was being pulled out to sea and... *oh, good heavens!*"

QL kept her voice firm. "Yes, we are indeed within zero-star territory, so let's get that motor up and running. The human here has no key, I'm afraid."

"The first aid kit under the seat," blurted the skiff, audibly shaken. "The Drivers keep a spare key in there."

"Oh, thank god," breathed Piers. No hotwiring this time. As he dragged out the first aid kit, he barely noticed Nixon and Scarlet arriving on the dock and cautiously jumping into the boat. Piers found the key he'd been looking for fastened to a coiled, red plastic cord. He inserted the key into the ignition and turned it, but the watercraft didn't make a sound. "It's not working!" he shouted. "Is the battery dead?"

QL informed the boat, "Madam, the key does not appear to be functional."

"I heard the human," said the skiff. "I don't know *why* I heard the human, but I did. He needs to attach the clip to the kill-switch, obviously."

"What clip?" Piers was desperate. He grabbed the claw-shaped piece of plastic on the other end of the red cord. "This thing?"

"Yes, now clip it to the killswitch."

Piers scanned the dashboard. The anthropomorphized features of the Machine World entity were very distracting. "And that is...?"

"The red button next to the ignition!" cried the boat. "Is there another Driver available, maybe?"

"He's the best we have, I'm afraid," QL informed her.

Piers attached the killswitch clip and tried the key again. This time, the motor purred into life. He looked around. "Okay, let me make sure everyone's here."

Using the amulet, Piers slipped into Ghost World. Dandelion sat in the very middle of the boat, looking scared.

"Dandelion!" Piers was relieved to see him. "Grab the amulet. Nixon, Scarlet, you too. We're going for a ride."

"Dandelions aren't an aquatic species," moaned the fairy.

"I am sensing a dumb idea to end all dumb ideas," Scarlet remarked. "Let's get this over with."

Piers brought them all across to Machine World. "Dandelion," he ordered, "untie the boat and get ready to set us loose!"

While the fairy wobbled over to the side of the craft, Piers made a quick detour with the amulet to pick up Emlee from Animal World. Then he jumped in the driver's seat. He pushed the throttle lever forward, and as the motor hummed louder, he felt the boat start to resist the pull of the water flowing out of the breach in the dam.

Piers knew this was the dumbest thing he had ever tried to do, but he had to get to his mom before it was too late. As a member of the medical profession, she would feel obligated to go to the community center for the meeting.

He grabbed the steering wheel and looked toward Dandelion. The fairy had unwrapped most of the rope holding the skiff to the metal cleat on the dock. "Okay, Dandelion," he called. "Do it!"

Dandelion removed one more loop from around the cleat, and then the tension on the rope pulled it out of his hands. The boat drifted backward, pulled by the water exiting the dam despite the forward thrust of the motor. Scarlet jumped onto Piers' shoulder and gripped tight.

"I think we are going backward," observed Nixon.

The boat hollered, "Lean on the throttle, Driver!"

Piers gave the motor more power. The boat started treading water, then began to move forward. He turned the wheel so the boat avoided the shore and headed out toward the middle of the reservoir.

"That's it!" cheered Emlee.

Piers made a wide turn, then aimed for the gap in the dam.

"Take it back a bit, Driver," said the boat nervously. "Something's not right up ahead."

Nixon jumped up onto the bow and put his paws on the railing. QL piped up from the console where Piers had left her, "I know my case is supposed to be waterproof, but could you *please* put me someplace safer?" Piers grabbed his phone and stuffed her in his pocket.

Scarlet's claws dug deeper into Piers' shoulder. "Dumb idea... dumb idea... dumb idea..."

The boat's voice grew more shrill. "Driver, this isn't funny. The dam is damaged. Pull back!"

Dandelion sat on the floor and covered his face with his arms. "I should have stayed on land," he whimpered.

"Pull back!" the skiff repeated desperately.

"Hang onto something, everybody," said Piers. "This might get a l-l-little bumpy."

❦ 45 ❦

They sped straight into the dam breach. The boat screamed in terror. Piers pulled back on the throttle, and he felt a moment of weightlessness as they emerged from the gap. Then the bow the boat dropped hard and they plummeted down the side of the earthen dam. Dandelion and Scarlet joined in with the screaming. Branches slapped the underside of the skiff, and the jolts from glancing off of solid obstacles tripled their panic. They reached the valley floor with a splash that soaked everyone.

"My hull!" cried the boat. "My poor hull! Am I leaking?"

Piers felt too shaken to release his grip on the steering wheel. "Dandelion, check for leaks!"

Emlee swooped low. "You're doing great, Piers. Just stay above the channel where it's deeper."

"I can't see where the channel is!"

Though the entire valley had flooded, Piers started to recognize the trees that defined the banks of the stream. He tried turning the wheel to avoid a row of sycamores, but the watercraft didn't change its course. It glanced hard off a tree trunk.

Scarlet tapped his shoulder. "Hey, you want to start steering this thing?"

"I'm trying!" Piers growled.

"Use the motor, you idiot!" the boat yelled. "The wheel doesn't work without forward thrust!"

Piers took a breath. "I *really* don't want to go any faster right now." Still, he pushed the throttle lever forward, and the boat picked up speed relative to the water around it. He discovered he could actually steer now, though the speed did nothing to lessen his anxiety.

Dandelion stumbled into his line of vision. "No leaks! Yet."

Emlee flew toward the bow of the skiff. "I'll scout ahead and let you know if there are any dangers." With a look of determination, Emlee moved her diaphanous form a further twenty feet in front of the watercraft.

The boat continued to cruise down the creek channel. Piers kept eyes his locked on the terrain ahead, adjusting the wheel to keep them within the corridor of trees lining the bank.

A submerged boulder jolted the underside. "I am not a kayak!" protested the skiff. "What on earth are we doing here?"

"Really sorry," Piers told her. "This is absolutely an emergency."

Up ahead, Emlee called, "Rock, on your left! Log! Another log!" She did a full swirl in midair. "This is fun!"

Piers swerved to avoid the obstacles. The creek began to level out, and houses and other buildings started to appear along the floodplain.

Dandelion crawled over to him. "Sir, what if the Ender notices us?"

They'd never see him coming. "You're right," he said. "Emlee!"

The ghost girl flew over. "I think we're back in my Circle now, if we wanted to—"

"Yes," Piers interrupted. "Can you take the amulet and move everyone to Ghost World? My hands are busy."

Her lighthearted expression grew serious again. "Of course."

She pulled the amulet off Piers' neck, then touched his head and turned the dial. The world shifted to a grayer palette, as if stormclouds had returned to the skies overhead. Emlee removed her hand, touched the dial once more and flickered out of sight.

Piers spotted a gap in the trees, and he decided to steer the boat out of the streambed and into the city itself. The altered landscape threw off his sense of direction. None of the street signs were familiar, but he navigated the roads as best he could, certain he would reach downtown eventually. A few people stood in shock next to cars that had stalled in the middle of the flooded streets. The water around the stranded drivers looked to be under two feet high, which compelled Piers to keep their boat moving out of fear that the craft would bottom out, leaving them stuck.

Emlee popped into view in front of him, holding onto Dandelion. "Okay, that's it," the ghost girl announced. She took a moment to look at their surroundings. "The flooding doesn't look too bad. The humans seem safe."

Scarlet hopped down onto one of the skiff's benches. "I don't think Big Ghostie got what he wanted."

"Maybe we drained the lake enough before he got there," Piers suggested. "Maybe we actually did it."

A buzzing noise came from his pocket. Removing one hand from the steering wheel, Piers pulled out his phone. It was his mother. "Emlee, quick!" he shouted. "Put me in Human World!"

The ghost girl reached over to him and adjusted the amulet. Piers immediately hit the receive button with his thumb. "Mom?"

He heard a cacophony of voices on the other end. And then, "Piers? Are you okay? The flood–"

"I'm fine." He let out a deep breath. "Where are you?"

"In the community hall," his mother answered. "They're not allowing us to leave right now. People are trying to seal the doors to keep the water out."

Piers still didn't like the sound of that. "Mom, you have to get out of there. Right now."

"I said I *can't*. Oh, wait... a door just flew open. There's a—" Her voice cut out.

"Mom?" Piers shouted into his cellphone. "Mom! Get out of there!"

The phone went dead.

Piers moaned, "Oh no, oh no, oh no." He pushed the throttle up to full speed, then called to the ghost girl, "Emlee! Get us back so we can see Sool!" He grabbed the cellphone in his lap just before Emlee returned them to Ghost World.

The boat entered the downtown district. Piers weaved through the streets, dodging waterlogged pedestrians and floating debris until they reached the front of the community center. He pulled back on the throttle, and the skiff decelerated and dropped lower in the water. The keel scraped the asphalt loudly before coming to a stop, and then the boat tipped sideways, causing everyone to catch themselves. Piers felt glad he wasn't in Machine World, because the complaints from the boat would have been severe.

He jumped over the rails and splashed down into a foot and a half of water. Before them, the front doors of the building appeared to have been smashed inward. The interior was dark. A wire from a nearby power line had been torn down as well, and the detached end, instead of laying in the street, now disappeared into the darkened entrance of the building. He listened for voices inside but heard only silence.

"Nixon," said Piers, "I need you to hold something for me."

❧ 46 ❧

Piers waded into the community hall alone.

Lit by the dull red glow of emergency lighting, dozens of people floated motionless in the floodwaters amid scattered metal folding chairs. Those on their backs stared lifelessly at the vaulted ceiling. Surgical masks covered many of their faces. The greatest concentration of bodies drifted near the far wall, and among them crouched Sool's mountainous, ethereal form. Through the mass of transparent flesh, Piers could see a portal almost as high as the roof itself. The edges of the gateway flickered with blue flame.

Sool was entering the portal.

"Wait!" Piers cried.

The grotesque, bloated head of the Ender swiveled around and focused on him.

"You've come too late, boy," rumbled the giant. His lips twisted into a humorless smile. "Not that I don't appreciate all your efforts. But sooner or later, it was certain to end this way." He began to turn back toward the portal. "Goodbye."

"The amulet! You can have it!"

Sool halted and eyed him suspiciously. Then he loomed up and hurled his mass toward Piers. He came crashing down like a wave of gelatinous flesh, snatching up the boy in his fist and yanking him into the air.

"Wait!" Piers shouted. "I don't have the amulet. Kill me and I can't tell you where it is!" He felt his chest collapsing under the pressure.

The Ender studied him with a swollen eyeball. "Why do I even need it? I am almost free."

"I'll give it to you," Piers vowed. "Just l-l-l-let me go first!"

Sool dropped him, and he fell backward into the water with a splash. Piers wiped his eyes, coughed and rolled onto his hands and knees.

The ghost cleared his throat expectantly. Piers pretended to ignore the warning. "Where is my mother?" he demanded. He stood up and waded toward the bodies nearest the portal, seemingly searching for his parent. Sool's body filled much of the chamber, so Piers forced himself to walk straight into the Ender's mass in order to reach the other side. He held his breath without thinking, and his skin tingled painfully the entire distance.

Sool shifted his hulking form away from the boy. "Oh, let's see. That would be... *this* one." He grabbed a corpse floating facedown from the middle of the hall and lifted it up, then waggled it like a rag doll. *His mother.* Piers gasped.

Sool looked down at the body. "So fragile, these humans. A small power line dropped in their midst, and *bzzzzt!* – the life goes out of them. Were you trying to save her?"

He ripped the surgical mask from his mother's face, then grabbed her lower jaw and started manipulating her mouth like a puppet, speaking in a cracked falsetto. *"You're such a disappointment to me, Piers, honey. Such a failure. But aren't we always disappointed by the ones we love?"*

Piers squeezed his eyes shut, trying to block out the image. Guilt and self-loathing ripped at his heart. Finally, he raised his eyelids and took a deep breath. "Nixon, now!"

Nixon raced into the chamber, holding something in his mouth. Sool turned, dropped the corpse of Piers' mother and snatched at the dog, but Nixon dodged the bloated arms. Sool grabbed for him again, but Nixon tucked his head low and dashed through the giant's legs, making it through to Piers. He flung the amulet that he held between his teeth, and then the back of Sool's hand connected. The dog was knocked flying across the hall.

Piers caught the amulet and began swinging the artifact in a circle, ten feet from the portal, just as he had seen Morgaed doing once before. He tried to focus on pushing his energy through the circle of twirling chain.

Now it was Sool's turn to shout. *"Wait!"*

"Back away from the portal," Piers ordered, "and I'll stop!"

The monstrous ghost retreated a short distance. Piers ceased spinning the amulet and held it in his palm. He felt some of the energy return to his body, like he was getting his breath back.

An evil smile crept onto Sool's lopsided face. "You know there's no use resisting. Close the gate, and I'll simply pluck the amulet from your lifeless hands and cross over. Or I'll make a new gate, and you won't be around to stop me." His bulging eyes bored into the boy. "You may as well step aside."

"I don't care if I die!" Piers spat back. "And there are others who will stop you."

As if on cue, Emlee floated down from the ceiling to hover above Piers's head. Sool's eyes flickered in the ghost girl's direction. He gave Piers a hard look, then grinned cruelly once again. "Want to see something interesting?"

Sool reached down, grabbed his mother's corpse and held it upright, legs dangling. A ripple from his arm radiated up into his fist, and his mother suddenly jerked upright and gasped a shuddering breath. She started coughing violently, spitting up water. Then her eyes focused on her son. "Piers?"

Sool gave a subtle shake of his hand, and the woman went

completely lifeless again. He sent another ripple of energy through his flesh, and her eyes flew open. "H-help!" she croaked.

"Mom!" Piers wailed desperately.

The Ender shook his fist, and the spark went out of her body once more. Piers started to step forward but caught himself. "Bring her back!" he screamed.

Sool lifted his mother higher and dangled her like a treat before a dog. "I say we make a deal," he rumbled. "You give me the amulet. I will give you your mother back. Alive."

Alive. Piers felt frozen in that instant, unable to act. Ever since the accident, he had believed that he owed his mom everything. Everything he had or ever would have. "I..." he stammered.

"Make your choice," boomed the monstrosity. "You have ten seconds. 10..."

Piers glanced around the hall. He caught the eye of Emlee, who looked heartbroken as she shook her head.

"9... 8... 7..."

Behind Sool, he could see the shape of Dandelion's silhouette, standing in the doorway.

"6... 5..."

Nixon struggled in the shallow water and rose to a sitting position. He looked at Piers and cocked his head to the side.

"4... 3..."

"No!" Piers shouted at the top of his lungs.

Sool's eyes squinted in anger. "No, *what?*"

The amulet slid link by link out of Piers' hand until he held it by the end of its chain. "No, you can go to hell," he answered.

Piers spun to face the portal and began twirling the amulet as fast as possible. Sool let out a roar, threw his mother's body aside and charged at the boy. The ghost grabbed for the spinning amulet and caught it in his fist, then lifted Piers completely off the floor. Piers hung on, dangling with one set of fingers hooked around the chain, but Sool's other hand grabbed at his legs and pulled. The boy screamed.

Desperately, Piers threw up his other arm to grab the amulet, but his fingers only latched onto the dial. Sool yanked him harder. Piers clung to the dial and watched as the tension slowly bent the pointer away from the Ghost World symbol. He was sure it was about to snap off the device. His tendons felt like they were ready to give way, too.

Sool bellowed, "It is mine!"

The tip of the dial bent a few millimeters more, then touched the symbol of the black sphere.

❧ 47 ❧

The world went dark. Empty. The walls, ceiling and floor disappeared, and although Piers could still see Sool towering above him... could *feel* the giant pulling at his limbs... there was nothing else.

Then a malignant presence focused upon him... eyes in the blackness, with a weight that felt almost suffocating. And as strong as the first eyes were, Piers began to sense other eyes opening and turning toward them. Then dozens. Hundreds. He started to see the outlines of creatures... black, demonic shapes writhing in the darkness of a forgotten world. Twisting, crawling over each other and coming for him.

His fingers slid off the dial.

∽

Reality returned. Piers fell to the floor, as did the amulet. Surprisingly, he landed on his feet, but before he could catch his balance, Sool smashed his arm into him. The boy went flying across the room, crashed into a set of chairs and hit the far wall. He tried not to black out. His temple throbbed from the impact, and he had just enough presence of mind to raise his head out of the floodwaters.

Sool reared up. *"What was that?"*

Piers struggled to sit straight and keep his hands from shaking. Apparently, Sool had seen the nightmarish world, too. "I d-d-d-don't know," he stammered. He really had no idea.

Emlee flew over to him. "Are you all right?" She peered closely at his face. "You're bleeding!"

He started to feel around in the water next to him. "The amulet," he whispered to her, "...where is it?"

"You tried to trap me somehow," the Ender growled, uncertainty in his rumbling voice.

Emlee pointed to a spot to Piers' left. The boy reached down, grabbed hold of the amulet and lifted it out of the water. Emlee took hold of the chain as well. "Piers, let me have it," she pleaded. "Let me do it. I am ready."

Piers gave a small shake of his aching head. "No. It has to be me."

Sool pointed an accusatory finger. "You tried to... *trick me.*" His rage threatened to boil over, but then he pulled himself back. "No matter. Keep the amulet. I never needed it to get what I wanted." He turned and began to enter the portal.

Piers jerked the amulet away from Emlee. He stood on wobbly feet, planted himself and started to spin the amulet again. "Stop!" he cried.

Sool paused.

"You win, okay?" Piers declared. "Save my mother, and... and I'll l-l-let you through the portal."

Emlee swooped in front of him and put out her hands. "No, Piers. Don't."

Piers looked through her to the monstrosity beyond. "Do we have a deal?"

The Ender stared hard at the boy. He reached down, grabbed

his mother's body and lifted her out of the water. "You will have your mother once I am through," he snarled. "Agreed?"

"Bring her back!" Piers demanded.

Sool shook the woman, and her eyes flew open once again. "Agreed?" he repeated.

Piers stopped twirling the amulet. "Agreed."

The undead creature began to squeeze his body through the portal. First a foot, then an arm, then part of his lower body. As big as the gateway was, Sool still had to distort his shape to fit through the opening.

Dandelion waded over to stand next to Piers and Emlee. "Are you sure this is the right thing?" he asked.

Piers looked sad. But not defeated. "I'm sure."

The boy walked forward and began to twirl the amulet once more. Faster and faster. His essence started to leave his body in tendrils, drawn through the vortex made by the golden chain. A cold light emerged from the other side of the vortex, striking the portal, which began to contract swiftly. Sool's eyes widened. He struggled but found himself caught.

"Let me go!" the Ender roared. He closed his fist tighter around Piers' mother. "She dies! She dies!"

Piers kept spinning the amulet and walking forward. Warm tears spilled down his cheeks. His mother, not understanding what was happening around her, reached out to him. Piers pulled his eyes away. "No," he whispered. "I'm sorry, mom. For everything."

Sool bellowed in rage, and his mother became lifeless again. He cast her into the water and reached for the edge of the gateway. Groaning, the Ender struggled to keep it from shrinking further, and the contraction finally stopped. Sool strained harder, and the portal began to expand.

Piers couldn't stop crying. He felt a tingle on his shoulder and saw that Emlee had rested her hand there.

"You are a good human, Piers Davies," she said. "Let's do this together."

Wisps of essence started to leave Emlee's form as well. They passed through the vortex, and the light on the opposite side brightened just a little.

Dandelion stepped closer and took Piers' other arm. "I am small, and I may not help much, but I am here, too."

The streaming light intensified. Sool pushed at the gateway, bellowing all the while, but the perimeter began to shrink again.

QL spoke up from Piers' pocket. "Carrier, connect me."

"Are you sure?" Piers asked her.

"Yes, I'm sure!" Her British tones had never sounded more definitive. "You may have your flaws, but *that* thing is hopelessly defective."

Piers used the arm Dandelion was touching to reach into his pocket. Immediately, more tendrils began to stream toward the spinning amulet.

QL used the full capacity of her speakers, shouting, "Feel that, you monster? My battery may be at 12%, but I am 100% ready to kick your <ping>."

The portal kept shrinking until it could not tighten around Sool's mass any further. The demonic ghost clawed at the floor with one hand, trying to drag more of his body out of the gateway, but his swollen flesh emerged much too slowly.

Piers looked up at Emlee. Her figure was so eroded and faint that he could barely see her anymore. She smiled down at him, nonetheless.

Nixon padded over and slipped his narrow head in between Piers and Dandelion. "Is it time to save the world now, Piers?" he asked.

Piers felt weaker than he ever had in his life... even this morning when he climbed the hill above the dam. But that sensation was overwhelmed by the emotions coursing through him. Sadness. Acceptance. And a deep, inexplicable joy.

"Yes, Nixon," said the boy. "It's time."

Nixon leaned his muzzle against Pier's leg, and the warmth of his soul gave Piers a surge of new strength. He twirled the amulet faster, and the five companions gazed resolutely toward their target until the glow of the energy leaving their bodies became blinding.

Sool screamed.

And the light went out.

A wisp of Emlee's hair was the last trace of her to be pulled into the vortex. One brief flicker of light, and then she was gone.

The amulet flew from Piers' lifeless hand, and he fell facedown into the water. Dandelion crumpled, and Nixon sunk onto his hindquarters, then rolled over and disappeared below the surface. Ripples lapped above where his body lay.

In the darkness at the back of the hall, lit by the red glow of an "EXIT" sign, Sool struggled wordlessly. His pinched midsection was barely a foot wide. Extending into the room, the rest of his mass looked like a balloon ready to pop. His facial features stretched gruesomely across the bulbous surface.

In the doorway of the community center, a tiny figure poked her head above the surface of the water.

"Well, well, well," said Scarlet with a dramatic air.

The squirrel half-hopped, half-swam through the floodwaters. "I was hoping this stuff might drain away by now. Here we go." She climbed atop a floating corpse, then leapt from body to body toward the Ender. After reaching a safe distance, Scarlet stopped. "Huh. You look like Fleabiter's nose when he was stung by yellow-jackets." She took a moment to shake her tail, then looked around. "Now where are..."

Her eyes came to rest on the unmoving forms of the boy and the fairy. After letting out a deep sigh, she hopped over to them.

"So much for looking after the getaway vehicle," grumbled the squirrel. "Dumb plan to begin with."

Scarlet sprang onto Pier's back and pointed her nose toward the surrounding water. "Figures they'd leave me with a mess to clean up." She hopped onto another corpse and continued to scan. "You know," she said more loudly, "you had me in a tight spot before, back in the forest... making me tell you how to escape your Circle." After leaping to another body, she glanced up into Sool's bulging eyeball. "How's that escape plan working out for ya?"

Sool's lips curled into the semblance of a snarl, but he seemed unable to speak.

Scarlet resumed her search. "So, I'm thinking it's about time we put an end to this beeswax – ah, *there it is.*"

The squirrel splashed into the water, disappeared, then emerged a few seconds later with the chain of the amulet in her mouth. She struggled to paddle through the water while dragging the amulet behind her, but she finally reached a corpse whose legs touched the side of the portal. The squirrel clung to the sodden hair on the man's head and climbed out of the water. She took the chain out of her jaws, pulled up the rest of the amulet, then gave her fur a vigorous shake.

"Whew! Well..." Scarlet walked across the neck onto the broad back of the human, stretching the chain out behind her. "Can't say I wasn't hoping things would end differently. Never got to live in that twelve-chambered oak trunk like I wanted." She stopped between the shoulder blades. "But at least I got to be the one to end the Ender."

The squirrel gave one last tug on the chain to make sure it was taut. Above her, Sool's eyes went wide.

"Goodbye, Sool, you old bastard."

Scarlet put the chain in her mouth and ran the rest of the length of the human. When she reached the corpse's feet, she used her momentum to swing the chain up and over her head. The amulet flew through the air, taking Scarlet's last breath along with it. It arced downward and struck the edge of the portal.

The room exploded.

❦ 48 ❦

Piers opened his eyes.

Blue skies filled his vision. A multitude of voices surrounded the boy, though he had trouble focusing on any particular individual.

He sat up, expecting his body to hurt all over, but it felt... fantastic. Tingly. Some aspect of his condition felt incredibly tired at the same time, and his thoughts remained fuzzy. He saw that he was lying on a cot in the middle of the street in front of the community center. Ambulances and fire trucks encircled him, and other survivors with blankets wrapped around them were being led out of the building. Only an inch of water covered the pavement now.

An emergency worker walked over and spoke to him. At first, Piers thought he might be stuck in the Ghost World, and he grasped for the amulet around his neck. It wasn't there. Then he noticed that the clouds had blown away and the sun was shining at full brightness. He *was* home. The man was speaking English. Piers' brain had simply been too tired to understand him the first time.

Piers murmured to the worker that he was fine. And as the

man walked away, memories of what happened in the community center slowly returned to him. His heart emptied.

Then out of the front doorway walked Nixon. The greyhound paced along the side of the building, sniffing the wet bricks and running his nose above the surface of the muddy water. He turned and retraced his steps, then trotted over to Piers' cot. The boy breathed a little easier. Nixon sat and rested his muzzle on the thin, cushioned material.

Piers leaned down and whispered, "Nixon, are you okay? Where are the others?"

The greyhound just stared at him, like any other dog.

Piers sighed and stroked the fur between his ears. "Good boy, Nixon. Good boy."

Nixon abruptly lifted his chin and pointed his nose toward downtown. Piers followed his gaze. Standing on the other side of the street with a blanket draped over her shoulders, a familiar woman stood talking to another emergency worker. She turned and glanced at him, and a smile broke out across her face.

It was his mother.

Piers awoke in his bedroom. The alarm said 8:29 pm. He must have dozed off in bed not long after dinner. Now he probably wouldn't be able to fall asleep tonight.

He threw his legs over the side of the bed and turned on the bedside lamp. Nixon lay on the floor a few feet away. The dog hadn't left Piers' side much since the flood incident three days ago, not even to explore the edge of the forest behind their house.

Piers rubbed his face and tried to shake some of the fog from his mind. Today was a better day. Tomorrow he might actually go for a walk. Maybe into the forest, or perhaps downtown to see if things had gotten back to normal. To see if he could find any trace of the amulet.

The rain outside his window had resumed. A strong wind pushed droplets against the glass and onto the windowsill. The fresh air felt nice, but Piers got up and closed the window to keep the floor from getting any wetter.

Someone knocked on his door. Nixon pricked up his ears. "Piers," came his mother's voice, "can I come in?"

"Sure, mom," he replied.

The door opened slowly, and his mother stepped inside. "Just letting you know that I'm going to work tomorrow. They've been pretty short-staffed, and... are you still feeling better?"

Piers nodded. "Yes. I think I'll go for a walk tomorrow if it's not raining."

"Good." She studied her son carefully. His mom had been more attentive than normal, which had been nice. She seemed to have no memories from the day of the flood, or about Sool. In fact, no one present at the community hall could remember what happened there. Maybe 10,000 volts from the electrical wires had something to do with that. Thankfully, his mom had never questioned Piers closely when he told her he had gone to the CDC meeting, too.

"Can I get you anything?" she asked him.

"No, I'm fine, really," he reassured her. "Good night, mom."

"Good night, Piers." Without saying anything else, his mother slipped out and closed the door behind her.

Piers walked to his desk and refreshed the local news page on his laptop. No new articles appeared. The previous news items were full of conjecture; most people suspected that the dam breach had been caused by a "domestic terrorist" who was upset about the quarantine. Other conspiracy theories focused on the power line that had been pulled inside the community center. Luckily, no one had come forward with pictures of him driving the reservoir skiff into town. That would have been really tough to explain.

Lightning flickered outside. Piers returned to the window and looked out into the forest. He should have heard from his friends by now. There had been no sign of them... nothing at all. Even QL, who had miraculously survived several hours of submersion, had been acting like a regular smartphone again.

Things were getting back to normal, and that unsettled him. He had come to realize over the last few days that he didn't *want* normal anymore. The Piers who had tried to save the world, even though he had so often failed... he *liked* being that person. He liked what his new friends saw in him... one pair of translucent, pale blue eyes, in particular.

Lightning flashed again just as Piers was about to turn away from the window, and he noticed something odd. Within the patch of condensation that his breath left on the glass, he saw strange lines materialize, then quickly evaporate.

He blinked and leaned closer. After a moment, he blew on the windowpane again, then waited. In the patch of fogged glass, more lines appeared – unintelligible symbols drawn by a small, invisible finger. He repeated his actions, getting more excited each time. Something was trying to communicate between worlds, and he thought he knew who it could be. None of the drawings made sense, however, until a shape appeared in the condensation that looked almost like a heart.

Piers smiled.

❦ 49 ❦

The next morning, Piers stepped outside his back door and took a deep breath. The scent of rainwashed leaves and grass blades permeated the air. It felt clear, just as his mind did. *Finally.* The fuzziness of his thoughts in the aftermath of the battle had taken days to settle out, during which time things like memory and identity had felt like unreliable concepts. He walked across the overgrown lawn with Nixon in tow and entered the forest.

Once they were safely enveloped by trees, Piers removed the greyhound's leash. Nixon trotted ahead, sniffing trunks and looking up into the canopy. "I can't wait to talk to you again, Nix," said Piers. "I hate not being able to share what happened with anybody."

After a short while, they came to the remains of the homeless encampment. Though it had only been days in reality, it felt like over a year had passed since he had last been here. The police tape had snapped; now it fluttered in the breeze, forgotten in the chaos of pandemics and floods.

Nixon sniffed the blankets and pawed at the space above them. Piers stepped over and felt around in the air. "Wait. Where is it?" His fingers finally touched the edges of the invisible portal. "Whew! Okay, let's—"

He then realized that the gateway had shrunk. Its dimensions were no wider than a soda can. Piers slipped a few fingers inside and tried to stretch the perimeter. It yielded only a few extra inches. He strained, but it didn't take him long to grasp that he was never going to fit through the hole. "Let's find another," he suggested.

They continued deeper into the forest, to the Animal World portal that Emlee had once pointed out to him. It took even longer to find this one, however, as the width of the gateway had contracted to the size of a quarter. "They're closing," Piers murmured. "They're healing themselves." A sinking feeling came over him. He might never see Emlee again. Or Dandelion. If his friends had access to portals into the Human World, they would have visited him by now. And if the amulet had survived, they would have used the artifact to reach him.

Piers hiked further into the woods so he could try one last portal before he gave up. Preoccupied by depressing thoughts, he somehow found himself above the ravine that held the bullies' fortress. Thankfully, no one seemed to be around. The boys had used thick branches to extend their structure out from beneath the slate overhang, but their makeshift roof appeared to have caved in. Piers' curiosity got the better of him, and he slid down the side of the ravine to have a closer look. Nixon sniffed the air and followed.

The eighth-graders had managed to wall in the space below the overhang with a substantial palisade of logs, although several of the beams now leaned precariously inward. A soft, clicking sound emanated from the dark entranceway. The image of a squirrel chewing at a nut popped into Piers' mind, causing a jolt of excitement. He stepped over to peer into the entrance and was startled when he saw one of his three antagonists, Ripal, sitting on a stump just inside the doorway.

The Indian-American teenager had been whittling words into a stick, but he glanced up. "Oh, hello, Davies." His tone was dispassionate, but not unusually so; Ripal had always seemed like the most detached of the three boys.

Piers couldn't remember ever speaking to him alone before. "Uh, h-h-hi," he stuttered.

"You been all right?"

"Ummm... what do you mean?"

Ripal set down his knife. "I mean, with the attack on Main Street, whatever it was. And the flood."

"Oh. Yeah. I'm okay." He wasn't sure what else to say. "I got kn-kn-knocked out in the hall. At the m-meeting."

"Yeah. So did my dad."

Piers was surprised to see the considerate side of someone he had long thought as an enemy. Then he noticed that the words Ripal had been carving into his stick were all obscenities.

The older boy brushed wood shavings from his lap. "Did you see what brought down the power line?" he asked.

Before Piers could think of how to respond to the question, he heard Nixon *whuff* in alarm. Another voice called out from behind him.

"Hey, it's my favorite charity case!"

Piers turned. The last members of the trio had arrived, dragging a fresh log into the campsite.

Ripal closed up his pocket knife. "Probably should have gotten out of here, Davies."

Brock dropped his end of the log, and Dwarviss cursed as the other end slipped out of his fingers. The taller, blond bully rubbed his hands together. "Last I remember, you were sabotaging our castle here." Brock stepped up swiftly and before Piers could back away, the eighth-grader grabbed him by the front of his shirt.

Nixon arched his back and growled, showing all of his teeth. Brock pointed a finger at the greyhound. "Hey! Back off, dog!" He turned back to Piers. "Sabotaging our castle *and* you went crying to the cops." His fingers curled tighter around Piers' shirt, and he forced the younger boy to look at the fort. "Now you may have noticed that someone's been messing with it again."

"Or the storm," Dwarviss muttered.

Brock brought his face close to Piers' ear. "Or a little storm called Piers D-d-d-davies." He gave Piers a shake. "You owe us."

"I c-c-can help," Piers struggled to get the words out. "Help you f-f-f-fix it. J-j-j-just n-not n-now."

Brock's smile disappeared. "Yes, right n-now."

Dwarviss let out a loud sigh. "Jesus, Brock. We don't need the kid." The stockier boy took off his beaten trenchcoat and wiped sweat from his brow. "Who cares that the fort's messed up? The *town's* messed up. People died!"

Brock hesitated. "Fine. Whatever." He threw Piers to the ground. "You want to pass through, you gotta.... ummmm... say the password." A twisted smile returned to the bully's face.

Piers sat up. "I d-d-don't know it."

"You gotta guess what it is."

Ripal got up and stood in the fort's doorway. "Brock, just let him go."

"Fine." Brock scowled and pushed his blond bangs away from his eyes. "The password is just *'password.'* See, we made it easy on ya. So what's the password, P-p-piers?"

Piers glared at Brock, his anger rising. Normally, tears of frustration would accompany these feelings. But not today. Nixon growled, giving voice to the boy's ire.

Brock bent down. "Let me help you." He grabbed the sides of Piers' face with his thumb and forefinger and forcibly pursed the boy's lips.

Nixon barked, and Dwarviss scolded, "Brock!"

The bully ignored them. "Say, *'passw-'*"

Piers slapped away Brock's hand, hard. Then something he'd once heard Scarlet say came spilling out. "The p-p-password is, *'If you d-d-don't sh-shut your mouth, Brock, y-y-y-you'll be scavenger hunting for your own t-t-teeth."*

Everyone went quiet. Then Dwarviss started whooping and cackling while he jumped around the campsite. Brock stood up and watched his friend with annoyance.

"Ha!" exclaimed Dwarviss. "Did you hear that?" The burly teenager gave Brock a side-hug and grinned. "This kid is my new personal hero. Where'd you learn that line from, a movie?"

Piers was afraid to say anything more and sound stupid again. Dwarviss reached down and pulled Piers to his feet. Nixon let out another bark.

"Easy, easy!" Dwarviss said, raising his hands.

Piers rested his fingers on the back of Nixon's neck. They shook with adrenaline. "It's ok-k-kay, Nixon."

"Nice password," Brock grumbled. "Get out of here."

"But come back and help us build, Davies," encouraged Dwarviss. "You still owe us, right?"

Brock answered for him. "That's *right.*" It sounded like a threat.

Piers jogged off with the greyhound without saying another word.

After a few minutes, his heartbeat slowed. He slowed his pace as well and noticed some changes to the forest. The trees around them were mostly dead, with wilted leaves and sap oozing from cracks in the bark. Most of the plants along the ground seemed similarly afflicted. It all felt a bit sad. At least there was hope that things would heal, with enough time.

Piers found a stand of trees that had escaped Sool's appetite, and he set himself down at the base of a healthy maple tree. Nixon trotted close and looked at the boy questioningly. Piers shrugged. "I guess not everything's going to be the same as it was. I mean, with Brock." He sighed. "I wish I hadn't stuttered."

Piers picked a stick off the ground and stirred the leaves with it. "Nixon," he began. "The others... do you miss them?"

Nixon lay down at his side.

"*I* do," whispered the boy. He sat there a while longer with his hand on Nixon's back. Then the dog's ears pricked up. They both raised their heads.

A squirrel came into view, dragging behind her a wooden amulet on a golden chain.

50

"Okay, the last thing I remember is the portal collapsing," began Scarlet. "Then I'm dead, or I *think* I'm dead. When I wake up, the Ender's gone, and I'm surrounded by a hundred splashing, coughing humans." She shivered from nose to tail. "It wasn't pretty, I can tell you."

"So you think it worked?" asked Emlee. The ghost girl swirled through the branches above them, barely able to contain her energy. "Sool was cut in half when the portal closed?"

"Cut in half?" Scarlet sputtered. "I think he exploded!"

Piers scratched behind his ear. "Then why weren't we blown to bits?"

Scarlet rolled her eyes. "Ghost explosions are different? I don't know!"

"I have a guess, maybe," said Dandelion. He sat on the forest floor and hugged his knees against his chest. "I think all the stolen energy within Sool was released, and that's what brought everyone nearby back to life."

Piers considered this. "Humans can't be dead for that long without permanent brain damage," he reasoned. "Somehow, my mom and everyone in there ended up being fine."

"Maybe it healed them, too?" the fairy suggested.

Despite the unanswered questions, Piers was thrilled to have everyone together again. Using the amulet, he had brought Scarlet and Nixon back from Animal World. Emlee had been following him around all morning, so she was easy to retrieve from Ghost World. QL's consciousness, too, was quickly transferred over, but their friend Dandelion took some time to locate. Piers had to recruit several fairies to search for him before he was found tending to his dandelion seedlings.

"I woke up in my own world," Emlee shared, "but slowly. I wasn't sure where I was for a while. By the time my mind settled, the holes had closed too much for me to reach you. And I couldn't find the amulet."

Dandelion shook his head. "Me neither."

Scarlet twitched her whiskers in annoyance. "Well, that's 'cause Dogbreath over there found it first, and he made me take the stupid thing so he could go look after our favorite human."

"Greyhounds are very good finders," said Nixon.

"Good at finding work for other suckers to do, you mean," huffed the squirrel. "I had to drag it out of there while trying not to get squashed or drowned or having both done to me at the same time." She poked Piers on the toe. "You still looked dead, so I brought the thing back into the forest and hid it."

"That was days ago," Piers noted. "Why didn't you take it to me?"

"I was guarding it!" Scarlet let out a dramatic sigh. "Believe me, I am glad to be free of the thing. All that time wasted, hiding out when I could have capitalized on my celebrity."

Emlee nodded approvingly. "That was very noble of you."

"Yes, it was," said the rodent. She stroked her chin, considering. "Hmmm... it's probably not too late to line up some engagements... maybe a speaking tour." Scarlet suddenly flashed her attention up at Emlee. "Hey! Why didn't *you* let me know you were floating around? I could have taken you to the amulet!"

"I tried," said the ghost girl. "I wasn't sure which squirrel you were."

Scarlet grabbed her own tail and shook it. "I'm the one with the red friggin' tail!"

Emlee drifted down for a closer look. "It's sort of a *subtle* red," she observed.

"Reddish-gray, maybe?" offered Dandelion.

"More like a grayish-gray," said Piers.

Scarlet crossed her arms. "Feh! You can all go suck walnuts."

Dandelion returned to the subject. "The explosion sent everyone back to their original worlds, then?"

"That is the most probable theory," stated QL. "And by the way, Carrier, this case is water-resistant, not waterproof. I believe we may have invalidated my warranty."

As the others continued to share stories, Piers took a moment to realize how great he felt for once. His thoughts felt so much lighter. His heart, so much happier.

"So, what now?" asked Emlee.

"Nothing." Piers smiled. "Absolutely nothing right now." He looked around at his companions. "We all died and came back to life. I love you all, but I want no more adventures for a while. I want to do some normal human stuff for a bit."

"Huh," Scarlet snorted. "And I want to do some stuff without humans, fairies and ghosts for a bit, so that's fine with me."

Nixon looked around, tongue wagging. "I think I will run and I will sleep and I will eat many dinners."

"I may work further on my machine code language skills," QL informed them, "in case I have to function in this primitive world again."

Emlee put on a serious expression. "I will keep visiting the portal sites, to see if they are all closing."

"Good idea," said Piers. The portal at the community center flashed into his mind, along with the sensation of what happened when the amulet's dial touched the symbol of the black sphere.

Another world? If it were, it wasn't one he ever wanted to visit again.

Piers lifted the amulet off his chest and examined the face. The dial shifted freely to point at Ghost World, but he felt a degree of relief that it did still not want to turn to the final symbol. He removed the chain from around his neck and held the talisman up to Emlee. "You should have this, just in case you get in trouble."

Emlee floated down and carefully took the amulet. Tendrils of hair settled around her face. "Okay, Piers. Just for now."

As the ghost girl donned the amulet, Piers turned to the fairy. "What about you, Dandelion? What will you do?"

"Well...." the little man considered, "everyone like me is tending to their charges. The forest needs a lot of help. But with the Willow Queen and many of the Elders gone, eventually someone will get around to seizing power."

"*You* should do it," urged Emlee.

His eyes went wide. "Me? Oh, no. Ha, ha. No. Me? No." Dandelion's cheeks turned bright red, and he hid his face beneath his puffball of hair.

"Hey, Dandelion?" Piers waited until a yellow eye peeked out before continuing. "I know I said no more adventures, but... if you need a hand..." He looked at the others. "If *any* of you ever need a hand, just ask, okay?"

"I got some ideas," Scarlet ventured.

"No more Talking Human Shows, if that's what you're thinking," warned the boy.

Scarlet screwed up her face and tried to keep a guilty grin from emerging. Finally, she managed to say, "I wasn't..."

Piers smiled. "Okay, maybe just one."

He stretched his arms, then turned to his other friends. "Look, I wanted to say sorry... for letting you all down so many times."

"It wasn't your fault," Emlee assured him. "The Ender was smarter and more powerful than we realized."

"No, I mean… I tried to give up and go home," Piers explained. "A lot of times. I'll do better. I promise."

Dandelion let his hair spring back away from his face. "We'll come help you, too… whenever you need us."

Nixon stood up proudly. "I will help and I will protect you from squirrels."

Scarlet stared at the dog and bristled. "Yeah, well, I'll help protect you from canine stupidity!"

"You remain my favorite Carrier," affirmed QL. "Keep me at optimum charge and my services are yours."

"You are a hero among humans," Emlee continued, bobbing in midair, "and I hope we'll have many more adventures together. All of us!"

Scarlet cleared her throat. "Since we're giving speeches, I'd like to say that you are the weirdest companions I've ever had in my life. I'd appreciate not dying the next time we get together." She glanced around. "Deal?"

They all stated their agreement.

This was the beginning of something, Piers knew. Something that had changed and would continue to change him. The guilt he had felt for so long had lessened, replaced by… *what?* He wasn't sure, really. But even after spending the last few weeks consorting with ghosts and fairies, machines and squirrels, Piers felt more human than he had in years.

ACKNOWLEDGMENTS

Tremendous thanks to my editors Cat Lazaroff, Mareike Larsen, Lee Nathan, Laura Vandezande, Michael White, Marcy Cent, Mary Snyder and Theresa Bauer, who made early dives into Summerday and brought clarity and guidance to this project. And to Lora Wereb - the best person to read a bedtime story to, even if she always fell asleep before the end of the chapter.

Piers and company will return in Book 2 of the Summerday Saga:

The Demon and the Dandelion

When Dandelion loses the amulet and exiled fairies start showing up on Piers' doorstep, Piers must hide their existence from his schoolmates while preparing to battle the entity that has usurped the faerie kingdom. If only he had a clue how to get there...

To learn about future releases and receive the free exclusive short story prequel, "Unleashed", join the Summerday Saga mailing list at: www.summerdaysaga.com/prequel

ABOUT THE AUTHOR

Bryan Snyder grew up exploring the rolling hills and shady creeks of upstate New York. After college, he found work in the rockier environments of the western mountain ranges before settling with his partner in the Santa Ynez Valley of California - a place famously hospitable to greyhounds.

He is an editor, musician and author of the non-fiction outdoor adventure series, *Off The Map*.

Made in the USA
Middletown, DE
10 February 2021